"A master storyteller."   —Nelson DeMille

A Midwinter's Tale

"In this deft addition to his shelf of novels, Greeley once again shows his knack for combining solid characterizations, folksy prose, a bantamweight sense of history and understated Catholic morality to make highly entertaining fiction."
                                        —*Publishers Weekly*

"Fans of Greeley's trademarked light touch will enjoy yet another tale of the trials and turmoils of Chicago's own."
                                        —*The Irish American Post*

Younger Than Springtime

"Pulled me in instantly and never let go. . . . You *will* want to read the next one. . . . Greeley certainly made me laugh."
                                        —*Chicago Tribune*

"The leisurely, enjoyable sequel to Greeley's *A Midwinter's Tale* again follows the O'Malley family of Chicago. . . . By the end, where Greeley skillfully ties up one plot line as he keeps the other aloft for the next book, readers may discover that they, too, have been romanced—by an expert storyteller."
                                        —*Publishers Weekly*

ANDREW M. GREELEY

❧ September ❧ Song

FORGE®

A TOM DOHERTY ASSOCIATES BOOK
NEW YORK

For Marilyn—after November there comes
June—eventually!

SEPTEMBER SONG

A Forge Book
Published by Tom Doherty Associates, LLC
175 Fifth Avenue
New York, NY 10010

www.tor.com

Forge® is a registered trademark of Tom Doherty Associates, LLC.

ISBN: 0-812-57945-3
Library of Congress Catalog Card Number: 2001033552

First edition: September 2001
First mass market edition: September 2002

Printed in the United States of America

0 9 8 7 6 5 4 3 2 1

1965

❧ ❧

❧ 1 ❧

"I told him that I wouldn't work for him because he is a vulgar, corrupt redneck."

"Chucky, you didn't!"

"I did!"

"He's the President of the United States!"

"Of America ... there are also United States of Mexico and of Brazil and Indonesia."

"Regardless!" I waved my hand in protest, one of my favorite gestures in dealing with my husband, especially when he's showing off how smart he is.

"I'm sorry ..."

"I should hope so!"

"That I didn't tell him that he was a lying son of a bitch."

I had been waiting for him in our suite at the Hay-Adams Hotel, across Lafayette Park from the White House. It was a suite because I had made the reservation. If my husband, Charles Cronin O'Malley, Ambassador of the United States of America to the Federal Republic of Germany, had made them we would have been in a double room with a double instead of a king-size bed. He would never get over the Great Depression. I've always had a little money, though I've paid a heavy price for it.

He sprawled on a chair, raincoat still on. Despite

his pose of nonchalance, he was upset, a little boy whose candy had been stolen from him by a bully—a bully almost a foot taller—in this case from Central Texas. He didn't want the candy anymore, but, as I would say, regardless, it had been taken away from him.

My husband will always be something of a little boy, which is one of the reasons I am dizzy in love with him, sawed-off little redheaded runt that he is.

"Woman," he said wearily, "I want me tea!"

Most men recovering from an encounter with Lyndon Baines Johnson would have wanted a drink. But Chuck doesn't drink, save for the occasional glass of wine at meals. I don't drink at all because I'm a drunk. So we brew tea late in the afternoon instead. Rather I brew it because Chuck, perhaps because of his partial South Side Irish heritage, is content with popping a tea bag into a cup of boiling water.

("Mommy," asked my daughter April Rosemary, "why don't you drink like the mothers of my friends do?"

"Does that bother you?"

"No, I'm glad you don't drink. Some of them act real silly."

"I did too before Daddy stopped me."

So soon had she forgotten!

"Daddy!"

Daddy was sweet and funny and adorable. And took real good pictures. But he never did anything really important.

"Daddy," I said firmly.

"How did he stop you?"

"He told me if I drank again, he'd make me take care of all you kids by myself!"

That was close enough to the truth. Actually he would have taken care of the four little monsters— that was before the fifth came along—by himself.

"He did NOT."

We both laughed and she hugged me and we loved and trusted one another till the next crisis of growing up came along.)

"Let it steep," I instructed him as I placed the teapot—ordered up from room service—on a coaster.

"Yes, ma'am . . . Rosemarie, that West Texas hillbilly is going to send 165,000 troops to Vietnam before the year is over!"

"Central Texas," I corrected. "West Texas is west of the Pecos, you know Judge Roy Bean's territory."

Chucky's eyes twinkled. Most men would resent such an interruption from a smart-mouth wife. For some odd reason he enjoyed them.

"He's forgotten about Korea!" I went on.

"I've been telling people for years that he is too shrewd a politician to make that mistake." Chuck reached for the plate of cookies I had brought out.

"Not till the tea is ready," I admonished him.

"Yes, ma'am." He sighed. "And the stupid generals who have no idea how to fight a guerrilla war will mess it up. It could go on for a decade. The Vietnamese have nothing to lose but lives. Good Communists never worry about such things. Bourgeois morality."

"Our kids . . ." I gasped.

"In ten years"—he rubbed his hand over his eyes—"the boys will all be of draft age . . . If we didn't have the damn draft, we wouldn't fight land wars in Asia. Your friend over at 1600 wouldn't have 165,000 men to send into the Asian jungles."

Paying little attention to what I was doing, I poured the tea.

"Dear God, Chuck . . ."

"God's pretty unpredictable, but I'd trust him more than I'd trust that lying redneck."

"*Deus absconditus,* a God who has absconded," I said in an automatic reference to St. Augustine.

In our marriage, Chuck and I trade citations. I usually win. Also I have to stay at least one book ahead of him. He says he doesn't want to fight it or I won't sleep with him, which isn't true.

(Some of my women friends tell me that my husband is oversexed. I don't know whether he is or not, but I tell them that's fine with me because I'm oversexed too.)

"Good tea, Rosemarie," he said, "not that it is a surprise."

"Tell me more about LBJ."

"He starts out by telling me that I have to help him get out of the mess in Vietnam, like I'm the only one in the country that can do it. I say that he should get rid of all the Kennedy holdovers and surround himself with Texas politicians who think the way he does. I didn't say Texas hillbillies because I was still being civil. He says that he thought that they were all my friends. I say that they are, but he still ought to have his own people in place."

"You were right of course . . . And he said?"

I had paid no attention to politics before we went to Germany. I had learned a lot on the subject since then, more than I really wanted to know.

"Changed the subject. Complained about Adlai up at the UN. Had to get someone else. Good man, but too much of an egghead. Soft as shit, an interesting mix of metaphors. I was supposed to rise to the bait like most of those people over there would. I didn't say a thing. He said he needed me back at Bonn for a couple of months, and then we'd see about the UN. I said I was submitting my resignation. Wanted to go home to Chicago and raise my kids. He said that he was the commander in chief and that he had to order young men to go to Vietnam and die for the country and he was ordering me to go back to my post as Ambassador to West Germany."

That sort of order would cut no ice with my Chucky.

"And you told him that you'd already done your

military service and you were going home?"

"How did you guess? . . . Then he asked me why and I told him what I thought of him. So he pulled his bathroom trick, door open, flushing toilet, and all . . . At least he flushed the toilet . . . So I silently rode off into the sunset. Only when I left the Oval Office did I regret that I hadn't called him a liar. He's escalating that war and not telling the public about it."

"The public doesn't want to know, Chuck."

He pondered that.

"You're right, Rosemarie my darling, you're right. But when they find out, they'll say that LBJ and his advisers lied to them. I don't want to be one of those advisers."

"Then what?"

"Then I went down to see Mac Bundy and told him what happened and he said they would need people like me around in the difficult times ahead and that he was sure that the UN appointment would come down by spring and I said that I didn't want it if it came down tomorrow."

Chuck had put aside his career as a photographer to enter public service during the Kennedy years like so many enthusiastic young Americans. "Ask not what you can do for your country, ask what your country can do for you." For one so young he was awarded a big prize, Ambassador to the Federal Republic of Germany. There had been moaning and groaning from the press (including the sainted *New York Times*) and the Republicans that despite his dissertation (on the Marshall Plan's economic impact on postwar Germany) and his photography books about Germany after the war he wasn't old enough or experienced enough for the job. The Embassy staff in Bonn were horrified. One of the senior staff resigned and a couple of others requested transfers. Everyone soon learned that with his quick wit, his quicker smile, and his even quicker tongue and his enormous charm my Chucky Ducky was a natural diplomat. Like he said, "when you're a sawed-off punk with red hair, you gotta be charming."

The Old One, Konrad Adenauer, the Chancellor of West Germany, who rarely smiled, had met Chuck in Bamberg when he was in the army of occupation and simply adored him. His face would light up in a happy grin whenever Chuck appeared.

"Ja, Ja, Herr Roter!"

"Ja, Herr Oberburgomeister!"

Adenauer, the frosty old democrat of whom even the Nazi were afraid and who, more than anyone else, was responsible for the political and economic revival of West Germany after the war, was terribly proud that he had been the Lord Mayor of Cologne since practically forever. Chuck, never one not to push his luck, suspected that he secretly liked the title, though officially—and Germany is a country where everything is official—he was Herr Reichkanzler. The marvelous old man beamed.

So Chuck merely had to pick up the phone and call his private line, as he did during the Cuban Missile Crisis in the spring of 1962. "Herr Reichkanzler, the Russians have missiles in Cuba. President Kennedy wants me to bring the pictures over to you. Now."

Adenauer knew from the use of the official title that this was serious business. He saw Chuck within a half hour. West Germany was the first country to sign on to the "boycott" of Russian ships, for which Chuck received considerable praise, even in the *New York Times*, which never really likes Irishmen, especially mouthy ones.

Those were scary days everywhere, especially in Bonn, because almost everyone feared that the Red Army would arrive at the Rhine in twenty-four hours. Chuck dissented. "They're in as bad a shape if not worse than our army is. Their machines will break down before they get through the Harz mountains."

Fortunately we never had to find out who was right in the argument.

I knew a fair amount of German and Chuck could cover up his mistakes with his usual infectious grin. We sent our four oldest to German schools instead of the local American one which also won us points. It was sink or swim for April Rosemary and her three brothers. Being O'Malleys, they swam of course. Being clowns like their father, they took great delight in imitating the seriousness of German teachers and students while at the same time entertaining them.

I stayed sober and played the *grande dame*, shanty-Irish style, got my picture in the papers almost as much as the local media stars, and sang German songs on every possible occasion. We both wore PT 109 pins.

We had, in other words, a great time and represented the United States of America with considerable grace, if I do say so myself.

It all fell apart for us on November 22, 1963, when Jack Kennedy was shot. As Pat Moynihan said we thought he had more time and so did he. Camelot, as people would later call it, was over. We were asleep when the first phone call came. We wept in each other's arms and then woke the kids and said the rosary with them.

"It's all over, Rosemarie," Chuck whispered to me. "The magic is finished."

We didn't know then how completely over it was.

Neither of us had any illusions about Jack Kennedy. We knew that he was a sick man and, like his father, an incorrigible womanizer. We also knew that he was the only one in Washington who, with some help from his brother, kept the missile crisis from turning into a nuclear war. He was witty and graceful and charming and Irish (though not Irish like the Chicago Irish) and we told ourselves that his sexual behavior was none of anyone's business.

He liked me and treated me with infinite respect. I guess the passes were reserved for movie actresses like Marilyn Monroe and Angie Dickinson. He probably realized that I would clobber him—literally—if he tried to hit on me.

At the time of his death the State Department told all its envoys to stay at their posts to reassure our allies and our enemies that America would weather the crisis. We ignored the rule and flew on one of the new Pan Am 747s from Frankfurt to New York for the wake and the funeral. Dean Rusk, the Secretary of State, a nice man but persnickety, was furious at Chuck, and told him so.

"Fine, Dean," my husband said. "You can have my resignation tomorrow morning if you want it. We Irish Catholics go to our friends' wakes."

Rusk backed down.

It was a terrible weekend. I have often thought that if I didn't get drunk then, I never would again.

Chuck never liked LBJ. On the way back to Frankfurt he told me he would resign immediately and we'd return to Chicago. I talked him out of it. He had to stay until the election next year. Johnson would push Jack's Civil Rights Bill through Congress. He kept all of the Camelot staff. We thought that perhaps some of our dreams might be salvaged. LBJ had words of high praise for Chuck when he visited Bonn. "Bullshit," my husband had whispered. The trial balloons went up that Chuck might go to the UN. We were both elated. The Camelot spirit of government service still drove us. We might yet make the world a better place; American ingenuity and enthusiasm were still alive and well.

Then we heard about the plans to escalate in Vietnam after the election. The public didn't vote for Barry Goldwater because they were afraid that he would start another war. Johnson and his advisers, the so-called "best and the brightest" and the military were secretly planing to do just that.

My husband decided it was time to sign off.

"And what did Mac say to that?"

"He seemed surprised. That whole crowd figures that they can keep Jack's ghost alive by working with LBJ. They're wrong, the dead refusing to bury the dead."

Pretty grim and gloomy sentiments from my cheery little leprechaun.

"More tea?"

"No thanks."

Chuck almost always wanted more tea.

"Another cookie?"

"No."

I waited to hear Gabriel blow his horn to indicate the world was about to come to an end. Chucky Ducky *always* wanted another cookie.

I curled up at his feet and took his hand in mine.

"Shitty," I said.

"Sure is." He sighed. "What was it that Pat said?"

"We'll laugh again but we'll never be young again."

"Yeah."

There was a dinner party scheduled that night. Chuck wanted to skip it. We belonged in Chicago, not this sick place, he insisted.

And I insisted that the Irish go out with smiles. I won, like I usually did when the issue was something important. In fact, generally when it was unimportant. So I dressed up in one of my sexier dresses and made Chuck wear a tie.

He whistled as I dressed. I told him not to be vulgar. He's seen me so often slightly naked, nearly naked, and totally naked, I don't know why it's such a big deal. He likes my little show, however. It's a wife's job to keep her husband happy.

I love my husband (madly), I enjoy sex (usually),

I am always modest (appropriately), and I'm delighted (generally) when, after all these years, I note that my husband is gaping at me.

"Isn't that a dress from our honeymoon?" he asks.

"Certainly not!"

"Same size though?"

"Regardless!" I waved my hand.

He likes to make the point when I tell him you can't give birth to five children and still be erotically attractive.

I retied his tie. He has never learned how to do it right and probably never will as long as I do it for him. He kissed me gently, a ceremony which always concludes the tie ritual.

At least I don't have to tie his shoes—very often.

The party was at a charming old home in Georgetown, all chandeliers and mirrors and crimson hangings and shining china and crystal. The guests were some of the last-ditch veterans of Camelot, witty, sophisticated, in-the-know, and almost as bright as they thought they were.

As usual we were the center of attention, not because I was beautiful, which I was not, and not even because Chuck was funny, which he was even in his grim mood, but because he was considered a marginal member of the "best and the brightest" and because the UN rumors were on everyone's lips.

"Are you looking at an apartment in New York, Rosemarie?" a woman with too much makeup asked.

Actually the Ambassador to the United Nations lives in a suite in the Waldorf Apartments.

"We have a nice home in Chicago," I said firmly.

Dead silence.

"You're really leaving the administration?" a very important journalist (whom Chucky and I both thought was a pompous fool) demanded.

"I'm going back to Chicago where I belong," my leprechaun said grimly.

Silence around the table.

"May one ask why?"

I was afraid that Chuck would repeat his line about LBJ being a corrupt and vulgar redneck.

"The administration," he said somberly, "is bungling into another land war in Asia. I want no part of that policy."

No longer Mr. Life of the Party.

"Surely we have to stand up to the Communists in Southeast Asia if we are to maintain our credibility," another journalist said as if that were as certain as a statement of papal infallibility. Later this jerk became a leading critic of the war. They all did.

"Our credibility to whom?"

"Well . . . World public opinion."

"There is no such thing."

"Our allies will say that we can't be counted on."

"Maybe our allies should learn to take care of themselves."

Gasp around the room. Even the second-string members of the "best and the brightest" shouldn't talk that way.

"We have to stand up to the Communists." One of the least intelligent women at the table repeated the line.

"We stood up to them in Greece and Turkey," my pint-sized lover replied. "And with the Marshall Plan and in Iran and in the Berlin airlift and in Korea and during the missile crisis. Isn't there a statute of limitations?"

"You sound like an isolationist!" she cried in alarm. "Didn't we stop them in Korea?"

"It cost us forty thousand lives! That's a small number compared to what we will lose in a guerrilla war in a jungle! And we won't win it either."

Someone changed the subject. Ambassador O'Malley was clearly wrong. The United States of America could do anything it wanted to do.

In the car returning to the Hay-Adams that night, he sighed loudly, and said, "I don't belong at a party like that, Rosemarie. You do, because you're a bright elegant woman. I'm a little punk from the West Side of Chicago who stumbled in by mistake."

When he's very discouraged, Chuck puts on that West-Side-punk-stumbling-in-by-mistake persona. The worst part of the act is that he half believes it, sometimes more than half.

A light snow was dusting the narrow streets of Georgetown. It fell on the living and the dead and covered the graves of our hopes.

"Don't be silly," I reply, as the scenario demanded. "You're a very distinguished American diplomat."

"Yeah, and I was an all-state quarterback too."

He was not all-state. In fact, he was fourth-string on a team that had only three strings. By a fluke he scored the touchdown which beat Carmel and enabled us to go on to take city. Chuck became a legend. He was never able to understand that myths transcend facts.

"Even the *New York Times* thinks you did a good job over there."

"The professional foreign service people didn't."

"What do they know."

He had said to me once that for someone like him, who had to rely on wit and charm to get by, being an Ambassador was easier than being a precinct captain for the Dick Daley organization.

Regardless, that was no reason to doubt his obvious intelligence—obvious to everyone but himself.

"I'm not the only one who has his doubts about Vietnam. Dean Rusk is the only one who has no questions. McNamara goes along because he thinks it's what the president wants. Mac Bundy tries to play a mediating game. The generals naturally want another war."

"That doesn't sound like an analysis that a stumbling punk would make."

He ignored my point.

"There's lots of doubt at the next level down—George Ball, John McNaughton. We're going to have half a million men in there for a five-year war before the American people even know that there's a war going on."

"No!"

"I think we'll be lucky to be out in ten years—1975."

"Chucky!"

"Yeah, I know, Rosemarie. It's all hard to believe. LBJ has heard those estimates. He doesn't believe them. He thinks he can control the military once they have a big army in the country. He's wrong . . ."

"You have no choice but to quit if that's what's going to happen."

"I know."

"Don't give me bullshit that you don't belong here, not if you can predict exactly what will happen."

"No points for being right five years early, Rosemarie my love . . ."

He put his arm around me and began to hum the music from *Rosemarie* as we turned off Connecticut Avenue. I knew what would happen to me when we were back in the fading opulence of the Hay-Adams. My husband is a very shrewd observer of people. As a red-haired runt he's had to be. There is nothing about me he doesn't know. When I stop to think about that, I feel totally naked. That's so embarrassing that I try not to think about it. Some of the time.

There is nothing in my sexuality that he hasn't figured out. Since the first time he kissed me at Lake Geneva when I was ten I have been mush in his hands. He knows when to leave me alone and when to seduce me and what kind of seductions to use at which times. He insists that all lovemaking is a kind

of seduction, which I suppose it is. The result is that
he can do to me whatever he wants whenever he
wants—that is, if I'm ready for it.

I don't like that. Well, I don't dislike it either.
However, I resent his confidence that he knows all
the things to say and all the buttons to push and all
the places to kiss and caress. It should be difficult for
him, should it not? What is left of my dignity and
independence when I act like a pushover? I tell myself that someday I must have it out with him. I must
insist that I'm not a pushover.

Then I see the glint in his eye and the confident
smile on his face and feel his fingers as they unzip
and unhook me and his lips as they explore me. He
has no right, no right at all to take everything away
from me, all my secrets, all my defenses, all my modesty, and turn me into a pile of pliant mush.

Except that I like being pliant mush.

In the early stages of his assault I want him to go
away and leave me alone. I am a drunk. I am an
addictive personality. I am a neurotic. My father
abused me sexually. My mother beat me, almost
killed me with a poker. I am a terrible mother and an
inadequate wife. I have had five children and am no
longer beautiful. I have no right to sexual pleasure. I
am a lousy lover. I don't say any of these things because I am incapable of saying anything. I need him,
I want him, I must have him. I've wanted him to make
love since he came back from the White House. I'd
been aroused ever since. No time for night prayers
today. Love is a prayer, Chucky argued long ago. Oh,
take me, Chucky Ducky. Please love me, even if I
am not worth loving. Push into me, fill me, drive me
out of my mind, let me be love, nothing but love,
love exploding in and around me, all over me, love
tearing me apart.

Love.

Love for this man who is everything for me. I want

to give myself completely to him. I reach for the gift. Suddenly it's there. We both shout for joy.

Then peace.

He's always very satisfied with himself after he's made love to me. He knows that he's done a good job and that I have been conquered again and loved it. That upsets me a little, but not very much because I am so complacent, so satisfied, so happy.

This time he says, "You're sensational, Rosemarie, more so every time."

I almost give a smart-ass Rosie answer, "You'd better say that."

Instead God makes me say, "You make me better, Chucky," and burst into tears.

He nurses me gently back to solid earth and sings to me. I lay my head on his chest and, undone again, pleasured completely, and filled with love, fall off to sleep.

Damn it, he should go to sleep first, but he never does.

For a few minutes of unbearably sweet ecstasy, I do not doubt myself.

❧ 2 ❧

"President Kennedy was always very fond of you two," the ethereal woman in black whispered as though we were at the gravesite in Arlington National Cemetery instead of in her flawlessly furnished drawing room in the Maryland hunt country. "He said that you Chicago Irish were different from the Boston Irish."

"Better," Chucky said with his most charming grin.

She laughed softly, something she didn't do often these days.

"He was very proud of your work in Bonn," she said, the mask of sadness slipping over her face again. "He said you were in the top ten of his appointments."

"Five," Chuck insisted.

She laughed again.

"Of course . . . I know he would understand the reason you're leaving government service. I merely wanted to tell you that."

I had never been able to understand her relationship with the President. I had figured she liked being first lady and tolerated his infidelities as a necessary price for her role. Now I did not doubt that she had loved him and that her grief was real. Maybe in the world in which she grew up Jack Kennedy's screwing around was accepted as the sort of thing husbands do.

I had warned Chuck that if he tried that sort of thing, I'd kill him. He had replied that probably that was the reason he became impotent every time he was tempted.

"Lyndon," Chuck said, "will do a lot for the civil rights movement. I support that, not that my support matters very much."

"It's the war," I said with a sigh.

"Yes, I understand. President Kennedy often said to me that he would pull our troops out after the 1964 election."

Now he was dead and we were sending more troops in. I hoped that God knew what He was doing.

Both of us were silent.

"I want to thank you both for your friendship and loyalty," she said, rising from her couch, like a queen from a throne. "I hope we will meet again sometime during better days."

Her eyes flooded with tears as she led us to the door.

"Life," my husband said, his voiced choked with sadness, "is too important ever to be anything but life."

"Oh, yes," she agreed.

We drove back to the Hay-Adams in driving rain. I was at the wheel because, as I had established, I was a better driver than he was. I think he let me win that argument because he found it easier not to drive. I turned on the local station that specialized in rock music, the Beach Boys singing "I Get Around" and the Beatles doing "I Feel Fine" and "Love Me, Do."

"Well," my Chuck murmured, "a little touch of royalty is nice in our society, isn't it?"

"We'll not see her like again," I countered, usurping one of his lines.

"I guess not." He sighed. "Rosemarie, do we have to listen to that noise?"

"You know the rules. The one who drives the car gets to pick the station."

"I can't remember voting on that rule."

"You didn't."

Chuck, like his father who knew Louis Armstrong and the other jazz greats of Chicago forty years before, was a jazz aficionado. Rock and roll music he told me was an effort at musical orgasm and I liked it because I was oversexed. That made me a little nervous because April Rosemary was in love with the Beatles.

"I know as well as you do what the word 'jazz' means."

"It's different."

"Why?"

"It just is."

Then, shifting emotional gears, I said, "I worry about A.R.'s obsession with the Beatles."

The three boys, growing into tall, rangy Black Irishmen who could be a junior unit in the Irish Republican Army, ignored rock and roll completely and concentrated on their horns, which they blew on every possible occasion, thus making our residence in Bonn sound like a school for retarded musicians. Moire, as in all things, strove to imitate her big sister.

"Music never ruined anyone," Chuck said, his mind elsewhere. "Not unless people use drugs with it."

That sent a chill through me. I was an addictive personality. What if my older daughter were too?

"I could have stayed in Bonn for Lyndon," he continued, "if it wasn't for this damn war."

The impulse to public service of the Kennedy years does not die easily. Perhaps that's why so many of his people stayed on with LBJ.

"Are you sure you have to quit?"

"Yep."

He sank deeper into his seat in the car and closed

his eyes, as if to blot out the Beatles, the rain, and the sad lines on a widow's face.

I didn't fully understand his opposition to the war. Everyone in Washington was saying that we had to take a stand in Southeast Asia to stop the spread of Communism. You'd think from the hindsight history written later that the people who wrote the history had been wiser than Lyndon and his staff and opposed it from the beginning. That's bullshit. People who thought like Chuck and George Ball were few and far between. Mostly they kept their mouths shut.

The O'Malleys had a long history of military service. His father had collapsed on the parade ground at Fort Leavenworth the day the war in Europe ended, a victim of the Spanish Influenza, and was almost buried alive. His grandfather had enlisted for the Spanish-American War, though he was, thank God, too old to be sent off to Cuba to die of malaria. His great-grandfather, the original Charles O'Malley had joined the Union Army as a raw immigrant boy at the age of eighteen. John Evangelist O'Malley (Chucky's delightful father, aka "Vangie"), having survived the flu, served in the Black Horse Troop National Guard unit between the two wars. He was called up two weeks after Pearl Harbor and was destined for the jungles of New Guinea. Chuck, then fourteen, somehow managed to persuade our local congressman to have him sent to Fort Sheridan. And Chuck himself had served in the Army of Occupation in Germany after the war, with considerable bravery as some of his friends from that era had whispered to me.

"Military service, yeah," Chuck said to me, "but none of us ever had a gun fired at them in anger."

"Except you in that black market roundup outside of Wurzburg."

"That doesn't count . . . Too many people I know died in Korea."

One person in particular, I thought—Christopher

Kurtz, the best male friend, maybe the only male friend, Chuck ever had was killed leading his platoon of Marines out of the trap Douglas MacArthur had sent them into at the Chosin Reservoir. Chris was killed attacking a Chinese machine-gun nest. As usual, in that strange core of the real Chucky Ducky, the arguments were always personal and local, no matter how good he was at articulating more sophisticated arguments.

"Not our kind of people," Chuck said, breaking a long silence.

"No," I agreed.

"Didn't have a neighborhood."

"Neither of them ever did."

"Well," my husband concluded the conversation, "we do and we're going back to it. That's where we belong. We'll stay there."

That it was where we belonged I did not doubt. However, my husband was a restless soul. I did not take seriously his vow never to leave the neighborhood again.

There were many layers beneath his quick-talking, pint-sized redhead persona, not that the top layer wasn't authentic. Chuck was a gifted artist, deeply sensitive and compassionate, incorrigibly romantic (he'd freed the magic princess from the tower and then ravaged her much to their mutual delight), and tough as they come when he had to be (as he had to be with me). He was also shrewd enough politically to be a precinct captain in Cook County and intellectually smart enough to turn down an appointment at THE University as we called it. I can't describe what the inner core of the man is because I don't know. However, down there in the subbasement of his soul is the reason why I love him.

Oversexed?

Maybe. If he is, like I say, so am I. That's why back in our suite at the Hay-Adams that terrible af-

ternoon we buried ourselves in one another in yet
another passionate obsequy for Camelot. The rain,
driven across Lafayette Park by a fierce wind, beat
mindlessly against the windows.

It was also raining the first Sunday in March in our
sprawling and comfortable Dutch Colonial house on
New England Avenue in Oak Park, technically beyond the boundaries of St. Ursula parish, but still
our parish because Chuck's father John Evangelist
O'Malley had designed it.

(We also maintained an official voting address in
Chicago in the basement of an apartment building I
owned on the east side of Austin Boulevard. We had
no intention of working for the city, but we figured it
was our legacy to vote in Chicago elections. The tiny
basement apartment was furnished so that it could be
used as an occasional getaway from the kids.)

Moreover, the house was quiet in early evening,
which it almost never is. Our daughters were over at
the Antonellis' house listening to the Beatles no doubt
with Carlotta Antonelli. Carlotta's mother Peg is
my closest friend in all the world and incidentally
Chuck's sister. The boys were watching a basketball
game upstairs on color television, something of an
innovation in those days. Chuck was reading some
dreary economics journal—he hadn't picked up his
camera or visited our darkroom since we came home.
I had thrown aside *Herzog* in disgust at Saul Bellow's
narcissism and picked up William Golding's *The
Spire*. We were both obviously in a bad mood. I
longed for summer and Long Beach.

Earlier in the morning, after we came home from
Mass and while Chuck was eating his usual breakfast
of bacon, eggs, waffles, cereal, and what he called his
"Sunday breakfast steak," I had read the *New York
Times* magazine article about him. We both knew it
was coming. My husband pretended to be indifferent.
I did not.

"How is it?" he asked casually.

"It's okay," I said, with equal aplomb. "They think you left the ship because of grief more than because of the war, but they have some good quotes about the war in there too. They also praise the work we did at Bonn and lament that perhaps principles that are a bit too lofty caused you to leave government service."

"Hmm," he said, soaking his already soggy waffle with syrup. "Lemme see."

I pushed the magazine in his direction. He glanced at the pictures, scanned the text, and placed it carefully next to his plate while he inhaled the waffle.

"Who was the Ambassador to the Federal Republic at that time?" he asked, his lips quivering with suppressed laughter.

"You were, dear."

"Most of the pictures are of my 'breathtaking' wife and my 'handsome' children. It would appear that they were responsible for the success of my work."

"You noticed?"

"I was busy with my lofty ideas and they wandered around charming the Germans."

He picked up the paper again.

"They don't mention my dissertation on the Marshall Plan, but they are obsessed with the clothes this breathtaking woman wore."

"Naturally."

"Gee, what would they have said if she was really beautiful and not the worn-out mother of five children?"

I threw the book review section at him.

Then we both laughed and dissolved into each other's arms.

"Isn't this a bitchin' picture of me?" April Rosemary stormed into the kitchen, waving a second copy of the *Times* that had somehow found its way into our house. "Daddy, you look kind of funny in this picture, don't you?"

"Daddy always looks that way, dear," I corrected her. "People call it cute, not funny."

"Yes, Mom," she said with a giggle.

Then the family poured in—Vangie, the good April, Peg and Vince and their kids. For an hour we were young again and happy again, despite Pat Moynihan's mordant predictions. All of us argued that Chuck's presence at Bonn had been unnecessary. He took the position that the assertion was absolutely true. His "breathtaking wife" and his "handsome" children had snatched the bacon of the United States out of the fire. He continued to eat bacon and butter English muffins with raspberry jam as the festival roared. It ended, as all O'Malley family festivals did, in song, the last of which, as usual, was "Rosemarie," as it usually is.

I loved seeing him happy again. I didn't mind the bias of the article. Fuck the *New York Times*!

Except I am not breathtaking. No way.

Then, when everyone went home, we settled down in front of the fireplace with our books and our memories and our grief.

Then the phone rang. Chuck ignored it. I picked it up.

"Rosemarie O'Malley," I said primly.

"Are you watching *Judgment at Nuremberg* on the tube?" asked Peg.

"We've had enough of Germany."

"They've broken into it with pictures from Alabama. The rednecks are murdering Negroes down there."

I dashed over to the TV and turned it on.

"Chuck!" I shouted. "Look!"

"We are replaying this incident," said Walter Cronkite, "because we believe it is a historic event in American history. Some six hundred civil rights demonstrators in Selma, Alabama, are preparing to cross the Edmund Pettus Bridge over the Alabama River and to march on to Montgomery fifty miles away. They are about to march two by two across the bridge, led by Hosea Williams of the Southern Christian Leadership Conference and John Lewis of the Student Non-Violent Coordinating Committee. They intend to protest the denial of voting rights to Negroes in Alabama. Across the river [the camera cut to the other side] Sheriff Jim Clark's mounted posse awaits them, accompanied by scores of state troopers."

As we watched, the Negro group marched onto the bridge. Someone ordered them to halt. They kept on marching till they were face-to-face with the white lawmen. They knelt to pray. Then there was an order to disperse. They did not move, then a voice—later we found out it was the Sheriff's—shouted, "Get those goddamned niggers!"

While the whole nation watched, the lawmen charged, swinging clubs, cattle prods, bullwhips, and rubber hoses. They pushed into the crowd, and amid Rebel yells, beat men, women, and children. They rode their horses into people and drove them off the bridge into the river. Clouds of tear gas drifted across the river. The crowd broke up and ran. The police continued their pursuit, smashing heads, trampling over bodies with horses, beating them with bullwhips.

The TV cameras caught the expressions of orgasmic satisfaction on the faces of the white cops and the pain and fear on the faces of the marchers.

"In Selma, Alabama," Cronkite went on solemnly, "the rule of law is Sheriff Jim Clark's order—'Get those goddamn niggers!'"

"My God," I said, "in the United States!"

Chuck was grinning.

"Lewis and Hosea got what they wanted," he said happily. "Now the whole country knows what the South is like! Sheriff Clark doesn't know what television can do."

"I have to go pack," I announced, tossing *The Spire* aside.

"Pack?" Chuck was still staring at the screen.

"I'm going down there. We'll teach those rednecks who won the Civil War."

"Lyndon will federalize the National Guard," he said still bemused. "It's all over. The Negroes will be voting in the next election."

"I'm going to be in the next march!" I yelled, charging for the stairs.

"Then I guess I'd better be too," he said, still confused.

"With your camera!"

Then, for the first time since he walked out on LBJ, my husband came alive.

"Hell yes!"

❦ 3 ❦

At Selma I realized that I was a radical, always had been a radical. I had a hell of a good time. I also understood, without Chuck telling me, that I could become a dangerous woman. I discovered that being a radical gave me an adrenaline high. When the white cops who looked and acted like they were characters out of a Faulkner novel shouted obscenities, you yelled back at them that they were redneck trash. When they clutched their batons as if they were going to club you or threatened to turn loose their guard dogs, you snarled that we were going to turn Selma over to the Negroes and drive them into the swamps where they belonged with the other animals.

Well, I said that. It was perhaps too literary an insult. Moreover, Peg, who was with me at all times to make sure I restrained my tongue, absolutely forbade me to use any obscenity.

"You must not sink to their level," she insisted.

"I didn't go to Rosary College," I told her, "so I don't know how to be a lady. I don't even wear gloves when it's not cold."

Peg ignored me as she always did when I said something stupid.

"Besides, you shouldn't shock these poor boys who are gritting their teeth and protecting us," she said, gesturing toward the teenagers of the Alabama National Guard, who were now under federal command.

"With the stars and bars pins on their uniform! They're as bad as Sheriff Clark's bozos!"

"They now work for the United States government," she insisted, "and they're obeying orders, no matter how hard it is. We should respect their integrity."

That's Peg for you. She was becoming more and more like her mother, the good April, a woman who thought benignly of everyone, even if they were not Irish, because after all, it wasn't their fault they weren't Irish. Occasionally I reflected that we were now older than the good April (Chuck's mother) was when I adopted their family—thereby as my shrinks have insisted saving my life. Just as I had deteriorated through the years, Peg had grown more lovely, a slender elegant symphony in brown just like her mother. I explained the contrast between us by the fact that she only had four children and I had five. Chuck once claimed that we were two forest animals, she a sleek timber wolf and I a prowling cougar. Now she was a grand duchess like her mother and I a shrewish, shanty-Irish fishwife—no matter what the *New York Times* said about my performance in Bonn.

When I announced to her on the phone that Chuck and I were flying to Selma to finish what the Civil War had not finished, she replied that she and Vince were coming with us, he to protect Chuck from being beaten up again like he was in Little Rock and she to help me keep my big mouth shut. "You must not call those poor people white trash," she had insisted, "it's just as bad as calling Negroes niggers."

The four of us were obviously crazy. Nine cousins in our two families—my five and Rosie's four—and we were going to Selma. There was no one in the crazy O'Malley family to tell us not to fly to Atlanta, rent a car, and drive to Selma. Father Ed O'Malley, my husband's youngest sibling, was organizing a group to respond to Martin Luther King's plea to people of all faiths to rally around those who wanted to march through Selma and on to Montgomery in support of the voting rights bill President Kennedy had pushed for. As the good April said, "Well, if Father Edward thinks it's all right, then it must be all right."

Lyndon, to give the devil his due as Chuck said, had delivered a powerful speech. Selma, he told the nation, was not a Negro problem or a Southern problem. It was an American problem. It was deadly wrong to deny anyone in America the right to vote. He ended by telling the people of the country in his rich Central Texas accent, "We shall overcome!"

He federalized the Alabama National Guard to protect the marchers and those who had come to support them. Now it will be safe, I told myself. Then I repeated the reassurance to my husband, who was having second thoughts.

"That," he replied, "is what the man said on Fort Sumter."

As we were departing the elder O'Malley house—having left the nine cousins in charge of their grandmother and grandfather, Chuck's doubts became more serious, surely because of his memories of Little Rock. He would go and the rest of us would stay at home. We vetoed that suggestion.

The cousins didn't mind a few days away from their parents. Grandma April spoiled them rotten and they knew it. Only April Rosemary had her doubts. "I wish you wouldn't go to that terrible place, Mom," she said as she hugged me, tears in her eyes.

I was too caught up in being part of a great turning point in American history to understand. You see, Chuck had been at the McCarthy hearings and in Korea and in Little Rock. All I had ever done was to smile at people in Bonn. It was time for me to become part of the action.

The Kennedy wake and funeral, for some reason, didn't count.

Peg's marriage had been rocky at first. When Vince came home from the prisoner of war camp in Korea, he had been a real problem—sorry for himself and angry that no one else seemed sorry for him. Well, I had straightened him out in my best shanty-Irish-shrew style and that was that. I never had any problems with Chuck . . . How could I? He had a hell of a lot of problems with me until I sobered up.

The atmosphere in the Negro section of Selma as we do-gooders swarmed in was unbearably exciting. The Negroes (as they were then called) could hardly believe that we white folks had come to support them. We could hardly believe how poor and oppressed they were. We hugged and kissed and sang "We Shall Overcome" all night long. I hardly saw my husband. He was scampering around, clutching his Leica (which Trudi, his German love when he was in the Constabulary, had given him) and blazing away fearlessly. No wonder the thugs had got him in Little Rock. He seemed to think that because he was short and boyish and innocent, the rednecks wouldn't see him. Twice, Vince later told me, groups of good ole boys closed in on him, with booze on their breath and murder in their eyes. Then they saw Vince, in the same shape he was in when he made All-American guard at Notre Dame, and reconsidered their options.

"Where were the soldiers?" I demanded, suddenly afraid.

"They can't be everywhere. The orders are that the marchers should stay on this side of the river till tomorrow and the white folk on the other side. Chuck figures that because he's press, he can go wherever he wants."

The adrenaline drained temporarily from my bloodstream. I wanted to go home.

Chuck was indeed press. His friends at the *New*

York Times had commissioned him to do a photographic essay to be called "Selma!"

"There's nothing to worry about," he reassured me. "I talked to Bobby this afternoon. Lyndon has persuaded Governor George Wallace to keep his big mouth shut and, just in case, he's put on alert a battalion of Marines at Camp Lejeune. Bobby doesn't think we'll need them."

Where, I wondered, had my exhausted and shivering husband found a line on which to talk to Bobby. Then I realized that Bobby had found him.

We huddled in a sharecropper's barn outside Selma the night before the march to Montgomery. It was cold, not as cold as Chicago in March but plenty cold. We sang most of the night. Some of the northern whites were drinking to stay warm, not plastered by any means but, as the Irish say, a bit of the drink had been taken. A few of the kids from New York were smoking pot, the first time I had ever seen that.

"Bobby has cut a deal between Dr. King and the cops. Only a hundred and fifty of us will actually cross the bridge with him tomorrow, most of them will be local Negroes plus some church people from the north, those two Corondolet nuns from St. Louis, up in the first row with him. Eddie will be right behind them. The rest of you will drive or bus down to Montgomery and meet us in front of the State House."

"What's this 'you and us' stuff?"

"You can't come," he replied, "because they don't need any shanty-Irish faces in the crowd and I can come because they need a photographer with an international reputation for courage under fire."

"You're not scared?" Vince asked.

"Terrified," my brave knight admitted.

"Why the small crowd?" Peg asked.

"Easier for the troops to protect on the march. To the TV camera, a handful of people crossing the river looks like a mob. Then in front of the State House, they'll open up the lens and everyone can see that there are thousands."

Then and there I made up my mind that I would be in the march. I had never walked fifty miles in my life. Well, it was time to try.

The next morning was cold and gray. At the car, where SCLC marshals were trying to line up the convoy to Montgomery, I kissed Peg and hugged her big lug.

"If I don't make it, take good care of the kids," I whispered, and then dashed away before they could talk me out of it. No way was I about to let Chucky Ducky have all the fun.

That shows how immature I was. I thought it was a movie and we were the good guys.

No one tried to stop me as I joined the band of marchers at the bridge. I found Ed in his Roman collar and one of Chuck's Ike jackets from Bamberg.

"Need a broken-down Irish housewife to walk with you, Father?"

He grinned at me, "I would have bet all the money I have that you'd show up . . . And I reject the adjective and the noun."

As Ed has matured in his priestly vocation, he has become talkative, not like Chuck, of course, but he has the flair even if he is less outrageous. He thinks I'm someone special because he claims I gave him good advice when he was thinking of leaving the priesthood. All I did was listen . . .

"Scared?" I asked him.

"Sure am . . . You?"

"On a high . . . I hope you or my pint-sized husband or someone is around when I come down off it."

Then Dr. King began to speak, his deep baritone voice drowning out the wind. I don't remember what he said. The important thing was that he said it. Then we joined hands, sang "We Shall Overcome," and marched onto the bridge.

I was sky-high. I wondered briefly whether my high was anything like getting drunk. I promised God that I would never permit such a high again—a promise I did not always keep—and asked him to take care of my husband and children.

It never occurred seriously to me for a moment that my husband's life might be in danger, much less my own.

The situation was scary. Sheriff Clark and his mounted police were lined up along the riverbank. The State Police were right behind them, their dogs—poor-white-trash dogs, I thought—were straining at their leashes. On the main street of the town, crowds of angry whites were shouting obscenities. Protecting our line of march were these poor kids in the National Guard, obeying their orders like good soldiers, though they probably would have been much happier if they were swinging their riffle butts against us.

Shut up you bitch, I told myself. They're brave young men doing their duty.

So far.

What if the strain was too much for them? What if the cries of the white crowd, the barking of the dogs, the singing of a hymn they must have hated, the determined march all proved too much for them? What if they broke ranks and joined the mob?

Where the hell was Lyndon's battalion of Marines when we really needed them?

Then I was off the bridge and on the street. We were marching through Selma!

"Smile for the camera, lady!" a familiar voice cried. "You too, fadder!"

"Charles Cronin O'Malley, act your age!"

"Yes, ma'am . . . We'll call this one 'priest marches with beautiful woman!' "

And off he scampered, like an organ grinder's little monkey.

Take good care of him, I instructed the Lord. What would I do without him.

I imagined that I heard a voice saying, don't worry!

I did just the same.

We managed to get through the town and out on the highway. The tension eased. Jim Clark's people had made their point and went home, unaware perhaps that the South, *their* South, would never be the same. The marchers were protected on all sides by the troops, State Police, the National Guard, and federal marshals—jeeps in front of us, jeeps on either side of us, jeeps behind us. Bobby meant business. He was not about to permit a single incident to plunge the march into bloody chaos.

This was after all, the United States of America, a hundred years, almost to the day since Appomattox Court House. I wanted to sing "The Battle Hymn of the Republic," but I figured that Dr. King would not approve.

Fifty miles is a long distance, longer than I would have thought possible. By the time our bedraggled band joined the huge throng in front of the State House, I was numb with cold and exhaustion and my voice was hoarse. At some points along the march only Dr. King and I were singing. I was ready to collapse. Indeed I would have collapsed if Ed had not grabbed me.

"I'm fine, Ed, just fine," I said bravely. "How many days have we been on the road?"

Chucky bounced by me and kissed me quickly.

"Proud of you, Rosemarie my darling." He hummed a few bars from our song and then dashed up to the podium. Somehow the soldiers knew that he should not be stopped.

He had to be twice as tired as I was. More adrenaline, I told myself.

"We'll take care of her, Ed," I heard Vince Antonelli say. "Could we give you a lift back?"

"I should stay with Dr. King," he said firmly. "Thanks anyway."

Peg and Vince supported me on either side. A lot of people talked. The crowd replied as Negroes did in church, "Oh yeah! You're right! Tell it like it is."

We sang hymns again. Astonishingly my adrenaline cut in yet again. My high surged back. I shouted and screamed as loudly as any Negro.

Then it was all over and, still supported by my best friend and her husband, I stumbled back toward our Hertz car. I almost fell on my face as I stepped over a low concrete barrier. A young guardsman reached out to grab my arm.

"Thank you, soldier," I said brightly. "Thank you for everything."

The kid's face split into a wide grin.

"Yes, MA'AM !"

"See, Rosemarie," Peg, like the good April, had to make their point, "some of them are nice boys, just like he is."

Chuck was waiting at the car.

"What took you so long? I have to get this last batch developed!"

He swept me up in his arms.

"Rosemarie, you're wonderful!"

"I just want to sleep for forty-eight hours and soak my feet in water while I'm sleeping."

I promptly went to sleep in the rear seat of the car, still in Chuck's arms.

Thank you, I told the Lord in my last waking moment. I am really an idiot to leave five kids at grandma's house and come on this crazy adventure. Thank you too that it's all over.

My final gratitude was premature.

I heard a sharp whine, something hit the window of the car and shattered it. Then there were several more whining sounds. The car leaped forward as though it had a turbocharger.

"They're shooting at us," Peg screamed.

"Hang on," Vince shouted.

My husband, who never swears, cried out a string of angry expletives I didn't think he knew. But this is a dream, I told myself, so it's all right.

There was one more whine but it didn't hit us.

"Peg?" Vince asked, a choke in his voice.

"Covered with shattered glass, but all right," she murmured, her voice small and unsteady.

"Chuck!"

More fearsome obscenities.

"Rosie?"

"This is a nightmare." I sighed. "So I won't tell the good April the terrible things my husband said."

When they all laughed nervously in response, I realized it wasn't a dream.

"Well," I said piously, "God didn't let them hit any of us."

I curled up and went back to sleep in my husband's brave arms.

Two people died on that road the next day.

I was exhausted the next morning, but my high was back. While Chuck worked in his makeshift darkroom, I bounced around the Negro quarter hugging people and singing with them, a weary Peg trailing behind me. Then she borrowed a Negro's fiddle and we went into our usual act to the delight of the locals.

Vince found us later and said that Chucky had finished his work and wanted to leave at once so he could begin producing prints. Suddenly I wanted to be home. Now. Back in peaceful Oak Park in my own Dutch Colonial home with my own children. Enough history for a while. Chuck was still riding high.

"Rosemarie, this will be a book, a historic archive for the peaceful triumph of the nonviolent Civil Rights Movement. The Negro problem in our country is over. Martin Luther King is one of the great Americans in the whole history of America. An American Gandhi!"

Chucky Ducky doesn't usually get grandiloquent

At the airport the man wanted to know what the fuck we'all done with his car.

"Some white trash shot at us," I told him before saner voices could be heard. "Almost killed us."

"Serves y'all right for not staying up North where you belong."

"You didn't hear what our Southern president said the other night?"

"Who's goin' to pay for what y'all done to my car?"

"It's Hertz's car, you redneck asshole, and their insurance company is going to pay for it because I didn't initial the waiver. I didn't figure it was safe riding down your focking white-trash roads."

"Rosemarie!" Peg snapped.

"I'm sorry, sir," I said, putting on my humble-pie face and voice. "You get shot at in the night, you get a little edgy."

"Yes, ma'am," he said, "I surenuf can understand that. Praise the Lord that none of y'all were hurt."

"AMEN to that," I replied fervently.

"He done delivered y'all from the valley of death."

"And keeps us under the shadow of his wings."

"Surenuf!"

"Chucky Ducky, where did you find this babe?" Peg asked.

"She used to hang around with my sister when we were kids."

Chuck worked on his negatives on the flight back to Chicago.

"Make the prints tomorrow and then ship them off to New York. They may want to use them next Sunday or the Sunday after."

We were met at the airport, like conquering heroes,

by Vangie and the good April. Of course there was a celebration at their house with the usual crazy O'Malley songfest and drinks all around, save for me and my husband, who sipped Lapsang Souchong tea. The nine cousins cheered us and sang with us. Poor little Moire of the flaming red hair hugged me, and said, "I saw you on television, Mommy. You were singing and you were really pretty."

Her big sister did not share her enthusiasm. I was going to have a problem there. Did she resent our risking our lives? Or perhaps leaving her and the others alone for a couple of days? There was no telling what the crazy and very risky adventure might do to a sensitive fifteen-year-old's head.

Tomorrow, I told myself. Tomorrow.

I woke up at least a dozen times that night. The rifle shots continued to whine by my head. I finally slept for a few hours and woke up, groggy and confused, about ten. I poured my morning cup of tea. Then suddenly it hit me. I had taken a reckless chance with my life and the lives of my friends. If it had not been for me, they would not have gone to Selma. If they had been killed, it was my fault.

I glanced at the newspaper and sipped some more tea.

The Marines had landed that day at Danang—the other side of Lyndon Baines Johnson.

I would not tell Chuck until the prints were finished.

I confessed my insanity to him as he worked feverishly in our darkroom.

"St. Crispin's Day," he muttered, as a print came up in the tray.

"What?"

"You know, Prince Hal, men abed in England . . . Selma will be our St. Crispin's Day for the rest of our lives. We were mad do it. But thank God we did it."

"And that we came home alive."

"That too!"

"You're not going to send that print of me and Eddie to the *Times*, are you?"

"No! Your picture's been in there too many times this year. I'll save it for the book."

"Well, at least I have all my clothes on."

Chuck suspended his frantic work for a moment.

"That really doesn't make any difference, Rosemarie, my darling."

I left, lest I get into another silly argument with him.

April Rosemary, in her plaid Trinity High School uniform, cornered me in my Edwardian, oak-paneled office where I was working on notes for my next conversation with my shrink. (Chuck had once insisted that it was more expensive than the Oval Office.)

"I want to have a *very* serious conversation with you, *Mother*."

When I'm *mother* I am generally in deep trouble

"Of course," I said with equal formality.

"Do you and Dad realize what you are doing to us?"

Oh, boy.

"Suppose you tell me."

"All the kids at school make fun of us because they say our parents are weirdos."

"The boys too?"

"*Mother*, that's not the point."

"And what is the point?"

"Why do you and Dad have to be *different* from everyone else's parents?"

She wasn't angry about the risk to our lives. She was angry because we were different.

"Do they make fun of your cousin Carlotta too?"

Carlotta was Peg's daugther and April Rosemary's "best friend."

"*Mother!* You know Carlotta is an airhead. Besides, her parents weren't on television yesterday like you and Daddy and Uncle Ed."

"You're embarrassed because we were on television yesterday . . . I'm sure we weren't on for more than a few moments, were we?"

"*Mother*, you don't understand! You're on television *all the time!*"

I thought about demanding to know what other times, but decided against it.

"Kids make fun of you because we're on television?"

Tears welled up in her eyes, tears of anger.

"Why can't you and Daddy just be like everyone else's parents?"

I bit my tongue. She was new in Trinity and different from the other kids, none of whom had spent almost four years in Germany. A few jerks were trying to put her down. At her age in life that meant that the whole world had suddenly turned cruel.

Little bitches. I hated them just like I hated those who made fun of me twenty years ago.

"Daddy is a very great man, April Rosemary. He doesn't quite realize it and he doesn't act like he's great, but he is. You have to let him be who he is. Maybe you could even be proud of him."

"I just wish you and Daddy would understand what his greatness is doing to my life!"

"There were very bad things happening down South, dear. Daddy felt . . . we all felt . . . that we ought to do something about it."

"Why couldn't the Southerners do it themselves?"

Tears were now pouring down her cheeks.

"The Negroes can't get their rights by themselves. They need our help."

"Why should you help them? If they can't help themselves, isn't it their fault?"

Ah, the little bitches were racist and had racists for parents.

I struggled to contain my temper.

"Jesus said that whatever we do to the least of the brothers and sisters we do to him."

"Did he also say that you had to make your children feel like fools!"

Angry sobs shaking her body, she jumped out of her chair and dashed from my office.

Selfish little bitch!

She would get over it.

Yet I had lost her. I went over my words. Was there anything I might have said that would have helped? Probably not. She wanted to punish us. And she had.

Not since I went sober had I thought that I might be an embarrassment to my children.

I sat silently in my chair, paralyzed. I felt like one of the bullets fired the night before last had hit me. I could not even cry.

Then a mass of red hair appeared at the doorway to my office, followed by the face of Moire as she peered around the corner.

"Morgen," she said in German. *"Wie gehts?"*

Our youngest had absorbed the German language more completely than the rest of us. Imp that she was— a womanly Chucky without any of the hangups—she loved to pretend that she knew no English. Unlike the Trinity girls, her first grade classmates thought she was hilariously funny.

One of her tricks was to enter a room with a fierce scowl as though she expected to fight someone and then, after giving the scowl time to have its impact, her face would light up like the Palmolive beacon on the top of the Drake Hotel and she'd rush at the nearest available lap.

In this case, mine was the only available one.

"Mommy, Mommy, Mommy!"

"What dear?"

"Can I be with you on television the next time!"

I tried to explain to her that there wouldn't be a next time.

Chuck dashed into the office, a large, neatly wrapped box propped up against his chest. He swooped down to hug and kiss his youngest child.

"Off to the airport to put this on a plane to New York," he said. "See you when I get back."

Everything Chuck did was neat. In reaction to the relaxed condition of his family life he had become almost compulsively fastidious. We had problems over this in our early days together because, in addition to being a drunk, I'm also a slob. I tried to get my act together, and I did improve. Then one day he said, "Rosemarie, there's no reason why you should be as compulsive as I am. I wish I could be a slob."

So of course I relaxed and improved considerably—I was about as neat as the good April and Peg, not very neat by the Polish American standards of "Missus" our wonderful housekeeper.

These thoughts did not distract me from the conviction that I had lost my daughter and might never get her back.

Then the boys and Moire erupted back into my office—the poor little tyke trailing behind them but running to keep up. Their teachers thought I had been wonderful on television and praised me for my courage. April Rosemary's problem was unique.

No, there were probably jerks in the grammar school too, racist kids with racist parents, but boys would simply laugh them off.

April Rosemary's problem was unique among our kids because of age and gender and sensitivity. Unique so far anyway.

I had lost her. It must be partly my fault.

I made some more notes for the shrink, a new one since Dr. Stone had moved to Boston.

Our dinner that night was typical—as many conversations as there were people. Except for April Rosemary. She sulked.

Later that night, I waited naked in bed, the covers folded down at my waist for Chucky to finish his work in the darkroom.

Finally, my husband ambled into our bedroom, so tired that he could barely walk a straight line. He closed the door softly.

"I am a mere shadow of my former self," he said, standing over me and smiling, "and the woman wants to make love."

He touched one of my breasts lightly. I winced as the electricity of desire rushed through my body.

"Ah," he said appreciatively, "the woman needs to make love. I should perhaps tease her ever so gently."

"You can do whatever you want to me, husband mine, but I must tell you about the conversation I had with your daughter this afternoon."

I told him as he undressed, slipped into bed next to me, and folded me into his arms.

"I've lost her, Chucky. I know I've lost her."

"She's trying out her role as an adult, Rosemarie," he said softly. "We're the first ones around to oppose. It's part of growing up."

"It will never be the same between us." I found that I was weeping, though I had sworn I would not. I did not want to spoil our bout of love.

"In a way you're right, Rosemarie. If we're patient with her, however, and love her no matter how much of a little idiot she is, we will develop a new relationship with her which will be much better. You've been wonderful with her so far. Now we both must learn to be patient."

Where had he picked up all this psychological mumbo jumbo? Doubtless he'd read a book.

"She hates us."

"For the moment. Someday soon she'll celebrate our St. Crispin's Day memories with us."

"How soon?"

"I don't know, Rosemarie. Maybe real soon. Maybe not for a long time. We have to believe in her and the faith and love we've had for her all her life."

"It's probably my fault because I was a drunk when she was a kid."

"I don't think so, Rosemarie. She loved you till last week. She'll work it out eventually. God gives us children to take care of for a few years, then He expects us to give them back to Him."

"She's too young."

"It will do us no good to try to push her. We never have."

"Maybe we shouldn't have gone to Selma."

"Don't say that, Rosemarie. Don't let her blackmail us."

"Where did you get all this wisdom?"

"Picked it up on the run, I guess . . . You still want to make love."

"OF COURSE I do."

So we lost ourselves in the deep well of passion. I slept soundly after. No more rifle bullets whining by my head.

The next morning I woke up worrying about my daughter, about all my children. Would they all have to leave us?

I also worried about my husband. He was as worried as I was about our kids. Since I am a neurotic and a drunk, he had to pretend not to worry.

That wasn't fair.

❧ 4 ❧

"Rosemarie, how many pounds have you gained since the last time we spoke with one another?"

I had spilled out to my shrink the madness of our Selma excursion and my terror over April Rosemary. She responded by asking me about my weight.

"Five pounds?" I suggested.

Her gray eyes twinkling, she shook her head, a mother superior with a dishonest but amusing novice.

"Three?"

Dr. Ward shook her head again as if the novice, however appealing, was chronically dishonest.

"A pound and a half," I admitted, feeling very guilty.

She sighed patiently.

Her office was a tiny room overlooking Harlem Avenue, and a park across the street struggling to emerge from a Chicago winter. Two chairs, a desk, and a shelf with books and a few snapshots were the only furniture, save for the photos, a perfect setting for my novice mistress. Or confessor.

"I thought we had agreed, Rosemarie, that, attractive as you may be when you look like an escapee from a prison camp, your physical and mental health require that you weigh ten pounds more than you do."

"I think I can remember that." I granted her point.

"You could at least snack on the way while you're rushing madly about."

"That's the way people my age get fat," I argued stubbornly.

"Shall we worry about that bridge in the unlikely event that we come to it?"

"Yes, ma'am."

"And, Rosemarie, I am not a mother superior even if sometimes I may sound like one."

"Yes, s'ter."

Margaret Mary Ward Keenan was a small pretty woman with long auburn hair and big gray eyes which seemed to burn with sympathy and warmth, a good fairy assigned to take care of me. Dr. Stone, who had been in charge of me when I had gone on the wagon, had betrayed me by taking an appointment at the Harvard Medical School.

"I strongly recommend Dr. Ward," she told me. "She is a psychologist and not a medical doctor. She is very unorthodox, but you, my dear, need someone very unorthodox."

I rebelled against this decision. Naturally. However, Dr. Ward's maternal smile—though she was my age—melted me. I needed a mother to take care of me.

Unorthodox she was. Somehow or the other we had agreed that I was regularly underweight because of low self-esteem. Some women hide their low self-valuation by putting on weight. Determined to be different from everyone, I did it by not being heavy enough. I would therefore put on weight, even if it meant a daily visit to Petersen's ice-cream parlor, a luxury of which I had often dreamed.

She and her husband Jerry Keenan lived in the parish just west of us. So I encounter her at various social occasions. She's not embarrassed by such meetings, but I am. Once I introduced her to Chucky.

"Dr. Ward, this is my husband Chuck O'Malley."

"All the good things she says about me are true," he said, "and all the bad things are false."

"Why, Mr. O'Malley . . . or to be proper, Dr. O'Malley, what would ever make you think we talk about you?"

My husband turned purple and laughed, "Touché!"

Later he whispered to me, "I hope that child doesn't have any male patients."

"What do you mean?" I turned on my thunder-and-lightning frown.

"Most men wouldn't be able to keep their hands off her . . . I would, of course, because I have such long practice at self-restraint, but . . ."

I shoved him with my elbow.

"Regardless! You have the dirtiest mind in the world," I told him.

"I don't know who keeps the list."

"I do and you be quiet!"

"Yes, ma'am." He giggled, content with himself.

In her office that day after Selma, I was trying to find an excuse for avoiding Petersen's.

"Well, I've been terribly busy . . ."

"Do we not have here," Maggie Ward (her *real* name), "Rosemarie, the perfect metaphor for your complex? I have given you license to indulge in your passion for malted milks, and you reject the license."

"I enjoy sex," I said defensively.

"Not as much as you might."

That hit home. I had admitted to her that there were times when Chucky and I were making love that I resisted the ecstasy that I might have enjoyed. I was afraid of what might happen. Moreover, I didn't deserve that much pleasure.

"Now," Dr. Maggie Ward said to me, "let us talk about your trip to Alabama."

She was silent for a moment, as was I. That meant I was supposed to say something.

"Well . . . It was a crazy risk . . . Wasn't it?"

"I thought we expected such behavior from the crazy O'Malleys."

"We could have all been killed."

"You weren't."

"I was responsible for Peg and Vince."

"Surely they have minds of their own. Indeed as you describe your sister-in-law to me she is a paladin of common sense."

"Well . . ."

"You would, of course, do it again, wouldn't you?"

Unfair question.

"I might not take so many chances . . ."

"One would hope not."

"I loved the excitement, the adventure, the adrenaline rush . . ."

"Which is to say that you are Rosemarie Helen Clancy O'Malley."

"I could have died . . ."

"We all die someday, Rosmarie."

"I know that."

Maybe after I was dead the demons racing around in my skull would leave me alone.

"All your life you have been taking risks, high risks, in defense of your selfhood. Have they not paid off?"

"We've been through this before, haven't we?"

"I believe so. Does it not seem possible to you that wise, if high risks, are your grace?"

"Like my karma?"

She grinned. "If you wish."

I didn't like this crazy Clancy broad who was good at taking wise if high risks.

"You'd probably be dead now, Rosemarie, if you hadn't taken a lot of risks when you were younger."

Maybe.

"What about April Rosemary?"

"What about her?"

"Am I going to lose her because I'm just a little crazy? Or maybe a lot crazy?"

"Do you expect your daughter to be just like you even if she looks like a clone?"

"Well . . ."

"Should she be fighting with the nuns and the other young women the way you did?"

"No . . ."

"Has she not grown up in a home where her parents loved one another and her?"

"So?"

"You tell me, Rosemarie."

"You always say that!"

She nodded and waited for my answer.

"She'll have different mountains to climb?"

"A nice metaphor."

"Actually a little trite, but it makes the point . . . Maybe I should say she'll have to swim across different bays with different sharks to avoid."

"Another nice metaphor, quite revealing actually."

"Will I lose her?"

"What do you think?"

"Maybe . . . I know what I'm supposed to say next. I'm supposed to say that I have to give her enough freedom so I might lose her if we're ever going to be adult friends."

"No one has ever questioned your intelligence, Rosemarie. Loss is always a risk with our children."

"Will I lose her?"

"No promises, Rosemarie."

Those luminous gray eyes turned sad. There were hints of some great loss in her own past. On one corner of the shelf behind her desk there was a frame with two pictures, one of a pathetically young sailor in World War II uniform and the other of a cute little girl baby.

"There can't be any promises, can there?"

"Time, Rosemarie. Stop at Petersen's on the way home."

I did. I discovered that a single malt was not nearly enough.

After supper, the boys were down in the basement blowing their horns. I found April Rosemary huddled over papers with her sister.

"I'm helping April Rosemary with her homework," the little redhead informed me proudly.

Big sister looked up at me and winked. Apparently we were friends again.

"Daddy and I are going over to Petersen's. Can you keep an eye on April Rosemary for me?"

"Yes, Mommy."

Big sister made a face as if she really didn't approve of such romantic nonsense from her parents, but she winked again.

"Don't worry about the boys," she said. "You know what they're like when they're making noise."

I pulled Chucky out of his darkroom. "Leave Selma alone for an hour and take your date over to Petersen's."

He put aside his magnifying glass and a stack of negatives and bounded out of his chair.

"Can I neck and pet with her like I used to?"

"Act your age, Charles Cronin O'Malley!"

"Yes, ma'am."

"And put on your Fenwick jacket. It's still April."

"Just like I was eighteen again!"

"I haven't noticed much change in you since 1946."

"I hope not."

Despite my warning that he act his age, he held my hand as we walked over to Chicago Avenue.

We were always welcome at the ice-cream parlor, the best on the West Side of Chicago as Chucky always said. Then he would add, "Nothing on the South Side even makes the cut."

The manager rushed to the door to shake hands as we entered. He reminisced about the good old days when we were teens and the Clancy/O'Malley duet used to burst into song like the ice-cream parlor was the set for a musical comedy.

So he prevailed upon us to do a bit of our old act, which meant singing songs from *South Pacific*. Actually it didn't take much persuasion. I wondered if some of the teenagers, the real ones that is, who stopped eating their ice cream long enough to stare at us, might be classmates or friends of April Rosemary. We were embarrassing her again. However, the applause was still favorable.

"Are you really April O'Malley's parents?" a wide-eyed blond kid asked us.

"No way," Chucky said. "Do we look old enough to have a daughter that's almost fifteen? My date is her big sister."

General laughter.

"Bitchin'," said the blond.

"Is that good?" Chucky asked, his hand sneaking up under my skirt.

"Charles Cronin O'Malley," I protested insincerely. "And yes, it's a compliment."

"You must have had a good interview with your gorgeous little shrink today," he suggested.

"I'm in trouble. I haven't put on the ten pounds she wants me to put on. So I have to come here more often."

"With me?"

"Not necessarily."

His fingers were approaching an area where, in my present horny state, I might react inappropriately.

"With who?"

"Whom."

"Regardless." He waved his hand, imitating me.

However, his fingers had stopped their exploration.

"With anyone I want. Usually by myself, if there's

no one around the house who can fit me into his schedule."

I gulped down the last sip of my malted milk.

"Charles Cronin O'Malley, finish your malt and take me home and make frenzied love to me."

"Really?" he said, faking surprise.

"Now."

So we went home. I checked on the children. Moire was in bed, the boys, dark-haired kids who looked like they might in a couple of years ride the Shenandoah Valley with Phil Sheridan, were still blasting away on their horns, April Rosemary was puzzling over an algebra problem. Despite my high level of sexual excitement, I said to her, "Some of your friends were over there."

"Hmm . . . Did you sing for them?"

"A little."

"They liked it?" She didn't look up from her algebra.

"They seemed to."

"Bitchin' . . ."

You never can tell.

As I entered the door of the master bedroom (which Chuck insisted on calling the mistress bedroom) I shed my blouse and reached for the hooks on my bra.

I would show that witch Maggie Ward that I could, sometimes, give myself over completely to pleasure.

Which I did. Up to a point.

That summer all our hopes for the political future
were obliterated. The casualties in Vietnam were increasing, but they were still low, just as they had been
in the early days of Korea. Each death of a boy from
our neighborhood caused a stir of unease. We did not,
could not, comprehend that such deaths would soon
become routine. However, Chuck and I found some
reassurance in the rapid progress of the Civil Rights
Movement.

The Voting Rights Act passed on August 10 in
1965. My husband was exultant. "The race problem
in America," he told me confidently, "will be solved.
The Negroes will come to political power, the Democratic majority in the South will be stronger, racial
peace and justice will emerge at a steady, gradual
pace. Selma was the turning point."

Chucky Ducky was rarely so pontifical. However,
he was telling me and especially himself that the
bright promise of the Kennedy years had not ended
with the rifle bullet that had crashed into the President's brain in Dallas, Texas, two years before.

The very next day, Chuck's predictions about the
solution of the Negro problem were proved wrong.

We were at our House on the Lake, which I had
missed desperately in Bonn and which had become

my favorite place in all the world, a place of peace and serenity and rebirth. I love it there; warm, drowsy days and cool, moist nights which soak the tensions out of my body and make me sink into a glowing pond of peace. And love.

"Rosie," my father-in-law had said, "I have the perfect house for you. It's a higgledy-piggledy, topsy-turvy place. You'll love it."

He knew that I wouldn't permit any external modifications on our house on New England Avenue in Oak Park because I insisted that its middle western copy of Dutch Colonial should not be violated. He also knew that I wanted to have a place I could do interesting things to.

"It's just down the Lake from us," he continued. "It needs a lot of work . . ."

Which was music to my ears.

"I don't know, Vangie. Will Chuck like it?"

"Who?"

"Your son, my husband."

"He doesn't get to vote."

The house was perfect. Once it had been a simple beach house, the outlines of which were dimly visible within the now sprawling and disorderly collection of additions, bedrooms, bathrooms, screen porches which had been incorporated into the house and new screen porches and galleries, and frequently improved electrical and water connections. And a cupola on the roof.

"Perfect," I had said to Chuck. "We can do wonderful things with the place."

"I'll get lost in there," he had said dyspeptically.

"You don't get to vote."

"I understand."

"You can advise, however. No consent permitted. You'll love it."

"Yes, ma'am."

I knew he'd love it because he loved me.

Anyway, I was buying the house. I had inherited money from both parental families. My father's money was dirty, so I gave it all to the Church. Mom's grandfather had owned about half of what is now the South Side. Wisely invested, it had survived the Crash and was now all my responsibility. I had set up some foundations and established trust funds for my kids which would provide for their education—even to graduate school—and their first home. I suppose I'm rich. I would have traded in all the money for a different family life when I was growing up. However, I never had that choice. I feel guilty about the money. I'm not an aristocrat. We live comfortably. I could live like an aristocrat (and that makes me feel guilty) but I don't and won't.

Chuck claimed that he had grown to love the place. "There's so many dead ends and alcoves in which I can trap you for my lascivious purposes," he argued.

He had learned that a little bit of tickling sent my body chemicals rampaging. Clever little imp that he is, he sensed when the chemicals were ready to rampage anyway.

The House at the Lake had become for me a place of new beginnings of second chances.

John Raven argues that our God is a God of infinite second chances. We always have the opportunity to start over again. At the Lake I could pause and reflect on my second chances. The O'Malleys had accepted a rich waif into their family. Chuck had married me despite my warnings that I was bad news. He made me stop drinking. That was a lot of second chances for one woman. How many more would I get?

So at the Lake I was more peaceful, more grateful, and more vulnerable.

The cupola had become Mom's Tower. Like Mom's Study at home, the door was always ajar, which meant that anyone in the family with a good reason (their call) could come in. This included at the

Lake Moire, who burst in several times a day to hug me and tell me how much she loved me and then dashed out at full speed.

Often that love made me cry. I didn't deserve it.

Mom's Tower was also a place where I could indulge in my secret vice. It was not sexual, at least not explicitly so.

I write. Stories. Lots of them. I have not shown them to anyone. Not Chuck, not Peg, not Maggie Ward. Not anyone. I never will. Nonetheless, I love writing them.

It was one of those sleepy humid days in August when everyone was pretending that summer would never end. The boys were blowing their horns down on the beach. As usual they had attracted a crowd of local urchins, some teenagers who liked their beat, and a few curious adults who thought they might be hearing a new sound. Also as usual April Rosemary was sulking. Her brothers were embarrassing her with her friends. They were decidedly not cool. In fact they were "space cadets."

"Complain to your father," I said, now weary of April Rosemary's endless embarrassment. "He turned them on to Louis Armstrong."

Chucky didn't like rock and roll. Believing, more or less, in letting his children develop their own tastes, he did not try to forbid them to listen to the "jungle music" as he called it. Rather he lurked silently in the background and awaited his opportunity to play the jazz card.

The opportunity came while we were still in Germany. The Louis Armstrong recording of "Hello, Dolly!" swept the Beatles temporarily out of first place on the charts. April Rosemary thought it was "totally gross."

"Dad," asked Kevin, then twelve years old, "who is this Satchmo person?"

"Actually his friends call him Pops," Chucky replied, not even opening his eyes on the couch.

"You know him?" James, age eleven, demanded. "He's famous!"

"Gramps and he are great friends from the time that Pops was playing early Chicago jazz in speakeasies in Chicago during the nineteen twenties."

"What's a speakeasy?" ten-year-old Sean asked.

Somehow I had never worried about my sons until the Vietnam War started. Even as kids they seemed sensible and stable. They treated me with grave respect, the way Chuck did. He was simply the oldest of the kids and hence one of them. All of them were or promised to be rangy, Black Irish young men, with deep, dark blue eyes, low hairlines, and bright smiles. They all looked like one another and like Colonel Brian O'Brien, my mother's grandfather who rode with Phil Sheridan during the Civil War, a giant bearded man with long black hair, a wicked smile, and hypnotic eyes. Despite his good looks and his trim cavalry uniform, he had managed to keep out of trouble during the war and after, though legends about his success in love and politics swirled around him.

I figured that if my sons had those genes, at least they wouldn't get caught.

Kevin, the oldest, was the leader, the planner, and the plotter. If I didn't know what they were up to, I would demand an explanation from Kevin.

"What are you three troublemakers up to now?" I would say.

"We're going to buy horns, Mom," he would say, the soul of innocence.

"Horns that make noise?"

"Not loud noise, Mom," he said with an impish grin that always won my heart. "We figured that the O'Malley clan is short on wind instruments. So we'd provide the wind."

They ended up with cheap and battered instruments, a trumpet, a trombone, and a sax (which I told them was not a wind instrument). Kev had not told me the truth. The noise was loud, very loud, to the dismay of the staff at our home on the Rhine. Each one of them seemed to be able to play by ear. They taught themselves how to play and seemed to concentrate on John Philip Sousa. The United States Marine Band they were not.

James, the second of the "Irish triplets" as they were often called, was the sensitive, affectionate one. He realized that Giovanni Batista Antonelli (Gianni) felt left out of the band when they came back to America and signed him on as the "little drummer boy."

Once he asked whether, "Dad was always like he is now when he was our age?"

"He hasn't changed much," I said, hugging him.

"He was a cool kid?"

"Coolest kid in the neighborhood."

"He really hasn't grown up much, has he?"

Aha, a delicate question.

"Well, he has graduated from a university and is a successful photographer and fine Ambassador for the United States of America, but he's still the coolest kid in the neighborhood."

"Great!" he whooped, and ran off with what he interpreted as good news.

I couldn't keep the conversation a secret from my husband. He did not seem surprised at either the question or my response.

"Not everyone realized I was cool," he said judiciously. "Indeed the adjective didn't have that meaning when we were their age. In fact, I was, however, the coolest kid in the neighborhood."

"Sometimes."

"Usually."

Seano was the clown of the group, like his father always ready with the quick quip. "Mom, can't we buy the neighbors earmuffs so they don't have to listen to us?"

They were a fun threesome, good kids, normal kids, got along fine with everyone, played at all the required sports, did well in school. The music, at first anyway, seemed a sideline.

I'm sure it started that day in Bonn when Chucky explained jazz to them.

"It's a mix of African and American music. It began with dancing and singing in a place in New Orleans called Congo Square where the slaves were free to be themselves for two hours on Sunday afternoon. Spread up to Chicago when Pops came up the Mississippi. It keeps changing as time goes on, yet it's always the same. It requires absolute mastery of the instruments and the ability to give form and structure to the music with improvisation. It's America's unique contribution to world music."

"Yucky," April Rosemary snorted, though she had listened carefully to Chuck's lecture.

"Do you have any of his records around?"

"I might have. I'll look for them tomorrow."

He knew exactly where the records were.

The triplets listened with rapt attention for several hours.

"Cool," they sighed in unison.

"Do you know him too, Dad?" James asked.

"Sure, when his band played in Cologne, your mother and I went up to listen and have a word with him. He recognized us immediately because your mother is so beautiful . . ."

"He recognized your father's hair."

". . . And he remembered the times when both your grandfathers used to come to listen to him in a speakeasy on Oakley Avenue during prohibition."

"Is he *famous*?" Seano asked, eyes wide.

"He's the most famous jazz musician in all the world."

"He shaped both instrumental and vocal perform-ances," I added. "Jazz is what it is because of Louis."

"Wow!"

"If he's famous," Kevin wanted to know, "how come he knows you, Dad?"

In his own country and among his own people . . . I'd let Chucky Ducky field that one.

"Because I'm Gramps's son," he replied gently. "Gramps is a famous architect and painter."

"Oh . . ."

"Your father is the Ambassador of the United States of America," I said with a touch of pride. "And he's published a lot of picture books."

Those accomplishments cut not a bit of ice.

Gradually, Chuck indoctrinated these three inno-cents into the theory and history of jazz with musical illustrations. They listened to the Duke and the Count, to Dizzy and Bix, to Miles Davis and Johnny Col-trane. Their education, after we came home, was sup-plemented by visits to Gramps, who spun wondrous yarns and produced old thirty-five-millimeter films of Pops and Sarah Vaughan and Billie Holiday.

I was astonished at my sons' fascination with jazz. They were only kids, basketball- and baseball-loving punks who constantly pushed each other around and were never quite free of trouble in school.

I guess they had been born with genes that de-manded sound. Jazz provided the sound for them.

So that catastrophic day in August, they were down on the beach serenading the community. Kevin's trumpet, always off-key, had the sound of Satchmo in it—still tentative, still youthful. Yet he was hearing the music, the way it ought to be heard.

Maybe I had a jazz trio on my hands.

Dear God, I prayed with a shiver, let them all live to develop and enjoy their talent.

I was lying on the porch under an umbrella in a bikini that was considerably more modest than those which my daughter's generation affected. I had put on five of that witch Maggie Ward's pounds, which made me figure I wasn't too skinny.

Chuck was taking a nap. For someone who is as hyperkinetic as he is, he has a damnable habit of being able to nap whenever he wants to.

With or without sex.

I was considering the possibility of complaining about the absence of sex on this perfect summer afternoon, when I heard him scream from inside, "Rosemarie!"

Always prepared for the worst when someone shouts my name that way, I hooked my bra and dashed into the parlor.

"What happened!

He gestured at the old black-and-white television, which we both agreed was fine for the beach.

Young Negroes were rushing the streets of what looked like a quiet suburban neighborhood with respectable single-family homes. They were burning cars, throwing gasoline bombs, smashing store windows, hurling rocks at the police.

The camera zoomed in on a kid no more than fifteen with an angelic face just as he threw a fire bomb at a passing car.

"Burn, baby, burn!"

"Chicago?" I gasped.

"Los Angeles . . . A place called Watts!"

"Why?"

"There was a rumor that the police beat a pregnant Negro woman. Apparently it wasn't true, but they started throwing rocks at the police last night. Somehow the cops were not able to restore order. Now it's totally out of hand!"

The TV people interviewed Negro "experts" Stokeley Carmichael and H. Rapp Brown. It was the end of "Uncle Tom" activism they both asserted. The black (first time I heard that word) kids in Watts had taken their destiny into their own hands. They were telling "whitey" that either America would give them what they wanted or they would "burn it all down!"

"Dear God, Chuck," I murmured. "What must Dr. King think?"

"He's probably as horrified as we are. They didn't understand anything he taught."

A "black" expert said to the TV camera. "Nonviolence doesn't work. So we're taking to the streets."

"But, Chuck, it looks like they're burning down their own neighborhood and looting their own stores!"

"Television is turning mass looting into a political statement. I don't understand it."

"It attracts people to watch, even if it does become a self-fulfilling prophecy."

As we watched a fire truck pulled up to a blazing television and appliance store. Men and women of every age and size were dashing out, appliances piled into their arms. The teens threw rocks at the fire truck. Gunfire rang out. The firemen wisely turned and ran.

"Whitey ain't no good," one rioter informed the national television audience. "His law and order don't be my law and order. Burn, whitey, burn!"

"Aren't you destroying your own neighborhood, your own stores?" an interviewer asked a bearded youth clad in an African costume.

"Those be Jew stores. Jews been exploiting us folk, you know. We're chasing Jews out of our community. Let them exploit someone else."

"Who will build new stores?"

"Don't matter none, you know. Jews be gone, you know! Whitey be gone too!"

"Anti-Semitism too," my husband groaned.

Not only was Watts burning; so too were the last ruins of the JFK Camelot dream.

Both of us were Democratic liberals, albeit of the Irish Catholic Chicago variety, Chucky by birth, I by conversion and conviction (and flaky, ex-drunk enthusiasm). We believed in racial and religious integration. We believed in peace and prosperity and American know-how that could create both. Our world was being torn apart.

Many of the Chicago Irish did not. They were racists and anti-Semites like my poor father. In the O'Malley house attitudes on race and religion were not a big deal. Chuck often told the story of how he had soaped the windows of a Jewish dry goods store up on Division Street with anti-Jewish slogans. He came home and bragged to the good April of his accomplishment. She ordered him to return to the store, apologize to the owners, and clean off the soap.

"They are as good as we are, Charles Cronin O'Malley. Better because they work harder and are smarter. You go up there this minute and apologize."

So he did. With the usual Chucky Ducky charm. They hired him to work at the store part-time. When he told the story to our kids, the explicit point usually was that you lose nothing by saying you're sorry. However, the other theme got through to them too.

"Just like Grams," April Rosemary said with admiration. "Be nice to everyone because people are people just like us."

That was not a very pure form of ideology. But it was enough. Chuck and I believed in it. During the early sixties we thought that it was where our country was going.

"Turn it off, Rosemarie." My husband sighed. "We've seen enough."

I flicked the switch on the television.

"We were wrong," he said grimly, face in his hands. "We underestimated the hatred and anger that a couple of centuries of oppression created. The Civil Rights Movement is finished. Black Power is the new way to go. Without people like us along for the ride."

"They can't win without allies, can they?"

"I don't see how."

"What happens next?" I sat on the couch next to him and put my arm around his skinny shoulders.

"More Watts!"

Appropriately a thick thunderhead moved in over the beach and temporarily extinguished the light of summer.

"If Jack Kennedy had lived . . . ?"

"Who knows." He sighed. "Now the crazies are running things."

"I hope you're not thinking of going out there with your camera?"

He looked up at me in surprise.

"What good could I do?"

Young Americans were dying in Vietnam. Blacks were burning down their own neighborhood and spouting anti-Semitism. We were both in our mid-thirties, yet our world was dying, just like summer was.

It took five days and sixteen thousand cops and National Guardsmen to bring peace back to Watts. Thirty-four people were dead, most of them Negroes. Two hundred and fifty buildings had burned to the ground. Martin Luther King was heckled by the young radicals when he suggested that they help re-build the neighborhood, their neighborhood. Watts never was rebuilt, despite all the federal money which was poured into it.

After I had clung to Chucky, I walked out on the deck. Against the chill wind I put on my robe. Down on the beach the sun was shining again. My sons were still blowing their horns. Mostly it was cacophony, but there were exciting moments. Little girls, including our Moire, were dancing together on the sand. Their mothers stood on the fringes of the crowd. Somehow they seemed to approve of the jam session. Perhaps because they could be sure where their kids would be when the Crazy O'Malleys, as the group called themselves, appeared. Even April Rosemary and her nearly naked bikini-clad gang watched some at a safe distance, enthralled despite themselves. I noted with transient pleasure that my child had the best body of them all.

Earlier in the summer she had praised me when I had appeared for the first time in my own, as I say far more modest, two-piece swimsuit. (Not, however, pathologically modest!)

"Mom," she said, eyeing me critically as we walked down the long flight of steps to the inviting sand, "you really are a beautiful woman!"

"I think I'm blushing, April Rosemary."

"That makes you even prettier. No wonder Dad loves you so much."

"He'll love me when I'm old and not beautiful anymore."

"You'll always be beautiful," she said definitively. "I suppose you and Daddy make love a lot?"

Ah, the question about which every teen worries, but lack the nerve to talk about.

"We are deeply in love, April Rosemary, as you can easily tell, so we do, though not anything like several times a day."

She giggled at that.

"Not enough privacy with us around . . . More than most of my friends' parents, I bet?"

"Probably," I said cautiously.

"I *hope* so."

She flounced off down the beach to her bevy of friends.

What was I to make of that exchange! It didn't fit any of the books I had read about adolescents and parental sex.

I told Chuck about the conversation in bed that night as we were both slipping into sleep.

"Hmm . . ." he replied.

"Is that all you can say?"

"Well, you did of course tell her that you weren't beautiful but a broken-down drunk!"

"Charles Cronin O'Malley! I'm serious!"

"I thought that was your standard response when someone tells you you're beautiful."

"You're scoring points against me and I'm trying to talk to you about our daughter!"

"Oh . . ."

"So what do you make of our conversation!"

"I think I'll have to take a lot of shots of the two of you together this summer. In fact, I'll even do a formal portrait of mother and daughter in alluring swimsuits!"

Chuck was doing formal portraits that summer. He had even built a small studio in one wing of our summer home.

"I'll never pose for it!"

"She'll be delighted to pose for it, so you will too."

"No way!"

I knew I would.

"Can I go to sleep now, please, ma'am?"

"You didn't answer my question."

"I did too."

"You did not!"

He sighed loudly.

"I implied that your daughter strongly identifies with you, which is no great secret, and indeed adores you. She's also trying to figure out how she can keep on adoring you and still become her own person."

"You read that in some book."

"It will work out all right but there may be a lot of heartache for both of you."

"So long as it works out . . ."

However, my husband by then was dead to the world.

I thought of that conversation on the day of the Watts riots as I looked down on the beach. Poor little Gianni Antonelli was pounding away on his drum, the only one of the gang who had any sense of tempo. The tune they were killing was, I thought, the "Notre Dame Victory March." It was kind of hard to tell.

Love flowed into me, love for my kids, for the joys of youth, for summer, for the Lake, the beach, everything. If only that moment of youthful fun could be preserved forever. If only I could protect them against the darkness which lay ahead for all of us. Perhaps if I were not a drunk and a neurotic I might be able to save them. As it was I could only watch in horror and tears.

Sunlight faded away on the beach. A front was coming through.

The future would be a lot worse than I expected.

6

"How many of you men have ever been married?" I demanded. "How many of you have ever lived with a woman or slept with a woman?"

A couple of laymen put up their hands. The rest of the group—bishops and theologians and a few captive laity—stared at me in silence. Next to me, my red-haired husband grinned happily. Clancy lowers the boom, he was thinking.

"Then how the hell can you claim to tell us married women what sex should mean in our lives?"

Dead silence. Packy Keenan, Maggie Ward's brother-in-law, was grinning. My shrink ought to be here instead of me. She wouldn't make a mess out of it like I would.

We had read Judge Noonan's book on contraception on the way over and realized that the Church had begun to make a really big deal out of birth control in 1930. In the previous century priests had been urged not to "trouble the consciences of the married laity."

"What do you think sexual love means to a married woman?" I continued my tirade. "Do you really think it's a debt I pay to my husband when his passions get out of hand? Do you actually believe that I could survive in my marriage if I gave up sleeping with my husband? Do you think that when a woman makes love with her husband she's actually hoping for another child when she already has five of them?"

We were at a meeting of the commission Pope Paul VI had established to advise him on the subject of birth control. On a hot June day we had assembled in a religious order retreat house a few miles outside of Rome. The nuns in charge had assigned priests and the laymen to one section of the stuffy building and the few women to another part. What right did women have to talk to bishops and priests about marital sex?

I had shouted in protest on arrival. I would stay only if my husband and I slept in the same bed. The other married couples had joined, somewhat hesitantly, in my protest. My husband had beamed his approval but remained silent.

"You didn't need me," he had argued when at last we were in our cramped sticky room, one with a bed designed at best for a large male retreatant. Or prisoner.

"Shut up, O'Malley," I had told him. "If you think I went to all that trouble to get you in the same bed with me and then would let you escape without making love you're crazy!"

I had pushed him back on the bed and fallen on top of him.

"I can't remember," he giggled, "that I had expressed any intention of denying you the marriage debt."

There were wide differences of opinion about what the commission was for. Some of the folks from the Vatican suggested that it was merely to confirm the existing Church policy on birth control. That's what commissions did in the Church. They told the Pope what he wanted to hear, certainly not what he needed to know. Others argued that, like Pope John, Pope Paul wanted a way out of the birth control crisis in the Church and the commission was supposed to find the way out for him.

Most of the theologians and bishops and cardinals on the commission were conservatives on the issue. The Church could not change its teaching on birth control, because it was the teaching of Jesus. When I asked them where Jesus had said anything on the subject, they mumbled nonsense about the "deposit of faith" and the "sacred tradition" and "the Pope as infallible teacher."

A few people, however, thought that the conservative tilt of the commission was a typical Pope Paul strategy. If those in favor of change could persuade men like London's Cardinal John Carmel Heenan that change was possible, then we would have persuaded everyone.

Chuck and I were in Bonn when Vatican Council II began. At first we were astonished by the headlines on the front page of the Paris *Herald Tribune*. What was happening to the Catholic Church? Were cardinals and bishops from around the world actually taking power away from the creeps in the Roman Curia? While we were living in Oak Park, we were involved in something called the Christian Family Movement, a moderately liberal (you couldn't be anything more in Oak Park in those days) Catholic discussion group which seemed to hint very vaguely that the laity might actually be the Church and should have something to say about what the Church taught, especially about marriage.

"Rank heresy," my husband muttered as we walked home on a chilly November evening from such a meeting. "What do the lay people know about marriage?"

"Or theology," I agreed, going along with his gag.

"Or anything else."

"All they should do is contribute money and obey the orders of their pastor, right?"

"Keep their mouths shut," he continued, "and their wallets open. It doesn't matter how much education they have, right?"

"Chucky Ducky, they really think that way, don't they?"

"I'm afraid so, Rosemarie my darling. They're going to have a lot of trouble in the years ahead if they don't change their minds."

It would turn out that there would be a lot more trouble than anyone could have imagined back in the days when Eisenhower was still President and Pius XII was still Pope.

For the laity, the big question was not an English Mass or making nice-nice with Protestants or how to interpret the Bible, but married sex since it happened at least once a week and sometimes (as in our case) more often. We really didn't expect a change. I had made up my mind that the Pope didn't understand anything about marriage but God did. I loved all five of my kids. I loved the fifth one especially, though there was so much to do that I could not find time to love the elfin little redhead the way I wanted. And I had help around the house, which is more than most young Catholic mothers with five kids had. I could not imagine that God wanted Chuck and me to give up love. So I said to him. "I'm with you and not with them." I assumed that he would understand. Most of the couples in our CFM group assumed, one way or another, the same thing, especially after The PILL went on the market.

Anyway, when we were in Bonn and Jack Kennedy was still alive, we read that one of those eastern Patriarchs in the funny clothes had said something like that on the floor of the Council and then some of the bishops, mostly from the third world countries, agreed. My husband and I decided to take a long weekend and sneak down from Bonn incognito to see what the hell was going on.

We arrived at St. Peter's at noon just as the session of the Council was breaking up. Under a clear blue sky a great crimson wave seemed to pour out of the Basilica as the bishops of the world, men of every hue and color under heaven emerged from the big, ugly church. Occasionally someone in a strange oriental robe would be swept along by the tide. It was quite an impressive show, the world leadership of the Church careening into the Piazza. My husband typically pulled a camera out of his jacket pocket and began to blaze away—in this case the Kodak I had given him when he left for the Army of Occupation in Germany, which he used for colored film.

I removed from my purse Trudi's Leica, rewound the Tri-X film, and replaced it with Agfachrome. When he had finished with the Kodak, he extended it in my direction without looking at me. I exchanged it with the Leica. He continued to fire away, not for a moment doubting that I had put in color film.

Since I had more or less conned him into his photographer's role, it was appropriate that I be his assistant.

"Marvelous!" he exclaimed, as the scarlet wave ebbed. "Someday I'll do a book on priests."

"If anyone up at that Vatican palace knew what you were up to," I told him, "they'd send out the Swiss Guard to confiscate that camera."

Puzzled, he glanced at me as he rewound the Kodak. "You think those guys looked funny?"

"I'm not sure Jesus would have approved of the successors of the Apostles parading around in those gaudy clothes."

Before he could answer, a young American priest joined us. "Ambassador O'Malley."

Chuck went through his act of glancing around to see if there was someone else to whom the priest might be talking.

"How could anyone think, Father," I said to the

priest, "that a little redhead with a camera in his hand could be an incognito Ambassador of the United States of America."

"Father Regan from the Catholic Conference in Washington," the priest put out his hand. "Good to meet you Mr. Ambassador. Welcome to Rome."

"You don't work for the Swiss Guard, do you?" Chuck said with fake anxiety as he shook hands with the priest.

"Hardly, sir. I'm a *peritus*, an adviser at the Council."

"What are you guys doing in there to our Church?" I asked with my most appealing smile. "Tearing it apart and remaking it, I hope?"

"Not exactly, Mrs. O'Malley. To quote Pope John we're just letting in a little fresh air."

"I'm Rosemarie and he's Chuck because we're both incognitio. If we buy you a cup of espresso, maybe you could tell us about it."

We found ourselves an open table at one of the sidewalk cafés along the Via Concilliazione, the wide street which ran from the Piazza down to the Tiber. There was a lot of heavy conversation going on among journalists and priests at the cafés.

"This is a really big deal, isn't it?" My husband began our conversation. "Are the bishops really pushing out the Curia?"

"Biggest deal in five hundred, maybe a thousand years," the young priest said, his face glowing. "We're *updating* the Church. The Pope calls it an *aggiornamento* because modernization might scare some people. The bishops are overwhelmingly in favor of change. As long as they're in Rome, the Curia can only play crooked games behind the scenes. The bishops are running things. When they go home . . ."

He shrugged his shoulders.

"What will the Church look like in five years?" I asked.

"Different. The Mass will be in English, we'll be on good terms with the Protestants and the Jews, we'll endorse religious freedom and the new ways of studying the Bible. Local bishops will have a lot more power. We'll look a little more like a democracy. Priests might be permitted to marry. There's even some talk of women priests."

"They already run the Church now," Chuck insisted, "especially if they're Irish. Might as well ordain them. It wouldn't add much to their power."

"Chucky!" I protested in vain.

"Birth control?" I asked lightly.

Father Regan hesitated.

"I'd say that there's a general sense around here that there's likely to be a change on the Pill. The Pope has set up a commission of advisers to look into it. Everyone says he wants to find a way to change."

"Father Regan," my husband asked, "do they sell chocolate ice cream in these stores?"

Chuck knew they did. He had told me often that when he was in Rome after the war the Italians had already produced the best *gelato chocolato* in the world. I went to buy us some.

"It's extremely exciting here now," Father Regan continued when I returned. "Nothing is certain. Every day the Curia tries some new trick. So far they've been beaten back, but everyone is worried about the Pope's health. He's a great old man . . . Would you like to meet him?"

Would we ever!

Father Regan must have lots of clout. Two days later we were in the Pope's office. Only Monsignore Capavilo, his secretary, and Father Regan were with us. The Embassy in Bonn, with considerable protest, had sent us a copy of Chuck's book on Germany after the war. (They hinted that we were engaging in unauthorized diplomacy with a man who was reputed to have pro-Russian, even Communist sympathies.)

Since I hadn't brought any black clothes from Bonn, I had to go on a shopping spree the day before, lest I violate Vatican protocol. I was strongly tempted to do that, but shopping overcame ideology.

The Pope was like Santa Claus, a jolly little old man, with a happy face and simple charm. He leafed slowly through the book.

"Very great talent, Excellency," he said, raising his fingers and rubbing them back and forth. "God has been good to you."

"That's what my wife tells me, Holy Father!"

Always Chucky Ducky!

The Pope laughed and smiled at me.

Then he turned to the picture that was captioned "Fidelity." It was a picture of a grieving woman waiting at the train station in Bamberg for her husband to return from Russia.

The Pope muttered something in Italian.

"Poor woman," Monsignore Capavilo translated for us. "One presumes he did not return?"

"Some stories have happy endings, Holy Father," Chuck said, suddenly dead serious. "He did come back. He is now the rector of the University in Bamberg."

There was a lot more to that story, one of Chucky's more gracious adventures.

The Pope smiled happily.

"So," he said, "you want to take my picture too?"

"If I may."

"Of course . . . Though I am not as good a model as that woman."

He glanced again at the pathos of the picture of Brigita and closed the book.

We shot with available light, only a half roll of Tri-X. The result is one of the most famous pictures of the Pope, one in which he looks very much like Santa Claus.

As we were walking out into the Belvedere Courtyard, Father Regan asked, "Could you do us a favor?"

"Name it," Chuck said in the best Chicago political style.

"Could you send a private note to your friend JFK and tell him that the Pope is not a crypto-Communist like some of his foreign service people are telling him."

"Consider it done. I'll send him a copy of the best of my shots."

And so it was done.

The good old man died in the spring. The next Pope, Paul VI, was more timid; my Hamlet, Pope John had called him. The Church unwisely began a slow retreat from the excitement of the Council, one that continues as I write this collection of memories.

Anyway four years later we were back in Rome to meet with the papal commission on birth control. I don't know how we got on the list of participants. Whoever made that mistake doubtless paid for it.

I wrote Peg a letter before my big explosion, which explains my mood at the time. A paper saver like her brother, she saved it and lent it to me.

Dearest Peg,

This is a terrible place, sticky, stuffy, humid, and uncomfortable besides. Most of the people here are priests, only a few laity around to represent those who are most likely to be affected by the decision. You don't want laypeople to decide about their own marriages, do you? Priests, bishops, and cardinals decide for them.

No one is wearing purple buttons, not even the creeps from the Curia. You can tell who the creeps are, however, because their body odor is worse than that of the rest of them. They are also the ones who looked the most shocked when I show up in a blouse with short sleeves.

Your brother, the man I sleep with, is up to something. So what else is new? He is buttering up the bishops and the theologians like he used to butter up the nuns at St.

Ursula and the priests at Fenwick and, I suppose, the officers when he was in Bamberg. His eyes are shining with mischief. I'm glad he's having a good time. I'm the one who has to carry on the fight. I don't understand the language much though one of the nuns around here translates for me sometimes. It's pretty clear that she disapproves of me.

Even when I understand the words, I usually don't know what the words mean. There is great concern about whether the marriage act is completed naturally, whatever that means. Apparently these men who have probably never completed a marriage act in their lives and probably couldn't if they had to think they know what is natural.

I gather that they have now decided that the Pill is just another form of contraception, as if that is going to change the minds of any of us. Those who favor change in the birth control teaching itself think that it is strategically wise not to settle for merely a victory on the Pill. Doesn't sound like a good idea to me. But what do I know about married love? One of these meetings I'm going to explode.

I wish I knew what Chucky Ducky is up to!

Love to Vince and the kids.

Rosie.

At the next session, I went into my tirade

"I hear some of you saying that we must beware of the danger of unbridled sex!" I ranted on. "Don't you know that the real problem for us married folk is too much bridled sex. Sexual pleasure is necessary to heal the hurts and the pains of living together. It renews and strengthens the love between man and woman. Can't you get it through you're heads that we're not libertines, but simply people trying to keep our love alive!"

I would have gone on but my ineffable husband began to applaud. The whole conference room joined in, except of course for the smelly creeps from the

Curia, many of whom were sound asleep anyway.

Apparently the people there who wanted to argue that a change in the birth control teaching was possible were waiting for an opening. They promptly took control of the meeting and began to outline the reasons for a change—the experience of the married laity, the world population problems, the health of women and children, the decline of infant mortality rates. Astonishingly the votes seemed to flow to their side. The Curia creeps shut up completely, figuring I guess that there was no point in fighting in this venue. They would save their arguments for the Pope himself.

Cardinal Heenan, good and pious man without much intelligence, kept worrying about how shocked the laity might be if there were a change. I told him that the men and women I knew would be shocked if there wasn't a change. He didn't get my point.

Meanwhile, the explanation for Chucky Ducky's game became clear. He was now scurrying around taking pictures. No one seemed to notice. He was such a sweet boy married to such a terrible woman, why not let him take a few pictures? Even the Curial creeps were happy to pose for him.

"So that's been the scheme, has it?" I accused him as we were strolling in the cool of the evening with the sickly strong scent of flowers all around us, the smell I thought, wrongly as it turned out of the old Church, which was dying all round us.

"I'm going to do a book someday called *Priests*. These guys are wonderful models."

"For a book of horrors?"

"We'll find some other types too. Actually some of those theologians are rather impressive-looking guys."

"If only they'd take showers more often!"

"Besides you don't need me to change their minds," he said in mock innocence. "I thought I would try to do something useful."

"I think I know what Dr. Frankenstein felt like."

The "majority" as it now called itself produced a very strong report. If Pope Paul wanted excuses which would legitimate a change in the birth control teaching, now he had them.

"Did we win, Chuck?" I asked him as we drove back to Rome and the swimming pool of the Rome Hilton up on the Monte Mario.

"We won the battle all right, with a lot of help from your lowering the boom. The war? I dunno. Some of those guys who never said anything, like that white-haired American Jesuit, reminded me of our friends on the West Side."

Which in Chicago talk meant the Boys, the Outfit, the Mob.

"They had the look of men who had decided to fight elsewhere, didn't they? Why are they so interested in dominating the sexual lives of people like us?"

"What's the point of having power unless you use it to control others?"

"Do they really think they can keep our report secret?"

Only the majority had submitted a report. Cardinal Heenan had not signed it. He told everyone, however, that he was in sympathy with it but worried about shocking the laity.

"They believe they can, Rosemarie. They don't understand that nothing is secret anymore. Your good friend Cardinal Heenan will go back to London and spill the beans by telling everyone that they must prepare the laity for change lest they be shocked when it happens."

Which it turned out is exactly what he did.

The next day we went down to the Vatican to meet the Pope. This time I had brought along my papal black clothes, economizing as I almost never do.

He was a charming and gracious little man, with

bright eyes and a wonderful smile. Alas, he was as agonized as Pope John had been cheerful. Try as he might, Chuck was not able to get a good picture of him—just like later he would be unable to get an adequate shot of Richard Nixon.

He thanked us for our work on the commission. It was, he said, a very difficult matter with enormous implications. As Pope he had to worry about the whole church and about the shock that a change would cause among the simple faithful. One had to balance so many different problems. He raised his hands in an almost despairing motion of a man trying to maintain a balance.

I could not help but like him. I even felt sorry for his heavy burden. Yet I also remembered the heavy burden of women who had too many children and whose health had been ruined by too many pregnancies. I also thought of the marriages that were being eaten up by the stress and strain of trying to cope with the birth control teaching and still salvaging their love life.

So I opened my big, shanty-Irish mouth again and said that I thought men and women I knew would be shocked if there wasn't a change.

He sighed and raised his hands again in the balancing motion.

"What do you think, Chuck?" I asked my husband as we rode back to the Monte Mario.

"We gave the poor little guy what he wanted and he's scared stiff of it."

"I hope you're wrong."

"So do I . . . Rosemarie." He put his arm around me. "You were absolutely sensational at that meeting. I was never more proud of you."

"I'm just a loudmouth, shanty-Irish fishwife," I said sadly.

"You don't believe that," he insisted.

But I did.

Well, at least I half believed it.

Finally, as we would later find out, birth control and married love would cease to be the issues, to be replaced by the issue of the authority of the Pope. The hard-core conservatives on the commission—the handful of Italian cardinals and bishops and a couple of their house theologians—would lose the argument about married love. They would win the argument about papal authority.

1966

❧ 7 ❧

"Martin," my husband said to Dr. King, "it's not a good idea. It won't work. You can't win and you'll be fighting the wrong people."

It was in December of 1965, the year all our trouble began. We were sitting in Dr. King's hotel room in downtown Chicago. Aware that his clout with younger blacks was slipping, he was planning to found a Chicago Freedom Movement to end segregated housing in Chicago, just as he had ended transportation segregation in the South.

"Chicago is the most segregated city in the North," he replied to my husband. "It's the place we must strike first."

Chuck sighed. He was no defender of Chicago housing practices, but he saw the problem in a wider context than did either the Civil Rights Movement or the national media, which always loved a chance to stick it to Chicago.

"Your enemies are not the poor ethnics who are trying to defend their neighborhoods and their homes from racial resegregation. Your enemies are the suburbs to which the rich can flee to escape what they see as the crime and the violence in the city. Gage Park and Marquette Park are not the right targets. You should be marching in Highland Park and Orland Park

and Palos Park and Lincoln Park and Lake Forest and
Kenilworth. Even our neighborhood Oak Park. If
those neighborhoods could be integrated, it would
take the pressure off the city housing markets and
white people would have nowhere to run. They would
have to stay in the city and adjust to integration."

Chuck and I were both strong believers in integration, though we had the feeling that we were losing
ground as we had that year on everything else.

"We will integrate Gage Park and Marquette Park,"
Dr. King insisted.

"I'm not sure you will, not yet anyway. In the end
blacks will move into those neighborhoods and like
all the other neighborhoods in the city where that has
happened they will promptly be resegregated. Eventually you will have an all-black city and all-white
suburbs. Do you want that?"

Dr. King hesitated.

"So long as our people will have decent housing,
we might be willing to take that chance."

The conversation was always calm and controlled,
but not exactly relaxed.

"Daley won't let you get away with it," I said.
"Like him or not, he doesn't intend to let that happen
and he has the votes and the power, even the black
votes."

"We've fought other strong men before."

"This is Chicago," Chuck said softly, "not Montgomery. Marches won't do it here. Housing is a different set of problems."

"We will force Chicago realtors to sell homes to
black people," he insisted.

The argument went nowhere. We parted as friends
who had agreed to disagree.

"There are racists in Marquette Park," I said to
Chuck as we rode home on the Lake Street L.

"Sure there are," he agreed. "And they will demon-
strate against the parades. But most of the Lithuanians

out there will stay home. They don't particularly want racial integration. They are afraid of crime and violence and falling property values. They love their neighborhood. They remember, as most folks don't, that they were victims of both the Nazis and the Communists during the war and that they are the survivors. But they don't like hate or violence. Martin is trying to stir them into violence like he did Sheriff Clark in Selma. It won't happen. Dick Daley won't let it happen."

"He did not seem to understand that the white working class are not the appropriate scapegoat. If he could integrate the suburbs . . ."

"Like Oak Park?"

"We'll integrate anyway, Chuck. It's already happening. And most of us won't panic. We have the resources to integrate without resegregating. Marquette Park doesn't."

"They're white ethnic Catholics, Rosemarie, the perfect scapegoat. It's not fair to go after them."

Chuck was right in principle. To select the Lithuanians and Slavs as targets and not go after the rich Lake Front Liberals or suburbanites was to misunderstand terribly who the real enemy was. However, Dr. King's strategy called for marches and demonstrations in the city. The white ethnics were the only available target, however questionable the morality of attacking them.

Whatever one might say about the theory of integrating Chicago housing by the strategies the Civil Rights Movement had used in the South, in practice I was right. In Chicago you don't fight City Hall. You make a deal with it. Richard J. Daley was not about to let Martin Luther King or anyone else take Chicago away from him. He was no racist and he believed in cautious racial integration—but in his style and his own terms. He would win. King would eventually have to leave town with an empty compromise.

"I feel like weeping," I said as the L train rumbled on.

"Me too," my husband admitted. "We're liberals in an era when radicalism is becoming chic. So we're losers."

It would later be said that, since we liberals were not part of the solution, we were part of the problem.

"What are we going to do?" I asked as we got off the Lake Street L at the Oak Park Avenue stop.

"We're not going to do anything. We'll sit it out. Like we're sitting everything out these days."

Naturally, my Chucky Ducky was not capable of sitting anything out. Not as long as he owned a camera.

(I pause to think that if any of my grandchildren should read these notes, they'll think we were crazy. How could we take politics so seriously? How could we worry about riots and marches and demonstrations and even about wars? Didn't we know that our convictions about politics were all wrong? Didn't we understand that you couldn't change the world or even our country much by political involvement? Where did we get this idealism that drove us during the 1960s? They will probably lump it with the very different idealism that the 1960s generated, which they now know had more to do with sex and drugs and rock and roll than it did with peace and justice. They won't understand that ours was the pragmatic idealism of the early 1960s, of the brief three years of John Kennedy's presidency.

How can I explain to them that we cared deeply about peace and racial justice but that we felt that you worked for both by winning allies, by making compromises, by dealing? Will that make any sense to them at all? Were our dreams so obliterated in the abyss of the 1960s that even the memory of them was lost and only our own personal heartaches survived.

Or perhaps the wheel will have turned again and

my great-grandchildren will perhaps understand why we suffered so much because our friend Dr. King and his colleagues never thought through their strategy for dealing with Chicago.

Maybe I'll erase these last paragraphs which I had to write, if only to explain to myself why I felt so sad that December evening we walked home from the L as a light snow dusted Oak Park.)

I'll put these lines in parentheses.

Chuck could not have sat out that summer of 1966 at the Lake, not when so many good photographs were demanding to be shot on the Southwest Side of Chicago. So we found ourselves on a hot summer day in 1966 on Marquette Road as Dr. King's marchers—mostly black, but not entirely—protected by vigilant, if unenthusiastic, police marched into the Lithuanian neighborhood of small and neat bungalows with carefully cropped lawns and statues of Mary standing in silent bafflement.

Martin believed in nonviolence. But nonviolence worked only if the violent attacked you. He challenged the violent to be violent.

We should have been at Long Beach. We were having April Rosemary problems again. Chuck didn't think they were all that serious. I did. Perhaps because I was a drunk and my mother had been a drunk, I was afraid that my daughter would become a drunk too. Didn't alcoholism run in families?

My daughter and I had been good friends at the end of the previous summer. Chuck had remembered his sleepy resolution to do a formal portrait of both of us in our swimsuits. I insisted that I would have no part of such indecencies. My daughter had determined that I would. She won of course. At first I bluntly refused to wear the new suit she had purchased for me.

"I will have no part in pornography," I said sternly.

"Mo-THER! You'll look sweet in it."

Chucky Ducky didn't help matters when he whistled like the wolf he is at me when he saw it.

"Doesn't she look totally sweet, Daddy!"

"Among other things." He sighed.

I had to admit that I wasn't totally grotesque. I had put on the ten pounds which that bitch Maggie Ward had prescribed. I was still exercising every day in the gym I had installed in the basement at home near the darkroom when I had bought the house in 1949.

While Chuck's journalism efforts involved snapping hundreds of pictures, now with a motor-driven feed on his Nikon, his portrait style was fastidious, not to say fussy. The background for our portrait was a mirror which reflected both our backsides (to which I objected in vain) and the Lake surging with white-caps under a cumulus sky. I figured that it was supposed to say something about the turbulence of femininity. I didn't like that either. Naturally I said so.

Chuck messed around with light readings—naturally he had set up a battery of lights. After all, it was a formal portrait even if the clients were dressed in virtually the ultimate in informality.

I complained about the delays, the repeated light readings, the rearrangements of lights, the interminable proofs he made with a Polaroid, the focusing and refocusing of the lens on his huge portrait camera, the glare from the light, and the whole silly, quasi-pornographic project.

"Mo-THER," my daughter reprimanded me, "you're being a total bitch."

"I think she looks gorgeous when she's being a bitch," Chuck said with a wink for April Rosemary's benefit.

"She's more gorgeous when she's laughing," the little brat said. "Make sure, Daddy, you take a picture when she's laughing."

I was outnumbered. My daughter and my husband

were conspiring against me. I felt awkward and embarrassed. Chucky had photographed me often. I was the wife-model of artistic legend. He had even captured me on film with my daughter. Now, however, that daughter had the body of an adult woman, if not the maturity. I didn't like the idea at all. My modesty was offended by the whole project. I had argued that morning to my husband that he should take only our child's picture. He dismissed me as a puritan.

Earlier in that summer, I had said to my daughter under our personal umbrella on the sand, "You made me blush yesterday, April Rosemary. It's my turn. You have the best teenage body on the beach."

Blush she did, down to the tops of her breasts.

"Mo-THER!"

"I admit I'm prejudiced, but I'm still right."

"I am NOT beautiful."

"Now I sound like you and you sound like me."

We both giggled. A few moments later she ran away from our umbrella to join her friends, embarrassed and pleased. Then she turned around and ran back to me.

"Thank you, Mom." She kissed my forehead and ran off again.

I wept.

So after an eternity of purgatorial fussing around, Chucky Ducky finally emerged from under the hood, grinned at us both, and said, "Laugh!"

April Rosemary buried her elbow in my ribs and chortled, "Làugh, Mo-THER!"

So we laughed.

The absurd hilarity of the situation exorcised my silly false modesty. I relaxed and enjoyed the fun. The scene was not pornographic, not erotic. It was only comic. My husband and daughter had perceived the comedy and I had not. Poor, dumb, stupid me. Anyway, I enjoyed the last several minutes of it as Chuck shot several packs of color plates.

"Now the two of you go down to the beach and leave me alone in the darkroom. I'll totally not tolerate distractions."

We both hugged him fiercely. Laughing, we ran down the steps and dove into the cold water of the Lake.

"That was fun, Mommy."

"Great fun!"

The portrait, which hangs in the parlor in our House on the Lake—and stops all traffic when strangers visit us—is, I must admit, a huge success: two gorgeous women laughing at themselves, the photographer, the mirror, the Lake, the whole world, and life itself. With little protest from us, he hung it at his next exhibition. I suggested that he call it "April and Rosemarie Revisited," the title of his first book. Instead he titled it, "Mother and Daughter Laughing."

I would look at it often in the terrible years to come and wonder whether the miracle of laughter would ever return.

My daughter and I were no longer buddies the summer when we were in Marquette Park watching the march of the Chicago Freedom Movement. It seemed to me that she was in constant trouble. She stayed out after curfew, she and her pack of friends harassed and tormented the cops, they lighted bonfires on the beach without permits, they blocked traffic on the streets, they threw rocks at the streetlights, they cavorted through people's yards at night.

The police brought her home to us twice, once for throwing rocks at a police car (a felony we were assured) and another time for disturbing the peace on the beach (only a misdemeanor) after she and her friends, having sneaked out of their homes after curfew, terrified a few of the local citizenry by the size of their beach bonfire.

By the time the police had dragged her into our house, awakening all of us, including her brothers, who were fascinated by the ability of their sister to raise hell, she was pale and contrite. She was very sorry, she regretted that she had embarrassed us. Actually she hadn't thrown any stones at the police car as, she insisted, her cousin Carlotta would testify in court. However, she shouldn't even have been with those who were throwing stones. She would never do anything like that again.

"Not till next time," I said bitterly.

Chuck frowned at me, a rare signal that I should keep my big mouth shut. We both knew that the stage of harassing the local police was a rite of passage for those in their mid-teens, taken seriously neither by the police nor the kids. Peg and I had pretty much done the same thing when we were that age. My husband, needless to say, never was a juvenile delinquent.

He reassured the police that we took the matter very seriously, that he was deeply troubled by his daughter's behavior, that she would be sternly punished, and that he personally would guarantee that she would never throw a stone at Long Beach ever again.

The cops left, expressing satisfaction with their night's work.

"What about Carlotta?" I demanded when they had left. I knew that April Rosemary and her cousin were as close as Peg and I had been at that age.

"She escaped capture," my daughter replied glumly, as if she were in a police lockup.

"How?"

"She ran. I stayed behind to tell the cops that none of our crowd had thrown any stones."

"Did Carlotta throw stones?" I demanded.

"I don't know."

"Young woman," Chuck said, imitating General Radford Mead under whom he had served in Bamberg after the war, "go to your room. I'll deal with you in the morning!"

"Yes, Daddy . . . I'm sorry, Mommy."

Off she went, head bowed in guilt.

"Now, Rosemarie," my husband began.

"Don't, 'now, Rosemarie' me!" I exploded.

"The only difference between you and my sister at the same age is that you two would never have stayed to proclaim the innocence of your friends."

That was only too true.

"My guess is that the main difference between now and then," he went on implacably, "is that you threw the stones, ineptly to be sure, in those days and Peg did not."

That also was only too true. Damn, why did I have to remember.

The next day, Chuck grounded her for the next two weekends, a punishment which she accepted quietly.

I called Peg.

"Apples don't fall very far from their trees, do they, Rosie?"

"They're both little brats," I insisted.

"So were we, though the good April worried about neither of us . . . Carlotta admits she threw a stone, but only a small one and she didn't hit anything. She also claims that your daughter is, like, totally innocent."

"Times have changed, Peg. We have to be more careful than the good April was."

"What does my all-wise brother say?"

I sighed.

"Same thing as you. We were as bad if not worse at the same age."

"How would he know? He was off in Germany, defending us from the dirty red Communists."

And getting his German mistress pregnant, I thought bitterly. I promptly reminded myself that Trudi and I were friends now and that I had no reason to be angry at Chuck, not being one to cast the first stone.

"He always has been good at guessing."

"I don't think you should worry as much as you do about April Rosemary. She's a good kid."

"I know she is, Peg, but these are bad times, and worse coming."

"I'm afraid of that too."

Neither of us knew how bad. Neither did anyone else.

Two weeks later, on a Friday night, April Rosemary returned home before the curfew. Chuck was reading *The Group* by Mary McCarthy, despite the fact that I told him that she made me furious. I had tossed aside *The Valley of the Dolls*, after forbidding him to read it on the grounds that it was a sinful waste of time, and had begun to plow through the *Collected Stories* of Katherine Anne Porter, my kind of writer. Charlie Parker was playing softly on the stereo, the boys were down on the beach, up to some mischief no doubt. Poor little Moire was sound asleep, worn-out by a day of constant running, like all her days. A light breeze was slipping in from the Lake.

"Young woman?" I said firmly.

"Yes, ma'am."

"Aren't you going to kiss your father and me good night?"

"Yes, ma'am."

She bussed Chuck's forehead.

"Terrible book, Daddy."

"So your mother tells me."

I thought he shifted uneasily.

As soon as she bent over me I smelled the beer.

"April Rosemary Cronin, you've been drinking!"

She sighed and sank into the couch. She bowed her head and stared at her sneakers. Chuck closed his book and watched carefully.

"Yes, ma'am. Only a half bottle of beer. I hated the taste and spit some of it out."

"You expect us to believe that?" I snapped.

Chuck frowned. I had gone too far.

"I took a couple of drags on a joint too. It made me sick. That's why I came home early."

"A joint!"

"You know, Mom, marijuana."

If she were confessing the truth about that, then she probably had told the truth about the half bottle of beer. I strove to control my terror.

"I didn't know that was available up here."

"Kids can get it easier than a bottle of beer. Most of our crowd takes a sniff or two and don't like it."

She was still staring at the floor, a penitent novice caught by an ever-vigilant mother superior.

"I'm sorry I said I didn't believe you, April Rosemary," I said. "We trust you completely, even if sometimes it sounds like we don't."

She looked up with a wan smile. "Don't do it completely. But don't worry about me either. I'll never become an alcoholic. I wouldn't have the willpower to beat it like you did."

"We don't recommend you try it, kid," Chuck interjected, saving the day for me. "Don't undersell the strength of your own character."

"I don't know how Mom did it," she replied to Chuck. "I mean her own mother would have murdered her with a poker if Aunt Peg hadn't pushed her down the stairs and killed her."

Total silence. The Bird on the stereo was the only sound for a moment or two. I had never told Chuck about that awful day. I assumed he knew about it. His face at the moment was as expressionless as that of a Greek statue down at the Art Institute.

"Who told you that story?" he asked finally.

"Carlotta. She heard her mother and father talking about it. So she told me. Don't worry, Daddy, we won't tell anyone else. We are as good at keeping secrets as Mom and Aunt Peg were at our age."

I bounded to the couch, threw my arms around her so we could both sob together.

"I'd better go bed," she said finally, easing out of my arms. "How long are you going to ground me, Daddy?"

Chuck eyes were shining.

"Let me think, kid . . . What about from five to six tomorrow night?"

She giggled and ran upstairs.

We were quiet again.

"You knew?"

"Yeah. I worried about that scene a few years ago and asked Peg what happened."

"I never could tell how much was a dream and how much actually happened. Your dad and Father Raven helped us to cover up. It wasn't murder, Chuck."

"I know that, Rosemarie." He replaced our daughter on the couch next to me. "It's none of my business, but have you told your shrinks about it?"

"No . . . Not yet. It's time now, I suppose . . . Long past time."

"What do I know?"

The next morning, Peg and I went for a sail on our beach boat. Carlotta and April Rosemary pushed the boat away from the shore for us. Carlotta looked like a luscious and sultry Italian actress. The impression was completely inaccurate. She was a sweetheart, not at all like her tempestuous, if wholesome-seeming cousin.

Peg steered the boat while I worked the sail, a routine that was almost twenty years old.

"April Rosemary knows about what happened at my house that day."

Peg frowned, displeased but not upset. "How did she find out?"

"Carlotta heard you and Vince talking about it."

"We weren't above eavesdropping were we? Kids are that way, my brother the worst of the lot."

Why did my best friend in all the world have to be so self-possessed *all the time*!

"The statute of limitations never expires, does it?"

"I asked Vince that once. He said that if the question ever arises, we'll do a polygraph test and that will be that. It wouldn't be fun, but no big deal . . . I suppose that was the conversation that the little brat heard."

"You told Vince long ago?"

"Sure. No point in being married to a lawyer if you don't get good legal advice free. Not right after we were married and not when he came home from Korea and was feeling sorry for himself until you told him off. Maybe eight, nine years ago . . . You tell Chucky?"

"No . . . He didn't seem too surprised last night though."

"He doesn't miss much."

There was a lot lurking behind that reply. Like true best friends we tell each other everything—except some things that it's better for the other not to know. We have an implicit agreement about that which meant I could not explore any further, not that I wanted to.

"He asked me if I had told my shrinks."

"And you haven't?"

We turned about and angled out into the Lake. We'd race back to the beach with our little spinnaker ballooning out ahead of us.

"I wasn't sure what really happened . . ."

"And now you are?"

"Now I realize that I knew all along."

"So?"

"I'll have to tell that Maggie Ward bitch. She won't seem a bit surprised. Don't all her patients tell her the same story?"

"I bet she'll be surprised. She just won't show it!"

We tacked out several times, so far out that the shore was a distant line against the horizon.

"We better go back, Rosie. Along about now the guys will start to worry."

"Good enough for them."

So we came about. I tugged on the spinnaker sheet and we raced toward the shore at maybe five knots an hour, which seemed like sixty on a highway.

"Thanks, Peg," I shouted over the rush of the wind.

She knew what I meant.

"A life well worth saving," she replied, tears streaming down her face.

We surged toward the beach, hooting and hollering. I pulled up the centerboard. The little boat tipped over just before it hit the beach and, with utter lack of respect, tossed us into the light surf. We laughed and yelled like we were sixteen again. Our daughters helped us up, then captured the boat. Our husbands looked up from their books and then looked back. The band made derisive brass sounds while poor little Gianni beat a fast tattoo on his drum.

That day at my house on Menard Avenue had been the St. Crispin's Day for Peg and me. I whispered a prayer for my poor mother as our daughters helped us drag the boat up on the beach.

"Mom," Carlotta informed her, "you and Aunt Rosie are as crazy as any teenagers on the beach."

No one disagreed.

So the next day, a sizzling Sunday afternoon, my husband and I proved who was really crazy on Marquette Boulevard.

Most of the crowd along the street watched silently as the black people, linked arm in arm, marched down the street, singing the spirituals I remembered from Selma. It felt strange to be on the other side. I told myself I hadn't changed, Martin had. No one was preventing the march. There were no police dogs or state troopers with bullwhips. The police were protecting the marchers. Couldn't the marchers see the difference? Still I was sick at heart.

A few stupid people shouted curses at the marchers. They were the ones the TV cameras were picking up. Naturally. You get a couple of guys shouting in your lens and it looked like a race riot. Chuck was concentrating on the real story—the impassive Slavic faces.

Then it happened suddenly and without warning as such things always do—like the rifle shots on the road from Montgomery back to Selma.

A big guy with dirty blond hair and a bloated beer belly underneath an old-fashioned undershirt smashed my husband in the face, first one punch and then another. Chuck was unprepared, he reeled back and collapsed, facedown, protecting the damn Kodak with his body. Another guy, cut from the same bolt of cloth, began to kick him.

I lost it. I can't believe I did what was on every television news program in Chicago that night. I went after the guy who was kicking my husband. I clawed his face, kicked his shins, and pushed him up against a lamppost. Then I kneed him in the groin. He kind of collapsed. The other guy, the one who had hit Chucky came after me. So I kicked him in his private parts, just as my husband reached out and grabbed his ankle.

The police arrived then, just a few moments too late, to see three men on the ground and one frothing hellcat, in expensive blouse and shorts, poised for further attacks.

"These bastards attacked my husband for taking pictures," I yelled at a big Irish cop. "He didn't waste his film on the fockers!"

Fortunately for me, the television sound track didn't pick up that outburst.

"Is he the little redhead?" the cop asked me.

Chuck, still clutching the Kodak, rolled over and looked up at the cop. His face was covered with blood and his eyes were woozy.

"O'Malley, Charles C., Staff Sergeant, First Constabulary, serial number . . ."

He drifted off into unconsciousness.

Later he denied all memory of the event. I have always suspected, however, that the military identification was not just his unconscious.

The cops, having learned from the TV people that Chuck was someone famous, rushed us over to Holy Cross Hospital, staffed by the Sisters of St. Casmir, whose founder, Maria Kuropas, had fled from Russian soldiers at the age of seventeen because she was determined to found a religious order in America.

Why not?

The doctors informed me that Chuck had a broken nose, a slight brain concussion, and possible internal injuries. They would set his nose, and keep him in the hospital overnight for observation. I called the Lake and told Peg what had happened and that she should not believe what she saw on television.

Then I addressed the media who were waiting outside.

"This is Holy Cross Hospital. It is owned by the Sisters of St. Casmir, who were founded by Mother Maria Kuropas. She fled from Russian soldiers at the age of seventeen because she believed that God wanted her to found a religious order. You will note how clean the hospital is: you could eat off the floor. It is arguably the cleanest hospital in America. I don't want you guys messing it up. It is very much part of this working-class community, which I think that Dr. King, with whom I marched at Selma, has mistakenly targeted for today's march when he might better have marched in Lincoln Park, Orland Park, Palos Park, or Highland Park. Or even Oak Park."

I was on a roll all right. I couldn't believe my diatribe when the kids enthusiastically showed me the tape when we returned to the Lake.

"How's your husband, Mrs. O'Malley?"

"We haven't asked Father to anoint him yet. The rednecks down in Little Rock did a much more thorough job on him."

"You weren't there, were you, Mrs. O'Malley?"

"No, I was not."

They laughed. Only when I saw this quite attractive, if I do say so, and wild-eyed matron on tape, did I understand why. Not Rosemarie Clancy O'Malley, but Grace O'Malley Pirate Queen.

Later in the evening when Chuck was conscious but not altogether clear about what happened, one of the nuns showed up at the door with five urchins trailing behind her.

"Children want to see their father," she said. "I'm boss here, so I say hokay."

April Rosemary led the urchins in.

"We made Aunt Peg and Uncle Vince drive us," my older daughter explained. "Mom, you were really sensational!"

Only poor little Moire, trailing her red-haired dolly behind her, kissed her daddy first.

"At least one of my kids," Chucky said, "thinks I was the hero!"

❦ 8 ❦

"Nonsense, Rosemarie," that bitch Maggie Ward informed me, "you were delighted with the warrior image you projected. You loved every second of it!"

I wanted to storm out of her office. I couldn't do that, however. She was my lifeline to sanity.

"I embarrassed my whole family."

"I don't believe that and neither do you. Your older daughter told you that you were the bravest woman in the world."

"How did you know that?"

"I have a teenage daughter too."

"She thinks I saved her father. She loves him more than she loves me."

"We won't even discuss such absurdities."

"You didn't see me on television."

"Rosemarie, everyone in Chicago saw you on television. You were, as your daughter doubtless told you, totally cool."

"I can't see myself that way. I mean if I did see myself that way, it's so different from my . . ."

"Self-image?"

"I guess," I said miserably.

"That is the problem we have been dealing with, isn't it?"

"Peg and I killed my mother," I said.

Her eyes flickered for just a second. Cool broad herself.

"Ah," she said.

"I suppose I repressed it before."

"Or didn't want to talk about it."

"My mother was a dear sweet woman when she was sober. A little vague maybe and ineffectual. She adored me the way she would adore a pretty little doll. She didn't know what to do about me, which is why I went down the street to the O'Malleys every time I had a chance. I think she knew my father was abusing me. She blamed me for it, especially when she was drunk, which was most of the time toward the end. This one day—Peg and I were fifteen—we were listening to Frank Sinatra records at my house. Mom, in a dressing gown, stormed into my room and ordered Peg out of the house. She called her a cheap little slut. Peg decided she'd better leave. You could call Peg anything you wanted, it was like water off a duck's back . . ."

"And . . . ?"

"I walked down to the door with Peg . . . It all gets kind of blurred now because I want to forget it . . . The stairs from the second floor ended just a few feet in front of the door to the basement stairs. Mom stumbled down the stairs and shouted that she wanted the little bitch out of her house. I was never to associate with her again. We didn't argue. We knew Mom would forget about it when she sobered up . . ."

My memory went blank. What happened next?

Maggie Ward's eyes seemed filled with warmth and reassurance. I had to go on, I had to tell the story at last.

"We weren't moving fast enough," I continued, my voice sounding like the croak of a sick hen. "Mom rushed into the parlor and grabbed a poker from the fireplace. She said something about my being a bold stump who needed to be taught a lesson. She swung the poker, I tried to duck, but it hit my side and I fell down, with a terrible pain in my ribs. She raised the poker again over her head. I tried to say the Act of Contrition because I thought I was going to die . . ."

"And Peg grabbed the poker?"

"They wrestled for it. Peg told me later that she knew Mom would kill me."

"And your mother fell against the door to the basement?"

"I think so . . ." I was sobbing now, close to hysteria. "I don't know exactly how it happened. The door never quite shut. She fell against the door and it sprang open. There was a terrible crash. Peg stood there, her face as white as the snow outside the house. She held the poker in her hand. She was staring at it blankly.

"We both dashed outside. Then Peg said we had to go into the basement to see how badly she was hurt. She wasn't breathing, there was a line of blood flowing from her mouth. We'd better go get Father Raven. We ran through the snow to the rectory, which was only two blocks away. Peg did all the talking. He drove us back to the house in his car. He prayed over her and anointed her and gave her the blessing for the dying. Then he said to me that my mother was dead and asked what happened. Peg told him in clear and careful detail. Dear God, Maggie, she was so . . . I'm sorry, Dr. Ward . . .

"I was wondering when you were going to get around to that," she said with a gentle smile. "I'm sure you call me that behind my back as in that bitch Maggie Ward."

We both had to laugh, which was probably her idea. I calmed down a little.

"So, Maggie, he nodded, and said that he'd better call the police and fire department ambulance. Peg asked him to call her father too. He said that we should tell the police the truth. We had been listening to records and when we came down the steps we saw the basement door open and went down the steps and found my mother. Peg wiped her fingerprints off the poker and put it back on the fireplace. The police didn't ask many questions. Mom, they said, had been drinking heavily and had tripped over her robe when she was going down the stairs to the basement. They asked why she would be walking down the stairs. I managed to remember that she hid her whiskey down there. The coroner ruled it death by accident. No one could have imagined that two frail-looking teenage girls had killed her, poor woman."

"They didn't kill her, Rosemarie," Maggie insisted. "Father Raven was right. It was an accident. As they struggled for the poker, your mother fell against the door, she lost her balance, tumbled down the stairs, and fractured her skull."

"Her robe was open when we found her. She looked so beautiful. We closed the robe . . ."

"You weren't listening to me, Rosemarie. I said that you and Peg did not kill her. It was an accident, a tragic, terrible accident. Peg was trying only to wrestle the potentially lethal poker out of your mother's hands."

"But . . ."

"No buts!"

I realized that she was right. A big, ugly glob broke loose in my brain.

"Yes," I said with a huge sigh of relief, "it was only a tragic, terrible accident."

"Why did you bring it up now? Surely not because of the incident at Marquette Park?"

"Oh, no. I learned the night before that my daughter and my niece know about it. Carlotta heard her parents discussing it one night. They won't tell anyone. They're as tight-lipped as we were at their age."

"You told your husband, of course?"

"No . . . He knew. Peg must have told him."

"Why didn't you tell him?"

"I was afraid that he'd be disgusted with me, maybe leave me . . ."

"Do you think he might really leave you?"

"He said he would if I didn't stop drinking."

"Is that what he said?"

We had been through this before.

"Not exactly . . ."

"Not at all . . . What did he really say?"

"That he would leave me if I didn't get help," I admitted, again feeling miserable.

"You got help, right?"

"Yes, ma'am."

I sounded like poor April Rosemary talking to me.

"And you still are getting help?"

"Yes, ma'am."

"So what if you went home tonight and drank half a bottle of whiskey?"

"He'd hold me in his arms and help me climb back on the wagon."

"You really believe that?"

"Probably . . . Maybe . . . I don't know . . ."

"You DO know . . ."

"Yes, I do know . . . Still, he didn't tell me about the child he sired in Germany!"

"Ah, today is the day for revelations."

"Her name was Trudi and she and her family were Germans who were fleeing from the Russians."

"Indeed."

She looked like she wished the time had run out. It had not.

I now felt very guilty.

"There was no reason to tell me. We weren't engaged or anything. He didn't know about the boy until I saw them in the art gallery in Stuttgart. He had to be Chucky's son."

"He denied it?"

"No, I tied on a real drunk and flew home."

"Ah."

"That's when he insisted I see a shrink, Dr. Stone and then you."

"Why did you get drunk?"

"Because," I admitted promptly, "I was ashamed of my behavior. Actually it was a very touching story. They were only kids. Chuck saved their lives. She disappeared when she found out she was pregnant because she knew he'd feel bound to bring her home and that would be a mistake. She's a fine woman. We've become friends. We visited them a couple of times when we were in Germany . . ."

"And all of this comes out today when you're trying to live down your image of yourself as the Pirate Queen of Marquette Boulevard?"

I sighed my agreement.

"Rosemarie," she said, "you are two different women: one is brave to the point of recklessness, forthright, articulate, charming, beautiful. The other is frightened, anxious, self-hating."

"I'm trying to bring them together."

"That is quite impossible. It would be much better if you could learn to cherish both of them. Now it's time."

Cherish both of them? I thought as I left her office. That would be the day.

1967

❧ 9 ❧

Ninety sixty-six slipped into 1967 quietly enough for the O'Malley clan. April Rosemary was on top of the junior class at Trinity, where I had once been. She was also active in the Oak Park Young Peoples' Anti-War Movement, which was as small as it was noisy. I was uneasy with her becoming a "radical." My husband insisted that we were against the war too. She had been able to do what I had failed at—she could simultaneously be a radical and keep the nuns happy. They were all against the war too, as the Fathers Berrigan and Sister Liz became the idols of nuns and priests all over the country.

Kevin, now a sophomore, was a towering forward on the Fenwick basketball team, his brother Jimmy, almost as tall, was point guard on the freshmen team. Sean was in eighth grade and leading the St. Ursula team toward a championship. They continued to blow their horns, now with considerably more skill and much better instruments. Gianni Antonelli now had a whole battery of drums. My three sons were charming, intelligent, studious young men. Kevin, the most studious of them all now, was reading "Catholic" novelists—Waugh, Mauriac, Green, Bloy, even Gabriel Fielding. I suspected that he had many deep thoughts, but he kept them to himself.

As for Moire, she had made her First Communion and was becoming more adorable every day, as for reasons of genes or conscious imitation, she grew into a womanly imitation of my husband.

Said husband refused to show any interest in photographing campus unrest or the race riots around the country. He was now a portrait photographer and nothing more. It was, he informed me, not our time anymore.

"Will it ever be our time again, Chuck?"

He pondered the question as though it had never occurred to him before, though he had been thinking about it every day.

"I don't know, Rosemarie. The barbarians are at the gate. Students take over administration buildings with the encouragement of the faculty. The administration backs down and gives in to their outrageous demands. The kids use highbrow rhetoric but they're mostly interested in sex and drugs."

"And rock and roll . . ."

"And rock and roll indeed."

Not all of the students were articulate. We got used to seeing them on television trying to explain why they had invaded the office of a university president and destroyed all his papers, including records of his life's research work.

"We had, you know, to protest, the, you know, genocidal policy of, you know, this university, against, you know, black Americans."

"Spoiled rich kid, thinking he's a radical because he's got long hair and old clothes," Chuck would sputter.

"Egged on by faculty," I would add, "who would sooner work out their father figure hangups than do their own work."

Meanwhile, there were a half million young Americans fighting in Vietnam, body bags coming home every day. The Democrats had been creamed in the 1966 congressional election.

"I couldn't believe he forgot the lessons of the 1950 off year," my husband moaned. "You don't have a war going on in Asia with draft troops when you're having an election." The Democratic ticket in Illinois and Cook County took a beating too. Some journalists said the Mayor was being punished by black voters for defeating Dr. King. Martin had left town with an empty "summit agreement" crafted with the mayor and various religious leaders of Chicago, some of whom actually believed in his campaign and others of whom were afraid not to be at the "summit."

The Mayor easily won reelection with a large majority of both whites and blacks voting for him. No one seemed to notice that.

Television, we were told by television people, had changed the nature of reality for Americans. Now we saw the burning and looting of the race riots, the campus violence, and the jungle combat in Vietnam on the national news. It seemed to me, however, that just the opposite was the case. The violence was assimilated to the prime-time programs and became no more real than they were. Ho-hum, one more city burning, one more shot of Vietnamese bodies. So what will happen on *Star Trek* tonight?

I did not like what it was doing to my normally effervescent Chucky. He had come to hate all reporters and anchormen. They were frauds, phonies, and fakers, he insisted, not without considerable reason. The special target of his dislike was Walter Cronkite, whose pose of gravity and responsibility deeply offended my husband, especially because when Cronkite pontificated about Germany he revealed his blatant ignorance.

"Hypocrite," Chuck would snarl.

"Charles Cronin O'Malley," I informed him in my Marquette Park persona, "I am on the verge of ordering you to give up the evening news and the *New York Times*."

It was a cold night in late January with a half foot of snow on the ground. It suited my mood perfectly.

He cocked his head and grinned at me. "On the verge of?"

"I don't propose to lose my comic little leprechaun to idiots like Cronkite!"

"On the verge of an order isn't an order."

"Okay, I order you not to watch the evening news or read the *New York Times*."

"Yes, ma'am," he said, and flipped off the TV. "What a relief!"

"How did we get hooked on all this stuff?" I asked, cuddling him in my arms.

"Jack Kennedy," he said. "He taught us we could make a difference. He was wrong."

"Will our time ever come again?" I asked, maybe for the hundredth time.

"Maybe, Rosemarie, maybe. It'll be many years into the future. We'll have a long conservative reaction before then. People will come along who will try to abolish the New Deal as well as poor Lyndon's Great Society. Americans don't like the war, but they don't like the looting blacks or the screaming kids or sex and drugs. It will all catch up with us. Twenty years to work that through the system."

"How long can Lyndon last, Chuck?"

"Not very long. For all his braggadocio, his skin is a lot thinner than was Jack Kennedy's. Young men are dying and their parents are blaming him. College kids are calling him a murderer, the blacks, for whom he thought he did so much, are tearing the cities apart. Because he's trying to run the war without increasing taxes, inflation is going up. McChesney Martin at the Fed has tightened interest rates, so there's a recession and unemployment and the workers have turned against him. That melancholy which is so much part of his personality will catch up to him. Then you can't tell what he will do."

"Will he run again?"

Chuck raised his hands as if balancing the odds, just as Pope Paul VI had done.

"Sixty/forty that he won't."

"Would you go back if he invited you?"

"You know what I said when Mac Bundy called and asked if I'd accept the UN when Adlai died in London?"

"You told them you'd come back only when we began to withdraw from Nam."

"Still stands."

Mac Bundy had left for the Ford Foundation and Bob McNamara for the World Bank. They couldn't take the war either. My Chucky and George Ball had left before there was any blood on their hands.

In the back of my head that cold January night in 1967 I worried about all my children. I worried about them all the time. In a couple of years all the boys would be eligible for the damn draft. What would happen to them!

What would happen to April Rosemary? Now she seemed to be moving to the left. She was currently interested in the Port Huron Statement of the Students for a Democratic Society. Written by someone named Tom Hayden (presumably Irish and Catholic), it was a lot of unintelligible nonsense, the kind of thing that some kid with a Catholic education and no experience of life might dream up.

"Isn't this wonderful, Mom?" she asked me, showing me a marked paragraph? Isn't it a wonderful vision!"

We are people of this generation, bred in at least modest comfort, housed in universities, looking uncomfortably to the world we will inherit . . . We regard *men* as infinitely precious and possessed of unfulfilled capacities for reason, freedom, and love. In affirming these principles we are aware of countering perhaps the dominant conceptions of man in the twentieth century: that he is a thing to be manipulated, and that he is inherently incapable of directing his own affairs . . . Men have unrealized potential for self-cultivation, self-direction, self-understanding, and creativity. It is this potential that we regard as crucial and to which we appeal . . .

"It's impressive, April Rosemary," I said. "A little obscure about details. It won't be easy to achieve those goals."

"Oh, we know that, Mom, but at least those are great goals!"

It was not up to me to tell her that her father and I had the same goals only a few years ago and we had discovered how easily human dreams go wrong.

In those days, SDS did not mean what it would later come to mean, young people blowing themselves up as they were manufacturing bombs in a New York house.

"Rosemarie my darling," Chuck said to me that night I had forbidden him to fume any more at Walter Cronkite, "I think we should walk down to Petersen's!"

"In the snow!"

"Why not? We'll have the place to ourselves!"

So we did and sang songs all the way to Chicago Avenue and all the way back. We were indeed the only customers. Still we sang the songs from *South Pacific* and *Rosemarie* like there was a huge, national audience listening to us.

For a few moments we were young again, without a care or worry in the world.

Except that when I was young I had many cares and worries, like how I was going to tell the man I loved that my father had sexually molested me.

What was I doing as 1966 slid into 1967 and 1967 stumbled toward 1968?

Besides worrying about my children?

I was still his assistant. I set up the studio for his portraits, I helped in processing the film, I kept the books, I paid the bills, both for the photography and for our house and children. I read a lot of books.

And when I could find a few spare moments, I would sneak off to my office on the first floor and write my little stories. I showed the stories to no one, not Chuck, not Peg, not the good April, who was for all practical purposes my mother, and not to my daughter.

I was afraid that they would all laugh. If I had spoken about that fear to Maggie Ward, she would have laughed at me.

We also turned down invitations from some Catholic liberal friends of ours to meet with Dan and Phil Berrigan. We were against the war as much as anyone. We were also against the doctrine of "liturgical protest" against the war.

We heard from Father Packy Keenan, who had been with us at the birth control meeting, that the word in Rome was that after two years of vacillating, Pope Paul had decided not to adopt our recommendations for change. The shadowy figures in the Vatican had warned him that he would destroy the credibility of the papacy if he did. The battle now was between those who wanted him to issue an encyclical reaffirming the traditional teaching and those who wanted him to do nothing because the issue was not sufficiently mature.

"That argument would fly with most Italian popes," Father Packy told us. "You never decide something that you don't absolutely have to decide. This man is too scrupulous to accept such an argument."

With all my other worries, the birth control issue

did not rank very high. All the laypeople I knew had already made up their minds.

We had a big birthday party for Peg and me. Everyone came. Music and tennis all day long. Kids played softball on the beach. Too many memories from the past. We can't be thirty-six I told my best friend, when she had laid aside her violin for a moment (concertmaster of the West Suburban Symphony now).

I feel much older, she said to me. So much has happened.

That was one way of looking at it.

Last summer we wore bikinis, I said.

Absolutely.

Summer at the Lake that year is a blur in my memory. The concerns that bothered me had not changed much, though I had a hard time recalling them precisely because of the following lunatic summer. The boys went to basketball camp, Moire took acting lessons, April Rosemary, who had loved the beach more than any of us, insisted on working in the city at the Oak Park Bank as a clerk. She had to save money, she told us, for her college education. She was planning on Harvard and she knew that cost a lot of money.

How like her father, I said to her father.

Neither of us, however, would have dared to tell her that we could easily pick up the whole tab for Harvard. She drove up to the Lake for long weekends in the Chevy convertible we had purchased for her. ("At least in modest comfort," the Port Huron Statement said.) "Missus," our Polish housekeeper, kept half an eye on her.

"April Rosemary," Chuck had said to her, "you're going off to college next year. We will have to trust in your taste and your judgment and in the values we taught you. There's no point at this stage in trying to control your life. We trust you now!"

She hugged us both and thanked us and promised

that we would never regret our trust. As it was she hung around with a crowd of kids, like Carlotta, who believed in getting a good night's sleep so they could play tennis, golf, and softball—and water-ski every day the Lake was moderately calm.

She was now able to give me a strong match on the tennis court and beat her father most of the time, though I think he let her win.

I also noted, I remember, with some desire to be able to deny it, the passage of the years. Next year my husband would be forty and I would be thirty-seven. Half our lives already gone.

Life is so short.

1968

✦ 10 ✦

In late October of 1967 Chuck began to talk about going to Vietnam. Somehow I wasn't surprised. I always thought he would. My stomach churned. Still, I said the right thing.

"I can understand that you feel you should."

I had truly become the sensitive sympathetic wife, one who almost but didn't quite say, "You damn fool, you're out of your mind, you should get a therapist too."

Antiwar protests were increasing at that time, though they were still smaller and less dramatic than they would become in the near future. April Rosemary, who not so long ago had felt that we were embarrassing her by marching at Selma, was now burning the American flag, and chanting, "Ho! Ho! Ho Chi Minh!"

"What's the matter with Sis, Mom?" Kevin asked me, a puzzled frown on his Fenian face.

"She's worried about all the Vietnamese who are being killed by our bombs."

He nodded thoughtfully.

"I guess that's worth worrying about . . . Will her protest marches end the war?"

"I don't think so. She figures that she has to do something."

He nodded again.

"Like you and Dad did when we went to Germany?"

"Something like that."

And something very different. We were carrying out government policy in the hope of making the world a better place. Our daughter was opposing government policy in the hope of keeping the world from becoming a worse place.

Both generations wasting their time?

We went to a meeting of "concerned Catholics" at Rosary College. It was a strange group, a dozen or so people, older Catholic liberals of *The Commonweal* variety, a couple of union types, a few CFM people, and some very angry nuns in lay garb. Well, the kind of garb nuns would wear and no laywoman would be seen dead in: ill-fitting pantsuits and "sensible" shoes which enabled them to feel that they were radical while enjoying the moral advantages nuns still enjoyed over most Catholic laypeople.

The nun in charge, a lean angular woman with thin lips and hard eyes, took an immediate dislike to me, too well dressed, too good looking. Spoiled Oak Park matron.

"We have the luxury of sitting here in a safe room in an affluent suburb," she began, "while black people are dying on the streets of Chicago."

Instantly I became Rosemarie the Obnoxious from my days at Trinity High School. Nuns do that to me. Well, to be fair, some nuns.

"I thought this meeting was supposed to be about the war."

My damn husband began to grin. He knew what was about to happen and settled back to enjoy it.

"Only someone who does not read the newspapers can deceive herself into thinking that the genocide in Vietnam and the genocide in Chicago are not the same thing."

"A rather complex sentence, Sister. You mean the war and the racial injustice in the city are the same thing?"

"What have you ever done to fight racial injustice?" she demanded.

"I don't think we solve anything by conflating issues which we ought to keep distinct," I replied.

Chucky Ducky, the bastard, sniggered at the word "conflating."

"You didn't answer my question!"

The group was getting restless. Instead of getting on with the business of figuring out how we were to end the war, we were letting two foolish women fight.

"Suppose you tell me what you've been doing, Sister."

They're always suckers for that question.

"I've been teaching racial justice in class, I march in protests, I sat down in the federal building, I've attended racial justice meetings, I'm advocating more black students in the college . . ."

"I'm impressed, Sister, I really am."

God forgive me for setting her up. God forgive my husband for the leprechaun gleam in his gorgeous blue eyes.

"And what have you done?"

"Not much since I crossed the bridge at Selma with Dr. King."

Dead silence.

Then the damnable blue-eyed husband joined the fray. "It wasn't really all that dangerous, except when the snipers shot at us on the road back to Selma from Montgomery."

The subject promptly changed to the war.

I don't know why I have this terrible aversion to priests and nuns. Perhaps it is their easy assumption that they are moral people and have the proper moral answers to all questions and that therefore it is their right and obligation to impose morality on the rest of

us. I don't include John Raven or my brother-in-law
in this condemnation or lots of other priests and nuns.
I just seem to attract the losers. Ed O'Malley was
undoubtedly at a similar peace meeting that night but
with a good deal of doubt because the O'Malleys turn
into pragmatists eventually. At that thought I said a
prayer for my April Rosemary that she would eventually discover pragmatism.

The group at Rosary that night decided that the
only way to end it was to dump LBJ in the election
which was two years away.

"I quite agree," my husband continued to muddy
the waters, behavior to which he was addicted in these
circumstances. "Dick Nixon is the man to bring us
peace."

The patent absurdity of such an assertion escaped
no one. Then another nun observed, "I don't see any
difference between him and John Kennedy and Lyndon Johnson."

We would hear similar idiocy—and not just from
priests and nuns—in the new year.

"That's right," Chucky agreed, "they're all running-
dog capitalists."

We stopped at Petersen's on the way home.
Chucky Ducky never put on weight. I was still under
Maggie Ward's mandate to keep my poundage at the
level she deemed appropriate.

We didn't sing that night.

"Silly people," I said.

"They mean well. They want to do something
about the war. I don't question their frustration. We
have to face the fact that we live in a Greek tragedy
and are powerless."

"Too bad Bundy and McNamara did not leave with
a noisy protest."

"Wouldn't have made any difference."

His hand caressed my thigh under my light autumn
dress. It was not the first time he had engaged in such

a maneuver in Petersen's. I sighed contentedly. It was good to have a husband who was fixated on your body, even if it were still a few pounds underweight.

"Who's left?"

"Townsend Hoopes, John McNaughton among the good guys. Rusk, Rostow, the military people among the bad guys. Lyndon never did follow my advice to bring in a bunch of West Texas sheriffs."

Dean Rusk and Walt Whitman Rostow were ardent cold warriors.

"How will it end, Chuck?"

"I said ten years, Rosemarie," his creeping fingers paused. "Nineteen seventy-five. Seven more years to go. People will finally turn against it. Well-meaning protesters like our daughter might prolong it a little."

"Our boys . . . They'll all be draft age . . ."

"I know. I keep asking myself what I can do . . . I hate panty hose by the way."

"So do all men. They'll just have to get used to them. I never like garters scratching . . . Chucky! That's a little too far!"

He did not desist, however. Nor was I of a mind to stop him. Sex defies death, as I tried to say in one of my secret stories. We faced death in our family. So we would have to make love to defy it—even if the threat seemed distant.

"Do you think I ought to go over there for a week or two and take some pictures? Or do people see it every night on television?"

Dear God in heaven!

"They would see it differently in your work, Chuck. More striking than any TV clip."

Later on, I wondered if I had actually spoken the truth under such circumstances. I had of course. All the more need to make love, passionate, violent love, the kind of love which thumbed its nose at death.

"I'll have to think about it," he said.

"If you continue what you're doing, I won't be able to think about anything."

"That's the general idea—finish your malt!"

"No seconds tonight? Oh . . . I guess not!"

We hurried home on the leaf-strewn sidewalk, slipped quietly up the stairs, and continued our passionate amusements in the safety of our bedroom.

We defied death all right. Spectacularly.

For the time being.

There were a lot more such exhausting nights, especially after December 1, when we announced the plan to the family. He would fly over after Christmas and be back at the latest by January 15. He wouldn't go anywhere near combat areas like Khe Sanh, where the Vietcong had surrounded the Marines just as they had the French at the battle of Dien Bien Phu, where the French were finally defeated in Vietnam.

Chuck probably meant the promise when he made it.

At first the family was quiet, accepting my acceptance of the harebrained scheme. Then April Rosemary began the discussion.

"Why do you have to go, Daddy?"

"Why do you have to go on protest marches?"

"Yes, but you already protested when you quit the administration and told the truth in that article in the *New York Times*."

So, the little brat remembered all that.

"I think my pictures will have more impact than the clips on television. The public is inured to them now."

"I'm sure they will," Kevin agreed. "But haven't you done enough?"

"Sometimes you have to do more than enough."

"Why?"

"Because we're Catholics."

That seemed to settle that.

"We'll go to Mass and Communion every day,"

Jimmy promised, "until you come back, won't we, Mommy?"

"You bet."

"It's a stupid war," Seano insisted, "isn't it, Daddy?"

"Very stupid."

"Promise you'll be careful."

"Cross my heart and hope to die."

I wished he hadn't said that.

We resolved that the trip would not ruin our Christmas. At the family party, Moire produced and directed a play for the whole sprawling O'Malley clan. It wasn't clear what it was about, but it was very funny.

At the end, she said, "We all know Daddy will come home safe and sound."

She had mentioned the unmentionable, doubtless quoting either me or the good April. We quickly changed the subject.

I wished I was as sure as she was.

It was silly, of course. Reporters, diplomats, movie and music stars had been through Saigon and Danang and Hue and none of them were casualties.

Charles Cronin O'Malley, however, had a certain genius for getting into trouble.

His trip, on a TWA commercial flight was delayed several times. Chuck finally arrived in Saigon on January 30, 1968, the day before the Vietcong violated their pledge of a cease fire for the Chinese New Year and threw almost a hundred thousand troops into a fierce attack on the cities of Vietnam. Later it would turn out that they expected that this offensive would end the war. They believed that the local populations of the city would rise to welcome them.

General Westmorland, the commander of the American forces, had told NBC that the Vietcong would launch an offensive at Tet. American intelligence knew it was coming. However, our officers were totally unprepared for a direct attack on Saigon and on the American Embassy, where my husband was spending his first night "in country."

❧ 11 ❧

Saigon
February 3, 1968

Rosemarie my darling,

I figured it would be easier for both of us if I recorded
my letters on a tape cassette and sent them off to you, so
you can tell that I'm in good shape, save today for the
usual jet lag.

You know from my phone call earlier that I'm fine and
utterly unfazed by arriving in the midst of a Vietcong
offensive. It's a disturbance on the tape medium that
makes it sound like I'm still scared.

I promised to stay away from danger. Danger, however,
came to me. I'm now the first O'Malley in several generations of uniform-wearing to find myself in combat. As
you have doubtless known for a long time, I'm a coward.

I endured a tedious conversation with the Ambassador
when I arrived here, a man who is not very bright and
perhaps a drunk. He called me Ambassador O'Malley all
evening. I think he suspects that I may take his place. He
informed me that there "was light at the end of the tunnel."

"We are winning the war," he said. "We've killed two

hundred thousand of them in the last year with negligible losses of our own."

"How many young men come of age in North Vietnam every year?"

"About two hundred thousand . . . However, no nation can afford to lose a cohort every year."

"If they're Communists, they can."

"The enemy is too weak now to mount a major offensive. It's just a matter of time."

I finally went to bed and sank immediately into a deep sleep.

I woke up in the morning to hear gunfire outside my window. Nightmare I thought. I opened the drapes and peeked out the window. In the bright sunshine people were shooting at one another on the Embassy grounds just one floor below me. I closed the drapes quickly.

How nice of good old Uncle Ho to arrange a welcome party for Staff Sergeant Charles C. O'Malley.

I guarantee you, Rosemarie, that I was in a daze. I firmly believed that it was a nightmare caused by jet lag. I didn't know what I was doing. So I threw on some clothes, grabbed Trudi's camera, and ran out into the corridor. There were a lot of people, military and civilians, running around like the proverbial headless chickens.

A women screamed that the Vietcong were everywhere. A man in Marine fatigues with a star on his shoulder shouted that the compound had been penetrated. A couple of grim-faced soldiers rushed down the corridor with automatic weapons in their hands.

I had held one of those in my own hands a couple of decades ago, but had never actually fired one.

It was, I thought, a dazzling nightmare. I figured that I should walk around and find a safe place, preferably in the company of a platoon of the United States Marines. Having served in the Army, I didn't trust the Army one bit.

I walked down a couple of flights of stairs, into a kind of sub-basement where I discovered a lot of communications equipment which had been abandoned. I knew then that it was a nightmare. We didn't abandon our precious technology, did we? Besides, how could an army that had lost two hundred thousand men break into the Embassy of the United States of America?

So I opened the door of the communications room and wandered down an equally empty corridor. I opened the door and found myself facing, maybe ten yards away, a wide-eyed Vietnamese lad, maybe Seano's age, with an AK-47 in his arm. Since we don't issue AK-47s, I figured he was one of theirs.

I remembered one of my basic rules of military life: when someone points a gun at you, fall on your face. I took the kid's picture as I went down. A burst of bees flew over my head. Then an M-1 rifle chattered in one of the offices which lined the corridor and the kid's head exploded.

Eternal rest, I said, and then I could not remember what came next.

A couple of more Vietnamese kids with AK-47s rushed through the door at the other end of the corridor maybe twenty yards away. Their eyes were wide-open and staring crazily. Drugged, I thought as I fired away with my Leica.

I was lying flat on my face in the darkness of the corridor I had entered from. The Vietcong were charging in from the bright sunlight outside. They couldn't possibly see me. One of them lifted a satchel charge as if to throw it. Before he could throw it, however, he was blown back out into the compound by a volley of M-1 fire.

The explosive detonated outside in the yard of the Embassy compound. I caught the blast with the last shot of Tri-X in the Leica. I hardly noticed the sound of the blast. My ears stopped ringing only a couple of hours ago.

No one stirred in the corridor. Then a Marine carefully peaked around the corner of one of the office doors.

"Sappers," he said.

Carefully, his back against the wall of the corridor,

which had been warped by the force of the blast, he eased toward the door, covered by several men with their M-1s at the ready.

Quickly he glanced out and then pulled his head back in.

"Sergeant, phone those idiots upstairs and tell them that we have repelled a wave of sappers who attempted to attack our communications facility. The charge they may have heard exploded harmlessly in the yard of the compound. They may want to send down a few more Marines."

"Yes, SIR," said a voice in one of the offices.

"Tell them no Marine casualties."

"YES, sir!"

I reloaded the Lecia, said a prayer of gratitude to every saint who might have been involved, and also a prayer for you and Trudi and pondered my next move.

A hasty redeployment, I decided.

I had now decided that it was most improbable that I was in a nightmare. Well, it was a nightmare all right, only it had not come from my unconscious.

I noticed the bits of the poor kid's brains and quietly vomited behind the door. Then I heard men thundering into the communications room. More Marines.

I hid behind the door. A dozen or so more Marines dashed through it, shouting orders to one another. They joined the half dozen and dashed out into the yard.

I slipped in after them and photographed the battered corridor, including the bodies of the invaders. Then I edged out into the yard, which looked like a bomb had exploded. Come to think of it, a bomb had exploded.

"What's happening, Captain?" one of the kids asked.

"The perimeter has been penetrated, son. I'm happy to assure you that the United States Marines have secured it. The enemy is being driven back by the ARVN and the police. We expect to have the city secure by nightfall."

I figured that now was the time for Staff Sergeant Charles C. O'Malley, late of the Army of the United

States, to redeploy himself very quickly before someone decided that they wanted his camera and the film in it.

The Embassy continued in chaos. I wandered around looking bemused, which I surely was.

"Ambassador O'Malley, is that you?" said a young man who was patently Foreign Service. What was his name?

"What would ever make you think that, Craig?" I responded.

"I'd hardly recognize you with all that black on your face, sir."

"Camouflage," I said . . . "What's it like outside?"

"Pretty secure in this area, sir. We're still fighting on the outskirts of the city."

"Would it be safe to walk over to the press headquarters?"

"Sure, Ambassador. No problem."

"Would you care to share with me a private evaluation of the situation?"

"In country, sir?"

"Yes."

"It's the greatest fuck-up in the history of the United States of America."

I continued my redeployment and finally found my room. Indeed, my face was covered with soot from the charge. Cheap munitions. I placed the Leica on the bureau, pointed it at myself, and pushed the button. I'm not sure that I will show it to you.

I also discovered to my horror that my rosary was not in the pocket of the slacks I had worn when I wandered downstairs.

I washed my face and discovered that it had not been altered appreciably. I donned khaki trousers and shirt which made me look vaguely but unthreateningly military. I made sure that this time I was carrying my rosary. Irish Catholic superstition or an act of faith? Maybe both.

If God were determined to protect me, as my family back in America was doubtlessly demanding that he do, it would matter little to him whether there was a rosary

on my person. However, it would matter to me, which
was probably the idea.

I stuffed more film in my pocket and ambled out into
the Embassy. It occurred to me that I might find a phone
and call you. I wandered into one office that looked like
it might belong to a third secretary. A very young woman,
Foreign Service assistant perhaps, sat staring at her type-
writer.

"Good morning," I said cheerfully, trying my best imitation of the high-level diplomat.

"Good morning, sir."

"You all right?" I asked.

"Oh, yes, sir, I'm fine. Just a little shook."

"Aren't we all . . . I am Ambassador Charles Cronin
O'Malley . . . Do you think I could make a phone call."

"Certainly, Mr. Ambassador."

She was too young to remember the legendary
O'Malley of Bonn.

"How do I get an outside line?"

"Dial nine, sir, and then the number you want. If you're
calling the States, just put eight-one before the number."

"Indeed."

So I called you and got you just before you went to
bed.

"Chuck," you said quite calmly, "what the hell is going
on over there?"

"I believe," I replied, "that our weakened and almost
defeated enemy launched a surprise attack to celebrate the
Chinese New Year. I'm happy to say it was repulsed."

"They were saying on the news that the American Embassy had been captured."

"Ridiculous, Rosemarie my darling. I'm calling you
from an office in the Embassy. Some sappers penetrated
the perimeter of the Chancery this morning, apparently
intending to blow the place up. However, they were repelled by some very brave United States Marines. The
perimeter is secure again. The whole city will be secure
by tomorrow morning."

(Actually it took two more days.)

"You sure you're all right?"

"Never in danger for a moment."

Even then, my love, I knew what I was going to do with my pictures and that you would see them on the front page of the *Tribune*. You would think I was in danger, but of course I never was. Not really. Nonetheless, I'm glad that everyone back home is going to Mass for me.

I asked the Marines at the door, in camouflage uniform and with automatic weapons, where the press office was.

"Well done, gyrenes," I said, still playing my role as Ambassador. "Good thing we had you guys around."

"Thank YOU, sir."

I had learned in Bonn, that you can never praise the Marines enough.

The street was littered with bodies, Vietcong bodies in civilian clothes just like the kids that were killed in the corridor where I had taken my photos. ARVN soldiers were methodically walking down the street and bayoneting the corpses under the blazing tropical sun. Then they scanned them with some sort of device to make sure that the bodies were not mined. I realized that I would not eat much that day.

I had photographed the dead Vietcong earlier without thinking about it. Now I hesitated. Ought not they be granted the privacy of those who had died bravely? I remembered what Oliver Wendell Holmes had said of Mathew Brady's pictures of the Civil War dead—"A repulsive brutal, sickening, hideous thing [war] is, this dashing together of two frantic mobs to which we give the name of armies."

Holmes was right. One had to tell the truth about war, about the young men who had died; even if had they lived, they would have slaughtered a lot of us.

The ARVN kids, also younger than Kevin, didn't seem to mind my camera. They giggled and pointed derisively at the bodies, serenely confident that no one would ever be poking them with cold steel to make sure they were dead.

The media center was crowded with angry men and women, celebrating the American defeat and damning the military for not doing a better job of protecting them. I wondered whether I hated the military more than I hated the media. It seemed a tight race.

In the last couple of days I realized that it wasn't so tight after all. I hated the media people a lot more. There were some brave and able people in the press corps, some who even went out in the jungle to cover the war. Most of them did their work in the local bars with their teenage concubines hanging all over them—children Maria Antonelli's age. They didn't like the war and neither did I. They positively lusted for an American humiliation, which I didn't. I just thought we ought to pack up and go home.

Anyway, a handsome spit-and-polish Army light Colonel strode up to the podium, rapped for attention, and began to talk. The chattering journalists continued to chatter.

"I am happy to report a great Allied victory," he began.

He was drowned out by obscenities and catcalls. He ignored them.

"Approximately a hundred thousand VC and NVA troops attacked twenty cities and numerous installations yesterday and this morning. All attacks were repulsed with heavy losses to the enemy and only light casualties to Allied troops. We interpret this attack as the last, dying gasp of the enemy and believe that now is the time to strike the final blow against them."

Laugher swept the room, which, I noted, was air-conditioned. You could cover the war here if you wanted without even working up a sweat.

I was fading in and out of consciousness, jet-lagged, exhausted, and sick.

"Why were we taken by surprise," a reporter interrupted, "when General Westmorland actually predicted the attack to NBC a few days ago?"

"I reject that interpretation. We were prepared for guerrilla attacks and repulsed them."

"How could they occupy part of the Chancery of the American Embassy."

"The Chancery was not occupied. A few suicide squads of sappers reached the outside of perimeter but were eliminated."

He was lying. I had proof in my camera, unless I had done some stupid thing and ruined the film. Did he know he was lying? Or did his job require that you not even think about truth?

"Whatever happened to the light at the end of the tunnel?"

More laughter.

I asked a grim woman where the bureau chief of the AP was. She looked up at me like I was some kind of leper.

"The tall guy with the gray hair over there against the wall," she sneered.

I strolled over to him.

"Chuck O'Malley," I said, extending my hand.

He glanced at me like I was an odd sort of vermin. Not a friendly crew around here.

Then a light went on in his brain. He smiled and shook hands.

"Chet Adams . . . I didn't know you were in country."

"I'm not . . . I got some dirty pictures here, you want to buy?"

"Of what?" he asked with interest.

"Of VC inside the Chancery of the Embassy."

"Exclusive for the AP?"

"Obviously."

"Why us?"

"I want them on the front page of every paper in the country tomorrow."

He nodded.

"How much do you want?"

"Free . . . I'll need a place to develop them."

He took me downstairs to a rabbit warren of dark-rooms. The familiar smell of chemicals, normally reassuring, made my stomach twist and turn.

"You look kind of sick, Ambassador."

"Chuck . . . Come back in two hours."

I wasn't sick, Rosemarie my love. You know what a stable stomach I have. I had to leave the darkroom only three times to rush to the rest room at the end of the rabbit warren and vomit. Another guy was in there the third time.

"Not a nice place, is it?"

"You should have seen Germany after the war!"

Kind of thing Chuck O'Malley might of said, huh?

Two hours later Chet Adams peered over my shoulders at the last shot coming up in the developer.

"My God!"

"I don't think he likes war much either."

I won't describe the pictures to you. You'll have seen them all by the time you get this letter. And doubtless be furious at me. But then you did know what I was like when you married me. Besides you made me a photographer. All I wanted to be was a safe and dependable accountant."

"These will be on every front page in the country tomorrow . . . We have to pay you for them, Chuck. They're Pulitzer material."

"Been there, done that. My wife's my agent. Talk to her. I didn't bring her along. Should have."

I thought of you again, Rosemarie my dearest. Indeed you had been in the back of my head all morning. Disapproving. But unspeakably proud.

"You look like you're going to pass out. Where are you staying?"

"Embassy of the United States," I murmured. "I don't think I'd better go back there."

"We'll get you a suite at the Grand Hotel. I'll try to

pry your luggage out of the Embassy before they find out about these photos."

"There's a mid-level staff guy there who knew me in Bonn. Craig something. He'll give you the stuff. Not much, film mostly."

So he led me over to the Grand Hotel-Saigon. The city was coming to life gain. You fought wars (as a journalist) from luxury hotels these days. I collapsed into bed and slept for several eternities. I've just come out of my trance and am dictating this to you before I find out what's happening outside.

I'm sorry if I've done dumb things. You and the kids keep going to Mass for me.

I'll love you always.

Scene: outside of the Grand Hotel. Sunny day, heavy traffic on streets. Bicycles weaving in and out. A pale, slightly confused Charles C. O'Malley blinks at the camera.

Q. Ambassador O'Malley, do you have any comment on rumors that both the American Embassy and General Westmorland want to send you home?

A. First-class ticket, nonstop or I won't go. Private jet. Maybe Air Force One.

Q. Are you aware of the controversy your photographs have stirred up in America?

A. Must have been someone else's work.

Q. Do you think we won the Tet battle?

A. Of course we won it. It doesn't mean we can win the war. I told the President that when I came home from Bonn. The other guys are not the good guys, but we can't beat them without a cost the American people won't pay. Nor should they.

Q. What did you think when you saw the VC point his AK-47 at you?

A. I thought that he was younger than my son Kevin and that he was terrified.

Q. What did you do?

A. Do? I had considerable military experience in Germany after the war. I did what any well-trained professional soldier does in such circumstances. I ducked.

Q. How close did the bullets come to you?

A. Who had a measuring tape?

Q. Have you heard that General Westmorland has asked for two hundred thousand more troops?

A. That sounds like something a general might do.

Q. Why did you come to Vietnam?

A. Do you know what Oliver Wendell Holmes said about my colleague Matt Brady's photos of the Civil War?—"A repulsive brutal, sickening, hideous thing war is, this dashing together of two frantic mobs to which we give the name of armies."

Ambassador O'Malley, on shaky legs, stumbles over to a table in the outdoor bar. He continues to sip from a tumbler of iced tea.

⤞ 13 ⤝

Saigon

Rosemarie my darling,

It is certainly all right with me if you want to have my tapes transcribed for history, as you suggested on the phone. Not that you are likely to wait for my approval

It was wonderful to talk to all of you last night. I expected to catch hell. Indeed I probably deserved to catch hell. Instead you guys all seem to think I was a hero. Actually the shots were the result of dumb luck and instinct. I also didn't think I was funny in that TV interview. I feel right now like I'll never be funny again.

I admit that I looked awful. I felt worse. However, I'm better now, almost feel like a human being. I suppose in February there's snow on the ground and it's bitter cold. Tell you the truth, I'd like the snow. I don't think my Irish blood can ever adjust to the tropics.

Your good friend Walter Cronkite was here yesterday pontificating, apparently on the basis of conversations in the bar of this hotel with media creeps. The war can't be won, he's saying. It's time to get out. Welcome to the club, Walter, you phony. I guess it's official now that this is the biggest fuck-up in American history.

He came over to my table where I was restoring myself

with a glass of iced tea and shook my hand. Brilliant photography, he said. We showed them all on the *Evening News*.

I was civil and correct, but not quite my genial leprechaun self. I thanked him politely.

I'm now doing the work that I had intended all along, studying the young Americans in this city to see what the war is doing to them. Most of them had not heard a shot fired in anger until Tet. They are young, innocent, frightened, spoiled, corrupt, lonely, pathetic. Many are hooked on heroin, which bodes ill for the future of our Republic. It's what comes of trying to fight a war with a draft army.

The joints in which they hang out are a Dali mural of hell. You'll see my shots when the AP sends them around. I don't imagine Lyndon will like them very much. He didn't like my Tet shots either, I'm sure. However, typical of that complicated man, he wouldn't let the MPs arrest me and put me on the first plane to anywhere.

By snooping around and listening to conversations I find that our intelligence people knew all about Tet. They warned that there would be a huge VC and NVA assault all over the country. Apparently these warnings didn't get to the command level. You don't want to worry a general about things he really doesn't want to know, do you?

There was a big NVA assault on Khe Sanh the day before they went after Saigon and the provincial capitals, several of which they still hold. The size of that attack should have been the tip-off that they are ready to throw everything at us. Their top commanders may well be almost as dumb as ours. Apparently they expected to capture Khe Sanh and that the whole country would rise to support them.

The Marines had little trouble turning them back up there. The country, which doesn't much like us and is not interested in fighting their own war, doesn't find the VC or the VNA all that attractive either.

A Marine officer told me that the sensible thing would be to pull out of Khe Sanh, "a focking dust bowl that isn't worth shit," he said. "Instead we're going to reenforce it. Westmorland and Lyndon are afraid of the comparison with Dien Bien Phu."

"Can you hold it?"

"The United States Marines lose a battle to the NVA, you gotta be kidding, General. We'll beat the focking shit out of the fockers. We're bombing the hills around the place twenty-four hours a day. The Frenchies didn't have anything like our air at Dien Bien Phu. They'll leave before we do. Then when they're gone we'll get on our transport planes and our choppers and get the fock out of there. Another big victory that's no better than shit."

The Marine brass are a lot more realistic about this place than the Army brass.

"The tip-off," says my friend with the salty if uncreative vocabulary, is "they're comparing Tet to the Battle of the Bulge . . . Were you there, General?"

I don't know where he got the idea that I was a general. Maybe he was putting me on. Maybe it was the heavy bodyguard that slinks along with me these days. Lyndon apparently doesn't want me to get shot up over here.

"No, my duty was resisting possible attacks by the Red Army after the war."

"Were they any good?"

"The Ruskies? They were worse than we were. They couldn't have made it halfway down the road from Leipzig to Bamberg."

"Anyway, the Army is still using the metaphors from the War in Europe twenty years ago. Massive American strength will crush the enemy. They can't figure out why Charlie keeps coming back."

I watch GIs walking down the street, arms around their pretty mistresses, kids who are still in their early teens. Maybe some of them think the girl is the love of their life and they will bring them home to America, like I thought I would bring Trudi home. Maybe it will even work out for them.

I'm told that half the eighty-five thousand troops that

the VC threw at us last week were killed. We lost only two thousand—two thousand brokenhearted parents and girlfriends and young wives.

This afternoon I went to a Catholic center here where a swarm of young soldiers, mostly Catholic kids, were teaching young orphans, playing basketball with them, and going to Mass with them at the end of the day. I went to Mass too, oops, participated in the Eucharist and for a few moments felt united in God's love with you guys back in St. Ursula. I hope God knows what He's doing over here.

Anyway, not all the kids are dope heads or rapists. All of them, however, are lonely.

So am I.

I can hardly wait to get home.

Love to all.

Khe Sanh

Rosemarie, April Rosemary, Kevin, Jimmy, Seano, Moire—all my darlings.

I really ought not to be here. I promised I would not come up here. However, I was told by my Marine friends that it was quite safe now, so I thought an overnight would be a good experience. Don't worry about me because by the time you get this tape I'll be out of here and almost on my way home.

This base started as an advance point to monitor any movement by the ANV into South Vietnam. Apparently General Giap—the genius behind Tet, a Pyrrhic defeat if there ever was one—felt a little nervous about our presence so he sent some of his regulars in to drive us out. The Marines wouldn't leave since they don't leave, they simply redeploy to the rear, as they said up at the Chosin Reservoir, where Chris Kurtz was killed.

So the twenty thousand troops settled down in the hills

around the base and began lobbing mortar shells in at odd hours and especially when transport planes or choppers landed. Occasionally they would test the perimeter, looking for weak spots. Once or twice they actually attacked with major forces, as they had at the time of Tet. That was a mistake. For once they were playing the American game instead of vice versa.

Then we responded to their mortars by sending jets to patrol the base twenty-four hours a day. Every time a mortar shell was fired, a jet dived at the source of the explosion and blasted it. They say up here that the rim of hills around us is the most bombed place in human history.

I'm constantly caught between conflicting emotions. I hate the war. I think we should never have got into it. On the other hand the Communists are butchers. In Hue before they were finally driven out they tortured and murdered three thousand men, women, and children, most of them Catholics. The difference between the Nazis and them is hard to figure out. I don't like our forces losing battles, but I don't like them being in a war that they can't possibly win.

Anyway our big transport plane with a load of Marine reinforcements flew up from Tonsunhut Air Base yesterday. The country is breathtaking from air, unbelievably beautiful. Its people don't deserve to be caught in a war that is foolish on both sides.

We circle the base once before coming in. A bevy of jets circle with us. I'm too dumb to know that I'm flying into a combat situation. I look out the window and see the ring of hills and this sprawling American base with its tents and tanks and artillery and fences and trenches. Lots of good shots I tell myself as we slip down on the runway. Nice landing. We turn and begin to taxi off the runway.

The dust puffs up next to us, harmless, if unexplained, little clouds.

"Mortars!" shouts the Colonel who is in command of

the detachment. "Prepare to take cover as soon as you disembark!"

He doesn't say where the cover is. I don't see it anywhere.

A jet curves lazily above us and then plummets toward the line of hills. Black clouds explode from the greenery. The plane turns around and sails through the smoke. Another explosion erupts and then a whole string of them. Three other planes follow the first jet. The whole ridge of hills is covered with smoke. There are no puffs of dust next to the plane.

What the hell am I doing here?

Rhetorical question.

"Step lively, now!" the Colonel orders. "Ground personnel will direct you to cover."

We jump out of the plane—no jetways in Khe Sanh—and run toward a bunker. It's too big a jump for Chucky, so I fall flat on my face. A black Marine with a big grin helps me up.

"Be careful, sir," he warns me. "This place could be a little dangerous."

Just a little.

Behind the bunker a Captain looks at the faces of the reinforcements. Then he sees a redhead civilian who really doesn't belong with the gyrenes.

"Colonel O'Malley, sir? Captain Ramirez, Third Marines," he salutes me, "welcome to Khe Sanh."

"Staff Sergeant, Captain, retired. First Constabulary Regiment."

The young man has no idea what the First Constabulary is, such is the short span of national memory. However, he is impressed and salutes me again.

"Charlie arranged a little reception for you, sir."

"So I noticed . . . Is he always that obliging?"

"Usually, sir. We welcome it. The reinforcements understand very quickly that we are at war up here."

I was shown my hooch, a wooden hut on legs to keep the crawling beasties away. In front of it was a foxhole in which I was expected to jump when someone shouted, "incoming" meaning that mortar shells were falling, or more likely had just fallen.

"That doesn't happen much anymore, sir," the Captain assured me. Charlie knows that as soon as he fires a mortar, our air will be all over him."

I was not completely reassured.

Later when I was eating dinner—K rations—with the one-star General who commanded the garrison I asked how long he expected the battle to continue.

He was a man who, save for the lines round his eyes, might have been a First Lieutenant.

"A month, sir. Maybe a little more. It may not have looked like it but we're winning. They're taking terrible casualties over there. They're regular army and not used to such losses. If Giap was smart, he'd pull out now. He's stubborn and not used to being outlasted. He's fighting our kind of war without our kind of resources. One morning we'll wake up and find that they have disappeared."

A roar, as of thunder right above our heads, detonated just outside the door of the CO's command post.

"Just our artillery, sir. We lay down intermittent barrages just to keep them on their toes. They're afraid to bring up their big pieces because they know we'll destroy them the day they appear. So they're limited to mortar fire and that at considerable risk. If Giap is thinking Dien Bien Phu, he is forgetting that the French didn't have much air and we have a hell of a lot of it."

"Are they likely to attack again?"

"Never can tell," he said lazily. "Probably. They don't care much about casualties. We do. That makes it a little hard for us."

"You're confident you'll hold the base?" I asked.

Just for a moment the General's eyes looked tired.

"Certainly, sir. We're Marines. However, when General Giap finally withdraws his troops, he'll quite correctly think he has won a major victory, no matter how heavy his losses. He has tricked the Americans the way he tricked the French, though with a different goal. He fooled the French by luring them into Dien Bien Phu and then defeating them. He tricked us by luring us out here to this useless place so that we would define it as another Dien Bien Phu. Here his goal is not to defeat us, but merely to hold us down so we cannot continue our attempts at winning over the people in the coastal lowlands. He's a brilliant fellow, all right."

"I guess I don't understand," I admitted.

"The Marines have a different image of the war than General Westmorland. He believes we should be out in the highlands searching and destroying the enemy resources. We believe that we should establish coastal lowland enclaves where we win the locals to our side by protecting them from Vietcong terrorism. Ninety percent of the people live in the lowlands. With all our resources up here on Route 9, our efforts in the enclaves are weakened. I'm afraid General Westmorland is doing exactly what Giap wants him to do. So are we, though we don't want to . . ."

With that unhappy thought preying on my mind, I wandered about the base, talking to the troops, taking pictures, and nervously glancing toward the hills. A Catholic chaplain joined me.

"Anyone ever fire ordnance at you, sir?"

"A couple of times," I replied casually. "A couple of days ago in Saigon a kid fired an AK-47 in my direction and once in Bamberg an officer working in the black market tried to kill me with a .45. Both, as is patent, missed."

"That's in Germany, isn't it?"

"Yeah, First Constabulary Regiment, Father."

Meant nothing to him either. He was a short bald man, in good condition and of indeterminate age, probably the oldest man in Khe Sanh. He spoke East Coast, probably Long Island.

"With a name like O'Malley, I would imagine you're a Catholic, sir."

"Sir is for officers, Father. I'm Chuck, Chucky to my

wife and sibs. And sure I'm a Catholic, brother a priest. Archdiocese of Chicago."

"I'm Tom Boyle . . . What brings you to Khe Sanh, Chuck?"

"I'm a photographer, Father. Getting some pictures."

"You're married?"

"I was when I left. Five kids. I think they may disown me when I come back. Wife is Irish-American too, bossy like they all are!"

We both laughed, as Irishmen must when they discuss the determination of their womenfolk.

"What do you think of this war, Chuck?"

"Folly. We may win all the battles. We will still lose the war. Shouldn't be here in the first place."

"Everyone over here thinks that, except some of the high brass and the dodos at the Embassy. It's not only folly, but sinful folly. It's destroying the moral fiber of the young men who have to fight it."

"Oh?"

"Up here, thank God, there are no bimbos and pimps. There's still heroin."

"Heroin!"

"It's all over. Most of the men use it, some of the officers. They're frying their brains because they're bored!"

"Wow!"

"Some night the Vietminh will come down out of the hills, all the alarms will ring, all the lights will go on, and nothing will happen. Our men will be so high on heroin that they won't fight back!"

"Scary!"

The good Father was exaggerating. I hoped.

"The Marines don't kill their officers. In the Army they do. They roll fragmentation grenades under the officers hooches. Call it fragging. Blacks especially."

"Why?"

"Sometimes because they don't want to go into combat with them. Sometimes because they just don't like them.

There's a race war going on here in country. The Marines won't tolerate it. The Army pretends it's not there."

How many American families had received notice of the death of a son or a husband "in action" when in fact he had died at the hands of his own men?

"These are kids," Father Boyle went on, "young men at the beginning of their lives with all the juices in their bloodstreams that come with being male and young. They are lonely, bored most of the time, in terrible danger on occasion, commanded often by dumb and cowardly officers, fighting an enemy they rarely see. They risk disease and addiction because they don't know what else to do. The war will haunt them for the rest of their lives."

So did all the wars we had fought, some of them dumb, some of them perhaps not so dumb.

"I would think they also lose some of their respect for human life. The enemy they can't see dies horribly, as are those men up in the hills. We're happy to see them die."

"They're the enemy, Chuck. You cheer when you know they're dying."

Yeah.

He explained to me the layout of the base. Barbed wire and mines created an outer perimeter. When someone tried to break through the wire, alarm bells went off, and floodlights illumined the location of the break. Then the machine-gun emplacements a hundred or a hundred and fifty yards farther in began to fire on the enemy who might have survived the minefields. The artillery several hundred yards farther back depressed the muzzles of their guns and fired into the area of the break. Infantry rushed to the bunkers around the machine guns to repel any attackers that managed to infiltrate.

"Slaughter," Father Boyle told me. "Human waves like in Korea. They just keep coming and we just keep killing them."

"Do we bury their bodies?"

"No place to bury them and no time. They've still got

mortars up in the hills. We douse them with gasoline and burn them."

The smell of burning bodies would remain with the young Marines for all of their lives.

I ate supper with the CO and his staff. They talked about why the NVA was wasting so many of its regulars on a battle they could not win.

I thought to myself that they might be wondering why we were wasting many of our young men on a war we could not win.

After supper I wandered about taking pictures of the young gyrenes, weapons next to them, writing letters home. I realized that I should be talking to the folks back home So I've talked into the recorder. I'll finish this tape before I leave in the morning.

I love you all. Pray for me.

Morning.

The sleeping bag in my hooch was not quite as comfortable as the bed in the Grand Hotel-Saigon, to say nothing of my marriage bed back home. So far away from home, I thought as I fell asleep. Almost as though it were not there. I'd be in country only for a couple of weeks. Most of the men out here would be away for a year—if they were not killed. I found my rosary and prayed myself to sleep.

It was not a quiet night—the thump of mortar rounds, the whine of a jet, the buzzing of mosquitoes and heaven knows what other beasties outside my net, an occasional angry burst of artillery kept me half-awake for several hours. Then I jolted up from deep sleep and very pleasant dreams about my wife.

The demons were loose. Sirens were sounding, a PA system was intoning the words "condition red, condition red, enemy within the perimeter, enemy within the perimeter," artillery was booming, men were shouting, troops were running by my hooch, jets were snarling overhead, searchlights were blinking on and off, machine guns were burping away—the first time I had heard an automatic weapon up close since my basic training at Fort Benning.

I considered my options. My stomach was tight, my mouth dry. I wanted to go back to sleep. There was too much noise. I pulled on my shoes. I forgot to shake them to get rid of scorpions. Fortunately, there weren't any. I remembered the watchtower near my hooch. Making sure that I had both the Leica and my rosary, I crept out of the hooch. Though it was still night, the lights outside illumined Khe Sanh like a ballpark at a night game. There weren't any men around me. They must be out there somewhere manning the inner perimeter.

I pondered the watchtower. It was maybe thirty feet above the ground. I don't like heights. So I climbed it anyway, not looking down the ladder till I made it to the top. I looked down then and immediately regretted it.

Clutching the rail for dear life I looked around at the battle scene, a nightmare worse than any night horror I'd ever experienced.

The breach in the perimeter was on our side of the base. Antlike figures were rushing, dashing through the barbed wire, across the minefields, and into a solid wall of American ordnance. Human waves. Pickett's charge at Gettysburg carried on at night under high-intensity light. Maybe the enemy was unprepared for the light. They had their own nightmares.

Khe Sanh was like a movie set, background for an improbable drama of brave men dying. The battle seemed illusory, hallucinatory, a pinball machine game. Reluctantly I dug out my camera and the telephoto lens. However, I was too far away to get any shots. The surrealist spectacle did not admit of photography. I would have to be down with the machine-gun emplacements.

That would not be a good idea.

I'm sure, dear ones, that you are happy to hear that for once Chucky was prudent.

The firefight might have lasted another half hour. Then

the ants stopped coming through the outer perimeter and the automatic weapons grew silent. The jets continued to whine overhead and the artillery continued to pound the hills.

Maybe the attack was over. However, no one on our side would take any chances. I lay down on the platform of the watchtower, just to rest my head, and despite the artillery fell asleep.

I woke to the rising sun and the smell of death. I looked around and discovered I was on the watchtower. Not a wise decision. I should never have tried it. Would someone please send a fire engine. Pretty please.

Since the Chicago Fire Department was halfway around the world, I realized that I would fry if I stayed on the tower as the sun rose in the sky. So with the bravery which has marked all my life I began to crawl down the ladder, step by trembling step. I resisted the impulse to cry for help, not because I was ashamed to but because no one would hear me.

I jumped the last several steps and, naturally fell on my rear end. Chucky Ducky as hero.

I staggered back toward my hooch, saw a puff of dust ahead of me and dove headfirst into an available foxhole. The soft barks of exploding mortar shells surrounded me. A furious jet whined over me, its guns clattering. Two rockets erupted from its wings. The mortar fell silent.

"Missed!" I chortled.

Gentle listeners, you will assume that Chucky Ducky had flipped out. I will not attempt to disabuse you of that conclusion.

Captain Ramirez appeared above the foxhole. "Are you all right, Colonel O'Malley, sir?"

"How did the NVA know this was my hooch?"

I scrambled out of the hole and glanced at the small craters which had crept almost to the edge of the foxhole.

"Well, they missed."

"Yes, Sir, SIR."

"Would it be safe, Captain, for me to photograph the battlefield?"

"The CO said you'd want to do that. The NVA is probably licking its wounds today."

Yeah, that was why they sent those mortar rounds over at me.

We walked through the camp. The gyrenes were sitting in little groups, heads bowed silently, weapons next to them. Occasionally they lifted a hand to brush a way a bug.

Victors.

The men at the bunkers were a little more alert. It was unlikely that there would be another attack. Still, Charlie had done crazier things. Beyond the bunkers men were emptying gasoline containers on the dead bodies.

"When will you restore the perimeter?" I asked.

"Tonight," Captain Ramirez replied. "In the dark. We'll sneak out there, fix the fences, and plant more mines."

"Dangerous duty."

"Yes, SIR. The men that will do it know their jobs."

"I would hope so."

"Charlie usually takes his dead with him," the Captain continued as we walked among the bodies. I didn't want to, but I was snapping away with the Kodak, striving to find some dignity, some hope, some promise in the dead bodies. A few of them wore Catholic medals.

"None of us like this burning stuff," the Captain continued. "We don't have much choice. Many of them are booby-trapped."

How do you go into battle with a booby trap on your body? You know you're going to die one way or another. Brave men? Or men who were afraid to argue with their officers?

"How many dead?"

"Over three hundred. Same number perhaps beyond the perimeter. They threw a battalion at us. That's unusual for them. If they had broken through, there would have been a lot more to push into the base."

"Did they come close?"

"No, SIR. We don't know why they thought they could. Life is cheap in this country."

The gunnery sergeant who was running the burial party, if it could be called that, ordered us back to the bunkers. He trailed a streak of gasoline away from the bodies and toward the bunker. Then he lit a cigarette, tossed it casually into the streak, and ran like hell.

I caught it all on the Kodak. Full color.

Then a dirty orange flame spread across the battlefield. The bodies blossomed like transient spring flowers. Many of them exploded as the booby traps went off. I caught those in the Kodak too. The stench of burning flesh floated in our direction on a light breeze. Some of the men with me vomited. Captain Ramirez himself looked sick. Perhaps hardened to war, I didn't feel anything at all.

Well, when I got back to my hooch I vomited all over the place.

The CO knocked on the doorjamb.

"Colonel O'Malley, there's been a development which might interest you. Our intelligence people have taken infrared pictures of the hills around us. They have located the tunnels and the bunkers and the ammunition stores. Our B-52s from Saipan are coming over to take them out. Would you care to watch from my command tower?"

I wasn't sure that I would. However, I followed him.

Despite the stench of the burning bodies and the smoldering fires at the site of last night's battle Khe Sanh seemed quiet, almost peaceful. The gyrenes were eating their K-ration lunches, a couple of kids were picking at their guitars and singing the blues. The CO watched the sky with powerful binoculars.

"They're coming," he said to me. "They're so high we will not be able to see them with the naked eye. Neither will Charlie. We'll know they're here only when the earth begins to shake."

Then the earth indeed began to shake. Our observation

tower quivered like it was hit by a tornado. The ridge of hills in front of us seemed to explode from end to end as if a volcano had erupted. Huge clouds of dust and smoke and flame shot skyward obscuring the blue sky and the sun. The ridge shuddered like a dying animal. Slowly the volcano spread in both directions, eventually forming a circle of fire all around us. Waves of sound enveloped us from all sides.

I hope they don't miss, I thought. There'd be nothing left in here. However, they didn't seem to miss.

The raid seemed to go on forever. The circle of fire rose higher. The ground quivered more violently. The sun darted in and out of sight. Secondary explosions ripped the ridges as ammunition and fuel stores blew up. My nose was clogged with the acrid smell of exploding bombs, my mouth as dry as the desert, my ears had stopped working. My stomach wanted to vomit, but it no longer knew how.

Make it stop, I begged whoever might have the power to make it stop.

Then suddenly it did stop. The CO, two of his aides, and I were lying on the deck of the watchtower, blown over by the blasts. For a few moments there was silence again as we waited to be sure that the B-52s had left.

"A little more than I expected," the CO observed. "Poor devils over there probably can't figure out what hit them."

Then our own artillery began to fire into the ring of dirty orange-and-black flame to remind the enemy that the firepower was all on our side. I remembered that I was a photographer and began to blaze away. I was furious at myself that I had taken no shots during the raid itself.

Finally, all the shooting was over. The smell of incinerated bodies, never blotted out by the raid, once more dominated Khe Sanh.

"They're going to get that every day from now on. It will make them think pretty seriously whether they're in the right place. Want to stay for the next show, Colonel O'Malley?"

I didn't.

My last memory of Khe Sanh was the stench of burnt human flesh as the transport plane hurried down the runway and lifted into the air. I am scribbling these lines on the ride back to Tonsunhut.

I didn't exactly cover myself with glory this time.

Keep praying for me.

Love to all.

Subic Bay, Philippines

All my loves,

Well, if you wanted me out of harm's way, the same has to be said of the United States of America. After the AP sent my pictures of "Burial Party Khe Sanh" around the United States, I was informed by a very officious Colonel that the Embassy wanted me out of country immediately.

I raised hell, of course. You can't do this to me. It's censorship. I'm an American citizen. I've served my country in both the military and civilian roles. I hold the Legion of Merit and the Medal of Freedom etc. etc. You'll have to remove me by force etc. etc.

The colonel retreated. I thought that perhaps I had done too good a job. I wanted out immediately too. However, to paraphrase the poet, I did not want to seem to be going too quietly into the daylight of home.

I called the AP and told them what was happening. They promised to raise hell. I packed my clothes and waited. The Colonel returned with a squad of soldiers. I protested loudly and obnoxiously as I was dragged from the hotel and placed in a staff car.

My behavior was atrocious at the entrance to the hotel, where NBC had thoughtfully placed a camera. I was wearing my Medal of Freedom, which I had brought along just in case I needed it.

"I am told that General Westmorland thinks my pictures are obscene," I informed the American public. "I think that his attempt to fight a guerrilla war like he is George Smith Patton Junior is obscene."

"Ambassador O'Malley, is it not true that you are opposed to war?"

"I made that clear when I left the administration. Can you tell me the name of any journalist here who is in favor of it?"

"Are you going to sue the government for this arrest?"

"Am I being arrested? Am I, soldiers?"

Grins and laughter from the GIs who were responsible for escorting me to Tonsunhut. They had already decided that I was cool.

"The budget deficit is too high as it is," I replied as the Colonel in charge shoved me into the car.

"Your career is already in jeopardy, Colonel," I warned him. "You touch me again and you will have had your last promotion."

The GIs looked away to suppress their giggles.

All in all, I had a grand time.

I have every intention of suing the government and General Westmorland when I return home. I must have really driven him up the wall. He's too smart a man to indulge in such a fit of pique. Ed Conway, I'm sure this letter will reach your eyes. Do we not have grounds to seek relief?

Anyway, instead of flying me to Chicago or to San Franciso or even Hong Kong, they dumped me at Clark Air Base which is near this place and left me to shift for myself. One more ground for action.

Clark Field, some of you may remember was the air base where that military genius Douglas MacArthur had all his B-17s lined up in a neat row for the Japanese to destroy eighteen hours after the attack on Pearl Harbor.

Anyway, I took a taxi down here to the huge naval air base built where John Wayne and his PT boats worked in *They Were Expendable*. It now has the honor of being known as the biggest whorehouse in the world, a ranking that was held by Naples when I was defending our Republic and the free world in the European Theater.

On the basis of what I see around here I am in no position to reject the claim. Indeed it makes Saigon look like a Trapestine cloister.

Those who defend it argue that the naval and Marine aviators who come here for "R and R" are men who live in constant danger of death. Even in peacetime, I am told by the few sober flyers I encounter, 10 percent of the aircrews perish during a cruise. Now the casualties are much higher—40, 50 percent. If they survive a crash, they face years (seven if my calculations are correct) in a Vietnamese prison. So Subic is a place to let off steam, to release tension, to defy death with booze and women, especially women.

I think of Father Boyle and the juices of life.

Yet the things they do to women, children really, are an abomination. Can they face death with easy consciences when they think of infidelity to their wives and cruelty to these children?

I ask my sober and chaste flier friend about this. He shrugs, "Captain, I don't know. They'd probably say that they just want to have a little fun before they die and that when they go home they'll be faithful to their wives."

Just like the GIs in country who say they'll stop using smack when they return home. Maybe they will. Yet I can't imagine that memory and conscience will let them off easily.

I do not believe that the title "Captain" represents a demotion. It is the naval equivalent of Colonel.

"Smack," by the way, is alleged to come from the Yiddish *schmeck* which in turn comes from the Old High German *smac* which means, not unreasonably, smell or perhaps taste. Stick with Ambassador O'Malley and you'll learn a lot.

I suppose the Roman Legionnaires had places like Subic to which they could repair for R and R during interludes between battle. It is still vile. Nonetheless, I have wandered about with both my cameras recording this extraordinary result of American imperialism during a foolish war. Tomorrow I will find a taxi driver to take me to Manila and try to negotiate a first-class fare to Chicago.

Yes, Rosemarie my darling, I said first-class. Out here I am willing to admit as a defensible hypothesis, but only temporarily, that the Great Depression is over.

I noted on the radio in my hotel (ABC Manila) that there is some contretemps in the United States about a former American Ambassador who was physically ejected from the country by the United States Army.

I can't image who it was!

I expect to see you all in a day or two. Please omit red carpets. Flowers will be acceptable.

All my love to everyone.

✥ 14 ✥

Tonsunhut Air Base

My loves,

I'm not sure that anyone is still listening to my letters. At any rate, as I said to my saintly wife on the phone, I never was missing. The United States Navy, which is no more efficient than the Army, it turns out, might have thought I was missing. However, I knew where I was all the time, even if they didn't. How can you be missing when you know exactly where you are?

In any case I am back in country, much I daresay to General Westmorland's dismay and with a whole new set of pictures. The United States Air Force is apparently favorably disposed to flying me to San Francisco. However, for some odd bureaucratic reason, it cannot do so until the United States Navy satisfies itself that I am not missing. I for my part am steadfastly refusing to leave until my luggage, which includes many rolls of film, are flown in from the *Kittyhawk*.

I give you my solemn word of honor—which most of you will with considerable reason discount—that I will not venture forth on any more photographic missions. I have, by the way, been promoted to Colonel again.

I must give you a brief account of Chuck O'Malley's

last ride in an F-14. Which was also his second such ride.

I should note that while the United States Navy didn't know where I was (still seems not to), the Vietnamese fishing boats did.

My sober naval aviator friend—Commander Tom McCarty by name—found me just before I was about to board the taxi for Manila and offered me an interesting bit of frosting on my cake—a flight in his F-14 to the *Kittyhawk*. The name of this carrier, I'm sure you will remember, is that of the beach on the Atlantic where the brothers Wright made their first flight.

I figured why not. I'd be flown back the next day or the day after. It might be the last time I had a chance to land on a carrier. Some of you might say that in retrospect that it could have been the last time I flew anywhere. But that is both unfair and untrue, in the strict literal sense of he word.

Was it crazy?

I will not dispute that charge.

Was I terrified at the prospect of landing on a carrier? Chucky O'Malley a coward?

The takeoff from the Naval Air Base at Subic was routine enough, save that I swallowed my nostrils, my tongue, and much of my throat and lungs, when the twin-engine jet pointed its nose at the sky and went straight up.

Motion sick?

Not with three marazene tablets in me.

I floated along in the sky and admired the beauty of the South China Sea, without a care or worry in the world. Thoroughly drugged, you might say. Alas, I do not know the Yiddish word for marazene, to say nothing of the Old High German word.

"There she is," Tom McCarty informed me on the intercom.

"What? Where?"

"The *Kittyhawk*! Down there!"

"I don't see anything."

He tilted the plane so that I was looking straight down. There was a patch of something white on the blue ocean, the wake of the carrier which trailed behind a black-and-gray dot. To call it a postage stamp would be to exaggerate its size.

"NO!"

"Yes, thank goodness it isn't a night trap. Those are really scary."

He engaged in some jargon with the ship. We went into a steep dive, pulled out of it off to one side, banked on one wing which, marazene or not, turned my stomach several times.

Then he pulled more or less level with the deck of the carrier—still an impossibly small softball field—and approached it all too rapidly. Like some crazy teenager driving at top speed into a bobbing garage. A line of lights on the left side of the ship blinking from green to red and back to green and a couple of people waving their hands.

I grabbed for my rosary, sure this time that I would see the face of God in five seconds and he would demand to know why I had left my deeply loved wife and children for this madness. There was not the slightest doubt that we would crash into the superstructure on the right-hand side of the ship. We were going much too rapidly to land. He had better turn around and try again. However, we hit the deck with a loud and vigorous thud. The plane lurched forward and then a massive and hidden hand reached up and slammed us to the deck.

It was called, I would later learn, the arresting gear.

God, it would seem, was giving me a second chance. Immediately I began to think of the stories I could regale my children with when I returned to Chicago.

Chicago? Where's that?

Commander McCarty maneuvered the plane toward the island as I learned the ungainly superstructure was called. Each twist of the aircraft (as these people call a plane) stirred up a troubled stomach. The plane stopped, the wings folded up, the engine shut down, as if in relief.

Another safe "trap"! The only issue now is how they would get me out of the plane.

Tom helped me out of the cockpit, which I left most reluctantly. Two men whose job was apparently to tend the plane and help inept landlubbers—I remembered the word—reached up their hands to steady my descent.

I was after all a former staff sergeant in the Army of the United States, former Ambassador of that great Republic to the Federal Republic of Germany, holder of the Legion of Merit and the Medal of Freedom. I had a certain dignity to maintain. Woozy head notwithstanding, I would disembark (if that were the correct word) from the F-14 with a certain elegance and grace.

Right?

Wrong! Of course.

I fell on my face. The only reason I didn't break my nose again was that a silver-haired officer with a broad smile caught me.

Captain, maybe Admiral.

I remembered the routine, probably from a movie.

"Permission to come aboard, sir," I said essaying a salute. It was not a sharp salute. However, even at its prime in Bamberg my salute was not very sharp.

"Welcome aboard!"

Some dignity preserved, though admittedly not a hell of a lot.

They put me to bed in the Captain's port cabin. Shot me full of some sort of chemical and permitted me to sleep for a day or so. I awakened periodically to hear a jet crash into the deck above me, and then went back to sleep. The next day they gave me the run of the ship with my cameras. A carrier is a fascinating phenomenon—a small city of five thousand people with its own hospital, dental office, chapel, kitchen, pastry chef. It plows through the ocean (in this case the South China Sea), cut off from the rest of the world, with the sole purpose of putting into the air every day five dozen aircraft (see!) which will deliver weapons of destruction on an unseen and perhaps nonexistent enemy and then reclaiming these aircraft when their work is done.

The carrier and almost all of its crew were in no danger from the enemy, which lacked the aircraft and the weapons to strike back. For the men who were not aircrew and had no responsibility for feeding and servicing the aircraft, this cruise, while not a pleasure trip by any stretch of the imagination, was hardly a war. If anything it was a more boring experience then waiting on land to attack the enemy or be attacked by them. There was sadness perhaps when a plane and its crew did not return or crashed on takeoff and landing. However, it seemed to me that after a while even these tragedies became part of the monotonous routine.

Truly terrifying, however, was the way the planes took off. They didn't roar down the flight deck and lift into the air with confident polish the way a 727 passenger jet would. Rather they were hurled into space by demonic steam catapults at the very front of the ship, a raw demonstration of brute power.

They would never do that to me I averred to myself. Obviously if I insisted on remaining on the ship until it returned to Subic I would have long since been divorced by my wife and children. I elected not to think about it.

They might divorce me anyway if they found out where I was.

I encountered a tall, husky civilian employee from the Center of Naval Analyses who told me that he had not seen the light of day for five months. Rather, he spent his day in the fluorescent beige-and-blue bowels of the ship calculating and recalculating arcane numbers on the performance of a certain new missile that the Navy was about to turn loose on the enemy.

"Does it work?" I asked him.

"Hell, no! It not only doesn't work, it would be an absolute menace to an aircrew that was carrying it. The Pentagon has a lot of money and a lot of prestige tied up in it."

"Like the torpedoes which didn't work during the War? We know they work because they have to work?"

"Something like that. I've talked the Admiral and the Captain out of trying it in combat. We'd just lose good men. I've sent in my report. I think some of the people who will read it might understand that there will be greater risks to their careers in using it than in scrubbing the whole project."

"Is anything we're doing out here having an impact on the war?"

"Very little. Bee stings to an elephant. However, the Navy feels that it has to be doing something to stay in the appropriations game."

"Even if it means the lives of the aircrews."

He nodded solemnly.

"Don't think the aircrews miss the point. Many of them just fly out from Delta One, drop their ordnance into the ocean, if they can. Hang around a little and return to the ship with a clear conscience. We know who some of them are. They'll hand in their wings eventually. Can't blame them."

"Does anyone out here believe in what we're doing?"

"They believe we're doing our duty as our superiors have told us. Affecting what happens in country? Maybe the Admiral and the Captain believe in it, though they keep their opinions to themselves. Virtually everyone else thinks it's crazy."

"Crazy but orders?"

"That's about it."

Like my young friend at the Embassy in Saigon said, the biggest fuck-up in the history of the United States.

Bigger than Bull Run? Bigger than Chancellorsville? Bigger than the Little Bighorn? Bigger than Pearl Harbor?

Quite an achievement.

Then I come to a part of my story of which I am heartily ashamed. At least I think I am. My wife and kids, my parents and siblings are all entitled to a divorce because of what I did next. Indeed, I'm sure my poor, long-suffering, gorgeous wife could have our marriage annulled on grounds of insanity because of this final part of my adventure.

So I have to say that I regret it. I really do. Some of the time.

It was, however, one hell of an adventure. I never talk about my adventures in Germany with the First Constab, maybe because there was a fair amount of tragedy as well as folly in them. This story, however, while it reveals culpable, indeed criminal behavior, is also in retrospect high comedy. And comedy in which no one got hurt.

Except Chucky Ducky, who may have pushed his luck with his family too far this one last time.

Note that I am seeking forgiveness on grounds of insanity.

The devil in the form of Tom McCarty, commander of VF 111, the fighter squadron of Air Wing 11, approached me my third day on the *Kittyhawk* with an appealing idea.

"Chuck, why don't you fly with me on today's mission. The other carrier out here is joining us in a major raid on what purports to be a concentration of NVA about fifty miles above the border. We'll be sending in about fifty planes. My job will be to sit offshore and direct them in and out. No one will shoot at us. There is absolutely no danger. Would you like to come along?"

No danger as long as the plane, uh, aircraft functioned properly.

That was a very important condition. It never occurred to me. I knew about the accidental losses of aircrew. But surely the plane I was on wouldn't be an accidental loss. Right?

It would involve being hurled into the air by the catapult monster. However, having done that once, I would not be frightened on my return flight to Subic. Right?

So I thought why not?

The good April, in an occasional show of impatience with me when I was growing up, would say, "Chuck, there are times when you don't think through what you say or do."

Well.

Anyway it seemed like a nice final chapter to my story. So I threw caution, to say nothing of common sense, to the winds, and said, "Sure, why not?"

After the words were out of my mouth I thought of a thousand reasons why not. It was too late unless I wanted to seem a coward.

Which we all know I am.

So clutching the rosary in my pocket, I was strapped in again to the rear seat on the F-14. We taxied to the front of the ship and were fastened on the steam catapult. No big deal. Tom McCarty said it was the most exciting moment of carrier flying. I would be slammed against the back of the seat and held down by a force of I forget how many Gs. I closed my eyes and pretended to doze and the aircraft shivered and shuddered in preparation for launch.

Then there was an abrupt explosion behind me, the engines on the jet roared to life, we were hurled forward by a demon not unlike the one that had slammed us down on the carrier deck.

It may be that the heavy weight of gravity and acceleration did pin me in my seat as we went from zero knots an hour to two hundred and fifty knots. I assume that did happen. All I can remember was clutching my rosary desperately as I waited for the South China Sea to engulf us.

Then the aircraft turned its nose toward the sky. I informed whatever power lurked behind my rosary that I was grateful for another miracle.

"All right back there, Chuck?"

"A piece of pie, er, I mean cake!"

"Told you it was a great thrill, didn't I?"

"You did indeed!"

I took my memory-laden Kodak out of the waterproof pouch in which I had placed it and tentatively began to snap some shots. You can't get very much from such a small camera in an F-14.

Across the horizon there appeared a ribbon of green which quickly grew larger as we sped toward it. Vietnam. Indeed North Vietnam.

Only a half hour away from the deck of the carrier. Too close, too close.

We were, I gathered from the chatter on the radio, Delta Leader One.

Tom directed the various groups of planes to hit the target. They reported back that they had delivered their ordnance and encountered no antiaircraft fire.

"Another dry target," Tom McCarty said evenly. "Well, everyone's going home alive."

Almost everyone.

Suddenly our engines stopped. Not one of them, but both of them. I told myself it was my imagination. They started again and then shut down. Definitively I thought. They'd had enough of this foolishness.

"This is Delta Leader One, Delta Leader One. Mayday, repeat mayday. Engines flamed out. We're going in."

Why did he seem so damned cool?

"We copy, Delta Leader One. We're informing Big Delta. Good luck."

"Don't worry, Chuck," he told me. "They'll have us picked up in a half hour. The seawater down there is warm."

"I need a swim," I replied, fooling no one.

He gave me instructions about "ditching." I paid no attention. All I knew was that I had to get out of the plane in a hurry.

The water came up with alarming speed. In another moment it would hit us. Lucky that water was soft.

Right?

Wrong!

It hit us like ten feet of solid concrete and began to tear the plane apart. I didn't have to jump out of the F-14. It tossed me into the South China Sea like I was bad luck and it wanted to be rid of me. I tumbled into the water and swallowed half of the South China Sea. Here is where I drown, I thought as I tried to remember what I was to do next. Fortunately Tom McCarty was next to me and he pushed something which made my life jacket inflate. A tiny raft appeared next to us. We clambered into it.

The water had indeed been warm, a lot warmer than Lake Michigan.

"Piece of pie," Commander McCarty said. "A lot better here than in country."

"Oh yes," I agreed.

"Delta Leader One," he spoke into some kind of mike. "Do you copy me?"

"We copy you, Delta Leader One. That aircraft went down in a hurry."

"Old one. I want a new one."

"We've got you marked. The cavalry will be out shortly."

The aircraft above us turned tail and raced back toward Big Delta.

We were alone in the middle of a very big ocean. It was no longer just the South China Sea. It was the Pacific.

"No real problem," Commander McCarty assured me. "The dye you see around us will mark our spot. The F-14s will be back in a half hour or so. They'll home in on our radio signal. No extra charge for the special thrill."

I was too paralyzed by fear to respond. We were alone in an empty ocean, somewhere off the coast of North Vietnam. On the opposite horizon a thin black cloud hovered.

"The weather people told us that the typhoon would hold off for another twenty-four, thirty-six hours."

First I had heard of a typhoon. Long-forgotten images from Joseph Conrad's novella surged into my consciousness. I would never see the Chicago skyline again, never walk over to Petersen's with my wife, never hear my children sing. My short life would end in a crowning act of folly. Thank heaven that Rosemarie had inherited a fortune from her parents. The family would survive. She would doubtless remarry and probably to a better choice. It would be tough but April and Peg and Dr. Ward would see her through.

Despair?

Something much worse to which I can't give a name.

It occurred to me that I ought to pray. Why bother? What good would it do? God had made up his mind that I was expendable. I couldn't really blame him. I was a wise guy, a smart-ass, a shitkicker, a professional voyeur. I'd done enough harm in the world.

Our raft rode up and down on the light chop, just enough to bring back my motion sickness. The water into which I had tumbled evaporated quickly, coating me with foul-smelling salt. I started to vomit. Routinely, every five minutes, I emptied everything in my stomach into the Pacific.

What a terrible name for an ocean that spawned typhoons!

"What's the name of that typhoon over there?" I asked Tom, who had been as quiet as I was.

"Rosie."

"Huh?"

"Typhoon Rosie."

God did have a sense of humor.

The sun was blistering my pale Irish complexion. My doctor would not approve of this much time under the tropical sun.

However, I would never see him again so it didn't matter much, now did it?

"I can't imagine what's keeping them. There must have been an accident on the ship. They know where we are even if we are not generating a radio signal . . . Don't worry, Chuck. The United States Navy hasn't forgotten us."

No, perhaps not. But if God had forgotten us, then who could blame the United States Navy?

The sun was slipping toward the distant smudge on the

horizon, which was North Vietnam. The day was running
out on us.

"They won't give up on us, Chuck, even if they don't
find us today. The Navy never lets its aircrews down."

I didn't believe that.

"Won't they be afraid of the typhoon?" I asked.

"There's at least twenty-four hours before that rolls in.
They'll find us before that."

If our radio beacon was still working.

"Maybe we should start praying, Tom?"

"It can't hurt." He grinned.

So I fished my rosary out of my trousers, now board
stiff, and we began to pray.

"You have a wife at home?" he asked me after our first
round of fifteen decades.

"Yeah, named Rosie, except that I always call her Rosemarie. She is the most beautiful woman I've ever seen.
We have five kids."

"A lot of responsibility . . . I'm married. Two children,
both under five. Good kids, great wife."

I hoped that all of both our families were storming
heaven.

"She approved of your being out here?"

"Not really. No woman in her right mind—and my
wife is very bright—would want her husband in an aircrew. I'm in fifteen years next week and due to go home
at the same time. I'm sure I'll make Captain back home.
Then I'll retire. I've paid my dues. What about you? Does
your Rosemarie approve of this adventure?"

"She didn't object very loudly when I told her I was
coming out here. She figures that my vocation is photography just like my brother Ed's is to be a priest. I don't
think she'd be delighted by this leg of the trip."

"Don't worry about us, Chuck. We'll make it home."

I began a second ride through the mysteries of the rosary. I had to stop several times to vomit.

What would death be like? I wasn't thinking so much
of my actual physical death. I would drown, an end which

is a lot quicker than cancer. I was worried about after-ward. There was some transcendental power behind the Universe. I didn't doubt that.

However, did the transcendent give a damn about any of his creatures? Most especially, in this instance, me.

"You said your wife is beautiful?" he asked.

"Yeah, I know. You're wondering how a radiantly beautiful woman would marry a foolish little guy like me. I never did understand that . . . To be in a room with my Rosemarie is to want to undress her, whether you're a man or a woman."

"I know the feeling," he said, his first hint of discour-agement.

If the skipper of our little island of humanity was losing his nerve, then his vomiting unable seaman could hardly be counted on.

"I can't figure out what's wrong," he said. "They should be out here now."

"How much time before sunset?"

"An hour maybe"

The sky burst into a brilliant sunset—red, gold, and purple.

"Hello!" Tom spoke sharply. "It looks like we have company."

He pointed toward the horizon where the sun was thinking about whether it ought to try again tomorrow. A couple of boats coming our way—from the North Viet-nam shore.

"Ours?"

"Unfortunately not. Vietnamese fishermen, NORTH Vietnamese. Their government pays them for every American aviator that they can pick up. Maybe someone onshore heard our beacon."

"Do we fight them?"

"With what?"

Prisoner of war. Civilian at that. Better the typhoon.

We watched with fatal fascination as the boats bumped

over the water in our direction. Vince had spent a couple of years in a North Korean prison.

"Lots of dreams about it still, Chuck," he had confided in me. "Dying from a bayonet wound in your gut would have been better."

That was when he had just returned home along with my friend Leo Devlin (who found his sweetheart married to someone else). Leo, who had lost a couple of fingers to his torturers, had not been missing in action. Rather he was reported as killed in action. Big surprise when he appeared in the neighborhood. Both of them were terribly haunted men. They grew out of North Korean prison more or less. Peg made sure that Vince recovered, though my lovely wife had to intervene once and tell him how dumb he was acting. Leo had gone off to Harvard to get his doctorate in political science. He was teaching somewhere on the East Coast. He had even married, though he'd never get over Jane, the first, and I thought only, love of his life.

Vince and Leo had survived, if maybe just barely. They were young and strong. I wasn't. Curtains for Chucky Ducky, a civilian prisoner at that.

I dried the Kodak, Rosemarie's gift when I went to Germany, fastened the telephoto lens, and pointed it at the boats. Poor Rosemarie. How much I loved her at that moment. I mean the moment she gave me the camera.

"What the hell are you doing?" Tom asked in surprise.

"Getting pictures of our captors."

He shook his head. Clearly the sun and the water and the dehydration had affected my brain.

"The Seventh Cavalry might show up in the nick of time. These could be great shots."

"No Seventh Cavalry this time," he said with a resigned sigh. "We're both missing in action."

The boats closed rapidly. They were maybe only fifty yards out when I began to shoot my last roll of film. Now the faces on both craft were clear. They didn't seem very friendly. Several of them where clutching iron bars and wooden clubs.

I kept shooting, concentrating on the fishermen with the most hate in their faces.

I never dropped any bombs on your family.

Something big and black whisked by, just over their heads, a dark Lincoln motorcar at full speed.

The Lincoln, in fact a helicopter painted black, stopped abruptly and turned around.

"Gyrenes," Tom said casually. "That's one of their Black Hughs—Huey painted black. No one seems to know what they do with them."

It didn't take the Marines in the copter long to analyze the situation. They turned again to head south.

Abandoned.

The copter banked again and raced toward us and the fishing boats. Ah, so they hadn't betrayed us. They flew in over us and fired automatic weapons on the boats, not hitting anyone, but scaring the life out of them. The fishing boats turned tail and ran. The Black Hugh trailed after them, like a dog dismissing a bunch of tomcats he had found in his master's front yard.

Then it banked back in our direction and hovered above us, maybe fifty feet in the air. The door opened and an American glanced down. He waved and grinned, and then went back into the cabin.

"Third Marines, not the Seventh Cavalry," Tom said exuberantly. "It must have been the rosary."

Rosary, Typhoon Rosie, Rosemarie my wife.

I did the obvious thing for Chuck O'Malley to do. I began to sing.

The Marine appeared again at the door and threw a rope ladder down at us.

I stopped singing.

"What's that for?"

"To climb up to their craft. You first, Chuck. Captain is the last to leave the ship."

The ladder swayed back and forth in the downdrafts

created by the copter's engines. No way, no way in the world I would climb up that thing. I couldn't even catch it.

Commander McCarty, who was at least a half foot taller than me, snagged it on its second pass over us and handed it to me.

"Up you go, Chuck. They'll be very careful."

Absolutely not, no way, out of the question.

So I thought of my wife, and, singing about Rosemarie my love, I began to pull myself up the ladder.

I'm sure I looked ridiculous—an all-purpose coward hanging on for dear life to a problematic ladder which now spun back and forth over the Pacific Ocean. The gyrene in the doorway grinned at my efforts. As well he might.

How many times did I think I was going to fall as I pulled myself up? Only once, but it lasted the whole trip up. I was astonishingly near the Marine, who was holding his hand out to me.

Then the wind caught us again and swung me around toward the front of the vehicle—as Tom had called it.

I knew I was going to plunge into the ocean. What an ignominious end to Charles Cronin O'Malley!

Then the rope swung back toward the door. I must have scurried up a couple of bars, because this time I was right at the door. The kid, no older than Kevin, reached out and pulled me into the darkness of the vehicle. We both fell on the floor.

"Permission to come aboard, sir," I said with an attempt to salute.

"Welcome aboard!"

He was laughing, as were the other two crew members.

"You never did this before, sir?" the kid asked as he picked me up.

"Elderly civilian," I said.

"You were great," he lied. Another Chuck legend was emerging.

"Navy plane?" he asked me.

"*Kittyhawk!*"

"Good thing," the pilot said over his shoulder. "If you were Air Force, we might have to throw you back in." More general laughter.

"You better sit down and fasten your seat belt, sir," my rescuer said, "while we bring up the other personnel. Name?"

"He's Commander Thomas Joseph McCarty, CO of VF 111."

"Big catch," he said, tossing the ladder back down to the raft. "Now we can't throw you back in. I meant your name."

"O'Malley, Charles C., Staff Sergeant First Constabulary, Army of the United States. Retired."

He thought that was funny too.

Tom scurried up the ladder with ease and composure. I got a picture of his grinning face just as it appeared

"Your vehicle arrived just in time," he said to the pilot, after he was directed to the seat next to him.

"Glad to be a help, SIR. Semper Fidelis, you know."

"Roger that . . . Can you take us back to the *Kittyhawk?*"

"Negative on that, SIR. Our base is Tonsunhut as quickly as we can. That typhoon is moving more rapidly than anyone expected that it would."

"Typhoon Rosie," I murmured

"Yes, SIR."

"You were coming from North to South," Tom McCarty said.

"Were we, SIR?"

Black Hugh indeed.

"Do you gentlemen have names?"

"No, SIR."

He heard my camera click and turned around quickly.

"Sorry, Captain O'Malley, SIR. No photos please."

I told him that I was a Staff Sergeant at best.

"You want the film?"

"No, SIR . . . Please refrain from taking any more till we are on the ground at Tonsunhut."

"Okay," I said, since I didn't know how a putative Captain was supposed to address a pilot with no name.

Then I remembered.

"Sorry I didn't ask permission first, son."

"No problem, SIR. Please refrain from taking any more till we are on the ground at Tonsunhut."

I thereupon did the sensible thing, given all my ailments. I curled up and went to sleep. I dreamed, naturally, of my poor, long-suffering wife.

Then suddenly we were on the ground. Tom was already out of the plane, uh aircraft.

"Thanks for the lift, son," I said as I took a very careful step to the ground. "Great limo service."

They waited till we were safely away from the rotor blades and then quickly left the ground and raced toward the control tower on the other side of the base.

"Spooks," I said.

"Super spooks. It may not be as secret as they would like to make it. Still they are first rate Marines. I'll see that the word gets to their CO."

"Where are we?"

"That building across the street is the headquarters of the naval attaché here. It's a job which requires no work at all. Glen Edmonds, one of my classmates, is in charge. He is, ah, a unique character."

"So long as he doesn't tell General Westmorland that I'm back in country."

"No danger of that."

Commander Edmonds, in a tailor-made white navy dress uniform—with epaulets—greeted us at the door of the house. He was a big, handsome guy with blond hair that was a little too long for the Navy rules, a crinkling smile, and a touch of what my mother the good April would have called the gombeen man about him.

"Welcome to both of you," he saluted us. "Great to have you both aboard . . . Tom, I figured that I had to really dress up to greet you. You're looking great, none the worse for wear. I'll try to make you feel at home here until Typhoon Rosie blows through . . . And Dr. O'Malley, it's a pleasure to meet you. Actually we have a couple of your volumes in the house. Nice to have a Pulitzer prizewinner aboard . . . You sure have been raising a lot of hell around here."

"Just so long as General Westmorland doesn't know I'm back."

"The General and I are not on speaking terms, I regret to say."

We were shown to our rooms by a tiny Vietnamese girl who spoke excellent English.

"Get yourselves cleaned up, have a little rest, and then we'll have a bit to eat and talk about Typhoon Rosie."

"Can we get a call to the United States from here?" I asked.

"Usually, but not just now with this typhoon messing up communications. We'll try to get a line, however."

The house, a big, luxurious remnant of French colonialism, complete with a gallery running around both floors, was furnished, not to say overfurnished, with expensive modern furniture.

"Glen," Tom whispered, "was the top of our class. He's a genius and an operator. Too bright, too clever, too ingenious to please the big brass. They may make him an admiral someday and then retire him the next day. In the meantime they let him do pretty much what he wants, because he's going to do it anyway. You get a picture of this place?"

"Navy money?"

"Not a penny of it, I'm sure. He's too smart to steal. He does very little around here. But what he does he does well. So both the Air Force and the Navy brass are content to have him here. At least they know where he is . . . And by the way, Chuck, thank you for leading the rosary. I'm sure it helped."

"Minimally, it didn't hurt."

I woke up about nine-thirty, tried to figure out where I was and why. Then I realized I was hungry and that Commander Edmonds had promised us food.

I looked in the closet. Sure enough. A white tropical-weight suit, just my size.

I showered again, put lotion on my face, dressed and ambled downstairs and into the parlor in which the president of France must have stayed if ever he came out here. A stunning woman in a white pantsuit, expensive, put aside a coffee table book, stood up with graceful ease, and extended her hand.

"Squadron leader Emily Dawson, Dr. O'Malley, I do liaison work for our people here. Glen is trying to get through to lines in America," she said in a remote approximation of English that had to be Australian. "I must say, this is a fascinating book."

It was my Bamberg collection.

"I was a lot younger then."

Chucky is not very good at first encounters with lovely and sexy women. He needs time to put his masks on.

Commander Edmonds, still in his dress whites, rushed in. "I think we are getting through to your house, Dr. O'Malley. Would you pass on this number to your wife so she can call Carrie, Tom's wife? We couldn't get their line at Miramar."

"O'Malley residence," you said with your usual cool self-possession.

"That's where I live!"

"Chucky, where are you?"

"In a gorgeous house being waited on by beautiful women."

"You're supposed to be missing in action!"

"I assure you, my love, that I was never missing. I knew where I was all the time."

"You sure you're all right?"

"Just had a great nap and am preparing for a huge supper. The noise you hear in the background is the wind from Typhoon Rosie, which is just coming through."

"I'm sure it will make a lot of noise," you said dryly. "Regardless . . . You are absolutely, positively certain that you're not missing?"

"How can I be missing if you're talking to me on the phone?"

You thought it over and admitted, "That's a good point. And you're not injured or hurt or anything?"

"Too much sun, nothing more."

"How many times do I have to tell you that you should wear a cap when you go out!"

"Actually I had one, but it went down with the plane, uh, aircraft . . . Rosemarie, will you call this number at Miramar, California, talk to Mrs. Carrie McCarty, and tell her that her husband Tom is not missing either, no matter what the Navy says. He will be in touch with her as soon as we can get a line through. Your typhoon namesake is raising hell with communications."

"Okay . . . We were afraid you were out on the ocean in the typhoon."

"Would I do anything that stupid?"

"I wouldn't bet against it . . . You're on dry land now?"

"Absolutely."

"And you're all right?"

"Just fine."

"I love you, Chucky."

"I love you too . . ."

And then the connection was cut.

You didn't seem too angry at me. In fact you didn't seem angry at all. However, I must be careful not to push my luck when I return to Chicago.

The cuisine that night was Vietnamese French, whatever that is. My appetite thoroughly restored I ate everything in sight. I limited my champagne to three glasses because I will never forget the humiliation of our wedding night. Never having tasted champagne before, I loved it and drank a lot more than three glasses. When it came time to drive to our wedding retreat at the Lake, I was thoroughly soused. Rosemarie drove us up there and then put me to bed. No consummation that night. You'd think a woman would have enough respect for her husband not to tell everyone about it.

So my drinking since then has been limited to an occasional glass of wine at dinner. However, here in the tropics, in a Joseph Conrad atmosphere, with no place to go for a couple of days, I thought I could renew my acquaintance with sparkling French wine. Glen Edmonds's champagne was much better than what we had served at the wedding.

Glen and Tom talked about their days at Annapolis. Tom observed that he would retire after he was made Captain and had twenty years of pension credit. No more sea duty. Glen said he'd hang around until they were forced to give him an Admiral's star. The subject then turned to my work. Emily asked many questions about the German book which I think I answered intelligently. Like everyone else, she was fascinated by Brigita and Trudi.

"Is one of them your wife now? Well, this one can't be because you said she waited for her husband till he finally came home."

"I married the girl down the street after I came home. Let me see, I have a picture of her in my wallet, not too damaged by the water of the South China Sea."

I showed them, of course, the picture of my wife and daughter in their swimsuits. There were a number of highly favorable comments, which I will not repeat.

Well, Emily did say something about how sexy you were. I said something like when Rosemarie is in the room all the men and some of the women, fantasize about taking her clothes off.

Then I probably—and you must remember I had several glasses of champagne—made a remark which conveyed something to the effect that every time I undressed my wife it was like the wedding night all over again.

"No wonder you were in such a rush to get through to her!" Glen observed.

"Was she angry at you for being lost at sea?" Emily wondered.

"Didn't seem to be."

That was the truth, but I didn't quite understand why.

They listened with rapt interest to my story of the German pilot who ran a photo shop.

"He really flew one of those ME 262 planes?" Glen asked.

"First operational jet fighter. Scared the hell out of us. If Hitler had put more money into it, things might have been very different."

"What did it look like?" Emily asked.

Was she his mistress? I wondered. Probably, but it was hard to tell for sure.

"Kind of like a traditional fighter aircraft (I didn't say "plane" despite the champagne) with two jet engines, one under either wing. Not much aerodynamically but unbelievably fast. We didn't have anything like it till we developed the Saberjet."

After dinner we sipped cognac (only one snifter for Chucky). Emily played the piano. It will come as a surprise to no one that I began to sing. I was sensational.

I slept well all night long. I can't remember quite who was in my dreams.

Rosie, the typhoon that is, tore at Tonsunhut the next two days. Tom and I continued to enjoy lives of well-deserved luxury. Finally, when the tropic sun broke through the clouds Glen, now in spotless Navy khaki, dashed in to announce that he had secured passage for both of us—a Marine courier plane would take Tom to Subic and an American Airlines commercial plane would bring me to Hawaii, where I would rendezvous with American 841 from Fiji to go on to Chicago.

I took pictures of everyone. Tom and I promised that we'd meet again with our wives to celebrate our own little comic St. Crispin's Day. Emily hugged me and advised me to tell my wife that she was a lucky woman.

Which, of course, I would never do.

"We'd better move now," Glen urged us. "The Air Force MPs are looking for you two."

"Why?"

"The Navy thinks you are both still missing in action."

As we drove down the little street in front of Glen's mansion, a jeep with MPs in it turned the corner and rolled up to it.

"Beat them!" Glen exulted.

We dropped Tom first at the Marine courier plane, one of whose propjet engines was already turning over. My 707 was ready to leave too. The door was shut as soon as I boarded. I barely had time to fasten my seat belt (in first-class, by myself, and with three cabin attendants to take care of me) before the aircraft, uh, plane, began to move out toward the runway. I saw an Air Force MP jeep pull up to the terminal building just as we took off.

Indeed we had beaten them.

I had no idea why it was necessary to beat them. I figured I shouldn't ask. It was a semicomic ending to a journey into tragedy.

It's been a long ride. I've spent it working on this final tape, which I will give you when I return. I took time off intermittently to eat, drink wine, and take pictures of the cabin attendants.

Even now as we vector over Lake Michigan and Chicago glows in the rising sun, it seems that none of these things ever happened.

❧ 15 ❧

Those who know more about these things than I do tell me that when a man comes home from war or from a great adventure or from grave danger to a woman he has not screwed for a long time, he wants instant sexual gratification. He thinks, they say, he's earned it because he has endured so much. No messing around. Right now!

Insofar as I expected anything from my husband on his triumphal return I figured it would be that. Silly me. All these years with Chucky Ducky and I didn't really know him yet.

Anyway we had a solemn high greeting for him at the airport—all the O'Malleys and their clan: the Antonellis and the Rizzos and the McCormacks and the Conways and all their children too, at least twenty of them counting babes in arms. Everyone brought their musical instruments too. The elder O'Malleys and Father Ed were there for the sake of *gravitas*. We also brought along a six-man contingent of the Shannon Rovers Irish War Pipe Band (with their drummers of course), who had played at our wedding.

When Chuck appeared at the end of the jetway, my sons began the fun with a horn fanfare they had written for the event. Then, Moire, on cue, rushed up to her daddy with a bouquet of roses and jumped into his arms. Heedless of the roses and my daughter I embraced him and kissed him soundly. The sons did the fanfare again, this time with jazz improvisations.

Then there was much hugging and kissing and embracing. My elder daughter clung to him for fear he was about to be swept up in a typhoon.

See the conquering hero comes.

The conquering hero, alas, looked liked death warmed over, maybe for the second time—tired, confused, anxious. Poor dear man. He might be an absolute idiot, but I loved him so very much.

Then the TV cameras arrived. Someone must have called the stations and told them that Charles Cronin O'Malley was returning from Vietnam. I wonder who . . .

"Mr. Ambassador, are we winning the war over there?"

"We are not losing it, but we're not winning it either."

"How long do you think it will last?"

"In 1965 I predicted that it would last ten years and we would have at least a million men in country. I see no reason to change my opinion now."

"Was Tet a major defeat for the United States?"

"No, sir, it was great victory, but that doesn't matter. We can win many more such victories and not win the war."

"Will we win in 1975?"

"My prayer is that the American people will force the government out of the war by then."

"Will you join the antiwar movement?"

"I'm against the war. However, I think the antiwar movement will prolong it."

Okay, we'd made our point. I signaled the Chief Rover, the drums pounded, and the pipes began to mourn for Ireland and all lost heroes, even those who always knew where they were even if other people thought they were missing.

"No one seems angry at me," Chuck said, his arm around my waist.

"No one is angry at a little kid that gets lost and then is found, are they?"

"True enough . . . Except I was never really lost . . ."

"You always knew exactly where you were, right?"

"Right . . ."

"I was never angry at you, Chucky Ducky. Scared maybe, terrified maybe. But not angry. Well, for no more than five minutes. I knew God would bring you back."

My husband shook his head as if he didn't quite understand.

"You have to be who you are, my beloved. It would be wrong for me to try to make you someone else."

I ignored the fact that all he wanted to be was an accountant and I made him a photographer. The point is, you see, that I did that only for his own good. Deep down he always *wanted* to be a world-famous photographer.

The party went on at our house. Chucky Ducky looked bemused as he sipped the iced tea I had made specially for him (from tea leaves no less, a returning hero is entitled to something more than tea bags, isn't he?). I worried about him because that's what women are supposed to do about their men and because he was, after all, thirty-nine years old and he'd been cavorting around like he was twenty again—not that he was much good at physical things when he was twenty.

Finally, the crowd drifted away, our kids discreetly withdrew, and we trudged up to the master bedroom, arm in arm.

"I have designs on your glorious body, fair matron."

"Funny thing, I thought you might."

The ensuing interlude was not at all like the macho

triumph I had expected. Chucky Ducky's love for me was gentle and delicate, healing kisses and caresses, a slow, leisurely renewal, a sweet rededication of passion. I felt like I was sinking into a luxurious swamp of dark chocolate.

He played with my boobs for the longest time. Noting that I was reveling in this attention, he sustained the game as the chocolate became darker and more luxurious. I had read in one of my books (I read every book I can find about sex) that in some situations if the man is patient enough and tender enough and determined enough and the woman in the mood (which is of course the critical variable in the game) sustained foreplay can lead the woman to the edge of the cliff, over which she then tumbles into orgasm.

Chucky never reads my books because he says they give him dirty thoughts.

As my arousal became more and more intense I wondered if maybe I was at the edge of the cliff (my metaphor). Why not see if it would happen? There was no hurry. We had nothing to do the next morning.

"Don't stop, Chucky," I begged.

"I wasn't planning to."

Then it happened.

Well, maybe I willed it to happen.

Anyway, it happened.

The result was an orgasmic wave, also chocolate, which swept through me, hot chocolate this time, warm, deep, full, and massive. Hot chocolate with rich whipped cream. For a few moments I wasn't there anymore. I don't know where I was, but it was wonderful. Then I found myself exhausted in Chucky Ducky's arms.

"Are you all right, Rosemarie?" he asked anxiously.

"Of course, I'm all right," I tried to sound snappish and managed only to sound deeply pleasured.

"Did I do that to you?"

I merely sighed. Or maybe groaned.

"Interesting," he murmured. "Is this in one of your books?"

I groaned again. I found that I was covered with sweat like after a bitterly fought tennis match.

"I think I'll have to start reading those books."

"No," I said weakly.

"Why not?"

"You already have too much power over me . . ."

He laughed softly and kissed me.

"I hope you're not about to stop," I said.

He was not.

Eventually we slept.

Then the phone rang. The February sun was shining through our drapes, rebuking us for being decadent sensualists. I sighed complacently. I had my little redhead leprechaun lover back. I murmured a lazy prayer of gratitude to God.

The phone kept on ringing. I picked it up on my side of the bed. Chuck's face was resting on my belly.

"O'Malley residence," I said, hoping that there was not too much sexual fog lurking in my voice.

"Rosemarie?" said a New England voice.

"Yes, it is."

"John McNaughton here. Is Chuck home from Asia yet?"

"Yes, he is. I warn you, John, we are prepared to resist any attempts of you Feds to take him away."

I was nudging my husband to wake up. He grunted in protest.

"Just now, Rosemarie," he said with a chuckle, "the Feds are terrified of Charles Cronin O'Malley . . . Do you think I might have a word with him?"

"I'll see if he's awake."

I put one hand over the phone and shook Chucky with the other.

"Go way," he ordered me.

"Chuck, John McNaughton wants to talk to you."

"Who?"

"You know, the Assistant Secretary of Defense."

"Why?"

"You ask him."

He tried to snuggle deeper into my belly.

I shook him again.

"All right, all right." He rolled over and reached for the phone.

I pulled it away and gestured toward the other side of the bed. I had every intention of eavesdropping.

"O'Malley," my husband murmured.

"John McNaughton here, Chuck."

"I have every intention of suing everyone in that building. I want Willy Westmorland's head on a silver platter."

"You might have that already . . ."

"I want it understood that no one over there gets blamed by the big brass, especially the people on the *Kittyhawk*, for my adventures."

"They won't, Chuck. I've seen to that."

"And I want my luggage back."

My beloved husband, I thought, was bluffing. He didn't have any high cards, so he compensated by being outrageous, a style which came easy for him.

"It's on the way."

"It had better be . . ."

"Now let me ask you a question," the Assistant Secretary of Defense went on. "Did you find anyone over there who thought we would eventually win the war?"

So maybe my husband did hold a card or two.

"Only the Ambassador and he was drunk, I think."

"Did we win at Tet?"

"Sure, it was Pyrrhic defeat for General Giap."

"Khe Sanh will hold?"

"Certainly."

"Is there any light at the end of the tunnel?"

"Not the slightest hint."

"Some of us down here have been pressing the same point. Town Hoopes has put together a memo which we arranged for the President to see."

"Around a lot of people's backs?"

"Well, we didn't want to worry them."

"And Lyndon begged you to get him out of the war, just as he begged me three years ago."

"Something like that . . . Anyway he has asked Clark Clifford, the new Secretary of Defense, to convene a group of, uh, wise men to reevaluate the whole situation. Candidly, I think Westy went too far by asking for two hundred thousand more troops. The military, of course, support him."

"That's generals for you. They don't do good things. They do the things they do well."

He chuckled again.

"This is a very important group, Chuck. The President accepted our suggestions about who should sit with it. Mr. Clifford offered some names. The President insisted that we include George Ball."

"Really!"

"And you . . . He was particularly taken by the pictures you sent back."

He caught my eye. I nodded vigorously.

"When is this meeting?"

"Week from tomorrow at the White House."

"An ill-omened place."

"Yes, indeed . . . Will you come?"

I nodded vigorously again. My husband grinned.

"Certainly!"

"Excellent! I'll send a messenger today with a copy of the memo Town wrote."

Chuck reached for one of my boobs. Glutton.

"See you then, John."

I tried without much sincerity to push his hand away.

"I want to insist, Charles Cronin O'Malley . . ."

"That you fly to Washington with me . . . Naturally,

I'll try to read more of those books of yours so we can amuse ourselves in our old love nest at the Hay-Adams. Now, let's have some breakfast."

He gave my boob one last light squeeze and relinquished it.

"I'll make pancakes and bacon."

"I'll help," he said with obvious lack of sincerity.

"We'll give you this morning off. You've had an exhausting time. Rest while you still can."

When I returned with the first tray for breakfast, I found him sound asleep, with a beatific smile on his face. I wept to myself with joy at my having him back.

❧ 16 ❧

"Daddy," April Rosemary asked, her brow furrowed in a deep frown, "why aren't you part of the peace movement?"

Chuck, clad in pajamas and robe and lying on the living room couch, had been reading and rereading the memo from John McNaughton, when our daughter had returned from Trinity High School in her plaid uniform. During his absence her relationship with me changed from day to day, sympathetic on one day, furious on the next because I was to blame because I had let him go. She had grimaced when Chuck had told the TV cameras at the airport that he thought the peace movement did more harm than good to the cause of peace.

He looked up from the memo with a bemused scowl.

"What?"

"If you are against the war, shouldn't you be for peace."

"I am for peace, darling."

"Why don't you join those who are demanding immediate withdrawal from Vietnam?"

"I thought my pictures made it clear where I was." He glanced down at the memo.

"Daddy! You are not paying any attention to me!"

He looked up again.

"There are different ways of opposing the war, darling. You have to persuade the American people that we should withdraw. We're not there yet. A lot of our people still think that we're doing God's will by resisting godless Communism. They need convincing. I'm afraid that protest marches by those they consider spoiled rich kids will delay their change of mind."

"I'm not a spoiled rich kid!" She stamped her foot angrily.

"I didn't say you were," he said gently. "I'm only saying that some of the people whose support we need will think you are."

"Why should we care what they think!"

"Because they vote in elections!"

"Maybe they shouldn't vote; maybe we need a revolution; maybe young people will have to take to the streets to force peace on the rest of the country!"

I was surprised. She'd never talked that way before. I wanted to slap her face. What would happen next?

"Doesn't forcing peace sound like a contradiction?"

"S'ter Anne Marie says that only people who are ready to take to the streets can stop the killing."

The new revolutionary line was coming from a nun. Probably one of those who had warned my generation against wearing patent leather shoes.

"What if those who still support the war take to the streets too?" Chuck folded the memo, put it on the end table, and sat up.

"Well . . . They have no right to take to the streets because they're morally wrong . . . They want the killing to continue."

"Suppose both sides take to the streets and your side loses. Then the war goes on forever?"

"We can't lose because we are the young people of the country!"

"My strategy," Chuck remained patient, "is to win people over against violence without using violence.

I think we have a chance to do this. Perhaps soon."

"Perhaps never!"

"I'll tell you my worst fear, April Rosemary. It's that Richard Nixon will win the election in November and the war will go on for seven or eight more years. Your brothers will all be drafted. Maybe some of them will be killed. Burning flags, tearing up draft cards, pouring blood on draft records as the Berrigan brothers do will help Nixon win. The demonstrators will feel good, but they'll prolong the war."

Our daughter had no patience with such political analysis.

"Bullshit, Daddy, just bullshit!" She raced out of the room and thundered up the stairs, sobbing hysterically.

"Chuck . . ."

"I know, Rosemarie. I know. She's torn apart. She's wrestling with complex and twisted problems and she doesn't have the experience or the emotional maturity to deal with them."

"The nuns are teaching her simpleminded morality."

"We can't talk her out of it, Rosemarie. We'll just have to hope she grows out of it. Probably she will."

Maybe she would have if it were not the year of Our Lord 1968.

Kevin appeared from the basement, coronet in hand.

"Trouble up here?" he asked. "Someone is making noise louder than ours."

He was so tall now, so handsome, so charming. All he needed was a blue uniform and a horse and he could ride down the Shenandoah with Phil Sheridan.

"Political argument between your sister and your father."

He fingered the valves on his instrument, as though he were trying to reason out the situation.

"She'll grow out of it."

He returned to the basement and his guys.

"What if she doesn't grow out of it?" I asked my husband. "These are bad times, Chucky."

"And I'm afraid," he said returning to the memo, "that they might get a lot worse."

Lyndon Johnson had won the New Hampshire primary, but Eugene McCarthy had captured several delegates. Suddenly, Johnson looked vulnerable. The Democrats had turned against the war. They had discovered that LBJ had deceived the American people, that he had led them into a major war without warning them or obtaining their consent. The most obvious development would be that he would lose to Bobby Kennedy in the primaries and Kennedy would win the election on an antiwar ticket.

It would be Camelot again.

We would never have believed in early March of 1968 how many things could go wrong.

"We'll lose her, Chuck," I warned solemnly.

"I hope not," he said, glancing up from the memo. "If we do, she'll come back eventually."

"Unless some redneck cop shoots her in the back."

He kept on reading.

That night Father Ed and Father Packy Keenan, both of them in secular garb, joined us for a late supper. They had high praise for Chuck's war photography.

"That'll do more good than a thousand peace marches," Ed said.

"Changed your mind on the marches, Ed?" I asked with an edge in my voice.

My brother-in-law is in love with me. Always has been. It's a different kind of love, however, than most loves, sort of a goddess-adoration kind of thing. He would never dream of making a pass. Rather he is content to worship me from a distance and absorb what he thinks is my wisdom. I've kept him in the priesthood with that alleged wisdom but only because he wants to stay in the priesthood. Nothing increases adoration more than help to do what you want to do anyway. Eddie, poor guy, is the only one of the Crazy O'Malleys who is short on what that bitch Maggie Ward calls ego-strength. Maybe that comes from being Chucky Ducky's little brother.

Packy, a burly giant like his brother Jerry, with a big smile and a bigger laugh, was a classmate of Chuck's in grammar school. He views me with that mix of amusement and respect reserved for sexy hellions. I'm not sexy anymore but he thinks I am. As for the hellion part, I'm not denying that. I want to establish that I always do the cooking when we have guests. I am proud of my cooking. Tonight it was Italian, northern Italian.

"I don't know, Rosie," he replied. "Some of the priests and nuns in the peace movement seem to be running away from their own religious problems. They're not certain about religious faith and since they need to be certain about something, they turn to political faith."

I was very proud of my slender, winsomely attractive boy priest. My husband, ignorant bastard that he can be on occasion, winked at me.

"How long, Chuck?" Ed went on, looking to his magical brother for answers, like he always did.

"Seven more years, more or less. The military told LBJ that they wanted a million men for seven years and he never said no to them."

"Can the country survive seven more years?" Packy asked.

Chucky Ducky loved playing the expert role. He took a deep breath, and said, "You remember the spring of 1945? I was reading the papers then, maybe you guys weren't. The war in Europe was over. The Japanese were using their suicide bombers against our ships at Okinawa. The public was growing tired of the war. Some anti-Roosevelt columnists were hinting that it was time to make some kind of arrangement with the Japanese. Our leaders should have learned then that the American people have no stomach for an extended land war in Asia. The atom bomb made the question moot. Today, the people are turning against this war. If the leadership does not have the courage to pull out, we're going to have lots of trouble ahead."

I felt a chill run up and down my spine.

"I hope you're wrong," Packy sighed.

"What do we hear from Rome?" I asked, deliberately changing the subject.

"Nothing good." Packy grimaced. "The Curia and Father Ford, you remember him that white-haired American Jesuit who sulked around the meeting, have persuaded the Pope to issue an encyclical which will reject the commission's report and reassert the traditional doctrine. The only question now is whether Pope Paul will make it an infallible teaching."

"In God's name why?" I demanded. "Don't they understand how the laity of the world will react?"

"They have persuaded the Pope that the authority and credibility of the papacy are at stake. If he reverses the teachings of the past, he will destroy his own credibility and that of his successors. The Pope would like to make a change but he feels he can't."

"How did they refute our arguments?" Chuck asked

"They don't discuss them. The issue isn't sex anymore, it's papal authority."

"So they dismiss married love and worry only about the authority of the Pope?" My husband now was truly angry.

Packy sighed. "That's about it. Ted Hesburg from Notre Dame called me from Rome the other day. He's trying to mobilize people to talk the Pope out of the idea of issuing the encyclical. He wasn't very hopeful."

"Don't they realize," I shouted, refilling the clerical

wineglasses like the good hostess I try to pretend that I am, "that they will destroy papal credibility? Why establish a commission, why debate the issue, unless there's a chance of change?"

"The Pope is absolutely convinced that the commission wasn't representative and that the simple Catholic laypeople will accept his teaching."

"How many good simple laypeople does he know!"

"Rosemarie, my darling," Chucky cautioned me, "that is expensive wine and this is your favorite Irish linen tablecloth."

"Regardless!" I waved my hand like a queen empress. "Eddie, what will you priests do?"

"Mostly ignore it. We've made up our minds already!"

"See!" I crowed triumphantly, as though poor Packy were Paul VI.

My husband deftly removed the wine bottle from my hand.

"Priests and nuns," Eddie went on, "are in a pressure cooker these days. There has been so much change in such a short period of time. They expect a lot more change, including celibacy. Many want to marry. They figure that change is just around the corner. When they discover it is not, they'll leave in droves to marry. They'll say they can't preach the encyclical. Those that stay won't preach it either. But it's a great excuse for looking for a widow or a nun or a rectory employee or a teenager to take to bed."

Pretty strong stuff from such a mild young man.

"You're not going to do that!" I shouted, pointing my finger at him.

"Yes, your holiness," he said, blushing.

I collapsed into my chair and laughed with the rest of them.

"Teenagers," Chucky Ducky observed with dancing eyes, "are notoriously unsatisfactory in bed."

More laughter. I was nineteen when we married.

"There are," he said archly, "some well-known exceptions."

"Are they really so cut off from reality over there, Packy?" Chuck continued.

"Why wouldn't they be? They have no contact with the world outside the Curia Romana, with its competitiveness, its ruthless envy, its backstabbing, its endlessly shifting cliques, its patronage. They think they don't need to be in contact with the rest of the world because they have a monopoly on the Holy Spirit."

"And its homosexual love affairs?" I asked.

"There's some of that too."

My husband deftly turned the discussion to one of his favorite subjects—Charles Cronin O'Malley, boy photographer in Southeast Asia.

We laughed not at the war, but at the hapless hero of the stories, a mask in which my poor husband devoutly believed.

Inside I was still steaming at the Pope.

After the priests had left, I went to April Rosemary's room. Dressed in a sweatshirt and Bermuda shorts, the required uniform in those prejean days, she was poring over her homework. The room was compulsively neat, a habit she had certainly not inherited from her mother.

"Hi, kid," I said.

"Hi, Mom."

"How's it coming?"

"Tough, I don't think I'll ever make it to Harvard."

"Radcliffe."

"Same difference."

"Our place would be delighted with you and they wouldn't treat you like a second-class citizen because you're a woman."

"But look what they did to the students that took over the administration building. Didn't they throw them out?"

Unlike Columbia and Berkeley, THE University did not cave in to the radicals. Chuck and I were secretly proud of that.

"They think that education is terribly important out there, April Rosemary."

"How can anything be more important than ending the war?"

"Your father is going to a meeting at the White House tomorrow to try to end it."

"I know"—she looked up from her book—"he's one of the good guys. I'm sorry I was rude to him this afternoon. I'm such a jerk . . ."

"No you're not," I said, hugging her.

It was still easy to reach out to her. She was still reaching back to us. How long, I wondered, would that last.

✎ 17 ✎

We flew from Midway Airport to Washington in a Vickers Viscount propjet on a lovely day. Chuck was poring over the Hoopes memo once again, making notes in the margins and on the reverse side of the printed pages.

"This is the revolt of the clerks," he said to me as we waited to board the plane. "The lower echelons of the Defense and State Departments have seized the opportunity of the present confusion to make the case that they have secretly been arguing for a long time."

"What do they intend to do?"

"Stage a coup d'etat against Lyndon."

"Bring him down?"

"Maybe."

We settled into our seats and ordered tea—black.

"Have anything to read?" he asked me.

"*Couples* by John Updike."

"Any good?"

"Dirty and dull. I don't see how anyone can make sex boring."

"Not everyone is married to a man like me."

I ignored him, as he deserved to be ignored.

"The creeps in this story screw a lot and don't have any fun."

"Updike is Protestant."

"I could write better erotic stories than these."

He glanced up from the memo and look at me intently.

"Why don't you? Then I would retire my cameras."

"Too busy," I lied.

"Well"—he pulled an envelope out of his jacket pocket—"here's my last tape from 'Nam. Finished on the plane back." He produced a tape player from his briefcase.

The Viscount, whining like an angry infant, started its takeoff run.

"Why did it take you so long to give it to me?" I demanded.

"You'll see when you listen to it."

I opened the envelope, removed the tape (which was labeled "Vietnam Tape" in Chuck's intolerably neat script), placed it in the recorder, and put on the earphones.

As I listened my hands began to perspire. The damn fool! Why take such terrible chances? Then I resolved that I would not be angry at him. Chuck, I told myself, as I had told his parents and my kids repeatedly, is Chuck. He's a weird little boy and God takes care of weird little boys.

A couple of times I turned to frown at him. He pretended to be poring over Town Hoopes's memo but he was watching me out of the corner of his eye.

I stopped the tape at the end and rewound it. My heart was pounding. I thought about his crazy adventures, especially the woman from the RAAF and the jeep chasing his plane out on the runway. Great danger maybe, but also low comedy.

Why the hell did he snap the Vietnamese fishermen with the bars in their hands?

When were they going to appear in the papers? Probably not for a long time. I would never look at them! Never!

Well, not till we returned to Chicago.

I began to listen to it again, this time in earnest.

Why was I terrified when I heard it the first time around? Don Quixote was sitting next to me on the Viscount, with a complacent smile on his face. Bastard.

When I finished the second time, I jammed tape and player back at him.

"About that Aussie woman?"

"I thought you'd ask that first."

"Well?"

"Well, what?"

"Would she have slept with you?"

"I was so tired after floating in the South China Sea for most of the day that I didn't think about it till the next morning. By then it was too late. I'd already shown her your picture."

"And told her that lie about everyone wanting to undress me!"

"Gospel truth!"

"And every time is like taking off my clothes on our wedding night!"

"More Gospel truth!"

"You forget that I had to put you to bed that night because you were wiped out by champagne!"

"I don't remember it that way." He giggled.

"You don't remember anything!"

"Did you really think I'd be angry when I heard the tape?"

He pondered that.

"Any sensible wife would be."

"Whatever made you think I was a sensible wife?"

"There's that."

"Maybe for five minutes, then I realized once again that God loves weird little boys and takes good care of them."

He chuckled.

"I was terrified when they said you were missing in action. Then even before the family swarmed over to our place, there you were on the phone saying that you knew exactly where you were and hence couldn't be missing."

"Like I said."

"The good April just sighed, and said, 'well isn't that just like Chucky, always playing his little joke.' "

"Sounds like her . . . You called Tom McCarty's wife?"

"Of course. Poor woman was sobbing. She didn't know whether to believe me or not. I put on my queen empress tone and then she did believe me, which of course she wanted to do."

"Did the Navy ever get around to telling you I was not missing?"

"Not yet."

"Figures."

We were silent for a few moments, as if digesting the story of a weird little boy snapping pictures of a fishing boat of people who might very well kill him.

They served us breakfast. Still tense, I gulped down my orange juice.

"No more combat photography, Chucky Ducky."

"No, ma'am."

"Were you ever scared?"

"All the time," he replied promptly.

"I'm glad you came home alive," I said, somewhat lamely.

"Yeah, you know, I'm kind of glad too."

Washington was awash in early cherry blossoms when we checked into the Hay-Adams. Chucky kissed me and departed for the White House. There would be briefings during the afternoon, then supper, then more briefings. The next day would be devoted to discussion and then the following day some of the participants would have lunch with the President and summarize the sense of the meeting. Chuck had argued, tongue in cheek, that he and Dean Acheson,

Harry Truman's Secretary of State, would do all the talking at the lunch.

"You think they'll let you into the Oval Office?"

"The day they start showing pornographic films at the Vatican . . . Look at this"—he handed me a piece of paper—"it is from a memo John McNaughton wrote. It tells the story":

> The ARVN is tired, passive, and accommodation-prone . . . The North Vietnamese/VC are matching our deployments . . . Pacification is stalled . . . The GVN political infrastructure is moribund and weaker than the VC infrastructure. . . . South Vietnam is near the edge of serious inflation and economic chaos. . . . *The present U.S. objective in Vietnam is to avoid humiliation.* The reasons why we *went into* Vietnam to the present depth . . . are now largely academic. Why we have not *withdrawn* from Vietnam is, by all odds, *one* reason: (1) to preserve our reputation as a guarantor, and thus to preserve our effectiveness in the rest of the world. We have not hung on (2) to save a friend, or (3) to deny the Communists the added acres and heads (because the dominoes don't fall for that reason in this case), or even (4) to prove that "wars of national liberation" won't work (except as our reputation is involved). . . . The ante (and commitment) is now very high. . . . *We are in an escalating military stalemate* . . .

"What will the people say when they find this out?"

"They'll vote for Richard M. Nixon," he said as he left our suite.

As soon as the door closed, I took off my clothes and dived into bed. Suddenly I was very tired. I had terrible dreams. I was on a raft in the South China Sea, naked, of course, as I usually am in my nightmares. The fishing boat was just a few yards away. April Rosemary was screaming obscenities at me and brandishing a crowbar. Then I was trapped in our house at Long Beach, which was burning down. I was trying to lead my children out of the burning building. A woman in an Air Force uniform was shooting an automatic weapon at us to prevent us from escaping. Fire engines were screeching outside. I woke up. They were still screeching. I rushed to the window and peeked out of the drapes. Lafayette Park in bright sunlight and awash in cherry blossoms was still there.

I fell back on the bed in a cold sweat and panting for breath. I covered myself with a sheet and willed myself to simmer down.

I would probably have to tell that snoopy little bitch Maggie Ward about the dream and then interpret it for her.

That wouldn't be hard.

She would want to know whether Chuck was in the house with me or had he abandoned us and left us to burn to death.

No, he wasn't there. The bastard!

After I had calmed down, I took a long and soothing shower, put on a comfortable terry cloth robe, and ordered supper from room service. The evening news on television reported that well-informed sources were saying that there was fierce controversy within the administration about the request General Earl Wheeler, Chairman of the Joint Chiefs of Staff, had brought back from Saigon for two hundred thousand more troops. According to the sources, the President was prepared to grant the request, over the strong opposition of junior level people in the State and Defense Departments. Unlike Robert McNamara, the new Defense Secretary, Clark Clifford, was a hawk on Vietnam and would endorse the military's request.

"Sure," I informed the fool on the screen, "that's why he's meeting with a crowd of people that have read Town Hoopes's memo."

"With Senator Robert Kennedy now formally in the race for President, the advisers closest to the President argue that he cannot afford to be seen as bending his Vietnam policy to win votes away from Senator Kennedy."

"Bullshit!" I shouted at the screen, just as room service knocked at the door.

I did not try to explain to the grinning black waiter that I was shouting at an electronic image.

"Dinner for one, ma'am?"

"Yes," I said, "my husband is on the other side of the park eating on the American taxpayer."

"Yes, ma'am. Chocolate ice cream for two, however?"

"Two chocolate ice creams for one. I'm on a diet."

I wrote a big tip for him on the check.

"Thank you, ma'am," he said, and departed, surely convinced that I was round the bend altogether.

I had lost five pounds during Chuck's excursion to 'Nam. I'd catch hell from that worthless snoop Maggie Ward.

After I had disposed of every ounce of steak and french fries and every bit of ice cream, I opened *Couples* again and with a sigh learned more about their joyless coupling.

How could one read a book about sexual romps, described vividly, and not experience even the slightest erotic feeling? Was Updike trying to say that sex was inherently boring or only the sexual games played by this particular crowd of dull people?

"To hell with them," I said, throwing the book aside. "I need a nice warm bath, a long warm bath."

I didn't expect that there would be sex tonight. More likely cuddling, which is often better than sex for me and, I think, for him too. Weird little boy that he is, my husband likes to be mothered.

Nonetheless in the tub I permitted myself some pleasant fantasies about the games he played with my boobs the first night he came home.

After the bath I powdered and anointed myself and

put on a very traditional gown and peignoir, with lots of lace, said my rosary, and settled down to read Phyllis McGinley's new collection of poems.

Someone knocked on the door about ten-thirty.

"Yes?"

"Chuck. I lost my key."

I opened the door.

"No, you forgot to take it with you."

"Figures." He slumped into a chair, his trench coat still on.

I insisted that he take it off, so I could hang it up. I did not, I told him, want to be blamed for making a mess in the room. He scanned the room with a quick glance.

"Someone took a long bubble bath," he said. "You look very pretty incidentally."

"Thank you . . . Hard meeting?"

"Terrible . . . The whole crowd was there. You'll be happy to know, Rosemarie, my darling, that your husband, little punk from the West Side that he is, can now claim to be one of the Senior Advisers to the President. They were all there—Dean Acheson, John McCloy, Clark Clifford, George Ball, Mac Bundy, Generals Omar Bradley, Matthew Ridgway, Maxwell Taylor, and Earl Wheeler, Cabot Lodge, Abe Fortas from the Supreme Court, Arthur Goldberg from the UN, Cyrus Vance, Douglas Dillon, Arthur Dean, Bob Murphy (the senior career Ambassador in the Foreign Service.) In short they were all there, the whole Establishment, everyone who was anyone in American foreign and defense policy in the last twenty years and was still alive."

"Sounds like a lot of clout."

"Yeah, some pretty pompous people, not all of them, mind you. And who walks into this august crowd but an inconspicuous and innocuous little redheaded punk from the West Side of Chicago."

"Right!" I said as I moved him to the couch where he could more readily cuddle.

"Don't agree so quickly! . . . I've met a few of them of course. Most of them didn't recognize me. Thought I was a waiter. Cabot Lodge gave me his coat to hang up, the phony jerk. He seemed surprised when I sat down at the table. Acheson, who didn't know me from Elvis Presley, asked us if we might go around the table and identify ourselves. So we did."

"And you said?" I asked knowing that in those circumstances he would say something outrageous.

He feigned surprise. "I said I was Chuck O'Malley from Chicago and I took pictures."

"And their reaction?"

"They seemed surprised. Dean Acheson grinned his frosty WASP grin, 'I believe you served in Germany on a couple of occasions, did you not, Dr. O'Malley? Once, unless my aging memory escapes me, as Ambassador to the BRD.' "

"And you said?"

" 'I was a Staff Sergeant in the First Constabulary Regiment the other time, Mr. Secretary.' They sniggered a little. Not a whole barrel of fun these guys. John McCloy, who was sitting right across from me and had visited us in Bonn, peered at me in surprise."

"Bad eyes . . . Then what?"

"Three guys briefed us till suppertime. Strictly objective reporting of the facts without the implication that Town Hoopes had put in his memo. Seemed to me that the facts alone made the case for getting out."

"Did they talk about it at supper?"

"Clark suggested we avoid discussion till the briefings were over."

"Clark is it?"

"Sure, everyone was on first-name basis. Dean Acheson was cooking up the Marshall Plan when I was still in Fenwick, but just the same he was Dean. And I, naturally enough, was Charles."

"Naturally."

"He took me aside at the drinks, one to a customer, and said, 'Charles, if you don't mind my saying so, you're a genius with that camera.' So I respond 'Thank you, Dean. I'm glad you like my work.' Matt Ridgeway, who was the General in Korea when I was over there with Eisenhower, said the same thing. He even remembered my shot of Ike climbing Mount Suribachi on Iwo Jima. Not your typical General. He's clearly in favor of pulling out."

"The others?"

"Hard to be sure. Bob Murphy is a hard-liner. So is Abe Fortas, though I think he is Lyndon's man in the room. Maxwell Taylor too."

"Bundy?"

I was kneading the back of his neck, which felt as tense as a two-by-four.

"He walked back here with me, said to give his very best to you. 'You were right all along, Chuck,' he says. 'I don't know how we could have been so wrong. Now Lyndon thinks we got him into it and are betraying him.' "

"And you said, Chucky?"

"I said, 'You weren't able to protect him from the military.' He agreed. He liked my pictures too."

I have argued on occasion that cuddling is one great advantage of marriage. With a lover you always have to screw. So we cuddled.

"Tomorrow?"

"We discuss and argue. The next day some of us go up to have lunch with LBJ in the Cabinet Room. Our formal charge is to render an opinion on Westmorland's request for two hundred thousand more men. Everyone knows, however, that this is a possible turning point. The issue really is whether we ought to wind down the war."

"Why now?"

"Combination of things—Tet, Clark Clifford's taking over Defense, Westmorland's request for two hundred thousand more men, the New Hampshire primary, Bobby's announcement, the unease of men like John McNaughton and Town Hoopes. What is it that Eddie would call it?"

"A chairos, a time of special grace . . . What's going to happen?"

"I don't know. Somehow I think Lyndon will mess it up if he can. Somehow I don't blame him for feeling let down."

"I didn't offer you a cup of tea, I'm sorry."

"Rosemarie, my darling, I'm dead tired. I just want to go to sleep and dream about that RAAF squadron leader—what was her name again?"

"Emily Dawson. Don't you dare dream about her."

So we went to bed. I slept pretty well. My husband tossed and turned all night long.

❦ 18 ❦

That night I had my rape dream. It comes in many forms. A hideous monster wakes me, tears off my gown, and brutalizes me. The monster always is my father in disguise. This time he was a Vietnamese fisherman who tried to force a crowbar into me. I woke up screaming.

Chuck stirred beside me, then folded me in his arms. I wept uncontrollably.

"It's all right, Rosemarie. I'm with you. It's all right."

He thinks that he can make the dream disappear. I let him think that. I permit him to caress me and calm me down because it makes him feel masterful. The horror will never go away. I have to live with it for the rest of my life. Dr. Ward says I have pretty much beaten it. The dream, she says, will come back only in times of crisis. I pretend to go back to sleep because Chuck has another hard day ahead of him and needs his sleep. In my head I damn my father to hell for all eternity. Then I tell God I don't mean it and I'm sorry. I say that I know He's forgiven my father and I'm trying to do the same thing.

I get up at five-thirty and take a shower. I order breakfast for the two of us, a small one for me because I know I'll vomit and a big one for Chuck.

Then, all bright and cheery, I wake him up.

"Rise and shine, Sergeant, you have duty today."

He rolls over and buries his head in a pillow.

"Go way."

"Blueberry waffles coming."

He groans, rolls over, and stares at me, like he doesn't know who I am or where he is.

"Squadron Leader Dawson?"

"Bastard!"

"Are you all right, Rosemarie?" he asks anxiously.

"I'm fine. It was the dream again. The next morning I'm always all right, you know that."

Except in the early days of our marriage, when I might go on a drunk. Now I don't even feel an impulse to do it.

In fact, I'm not all right. However, I have been lying to him about the dreams since we were married and I don't know how to tell him the truth now. After I vomit I'll be okay until the next time. Fortunately they don't come very often.

As soon as he leaves for the White House, I put out a "do not disturb" sign, tell the switchboard to hold my calls, and do my vomit thing. Then I fall into bed and sleep for a couple of hours. I take another shower, dress up like an important Washington matron, and go out on a shopping expedition (during which I buy nothing except a couple of miniskirts) and return to our suite at the Hay-Adams feeling like a new woman. Almost.

Whenever the dream comes, I tell myself how fortunate I am to have survived and to have a fine husband, a wonderful family, and a good life. More or less.

In the afternoon, I called home to talk to the kids. April Rosemary squealed with joy.

"MOMMY! I just got my acceptance from HARVARD!"

"Wonderful!" I squealed back, resisting my impulse to say that it was actually from Radcliffe. "We're proud of you! We'll have a big party as soon as your father and I get back!"

"How are his meetings coming?" she asked, completely uninterested in anything but her triumph.

"He thinks they're making progress. I'll have him call you as soon as he comes back."

I sat at the window of our parlor, with Phyllis McGinley on my lap, and stared at the cherry blossoms which framed the White House like a Japanese watercolor. I had hoped that my daughter would have attended some middle western Catholic liberal arts college. Somehow she seemed too fragile for a place like Harvard, a hangout for crazies and freaks, albeit bright crazies and freaks. I was in no position, however, to be critical of elite secular universities, alumna of THE University that I am. I was a lot less mature at seventeen than my daughter and I survived easily enough.

But times were different then—the mother's endless lament!

Chucky knocked at the door late in the afternoon. Naturally he had forgotten the room key again.

His shoulders were slumped, his head bowed, his face glum. I kissed him gently.

"Bad day?"

"Good day, I think." He sighed as he took off the utterly unnecessary raincoat and gave it to me to hang up. "But who knows?"

He slumped into the couch. I sat next to him. After the Dream I was not very interested in sex for a couple of days. Yet I loved my husband. So I had arrayed myself in frilly underwear beneath my robe.

He handed me a sheet of letterhead with "White House" embossed in blue at the top.

"During my recent trip to Vietnam, an American familiar with the situation characterized it as the greatest fuck-up in American history. I concur with that evaluation. Nothing I have heard in the briefings or in our discussions has caused me to change my mind. We are trapped in a quagmire that we have created for ourselves. At some point when the public realizes how it has been deceived there will be a demand that someone be blamed. I don't believe there will be any point in a search for blame. Every administration since 1945 made decisions which led with a high degree of probability to the present situation. We could have blocked the French when they tried to return to Indochina after the war. We could have refused to support them in their war against the Vietminh. We could have declined to assume responsibility for that part of the world when they left. We might have refused to send more military assistance in the first year of the Kennedy administration. Yet we did none of these things, indeed we barely considered them. Our decisions about Vietnam were as natural and as logical as our decisions about Greece and Turkey immediately after the war and about Korea in 1950. What is done is done.

"The question today is whether we are prepared to recommend that the President decisively change course and that he admit in effect that we made a very serious mistake. As someone has said, the cost of victory in Vietnam would be so high that the American people would refuse to pay it. I sense very little disagreement in this room with that conclusion.

"The question becomes how we implement our conclusion and how we tell the American people about it. I propose that we begin withdrawing our troops and set a deadline for completing that withdrawal, say a year from now. We tell the people the truth, something that we haven't done thus far. Does that mean we have lost the war? No, it only means that we can't win it and do not propose to spend more lives to maintain our credibility. We have learned that there are limits to our power to intervene, one of which is the stability and strength of purpose of the government on whose side we are intervening. We must cut our losses and get out now.

"I question whether there is the will to tell this dramatic truth and take this dramatic action. We will try to fudge and compromise. We will try to appease the President's wrath. We will not tell him the full truth, which among other things is that we either begin a withdrawal now or Richard Nixon will be sitting in the Oval Office a year from now and the war will continue for many more years and with many more casualties. Can anyone seriously dispute the fact that eventually we will have to leave? Is it not true that the longer we cling to the illusion that we can solve the problems of the Vietnamese that they were not willing to solve themselves, the more disorderly our departure will be and the more calamitous the blow to the nation's prestige and perhaps to its self-confidence.

"It is not enough to refuse to approve the military's request for another quarter million men. That is not enough. We must strongly advise the President that he should begin a withdrawal now.

"That will be difficult to do because he is sensitive to the appearances of betrayal, even though we have been candid with him in the past, if not as bluntly candid as we might have been. Nevertheless, this is a decisive time. Either we begin to leave now, with whatever humiliation and embarrassment, for we will leave later, much later with more humiliation and embarrassment and many more dead young men."

"Did they applaud?" I asked.

He grinned, his terribly sexy little leprechaun grin, which always makes my heart ache with love. "Not exactly. Everyone was kind of quiet and serious for a moment. Dean said something like, 'Charles, your prose style is as clear as your photographs,' and they kind of sniggered and the discussion went on."

"You don't mention Bull Run or the Little Bighorn or Pearl Harbor?"

"I threw them in as an ad-lib. Too good a line to miss."

"You pushed the agenda farther than they want it to go?"

"I think"—he put his arm around me—"we may edge toward my position tomorrow when we have lunch with the President in the Cabinet Room. Heaven only knows what he'll do."

"So they're letting you attend the lunch."

"I don't want to go, but I don't have much choice. LBJ wanted me on the committee, so he must want to see me."

"You'd better call home right now!" I said, remembering my conversation with our daughter.

"About what?"

"I want you to be surprised."

So he called and smiled happily when April Rosemary told him her good news.

"I'm not surprised, darling, but I am terribly proud. You'll show all those East Coast brats how bright we middle westerners are. Don't ever become a Republican!"

She must have sworn that she would not because he laughed loudly.

"One happy kid," he said to me. "What do you think about it, Rosemarie?"

"I wish it was some other time. However, it's her time and her era. She has to make her own decisions. We'll do what we can to help her."

"So young to decide."

"Weren't we all!"

"I need a shower and then we'll go out for supper."

"I've made a reservation at the Versailles. And bath, not shower, it's more relaxing."

I stood up and removed my robe.

"As always"—he sighed—"you're the boss."

My heart was not in the project. The Dream continued to lurk on the fringes of consciousness. However, I loved my husband and I knew that he needed love. As it turned out our games in the tub, while not spectacular, were rewarding enough. A woman often finds that what starts out as mostly an act easily turns into the real thing, especially if she is deeply in love.

"We acted like a pair of silly teenagers," I said at the Versailles, blushing at the memory of the interlude in the tub.

"Hmn . . . ?"

"You know what I mean."

"I doubt that teens would have the patience or the creativity we displayed. I hope not."

"A lot of women my age would say we were too old for that sort of stuff."

"You don't seem to be too old." He grinned wickedly. "As I remember you started it."

"They say that we betray other women when we give in to male fantasies."

"All women say that?"

"Those of us who disagree keep our mouths shut."

"Don't women have fantasies too?"

"Oh yes."

"You indulged in some of them today, if I'm not mistaken."

"Probably."

"I should like to learn about all of them."

"You know most already . . . Anyway, the strongest fantasy is to be desperately wanted by a man who loves you."

"I can indulge you in that one forever."

We had no idea then how difficult that would be in the terrible years ahead of us.

"Besides," he continued, "what's the point in being in a nice hotel suite with your spouse, unless you engage in a little extracurricular activity."

"Especially when to be in the same room with your

spouse is to want to undress her like you did on our wedding night."

I wondered whether he had really said that at Tonsunhut or he had inserted it in his tape to excite me.

"I'll never live that line down. It's true just the same."

I didn't believe that for a moment. However, he did. I felt warm and complacent.

"The future of our country and our family are at stake these days, Chuck."

"All the more reason to defy death with love."

The next morning he was anything but eager to walk across the park to the Cabinet Room in the West Wing.

"Lyndon will mess it up, Rosemarie. Somehow, some way, he'll keep the war going to punish the country for not supporting him."

When he returned that evening, he wrote out for me an account of the day, which I have saved.

"Mac Bundy was the reporter. He presented our consensus delicately and gracefully. The present policy was not working. We could not continue it without a virtually unlimited application of resources. The American people would not support that. Much of the business, academic, religious, and political communities in the country did not even support the present limited war. Military victory in Vietnam is impossible under conditions compatible with the country's larger interests. The fundamental goal should be to get out rather than to get in. Insistence on a military solution had dragged the President and the country into a morass from which escape was possible only if the goals and purpose of the war were changed.

"That, I thought, is pretty tough stuff. LBJ doesn't like it one bit. This is not going to be a pleasant afternoon.

"Abe Fortas, who was the President's man within the group objected that Mac's summary had not accurately reflected the sense of the discussion. Dean Acheson responded that the summary did indeed accurately summarize the consensus. The President argued that the men who had briefed us were not the same ones who had briefed him. Clark Clifford replied that they were indeed the same men and they had given the same briefing. He had told me privately later that Walt Rostow, Bundy's successor at the National Security Council and an ardent supporter of the war, had doubtless followed the usual bureaucratic practice of underlining the parts of the briefing that suited his policy.

"The President announced that he wanted to hear what each of us thought. As he went around the room it became clear to him that his trusted advisers had, with few exceptions, turned against the war. Only Bob Murphy argued that the President ought not to permit a civilian group to intervene between himself and his military advisers during wartime. General Ridgeway replied that we were still a society in which the military must be subservient to civilians.

"Finally, he came to me.

'I don't suppose you've changed your mind in the last three years, Chuck?'

'No sir, Mr. President.'

'At least you've been consistent . . . Do you want to add anything else now?'

"The consistency line was a jab at those in the room who had changed their minds on him.

" 'Yes, sir. I said at the meeting and I must repeat that I am convinced that you should not only decline the request for more troops. You should announce plans for a phased withdrawal. That is the only policy which will protect the country from being torn apart and the only policy which will keep Richard Nixon out of this building.'

"He nodded and went on to the next man.

"We left the West Wing in gloomy silence after a

tough afternoon's discussion. We had done our part
to tell the President the truth. He did not want to hear
the truth. He was angry at most of us because it was
a different version of the truth than he had heard before from them. He is a stubborn, bitter, and weary
man. His future behavior is unpredictable. I am terrified that he might make matters worse instead of
better.

"However, let it be recorded that on the Ides of
March in 1968, the Senior Advisers told him that the
war could not be won. Any continuation of it over a
substantial period of time for whatever reason is absolute folly."

As we all know now the war went on for seven
more years. More men died in those years than had
already died. They died for a cause that the leadership
knew was lost. Terrible harm was done to the whole
country.

It is very hard to understand why this could be so.
The "best and the brightest" got us into the war. They
tried on that lovely March Saturday to get us out.
Who were the men who kept us in Vietnam? Their
names are well-known.

I weep when I read Chuck's memo. He was thirty-
nine years old when he wrote it. He was absolutely
correct in his prediction. If Lyndon Baines Johnson
had listened to him, our family would have been
spared terrible tragedy.

"What happens next?" I asked my downcast husband when he had returned from the West Wing of
the White House.

"Lyndon will give a major address to the nation on
March thirty-first."

"What will he say?"

"Clifford will have to fight with Rusk for control
of the text. Lyndon will make the final decision himself. My guess is that he'll fuck up the fuck-up."

As our Vickers Viscount heaved itself into the sky

just before it plunged into the Potomac (or so it always seemed) I glanced out the window at the fleeting picture of the Capitol, at one of the Mall. Under the somber gray sky, it looked lifeless, barren, dull. All the excitement had gone out of being American.

We sat around the small color television in the elder
O'Malleys' apartment in Naples, Florida, to listen to
Johnson's "historic" address, as the media cliché
mongers had insisted on calling it all day.

The apartment was a haven that Vangie and the
good April used to escape from Chicago winters and
to spend time with their children free from the demands and the noise of the swarms of adored grandchildren. With all that we had on our minds, Chuck
and I hesitated about flying to Florida. We would,
against all sense, be deeply involved in the Robert
Kennedy campaign. Yet they were my real parents
and I would not, could not disappoint them.

They were both in their early sixties now, handsome, attractive people for whom the Great Depression had been an unpleasant but forgotten interlude
and not the formative experience it had been for my
poor dear husband. He was once again a wealthy architect, she a gifted music teacher. She was a slender,
elegant woman who, my husband had said, was secretly a Russian archduchess, though contact lenses
had deprived her of her faintly perplexed expression.

She was also the original Dr. Panglossa, especially
when the subject was her grandchildren. "I'm sure
that poor dear April Rosemary will come back from

that Harvard place just the same sweet little girl she is now."

Or, "I think it's cute that dear little Kevin is interested in jazz. On our first date, Vangie took me to hear Mr. Armstrong."

Dear Little Kevin was now as tall as her husband and five inches taller than his father.

She is a perennially beautiful woman. I'm not as good-looking as she is and I'm a quarter century younger.

"Did you ever notice that when your mother drifts into a restaurant, men turn to look at her, and not only older men."

"The good April," my husband replied, "is one very sexy broad. It took me a long time to come to terms with that. She has shared her grace with Peg and of course with this foster daughter that tends to sleep in my bed."

"Nonsense," I protested.

"I won't argue . . . Do you think she knows men are admiring her."

"The good April is oblivious, but not that oblivious."

"They certainly don't do silly teenage things together, do they?"

I snorted in derision. The guest bedroom was at the opposite end of the apartment, so that both couples could have all the privacy they wanted. Chuck and I took full advantage of it . . . Though I felt guilty about being away from my kids.

Vangie—John the Evangelist O'Malley—is a big, bald man with a dangerous red beard. He looks like a pirate and is the least dangerous of humans. He lives in a world where colors and shapes blend in a harmony that obscures, if it does not hide completely, ugliness. So much of what my poor dear husband is was shaped by this somewhat ethereal couple. Surely the mixture of endless patience and often berserk passion with which he copes with his flaky wife was learned from his parents' marriage.

Thanks be to God.

So we were sitting in front of the small television—"no need, darling, for a big one in this tiny apartment"—waiting for the President. Chuck's information from Washington left very much in doubt which turn the talk would take.

We were in our swimsuits, drinking iced tea and eating cheese and crackers after a delightful day in the Gulf Coast warmth.

"I'm sure the poor dear man will end the war," the good April said, picking up her knitting.

"It doesn't make sense not to," Vangie agreed.

"You don't know Lyndon," my husband cautioned. "He's just a little crazy."

The picture of Lyndon in the Oval Office filled the screen. I was shocked at how old and how tired he seemed.

"Good evening, my fellow Americans. Tonight I want to talk to you of peace in Vietnam and Southeast Asia." He reviewed his administration's efforts "to find a basis for peace talks," and said that there was "no need to delay the talks that could bring an end to this long and bloody war . . . So, tonight . . . I am taking the first step to de-escalate the conflict. We are reducing—substantially reducing—the present level of hostilities . . . unilaterally and at once. Tonight, I have ordered our aircraft and our naval vessels to make no attacks on North Vietnam, except in the area north of the Demilitarized Zone, where the continuing enemy buildup directly threatens allied forward positions. I call upon President Ho Chi Minh to respond positively, and favorably, to this new step toward peace."

He settled the question of the request for a quarter of million more troops as though it had never existed "We should prepare to send—during the next five months—support troops totaling approximately 13,500 men." President Thieu he told us had, in the previous week, ordered the mobilization of 135,000 additional South Vietnamese, which would bring the total strength of ARVN to more than 800,000, and he pledged an effort to "accelerate the reequipment of South Vietnam's armed forces which will enable them progressively to undertake a larger share of combat operations against the Communist invaders." The tentative estimate of these additional US and ARVN costs was, he said, $2.5 billion in 1968 and $2.6 billion the following year. He then made a strong pitch for a 10 percent surtax, saying "The passage of a tax bill now, together with expenditure control that the Congress may desire and dictate, is absolutely necessary to protect this nation's security, to continue our prosperity, and to meet the needs of our people."

He went on,

"As Hanoi considers its course, it should be in no doubt of our intentions.... We have no intention of widening this war. But the United States will never accept a fake solution to this long and arduous struggle and call it peace ... Peace will come because Asians were willing to work for it, and to sacrifice for it, and to die by the thousands for it. But let it never be forgotten: Peace will come also because America lent her sons to help secure it."

Finally, and as an anticlimax, came the big surprise. "There is division in the American house now. There is divisiveness among us all tonight. And holding the trust that is mine, as President of all the people, I cannot disregard the peril to the progress of the American people and the hope and prospect of peace for all people.... With America's sons in the fields faraway, with America's future under challenge right here at home ... I do not believe that I should devote an hour or a day of my time to any personal partisan causes.... Accordingly, I shall not seek, and I will not accept, the nomination of my party for another term as your President."

The good April and I applauded. Vangie shouted. Chuck sat in his chair, his face in his hands, and peered through his fingers at the screen.

"It's good news, isn't it, Chuck?" I asked.

"Maybe," he said softly. "Maybe."

"Bobby will be nominated and win and end the war," I said jubilantly.

"Lyndon will do all in his power to stop Bobby. He'll throw his weight behind Hubert Humphrey, who won't dare denounce the war before he's elected . . . It's all more confused than ever . . . He's still lying. I don't care how large the Vietnamese Army is it can't fight worth a darn."

We would not let his pessimism ruin our happiness. Peg called and then Jane and then Father Ed. Finally, April Rosemary who shouted to me, "Daddy did it, didn't he? He ended the war!"

Chuck shook his head.

"Lyndon," he said, "is still a mean, nasty, son of a bitch. He didn't announce a withdrawal and that's what really matters. We have to get the hell out of that quagmire."

Four days later, we came in from golf at supper-time. I had won, much to the dismay of my husband and father-in-law and to the delight of my mother-in-law.

"Poor little Rosie was always a wonderful athlete," the good April insisted.

"She cheats," my husband protested.

"Now, Chucky dear, you should always be a good sport."

The phone was ringing as we entered the apartment. Always in charge, I picked it up.

"Peg, Rosie. They shot Martin Luther King today. The city is burning already."

I burst into tears.

"Martin is dead," I shouted at Chuck. "Chicago is on fire. We should fly home right away."

"I don't think we can put out the fires. Is Vince there?" he asked Peg, as he took the phone away from me. "Okay, would you have him call us down here when he gets a chance?"

Vince had agreed to work in the Mayor's office for a year.

I grabbed the phone away from him.

"Is it all right out there, Peg?"

"Sure. You wouldn't know there's a riot if it wasn't for television. Stokeley Carmichael told the kids to go home and get their guns."

We turned on the television. There were riots all over the country. Washington was in flames, Chicago was in flames, the country was in flames.

"If you look carefully," Chuck said, "all the violence is in black neighborhoods. They're burning down the stores and the buildings and looting everything they can get their hands on. Funny kind of mourning for a man who preached nonviolence."

"We should kneel and say the rosary for the repose of his soul," April informed us.

That was the first sensible thing anyone had said.

Vince interrupted it.

"It's pretty bad out on the West Side," he told us. "Relatively quiet on the South Side. Out in Garfield Park we've lost control. Molotov cocktails all over the place. The National Guard is coming. The mayor has asked Lyndon for federal troops."

"Burning and looting?" I asked.

"Stores especially, the black radicals are telling them to go after the Sheeny storekeepers. You won't hear that on television. They don't seem to care that a lot of black storekeepers are losing their stock and their stores. It's all crazy. They're destroying their own neighborhoods."

"Are they attacking whites?"

"A few incidents, nothing serious."

"I hope God doesn't let Martin know what his people are doing," I said to Chuck.

He just shook his head.

"Damn media are stoking the fires. They love it."

That night the evening news reported that America was burning down. In fact blacks were burning down their own neighborhoods in a burst of anti-Semitism. They were undoubtedly angry about the poverty and discrimination and saddened by Martin's death. Yet their frustration and rage turned on themselves. The report of the Kerner Commission on the riots, which had just come out, blamed the riots on white racism, true enough in some fashion, but not one likely to win much support as whites watched blacks destroy their own neighborhoods in memory of a man of peace.

"Should we go to the funeral?" I asked my husband in bed that night.

"I don't think we'd be welcome."

I didn't argue. He was probably right.

The next morning, Saturday, I called home.

Kevin answered.

"What's going on, Kev?"

"What do you mean, Mom?" he asked, confused by my question.

"The riots!"

"Oh, that," he said calmly. "It was bad again last night, I guess. Troops are coming in today. Uncle Vince says that the Mayor is incoherent. Can't blame him. Bad way to honor a great man, isn't it?"

"Any trouble there?"

"In Oak Park! Mom, you gotta be kidding! This is a great center of urban rest."

"You guys stay away from the West Side, you hear!"

"When was the last time we went down there?"

"April Rosemary?"

"She's frightened. Thinks the country is pulling itself apart. But you know how she is, Mom."

"She hasn't gone to the West Side, has she?"

"Nah, she's up in her room weeping, poor kid."

"I think we should go home," I told my husband. He thought about it.

"It won't do any good," he said.

"I want to go home."

"Okay, I'll see if I can change our reservations from tomorrow to today."

He couldn't. I didn't enjoy that lovely Saturday much. Too many worries. Things can't get any worse I told myself. I was wrong. They would get much worse before the summer was over.

We left on Palm Sunday just before noon. Flying into Chicago late in the afternoon we saw columns of smoke rising from the West Side of Chicago, along Madison Street. Ugly and sad.

"Tragic," I murmured.

"Tragic," Chuck agreed somberly, "but not exactly a city burning down, much less a revolution. In a real revolution they would have burned white neighborhoods and looted stores in those neighborhoods."

"Will they ever do that?"

"I don't think so. Older black folks might not like whites, but they don't hate us that much. The kids know they could be killed. Too much at stake for everyone."

"Not a prerevolutionary situation?"

"Despite the media efforts to make it one, no. Not likely to be either."

Peg, looking harassed, met us at O'Hare. (The O'Malley clan always assumed that no one should drive their own cars to the airport.)

"I haven't seen my husband since it started," she said. "It's all so sad and so crazy. What do those Black Power guys hope to accomplish?"

"Stick it to whitey, then negotiate with them," my increasingly mordant husband observed.

"The Mayor is already talking about grants to rebuild the neighborhoods," Peg told us. "There won't be any storekeepers anymore."

"Did the Jews really overcharge them?" I asked.

"No more than their own black shopkeepers. The costs of doing business on places like Madison Street are higher than elsewhere—bars and alarms and insurance. It's not a good way to earn a living. They'll collect their insurance and never go back."

"When will it ever stop?" I wondered.

Neither my husband nor my sister-in-law answered. We drove back to the neighborhood as darkness fell, each of us with our morose thoughts.

Martin died on Thursday. By Friday evening, the police had lost control of the West Side areas along Madison and parallel streets. Thousands of looters ravaged all the stores in the neighborhoods. The Mayor asked for the National Guard on Saturday. Thirty-six major fires were burning and the looting continued. Some black leaders proclaimed on television that the revolution had begun. They were going to burn Chicago down. However, they only burned one neighborhood, a black one at that.

On Sunday, the federal troops arrived, five thousand of them from Fort Hood, Armored Division. Whether the tanks and bayonets of the soldiers frightened the rioters or whether they had taken everything that was available, an uneasy peace descended on Chicago.

Despite his promise to avoid combat zones, Chuck spent most of Sunday photographing the ruins and the grim-looking Feds. He managed to discover an officer that had been with him in Bamberg.

How did I know that?

Well, I couldn't let him drive into those neighborhoods by himself, could I?

We watched the funeral on television. It was like the congregation and the watching country had briefly entered the world of the Negro spiritual—sadness, color, hope all blended into a seamless robe. Perhaps the seamless robe of Christ.

"Greatest liturgy in the history of our country," Chuck said.

I had cried myself out and was now crying again. Vince and Peg and the band were there with us. The kids somehow knew that their music was in communion with the funeral music.

"Will it ever get better, Dad?" Jimmy asked. "This race thing. The kids that rioted on Madison Street are our age. We play their music and they are too poor to know the music. Can we do anything?"

I thanked the angels that he hadn't asked me.

"Louis Armstrong and Billie Holiday were a lot poorer. Probably there are future great musicians on the West Side. Not everybody your age rioted, only a small proportion. It doesn't take a lot of people to burn down a neighborhood . . . I'm not answering your question, am I?"

The poor boys shook their heads solemnly.

"I don't know, guys. I just don't know. We tried to do something at Selma and it didn't work. The man who preached nonviolence died violently. In his memory kids your age did violence. Maybe the anger has to run its course. Then maybe again we can work together on a better life for the blacks. Now is not the time when any white person is welcome. They feel they don't need us. Please God that will change."

They nodded solemnly. We were four white Catholic liberals, three Irish and an Italian. We all grew up despising racism—which was not true of many of our contemporaries. We had tried and we had failed. Now we were irrelevant. We might be irrelevant for the rest of our lives. We had no answers to give to our children.

✻ 20 ✻

"He said that anyone who came into a room where you were wanted to undress you?" Maggie Ward raised a skeptical eyebrow.

"Men, he said, and a lot of women too."

"My," she said softly, "that is an outrageous statement. And he put it in the tape to you?"

"Right!"

I was strung out, really strung out.

I needed help. We had worked hard on the Kennedy campaign in Indiana. All the kids except Moire were out there in the bitter cold and the spring snow every weekend, passing out leaflets, knocking on doors, telling people that we had to end the war and eliminate racial conflict. Northwest Indiana seemed to like what we were saying. When Bobby showed up in Gary, a huge crowd appeared to cheer him. He seemed genuinely moved. Suddenly he was a populist, a champion of ordinary folk, a man more sensitive and open to people than his brother could ever have been. His shy, boyish smile and his radiant eyes captivated everyone. He remembered Chuck and me and even the names of our kids.

I was out there every weekend too, bringing Moire, who threatened to disown the family if she couldn't come. It somehow seemed surrealistic, another dream,

Camelot reborn. In my heart I wondered if it was not a pipe dream. Gene McCarthy, who had entered the race when it seemed there was no chance, felt he had a legitimate claim on the nomination. There was no divine right of the Kennedys. Bobby didn't have a claim on the presidency.

The truth was, as Chuck said, that McCarthy had no chance to win the nomination and Kennedy did. All McCarthy could do was deny it to Bobby and leave the nomination to Vice President Humphrey, who was Lyndon's man and who would surely lose to Nixon. As far as one could tell Gene McCarthy was too vain to care about that.

The Kennedy volunteers from Chicago bonded together with the happy expectation that they would be lifelong friends who would remember their own St. Crispin's Day when they campaigned to end the war and to promote racial justice.

Our family bonded too, especially the boys and their father. As we drove home in our station wagon, Kev engaged his father in a conversation about music.

"Dad, why is it that early jazz seems so pure compared to what came later?"

"Pure?"

"I like Miles Davis and John Coltrane, but somehow their music doesn't have the fire and the energy of the early stuff, like Pops or Lady or Jelly Roll."

"Pops" was what the initiate called Louis Armstrong, "Lady" was Billie Holiday, and "Jelly Roll" was the fabled Jelly Roll Morton.

Chuck took a deep breath and tried to reply

"Early jazz as you know came up to Chicago directly from the poor neighborhoods of New Orleans. It wasn't new to those who played it. It was new to us and the first hint any Northerners had of black culture. I wasn't around then, but from what your grandfather said, it bowled people over. The next generation of black—and eventually white—musicians couldn't simply repeat the first generation. In line with the jazz principle of improvisation, they developed their own styles of jazz. Necessarily I think jazz became more elaborate, but it was still jazz."

"Rock and roll is better," April Rosemary said, looking for an argument.

The males in the family ignored her.

"They never should have left Chicago," Jimmy complained. "Nothing good ever happens in New York. Look what they did to Billie Holiday."

So the conversation would go. My elder daughter sulked, my younger daughter fell asleep, as she would do with the slightest provocation. My husband did his best to maintain the fiction that he knew a little bit more about music than my sons.

I was so strung out in those days that I wondered about whether I was losing my hold on reality. The monster didn't come in my dreams anymore. Rather my dreams were quirky, faces and places I had never seen before. A city like Chicago except different. People like my friends and family, only not quite. There was nothing hostile about either the people or the city. Yet I was running constantly down strange streets, through homes of people I didn't know, over fences, into alleys. I didn't understand why I was running, yet I was always falling behind. Mostly I was trying to catch a bus, but it always pulled away just as I got there. Often, during these runs I had a baby in my arms.

So I went to see Maggie Ward again and like an idiot complained about Chuck instead of telling her about my dreams.

"Do you think he really said that to people or he put it in the tape to please you?"

"Please me!"

"I should think it is a rather strong if perhaps erotic compliment."

"I don't!"

"Come now, Rosemarie, of course you do!"

"It embarrasses me."

"Sexual compliments tend to do that."

"I don't think my husband should go around saying things like that about me."

"The woman doth protest too much."

My face was aflame.

"Surely you notice that people find you sexually attractive?"

"I do not!"

"Come now, Rosemarie, you certainly do. And it pleases you too. Otherwise, you would not dress in such a way that emphasizes your erotic appeal."

"I do not!"

"I wonder why you so vehemently deny that which is self-evident."

"Because I'm afraid that it's all true," I blurted.

"Ah, now we come to the truth again, the same truth if you will, but the truth. What would follow if it is the truth?"

"That I'm an important and powerful person . . . I don't want to be that just because of my looks."

"Not a very good response to God's generosity to you, is it?"

"Stop raising religious issues!"

"I am also intrigued by the fact that you have been through so much pain in your life recently and yet you mention this obiter dictum of your husband at the beginning of our conversation."

"It's the most important thing," I sulked.

"Why?"

"Because it's about the way I see myself . . . About who I am."

"As always, Rosemarie, we get around to the truth."

I was afraid she would ask me who I was. She didn't, however, the little bitch. She'd made her point.

Then I told her about my running dreams. As usual she zeroed in on the heart of the matter.

"Who is the child you have in your arms during all your dashing about?"

"April Rosemary I suppose. Maybe Moire, though she doesn't have red hair."

"Could it be someone else?"

"I don't know . . . ?"

"Are you protecting the child?"

"Certainly!"

"From whom?"

"People who would hurt her."

"And what would happen if you caught the bus?"

"She'd be safe."

"Ah."

I knew where we were going. I didn't want to go there. Yet I figured I might as well admit it.

"I'm the baby," I murmured.

"Are you very good to her?"

"I'm careful with her. I'm impatient with her because she slows me down . . . Sometimes she's very heavy . . ."

"So . . ."

"So," I said, "I should be very nice to that poor little kid because she's really wonderful. Is that what you want me to say?"

"The question is whether that is the truth."

My eyes filled up with tears.

"Maybe . . . Probably . . . It'll take time to accept that idea . . ."

"I'm not holding a stopwatch, Rosemarie, except to say that it's time."

"Do you image me naked during these conversations?" I said at the door.

"What makes you think, Rosemarie, that you're not!"

Touché. The little bitch had nailed me again.

So much happened that year. I can't remember whether the dreams stopped right after that conversation. Nor do I know whether I was nicer to the child I was lugging around. I think I tried and then kind of dropped her.

April Rosemary refused to go to the Trinity or the Fenwick proms with Bill Enright, a Fenwick basketball player and a nice if rather dull boy. He called me, baffled.

"How will it help end the war?" he asked.

"I don't know, Bill. I do know she won't listen to me."

In part because I hadn't gone to my own prom either because I hated the school and the nuns so much.

"It would be a sin," April Rosemary told me, "to go to a dance while boys my age are dying in that terrible war."

Somehow I couldn't tell her that she was completely wrong. I didn't add that some of the boys at the prom would be dead in another year.

Bobby asked Chuck to photograph the Oregon and California campaigns. Since there were no Vietnamese fishing boats or women from the Royal Australian Air Force in either state, I urged him to go. I had to stay home to prepare for the family milestone of our first high school graduation.

Oregon delivered a savage blow to the Kennedy campaign. McCarthy won 46 percent to 39 percent. A lot of Oregonians told the media that it was not fair for Bobby to enter the race after McCarthy did. First come, first served. It was a strange political philosophy. The media folks, who thought Bobby was an "opportunist," pushed the theme hard. McCarthy had the right to the nomination, not Bobby. There was less excuse for them than for the Oregon voters. The media people, especially those from Washington, knew that McCarthy was vain and lazy and would be a terrible president.

Senator Kennedy himself said that California

would make or break his campaign. He had to win there to have a chance at the nomination.

In Chicago, the Mayor had indicated his support for Bobby, which was a case of the leader following his followers.

Chuck flew home for the graduation. It was a glorious spring day. He told me that Frank Mankiewicz, Bobby's Press Secretary, was a mean man who hated Chicago and everyone from Chicago.

April Rosemary looked lovely in her graduation dress. We beamed proudly at her academic awards. Alas, one of the younger nuns organized an antiwar demonstration in which a group of the graduates, our daughter included, broke out banners and chanted, "Hell no, we won't go!" as if there were any chance of them going to Vietnam.

The demonstration did not contribute to the eventual end of the war—none of the demonstrations ever did. Quite the contrary. During the Nixon administration support for the war as measured by the polls went up whenever there was a major demonstration. The one at Trinity affronted many of the parents, which was perhaps what the nun and the kids had in mind.

"They ought to rescind their diplomas," a fat, pompous, red-faced Irishman informed us after the ceremony.

Chuck could not resist a response. Well, he never could resist a response.

"It's their brothers and their boyfriends that will die over there," he informed the asshole.

It shut him up. However, it made it impossible for us to remonstrate with our daughter, who, having heard her father rebuke the man who wanted to take away her diploma, hugged her father fiercely.

Her cousin Carlotta shook her head sadly and whispered in my ear, "It's just a phase, Aunt Rosie, she'll get over it."

Chuck flew back to Los Angeles the next morning.

I joined him the day before the June 5 election. We watched the returns anxiously as they appeared on the big blackboards in the hotel ballroom. A lot of people in California also seemed to think that McCarthy had a right to the nomination and that Kennedy was an opportunist.

Finally, late in the evening, it became clear that Bobby had won 55 percent to 45 percent. We all cheered enthusiastically. Camelot was still moving forward.

"I bet TV people are already calling it a squeaker," Chuck whispered to me.

The Senator, looking drained, made a weary victory speech in which he thanked everyone and promised that we would go on to the convention in Chicago and then to Washington in January.

The crowd—young, dedicated, and enthusiastic—went wild. For us Catholic liberals of the Camelot generation it was our last hurrah.

"We're supposed to join the family in their suite for a smaller celebration," Chuck took my arm. "The happy expressions on their faces should make great shots . . . We're going out through the kitchen."

The Secret Service checked our passes and waved us into the kitchen. Other Secret Service people and the Senator's own guards were rushing him rapidly toward the door.

Then the shots rang out, like explosions from a Fourth of July cap pistol. Screams of rage and horror. I knew what happened without being told. I leaned against the wall and closed my eyes. It had all been too wonderful to be true. We had enjoyed a few shimmering months of hope. It was all over now. Nixon would be elected and the war would go on. The screams of horror, the smell of the kitchen, the shouts of the Secret Service and the press were all pouring out of the mouth of hell. Dante Alighieri where are you when I really need you? I could feel the flames, hear the shrieks of the damned, sense their despair.

"Rosemarie."

I opened my eyes. My husband's face was ashen. A rosary wrapped around his hand. Astonishingly, I was clutching my rosary.

"Chuck . . . Did you get some pictures?"

"Yeah, enough. The killer is some skinny little kid with dark skin . . . Let's get out of here."

"I want to go home," I agreed.

So we went home, too numb even to grieve. We went to the funeral of course. The new English liturgy was so much better than the Latin liturgy at JFK's funeral. We didn't go to the burial. Days later we could not talk about it or indeed about anything else. The kids respected our grief with astonishing sensitivity.

In July the Pope issued the long-feared birth control encyclical, locking the barn door as Peg had said, long after the stallion and the mare had run off. I wouldn't even read the damn thing.

We were at the Lake, trying to recover from the tragedies of 1968 without much success. I felt terribly old. Facing forty on September 17, Chuck could not work up enough energy for either tennis or golf. I had to go water-skiing with the kids.

"Well," Chuck said, "at least he cut the line about infallible authority."

"It doesn't make any difference. People would ignore him. Married laypeople might be infallible about sex but no celibate pope is."

"He mentions all our reasons for change."

"And says by way of reply?"

"Nothing."

"He dismisses them?" I felt my temper rising. "How can he do that?"

"He appeals to the authority of the Church."

"Does he think that will work?"

"Apparently . . . He has some stuff about the importance of the personal relationship in marriage and how artificial contraception interferes with it."

"How does he know?" I screamed.

"Hey, don't blame me. Am I the Pope?"

"You're a man!"

"The very kind of person from whose unbridled lusts the Pope is trying to protect women?"

"Does he say *that*?"

"He kind of hints at it."

"Asshole."

TV came to our front door to talk to us. Our youngest child answered their ring and glared at them.

"Go way!"

"Is your daddy home?

"Go way!"

"Your mommy?

"Bad people! Go way!"

"Bad?"

"My daddy says you're bastards!"

Then she giggled and ran into the house. Her father's daughter all right.

"Do you have a reaction to the new encyclical, Dr. O'Malley?"

The airhead blond pronounced the word like it was sigh-ike-el.

"I think the Pope has taken a somewhat greater risk than he might have imagined."

"How is that?"

"He believes that his own personal authority will outweigh the common experience of married people about the importance of sex in their lives."

"Do you think that the Catholic laypeople will accept his authority?"

"That remains to be seen. My impression is that they've already made up their minds. This decision has come too late for them to change their minds.

"And priests?"

"I would suspect that in the confessional many

priests will continue to tell the laity that they should follow their consciences."

"Will many people leave the Church because of the encyclical?"

"I doubt it."

"How can they remain Catholics and disobey the Pope?"

"There's a long history of Catholics remaining Catholic on their own terms. I would not be surprised if many American Catholics will now join that history."

"Mrs. O'Malley, how do you think Catholic women will react?"

Ah, so I am not invisible. I must be careful, controlled, calm.

"I don't know how others might feel. I wonder how the Pope can make such an important decision which will affect my life and the life of every Catholic woman in the world without consulting us."

So far, so good, Rosemarie. Stay cool.

"Do you feel that the Pope does not understand women?"

"What troubles me is that he seems to assume that it is unnecessary for him to understand women!"

Clancy lowered the boom, boom, boom, boom!

Which is precisely what my husband sang when the media left.

Clancy, I must confess, was inordinately proud of herself. There were many phone calls after the interview aired. They had rearranged it so I received top billing. They used both of my sound bites before they gave Chucky Ducky any airtime.

"Well," he said, "at least I had the last word!"

"We will make love tonight," I informed him, "to respond personally to the Pope."

"If you insist!"

"I insist."

"I wanted to tell those people it was the biggest

fuck-up in the history of the Catholic Church."

In retrospect it surely was. Reaction from the various conferences of bishops around the world to the encyclical was at best lukewarm. Some (like the Canadian) actually seemed to reject it. Groups of theologians pointed out ways around it. Most parish clergy ignored it in their sermons the following Sunday. Priests who were waiting for an excuse to leave the priesthood and marry departed in droves. Instead of confirming papal teaching authority, the encyclical damaged it badly. Catholics stopped listening to the Popes when they spoke on sex. Maybe they should have done that long ago.

The Pope was so astonished by the reaction that he never wrote another encyclical. Indeed, one of his biographers later reported that he even considered resigning, which is what he should have done. He decided against it, however, on the grounds that he was the "father" of the Church and that one cannot resign from fatherhood. That argument, it seemed to me, was of the same validity as the arguments in his encyclical.

Chuck and I would discover that our presence on the birth control commission made us pariahs in some ecclesiastical quarters. A small Catholic college revoked an offer of an honorary degree. The local bishop ordered a larger university to ban him as a commencement speaker. A couple of Catholic papers attacked his photography, which they had not noticed before, as prurient.

"Mr. O'Malley," a clerical editorialist wrote, "is obsessed with womanly flesh."

"I should hope so," I commented. "Isn't that how God made men to be?"

Chuck wouldn't let me send the letter.

"Rosemarie my darling, you have lowered enough booms on this issue."

"That's what you get for giving the Pope honest

advice, which presumably he was seeking!"

I got even with all of them by writing one of my secret short stories about a couple who engage in spectacular lovemaking the day the encyclical appeared. The story was a comedy because sex, I believe, is of its very nature comic. It was not a completely autobiographical story.

I did not, however, show it to my husband. Or anyone else.

❦ 21 ❦

"They're planning on tearing the city apart," Vince said at supper a couple of days before the Democratic Convention in Chicago.

We were having supper at a small fish restaurant up the Lake from our homes. All four of us had tired for the moment of the Country Club. There were just too many people there who did not share our heart-aches.

"Why?" I asked. "What do they hope to accomplish?"

"The kids want to protest the war."

"How do they think breaking up the Democratic Convention will stop the war?"

"They don't think, Rosemarie," Chuck said sadly. "Does our daughter think? The horror of the war overwhelms them. They believe that if they will it strongly enough, the war will stop."

"They'll elect Nixon," I protested.

"They don't care. They think there is no difference between Nixon and Hubert."

"If I hear that once more," I complained, "I'll scream."

"Like my brother says all the time"—Peg shook her head sadly—"they lack experience, a sense of history, political realism, and teachers who will challenge their naïveté."

"It's an interlude," her brother said. "We'll get through it. In years to come their own children will look back on their parents' behavior and be embarrassed."

"If they live to have children."

"Some of their leaders are far more cynical," Vince said as he polished off a plate of sea bass and looked at the empty plate like he wanted more. "We've received warnings from the FBI and the CIA that some of the leaders have phone conversations with the Russian Embassy every week."

Chuck had learned to be skeptical of both agencies during our years in Bonn.

"Red baiting?"

"I don't know, Chuck. The documents look pretty good to me. The Mayor thinks they're Communist agents. I doubt that. I wouldn't be sure that they're not getting some money from our friends over in Moscow."

"Why, Vince? Why should they care?"

"Anything that disrupts American society makes them feel good. Tearing a city like Chicago apart is worth a few extra rubles even if it does not have long-term effects."

"They'd rather deal with Tricky Dicky?" I demanded.

"Like the kids, they don't think."

"What about the cops?" Chuck sipped at his iced tea.

"You mean are they capable of protecting the city? Sure they are. We'll have the National Guard in town too."

"They didn't do too good a job during the riot . . ." Vince hesitated.

"I'm not sure that they have enough training yet to

restrain themselves when young women shout obscenities and throw feces at them."

"We might have a couple of riots, one of them involving the police?" Chuck pushed his point.

"I've warned the Mayor. He has a lot of confidence in the Chicago police."

"Too much?"

"Perhaps."

"Sounds like a bad scene," I whispered to my husband, after we had made love that night.

"We'll stay up here," he murmured, his mind on other things at the moment. Like me.

"We will NOT," I said. "You'll be in Chicago taking pictures and I will be with you."

"Anything you say, woman"—he sighed—"as long as you keep doing things like that to me."

"Silly!"

It was not only the crazies like Jerry Rubin's Yippies who planned to make trouble for Chicago. The media came prepared to attack the city relentlessly and did so without any regard for fairness or even truth. Unfortunately the Mayor and the cops played into their hands.

It's hard to understand their reasons. Did they want to elect Nixon? Hardly, but then like the kids and like the Russians, if they were supporting the protesters with their money, they weren't thinking beyond the spectacle of the event. Their paradigm was simple enough. Because of Mayor Daley and the city of Chicago, the Democratic Convention was a disaster and the Democrats lost the votes of those who were appalled by the behavior of the city.

Whence that paradigm? I think some of them, like that faker Walter Cronkite, really hated the city, for no other reason than, like the man said about Mount Everest, it was there. In their WASP (and Jewish) minds Irish Catholic politicians like the Mayor were an inherently evil people as were the "white ethnic hard hats" who voted for him. They were the people who the media blamed for the war. Hence they must be punished. So the media made common cause with the crazies and the kids and in favor of the disruption of the convention.

It was also, as my astute husband said, a great story, a "historic story."

They ignored the facts that the Mayor was antiwar as were the "white ethnics" whose sons were fighting it. Such facts never bothered people like Cronkite when they made up their minds.

Upon arrival in Chicago, Cronkite blamed the Mayor for a strike which inhibited the networks from establishing their bases at the convention till the last moment. The strike, he argued, was a tactic the Mayor was using to censor the national media in a city which was becoming an armed camp.

He knew nothing about Chicago labor relations, or he wouldn't have said something so foolish on national television. But the temper of the times was such that no one cared about even the semblance of journalistic ethics. Some TV crews staged fake shots of kids who had been beaten by police in Lincoln Park, then unwrapped the bandages as soon as the shot was over.

Chuck and I wandered through the park, which was occupied by the Yippies of Abbie Hoffman and Jerry Rubin, comic anarchists who were perhaps more of a serious threat to the city than the serious protesters. For the most part they were rich kids playing at revolution, and a stylistic one at that. Dirty skin, body stench, bizarre clothes, foul language, the beat of rock and roll on portable radios, and drug-induced dreamy faces made them revolutionaries—as of course did excreting their bodily wastes on the grass of Lincoln Park.

Scotty Reston, the pompous jerk from the *New York Times*, would later cry that the protesters on the streets of Chicago were "our children!" They were not his children in fact or my children, in the latter case not yet anyway. Nor were they the children of most Americans or of typical Americans. Lincoln Park in those days before the convention was a preview of what Woodstock would be in 1969—a youth culture more interested in sex and drugs than politics.

Some of them murmured sleepy and incoherent obscenities at us as we toured the park. None seemed to object to Chuck's camera. "Make love, not war," others would mumble at us. We found an occasional child who was prepared to argue coherently with us, using only a minimum of "you knows."

"Like, man," one girl with a strong New York accent said, "we want to show the absurdity of capitalism and laugh the country out of war. We don't hate anyone. Hatred is not cool, you know?"

"You hate the cops, don't you?"

"The pigs, well, they're not really human, you know, but we don't want to hate them, just make them laugh."

"In five years," Chuck said, "she'll be an upperclass matron in Westchester County and belong to a country club. Now she's sticking it to her parents."

"Most of them will be. Not all. Some are hooked on drugs forever. Look at that kid over there against the tree. He's in another world, spaced out completely . . . Do you think that will happen to any of ours?"

"I hope not."

"If it does, do you think they will come back?"

"I hope so."

We stopped on Clark Street to talk to some of the cops.

"Fucking spoiled brats," one said.

"Deserve a good spanking," another told us.

"And a solid clout on the head with a billy club and a night in jail," a third claimed. "Rich white trash."

He was black.

"I can hardly wait till we get the word," the first concluded, "to drive these dirty vermin out of our park."

"I don't like the sound of that," Chuck said, as we walked down to Grant Park. "This could get bloody before it's over."

"What if a hundred kids are killed?" I asked, thinking that one of mine might be among them.

"Let's hope and pray not."

"It's a volcano ready to explode, Chuck. What can we do?"

"Rosemarie, we've learned by now that we can't do much of anything."

"Except stop by the Cathedral and pray."

So we did.

The only difference between us and most of the crowd in Grant Park was that they thought they could do something. A few of them were spaced out on drugs, rock and roll continued to play, they wore ragged clothes, bags of excrement were ready to throw at the pigs. Yet most of them were relatively ordinary kids who didn't want to start riots. They wanted only to stop the war—and believed that disrupting the Democratic Convention in Chicago was a strategic way of doing it.

"We're going to march on Mayor Daley's home in Bridgeport tonight with candles to protest," a young woman with a Kansas accent and corn-colored hair to match informed us with shining eyes. "We'll let him know how the young people of America feel about the war."

"Do you think he doesn't know?" I asked gently.

"He supports the war," she said stubbornly.

"No, he doesn't."

"Well maybe when he sees us in front of his house singing peace songs he'll oppose it even more."

She was pretty, she was innocent, and she was trying.

Our daughter was not in the crowd across from the Conrad Hilton Hotel facing cops across the street in front of the hotel. She was up on the fifteenth floor in the McCarthy headquarters. Both of us had our doubts about Gene. It was irrational perhaps to blame him for Bobby's death. Yet it was hard to forget that he'd been a spoiler. Moreover, his indifferent response to the Russian invasion of Czechoslovakia, suggested what a lazy president he would be. Yet April Rosemary was still choosing politics over riot. Anyway, she had to make her own decisions, didn't she?

I yearned for the days a few years ago, when we made some of the decisions or at least talked her out of the bad ones.

We had a quick sandwich with Vince at Berghof's.

"The Mayor," he told us, "is trying desperately to persuade Ted Kennedy to run. This morning he thinks he made some progress."

"Ted's terribly young," I said. "Isn't the Mayor exploiting the name?"

"The Mayor wants to pull the country together," Vince replied. "He thinks Ted can do it."

"He also wants to win the election," Chuck said. "Don't we all?"

"Any more assassination rumors?"

"Lots of them, Rosie. There are plans to kill the Mayor and McCarthy and Hubert. There is a plot to trick the cops into killing one of the young women in McCarthy's campaign, preferably a black one."

I would remember that plot the last night of the convention.

"Any truth in them?"

"In the present circumstances, Chuck, we can't afford to ignore them. It's explosive."

"People are going to be killed!" I said shivering.

"I'm afraid of that too."

We went home with heavy hearts, I to my exercise room, Chuck to his darkroom.

"Daughter on phone," Missus informed me. "Too much sweat. Too much exercise is too much, ain't it?"

"You're right, Missus, as always."

"Hi, Mom," April Rosemary said. "I'm staying down a little late. We're going to march on Bridgeport with lighted candles tonight. All very peaceful."

She wasn't exactly asking my permission, but she was seeking my approval. It was Martin's strategy. Stir up a riot with a peaceful march: nonviolence generating violence.

"Do you think the ordinary people in Bridgeport support the war? It's their sons who are dying in it."

"I don't know, Mom. Probably not."

"Then why invade their neighborhood? They're not the enemy. Neither is the Mayor. He has spent the whole day trying to persuade Senator Kennedy to run."

"REALLY!"

"Missus is from Bridgeport. Is she the enemy? Is she responsible for the war?"

"No . . ."

"What's the purpose of the march, then, except to get your pictures on television and maybe to incite some crazy cops to riot?"

"They won't, will they?"

"We talked to some of them today. They think their city has been invaded by obscenity-shouting, shit-throwing revolutionaries. No telling what they might do."

Silence.

"We have to do something, Mom."

"And you're doing that by working for Senator McCarthy."

"We have to do more. Kids our age are dying right now in 'Nam."

"We know that April Rosemary."

"I'll be careful . . . I promise."

"You'll be staying at the hotel tonight?"

"I thought I would . . . They're good kids here, really, Mom. No"—she giggled—"shit-throwing revolutionaries."

"Call us when you get back."

"I will, Mom."

Dear God, I prayed, we're wrestling for her soul and the match seems fixed against us.

I knocked on the door to the darkroom.

"Come in, Rosemarie," my husband shouted.

"Hey, look what I got," he exulted.

When his prints come up, Chucky is still the little boy with the Brownie, reveling in the magic he has worked. I love him specially at those times.

Isolated from the televised crowds, even the Yippies looked forlorn and pathetic.

"So sad," I said with a sigh.

"Aren't they? This is the other side of what's happening here now. Some of those poor kids are zonked out on drugs, others are just homesick . . . I must say you look fetching as usual in those rather skimpy exercise clothes."

"Missus says too much sweat is too much."

"I have a different perspective."

He rested his hand on my rear end. For a moment I relaxed in his admiration. Then I delivered my message.

"April Rosemary wants to join the march on Bridgeport tonight."

"Figures . . . What did you tell her?"

"I followed your strategy. I argued with her respectfully. She said she had to do something because boys her age were dying right now in Vietnam, which

God knows is true. I told her to be careful and to call us when she got back to the hotel."

"I'd better go down there and take some shots."

"No," I said firmly.

"What?" He seemed surprised, not that I would prevent him from doing something stupid. Like most wives, I do that all the time. Rather he was surprised because I had given him a flat order.

"You're telling me," he feigned bemusement, "that you didn't forbid your daughter to march on Bridgeport, but you're forbidding me to go down there and take a few shots?"

"That's right," I said firmly.

"Why the discrimination?"

"Because I can't control her and I can control you."

"Oh, that . . ."

"I'm not about to risk the two of you down there tonight."

His fingers moved to tickle my belly, a gesture which he well knew would begin arousal in key regions of my body.

"No, Chucky"—I backed away—"not now."

A few more such tickles and I would be putty for him to mold. He would ravish me on the darkroom couch as he had done many times before. Including the night I had conceived April Rosemary.

Back on the bicycle, I told myself I was an idiot for missing the opportunity. Defy death.

Later the boys tripped in from pickup basketball games at Skelton Park. The exciting news today was that Seano was really hustling for rebounds. They fell on chairs around the kitchen table and demanded ice cream.

They could have served it up themselves, but I loved them too much to tell them that. (I had, by the way, put a sweat suit on over my minimal exercise clothes.) Besides I wanted some myself.

"What's happening downtown?" Jimmy asked casually.

"Nothing good. I'm afraid that there will be a confrontation between the hippies and the cops and some people will be killed."

"Why?" Kevin asked, a vast scoop of chocolate ice cream suspended at his mouth.

"The hippies because they have to do something about the war and the cops because they resent these spoiled rich kids invading their city and throwing piles of shit at them."

"And this is supposed to end the war?"

"Don't expect me to disagree, Kev."

"What's Sis doing?" Jimmy inquired. "Not throwing shit, is she? I can't imagine that. She'd get her hands dirty that way."

Yucking male laughter around the table.

"She's marching in a candlelight procession to the Mayor's house tonight."

"Why?" Jimmy frowned.

"Because she has to do something," Kevin replied.

"Well"—Jimmy sighed—"Sis is Sis. She has to do what she has to do."

"Your father wanted to take pictures of the procession."

Instant outrage from the group.

"I hope you told him he couldn't."

"You did stop him, didn't you?"

"Dad's crazy."

"He ought to act his age."

They shared amused tolerance for their sister and fury at their dad.

"He's not going to do it," I said calmly.

"Some one of these days his luck is going to run out."

Sisters are immortal. Dads are not.

The talk turned to the jazz band they were organizing for the coming school year. It seemed that there was "this girl" who wanted to sing with them.

Aha.

"Is she any good?"

The boys laughed.

"You mean as a singer?" Kev said.

"What else could I possibly mean?"

More laughter.

"Well, yeah," he said, "she is very good. I don't know where she learned how to sing the blues. Sometimes she sounds like Billie Holiday."

"That I doubt," I said.

"She's also gorgeous," Jimmy said, "which is what you want to know, Mom. Sophomore at Providence."

"Only fifteen?"

"Well almost."

"Name?"

"Maria Elena Cortez," Jimmy said promptly.

"Lopez," Kevin corrected him.

"Latina?"

"Huh?"

"Uh, Mexican?"

"Yeah, probably," Kevin said as though ethnicity didn't matter when a young woman could sing like Billie Holiday. "You'll like her, Mom."

"What makes you think her parents will let their lovely young daughter sing with you pack of Irish ruffians?"

"Well . . ."

"We kind of thought . . ."

"Maybe you could talk to her parents . . ."

"And tell her that we're all right, you know . . ."

"I will tell her that you're a pack of hormone-filled adolescent males whose heads are constantly filled with dirty thoughts."

They thought that was hilariously funny.

When they stopped laughing, Kevin said seriously, "She's not that kind of a girl, Mom."

"What kind of girl is she?"

"The kind guys like us," Jimmy argued, "want to respect and protect."

"Not that she can't take care of herself," Seano added.

"Kevin stares at her tits all the time," Jimmy said with a sly wink at me.

"Breasts," I insisted.

"All right!"

"I do not," said Kevin. "Besides there's nothing wrong with that, is there Mom?"

"Depends on how you do it."

"Adoringly?"

I didn't like that.

"Too young."

"We won't always be . . . Anyway we invited her up to Long Beach for a few days so we could practice. Her mother said absolutely not . . . Would you ever . . ."

"I would not."

I would have to meet the young woman first.

Music and youthful romance were a pleasant escape from the confrontations in downtown Chicago.

The boys went out to find Gianni Antonelli. I went back to my exercises. I thought about young romance. I had been fourteen once and in love with a boy a couple years older than me. He was a jerk a lot of the time, not the mature, poised young man that my son was. He was always respectful, however. Still was.

I stopped my work. I had stirred him up an hour ago and then backed out. Shame on me, shame, shame on me. I ought to have been delighted that after all these years he wanted me virtually on sight.

Dr. Ward would have disapproved strongly of my behavior.

That was a rationalization.

I stopped the exercise machine and put on the pants

of my sweat suit. Give him a little more to contend with.

I went back to the darkroom with the excuse that I had to tell him about this Maria Elena Lopez girl.

I did. He shook his head.

"Here we go again."

"I'll check her out first," I assured him.

"I wouldn't worry about Kevin."

"Just the same. The boys tell me she has gorgeous breasts."

"They said that to you?"

"We're buddies."

"I'd never have said that to April about you," he muttered.

"You didn't have to . . . What are you working on there?"

I leaned over the tray.

"Cops!"

"Chuck! They're terrible!"

"Yeah, they are . . . you're not, however."

He tickled me again, this time seriously. I gasped for breath as my body chemistry went crazy.

"Why did you change your mind?" he asked.

"Because I love you so much."

A spasm of almost unbearable delight spread across his face. So easy to make him happy.

The march on Bridgeport was peaceful. The local cops doubtless had been given strict orders on how to behave. My daughter was at the head of the march. She chatted amiably with the cops. Smart politician my girl. Some of the time, anyway.

The spokesman, perhaps self-anointed, for the crowd was Michael Novak, a "Catholic philosopher" in beads and a beard with a high-pitched voice.

"We let the Mayor and his community know," he said pompously, "that the young people of America are demanding peace."

Later, beads and beard shed, he worked for Sarge

Shriver in the disastrous 1972 campaign and then, sensing which way the political wind was blowing, became a conservative Republican defender of capitalism.

A Catholic Sammy Glick, my husband had dubbed him.

April Rosemary called long after midnight from the Hilton.

"I didn't want to wake you, Mom," she said, "but I promised I would call. I'm at the Hilton and fine. I'm going to bed now. In a room with *girls*!"

"I know that April Rosemary."

"I know you do, but I thought"—she giggled—"I'd say it for the record . . . Did you watch us on television?"

"I saw you chatting with your good friends from the Chicago Police Department."

"Was that on television?" she said in horror. "Oh, Mom, I didn't know that! I'm so sorry! Actually they were very nice men."

"We don't have anything to worry about," my husband assured me. "She's one of us."

For a moment I thought he was right.

The next day came to be known as the battle of Chicago. Or maybe the police riot of Chicago.

22

"They've gone crazy!" I shouted at Chuck as a group of cops in hard hats seized a young couple who had been strolling along Michigan Avenue, shoved them up against the window of a Conrad Hilton Café, beat them with clubs, and then shoved them through a plate-glass window. They were quite oblivious to my husband's clicking power-drive Nikon.

It was a thick, airless night, the kind on which you have to fight your way through curtains of humidity, the sort on which you want to fight or have sex. Both urges were playing on Michigan Avenue.

Later I learned from one of the Red Cross people that the broken glass had cut an artery in the young woman's leg. Some of the Red Cross volunteers were also beaten, including one who had served as a corpsman with the Marines in Korea.

Cops were everywhere, smashing heads, cracking ribs, kicking people on the ground—old people, young people, passersby, protesters, anyone they could grab. Reporters, or anyone who looked like a reporter, were a specially favored target.

Vince had provided Chuck and me with City of Chicago badges which protected us, though only just barely from the rampaging cops.

Some idiot had ordered the cops to fire tear gas

into the crowd across the street from the Hilton. This provided the TV cameras with wonderful shots of clouds of smoke and kids running away from the tear gas.

There would be much debate afterward about who started the battle, the cops lined up in front of the Conrad Hilton or the howling kids across the street. Chuck and I thought that a group of kids had stormed across the street and thrown feces at the cops before the cops went berserk. The issue patently was irrelevant. The cops lost their cool on national television and gave the city of Chicago a bad name which perhaps it deserved.

It was August 28, the presidential voting was taking place at the Amphitheater. The networks ingeniously would cut back and forth from tapes of the riot to the proceedings on the convention floor. Senator Ribicoff, playing to his Connecticut supporters watching TV, insulted the Mayor from the podium. Daley shouted something at him, faker, fucker, or kike depending on whom you believed. Vince, who was furious at the Mayor for letting the police get out of control, has always insisted that the Mayor would never use the last two words because they weren't part of his vocabulary. I figured he was right. Even furiously angry, he was too smart a politician to lose his cool that completely. Not all the police rioted. Probably only a minority. It takes only a handful of angry cops to create a riot, especially on television. That's no excuse. The police leadership lost control.

The cops were tired, hungry, disgusted by the obscene taunts of the protesters, the sense that they were spoiled rich kids, and the filth which the kids threw at them. That's no excuse either. It does help to understand what went wrong. Chuck's pictures show a look of orgasmic satisfaction on the faces of some cops as they beat kids into the ground.

The Chicago Police Department never let that happen again. However, the harm was done. The "Battle of Chicago" lasted no longer than forty-five minutes, maybe only a half hour. Yet magnified by the media it became a lasting icon of those years. When Hubert Humphrey was finally nominated early the next morning, the media people told those who were still listening that the nomination was not worth having because of the brutality of Mayor Daley's police to peaceful protesters.

The next night two hundred Illinois National Guardsmen lined up in front of the Conrad Hilton across the street from the jeering crowds, triumphant over their "victory" of the previous night. Whether the Guard was there to protect police from the protesters or the protesters from the police was not clear. They carried rifles with bayonets but without ammunition. Moreover, unlike the cops, they were the same age as the protesters. There was not much chance of them using their bayonets, especially as a Guardsman said to me, "we've never had any practice with these things."

"Let's get out of here," Chuck muttered to me when things on Michigan Avenue had settled down.

The whiff of tear gas had made me slightly sick.

"I have enough nightmares of my own," I replied. "I don't need this one."

As we turned on to Wabash Avenue and walked toward the garage where our car was parked, the world became quiet again. A peaceful night a block away from Michigan Avenue with maybe some kind of festival in Grant Park. It was an eerie experience, like we had stepped into another planet. Suddenly the silence was violated by the piercing cry of a woman under assault. A girl rushed around the corner only a few yards ahead of us with a club-wielding cop right behind her. As we watched he caught up with and slashed at her shoulder with his club. She collapsed on the sidewalk, still screaming.

Chuck pulled out his camera and began to fire away, as the cop hit her on the head. I charged in and waved my badge at him.

"You'd better stop, Officer, if you want to keep your job."

"Who the fuck are you?" he demanded as he pondered whether to hit me. "Some fucking rich liberal bitch?"

"Take a good look at my badge, Officer."

He swung his club back as though he were about to swat me. I braced for the blow. He hesitated, his face reveling in the possible joy of clubbing a rich bitch.

Chuck stepped between us.

"Do that, Officer, and you're dead."

I had no idea how Chuck would kill him. However, he sounded so ominous, so dangerous that the cop walked away muttering curses.

We helped the young woman to her feet. She smelled of marijuana. She was surely no older than April Rosemary.

"Fucking pig," she shouted after the cop.

Then she turned on us, and sneered, "I don't need help from fucking capitalists like you."

"You don't have to curse at us," I replied. "We're not your parents."

It hit home. She gasped, then ran in the other direction.

"You scared the shit out of that cop, Chucky," I said.

"That was the face and command presence of Staff Sergeant Charles C. Cronin, First Constabulary Regiment, Army of the United States, at your service, ma'am."

"What would you have done?"

"He was fat and slow. My first move would have been to smash my camera into his genitals."

I had no doubt that he would have done just that.

"Did you get any good shots?"

"Fast film . . . I think got a good one of his face."

The next night we became part of the Battle of Chicago.

The beginning of that night was splendid: Walter Cronkite took on the Mayor on the *Evening news*. The Mayor creamed him. Poor Walter believed his own lies—the Mayor was a throwback, a cheap party hack who couldn't speak good English, an inarticulate and brutal goon given to hilarious malapropisms (such as "the police don't cause disorder, they preserve disorder.") It would be easy to make him look like an idiot. Instead Walter hardly got a word in edgewise as the Mayor rolled over him with waves of soft-spoken complaints about how Walter came into the Daley family home every night and how much his family and the people of Chicago respected him and how disappointed in him they were because he had misled his viewers about the great city of Chicago and how difficult it was to maintain order when outsiders were trying to tear the great city apart. The Mayor appeared as the man he really was, quick-witted, hurt by what the media were saying, doing his best to stay calm under enormous pressure, but normally in complete control of his temper.

Around our supper table we whooped and hollered. Chicago had been taking it on the chin all week. Now we were giving some of it back.

Unfortunately for CBS, it was a live interview, so they couldn't edit it to make Walter seem triumphant. When he returned to the CBS headquarters he apparently expected applause for having disposed of the Mayor. It is hard to understand how he could have, but he did. He was greeted with boos and catcalls. Alas, his defeat did not make him question his assumptions about Chicago.

Earlier in the day I had spoken on the phone with an exhausted and disillusioned April Rosemary. Senator McCarthy was a fine man, he'd studied to be a monk, he supported peace, he was the first one to run in the primaries, he should be President. In a democracy, I said, you need a majority of the votes—Rosie the ex-radical and ex-liberal falling back on the high school civics course I had denounced when I had been her age.

"It isn't fair," she argued stubbornly.

"What about his comments on the Russian invasion of Czechoslovakia?"

"Doesn't America already have one war? Isn't one war enough?"

"Kind of hard on the poor Czechs . . . Can we give you a ride home tonight?"

"That would be wonderful, Mom. I'm asleep on my feet."

"Ten o'clock?"

"Wonderful!"

Driving down in my Benz, I thought about the shift from the angry radical who was willing to write off the Czechs to a grateful daughter who wanted to ride home with her parents.

"If I were her age today," I said to Chuck, "I'd probably be as bad as she is."

"Much worse," he said with a laugh.

"You're right," I agreed. "I had no common sense at all, just a loud Irish mouth."

"And good taste in men."

"That's debatable."

I was driving because Chuck is not the world's best driver and he claims to freeze up at the wheel of an expensive car. I think he's lazy. Still, I'm not about to trust him with the Benz.

It was another sticky night without a hint of a breeze. The faint aroma of tear gas still hung in the air. Many of the protesters had left already, their work done. The Guard, hot and tired, stood listlessly in a line that didn't look very military. Cops walked around, fingering their clubs as though they were waiting for another hippie head to bash.

"Why does Daley continue to support these goons?" I asked.

"Probably figures that when your back is to the wall, you don't give an inch. There'll be a reckoning afterward with the cops that lost it, but it will be done very quietly."

"You're going to give him your pictures?"

"Turned the prints over to Vince this afternoon."

"Not the negatives, I hope."

"I never give anyone the negatives, Rosemarie my darling . . . I'm thinking of an exhibition next year called *1968—Year of Violence*."

"What a great idea!"

"And the year still has four months to go!"

The fifteenth floor of the Conrad Hilton was quiet. Vice presidential voting was not very interesting, especially since TV had said that the presidential nomination was worthless after the "Battle of Chicago." Many of the McCarthy volunteers, some of whom had been with him since the first days in New Hampshire, had not left.

Our daughter proudly introduced us to her young colleagues. She told them, with a perfectly straight face, that we had been with Dr. King at Selma. Chuck turned on his very considerable charm and I tried my best to keep up. We were both, perhaps foolishly given the venue, wearing shorts and tee shirts. One of April Rosemary's friends said that we looked more like an older brother and sister than a mother and father. Chuck went through his usual dippy line about being a child bridegroom.

Then the doors of the elevators swung open and a dozen cops in hard hat helmets and without name plates charged into the lobby of the fifteenth floor like the troops of Genghis Khan. The "Battle of Chicago Part II."

Kids, screaming in agony, fell to the floor. Chuck's power drive clicked away.

"Get the fucker with the camera," a black sergeant shouted.

"He means you, Chuck," I gasped.

My husband looked up, saw a cop with a billy club raised over his head closing in on him, and flipped the camera to our daughter.

"Get out of here, kid," he ordered and turned his shoulder to deflect the cop's blow. The cop, a sneering little Mick with a whiskey nose, swung again, this time hitting the side of Chuck's head. He collapsed to the floor in an untidy pile like a discarded Raggedy Andy doll. Remembering the scenario from Marquette Park, I jumped on the cop, scratching, screaming, kicking, clawing. Out of the corner of my eye I saw that we had created enough of a diversion for April Rosemary, who was running down the corridor toward the stairway to the first floor. We had saved the Nikon and the film in it. Big deal!

I wasn't as lucky as I had been in Marquette Park. Another cop, a burly Italian, pulled me off his buddy and pounded his club against my chest. He was aiming for my boobs but missed. Still a sharp pain sliced through my torso, like I had been jabbed by a lance— not that I have ever been jabbed by a lance.

"Fucking rich bitch, I'm going to smash your face."

The cop I had clawed kicked me a couple of times in the stomach. I thought he might kill me. Curiously I was not afraid to die. All the guilt and all the obligations would die with me.

"Let's do her face," the Irish cop said. "Smash it to pieces."

"Yeah, that would beat fucking her."

I thought of poor Chucky trying to get along without me and wanted to live. I reached into the pocket of my shorts and pulled out my Mayor Daley ID.

"Geez," said the Italian, "she works for the fucking Mayor."

"What the fuck is she doing here?"

"You're dead, you fucking asshole," I said through my clenched teeth.

"Let's get out of here," the Italian said. "She doesn't know our names."

Yeah, asshole, but we have your faces on film.

"We ought work her over a little bit more . . ."

"You want the Mayor up your ass? Let's get out of here!"

So I was spared to live a little longer with my normal face for whatever that was worth.

Chucky stirred next to me. Out like a light when I really needed him.

"Rosemarie . . ."

"Ribs," I muttered.

We struggled to our feet and, his arms around me, stumbled toward the elevators. I cried out with each step.

"Where do you think you're going?" said the black sergeant.

"To the hospital. My wife is badly hurt."

"You're not going to any fucking hospital, you're going to the fucking lockup."

I showed him my ID.

"You're dead, you fucking asshole," I informed him.

"What the fuck you doing up here throwing things out the window?"

He backed off, turning his face away so we might not recognize him again.

Chuck pushed the button for the elevator. As we waited for the door to open, he pulled Trudi's Leica out of his pocket, leaned against the wall, and quickly fired off most of the roll. If in his woozy state he could still take pictures, a lot of cops were in deep shit.

'Scuse me, I meant hot water.

Then the elevator door opened. We lurched into it. Chuck leaned against the door so it would not close.

"Hey, Sarge," he yelled.

The cop turned around, his face twisted in a hellish glare.

"Smile for the birdie!"

Chuck fired off three quick shots and the sergeant rushed toward us. Then the elevator closed in his face.

"Damn," Chuck said sleepily. "I could have got one more just as the door closed."

"I'm hurt," I groaned.

"I'll take you over to Mercy Hospital right away."

"NO! I want to die near home! Take me to Oak Park Hospital!"

Dumb idea. Chucky, however, is used to doing what I tell him to do.

We should have taken a cab. Instead we stumbled and bumbled toward the garage where the Benz was parked. We couldn't find it. So we argued about what floor it was on. I was right, naturally.

Then we argued about who should drive the car. I'm afraid that, because doubtless of the bad influence of the cops we swore at each other, so I will not repeat the exact words. In effect I told him I was not about to risk my Benz with him at the wheel. He insisted that with my broken (as he diagnosed the situation) ribs I couldn't even turn the wheel. I replied that even with banged-up ribs I was a better driver than he was. He responded by saying that he would wrestle me for the keys. I gave in.

He was right, for one of those rare times, though I never admitted it to him.

We both were patently out of our minds.

The Lord God must have assigned some of his most skillful angels to protect us as we weaved down the Congress Expressway to Harlem and then up Harlem to the hospital.

Finally, we dragged ourselves into the emergency room.

"What happened to you two?" demanded the resident in charge.

"My wife hit me over the head with a rolling pin and I had to fight back."

I laughed. Mistake. The lanced jabbed my body again.

"A confrontation with Mayor Daley's cops," I said through gritted teeth."

They took all kinds of X rays, gave us painkiller pills, and then took more X rays. I remembered, in the nick of time, the camera in Chuck's pocket.

"Has someone left a Mercedes outside with the engine running?" a nurse asked.

"My wife did," Chuck said.

They told me that my ribs were badly bruised but neither broken nor cracked. Chuck had lacerations on his head but no concussion. They bound my torso up like I was an Egyptian mummy. It appeared that neither of us had any internal injuries.

"The Mayor's thugs are losing it," I muttered. "Okay, Chucky Ducky, lets go home."

"Oh, no you don't," said the very young nurse who had tied me up. "Not with all those painkillers in you . . . You were crazy to drive yourselves out here. You might have had internal injuries . . ."

"Oh," we said in unison.

"Rosemarie, my darling," my husband mumbled, "maybe you should call the kids."

"Good thinking," I said. "They can come and pick us up."

On the third try I managed to spin the right numbers.

"O'Malley residence," said a businesslike voice which sounded much like my own.

"Hi, honey, Mom . . ."

"MOM! Where are you!"

"Oak Park Hospital. We're both okay. They won't let us drive home because of the painkillers they've given us."

"PAINKILLERS!

"No big deal. Do you think you and Kevin can drive down in the Mustang and pick us up?"

"SURE!"

"Then call Aunt Peg and tell her to tell Uncle Vince that we are going to sue him and the Mayor for every penny in the city treasury."

"I already talked to Uncle Vince, Mom, and told him about the pictures. He's coming over."

"Oh . . . Did someone develop the pictures?"

"I did, Mom. I had to do some special stuff to bring them up because of the low light level. They look fine."

"Where did you learn to develop film?"

"At school."

"Oh."

"We'll be right down, Mom."

"I am drugged," my husband said, "and I imagine things. Our daughter didn't mess with my film, did she?"

"Of course she did, dear. What else would you expect? It's in her genes."

"Oh," he said, then dropped off to sleep.

Almost instantly our two eldest were on the scene, in charge of the whole operation.

"Seniority counts," April Rosemary announced. "I'll drive the Benz home, bro. You can take my Mustang."

"*Our* Mustang, Sis . . . Mom, I should drive the Benz, I'm a better driver."

"You are not!"

"You can do it the next time we're in an emergency room, Kev. She's older."

"Rats!" he said, with a good-sport shrug of his shoulders.

In the car, our daughter gave Chuck the prints she had made.

Did everyone in the family have secrets?

Her father looked at the prints with the best critical frown he could muster in the circumstances.

"Couldn't have done any better myself, kid. You've inherited the family talent."

"Thanks, Dad," she said happily.

"Tell you what, kid. There's some more film in my Leica." He fumbled in his pockets for Trudi's camera.

"It's in my purse. You almost left it at the hospital." I turned my purse over to my daughter.

"Yeah . . . anyway . . . there's some more shots in it. Why don't you develop them too. The light's probably even worse . . ."

"Now, dear," I said. "Please drive us home."

"Stop at Petersen's," my husband insisted. "Your mother and I need a couple malts to keep us going."

"Dad"—April Rosemary giggled—"it's closed at this hour of the night."

"Make them open up . . . We're special customers."

Then, because with the bandage on his head and the wrappings under my tee shirt we looked like walking war wounded, he began singing "Lili Marlene."

"It's lucky Dad doesn't drink much, isn't it, Mom?"

We were so very close that night. Afterward I wished with all the power of my soul that we had been able to preserve that closeness forever.

"He is cute, isn't he?"

Peg and Carlotta were waiting for us as our older children helped us into the house. Jimmy and Seano rushed to the door, ready for a fight. Phil Sheridan's cavalry riding toward the Shenadoah. Moire was sound asleep.

"Don't hug Mom," April Rosemary ordered. "Her ribs are badly broken."

"Bruised," I said in a tone of voice which must have sounded pitiable. "You can hug Daddy, it's only his head."

"Rosie!" Peg screamed in horror.

"Aunt Rosie!" her daughter echoed her.

"I gotta develop some more film." Our daughter rushed for the basement.

"The kid has some talent," Chuck admitted, a benign—and drugged—smile on his face.

"Everyone knows *that*, Uncle Chuck," Carlotta informed him. "She took all the pictures for our yearbook."

And never told us a word. Why are there so many secrets?

Vince was coming from City Hall. We would wait for him. I wanted in the worst way to collapse in my bed. However, my husband was quite incoherent, if very funny, and it fell to my lot to tell our story

"Those bastards!" Peg exploded.

"Not in front of the children, Peg," Chuck warned her.

We ignored him like we usually do.

"Does it hurt much?"

"I'm all doped up so I don't feel anything. I'm not even angry at the poor goons."

"Fucking goons," Chuck cut in.

"Not in front of the children, Uncle Chuck," Carlotta warned him.

I showed her the pictures. As usual my husband, under extreme pressure, proved himself a genius. There were five or six shots that were front-page material.

"Well, Vince had *better* do something about this!" Peg said, her lips a thin, dangerous line.

"Or we'll divorce him," Chuck added.

The doorbell rang, Carlotta let her father in.

"Daddy, you better do something about this!"

Vince was ashen. "The Mayor is horrified. He

asked me to express his personal apologies. He will talk to you eventually. It was the first he heard of the raid on McCarthy's headquarters . . . My God, Rosie," he added as he looked at the pictures, "this is awful!"

"All cops' heads on silver platters!" Chuck demanded, and then fell asleep.

Vince sank into a chair and slowly and carefully reviewed all the pictures.

"You could get indictments on the strength of these pictures alone," he murmured. "There'll be no problem putting a name on these dolts."

"Uncle Chuck says they're fucking bastards, Daddy," Carlotta observed.

"Uncle Chuck is always right."

April Rosemary burst into the room waving a handful of prints from the Leica roll.

"Wait till you see these, Uncle Vince!"

Vince sifted through the prints and slumped into the chair.

"This sergeant is about to swing his club at Chuck! Look at that evil face! What stopped him!"

"The elevator door," I said. "Boy genius wanted to get one more shot. Thank God the door closed in time."

"Rosie"—Vince took a deep breath—"candidly you could file a complaint with these pictures and the State's Attorney would have to indict these guys!"

"Uh."

"Moreover—and I continue to abuse the rules of conflict of interest—you could sue the city of Chicago for tens of millions of dollars."

"We don't need or want the money," I said. "I don't want to embarrass those men's poor families."

Bleeding heart liberal, huh?

Or maybe only a Christian.

Anyway, I couldn't believe I'd said that.

"Make a deal with the Mayor," Chuck said, waking up suddenly. "See that these guys are punished. We don't care how and don't want to know. If it ever happens again before the statute of limitations runs out, we'll sue for so much that we will take away his home in Bridgeport and maybe the church down the street too."

"Do you mean that, Chuck, or is it the Empirin and Tylenol talking?"

"Gotta defend the city against Cronkite."

He closed his eyes again.

"Rosie?"

"I'm in."

"The Mayor will be very grateful."

"He damn well better be."

"Kid ran like Gayle Sayers with the camera," Chucky said, his eyes still closed. "Then came back here and did the prints for us. Genius genes."

1969

❦ 23 ❧

"How you doing?" My husband, bright and lively and elegant in the dressing gown I had bought him which he never wears, handed me my morning cup of coffee.

I refused to open my eyes.

"I ache in every bone of my body," I said.

"More medicine?"

I took a deep breath.

"Ouch! . . . Yes, immediately!"

"How are you?" I said after I swallowed the pills he gave me.

"Headache . . . Sometimes I see double which is all right when it's two Rosemaries. Otherwise, I've been worse."

"Like at Little Rock . . . What time is it?"

"Around noon . . . I thought I had better tell you. The sons have planned a concert here this afternoon featuring this Hispanic girl who sings like Billie Holiday, if you can believe it. I told them I didn't think you'd want to cancel it. I knew you'd want to get a look at her."

"Certainly!"

How dare this little tramp try to vamp my oldest son!

A tramp it turned out she wasn't.

Quite the contrary, she seemed a sweet freshman turning sophomore, a shy child, tall and slender with a café au lait complexion and a lovely figure in her gray shift.

"I'm happy to meet you, Mrs. O'Malley. I'm sorry you were hurt last night."

Sitting at our grand piano, the good April was an addition to the band. Clearly the guys had been working out with Grandma, who had been there in the beginning when Pops Armstrong was playing in the speakeasies on the West Side.

More secrets.

"We're going to experiment today with some Latin blues"—Kevin played the smooth master of ceremonies—"which Maria Elena taught us and which we think are pretty cool."

The music began. Pops was present in our parlor, not perfectly smooth by any means but still real. The kids were imitating still. They were getting better at it.

Then the awkward almost-fifteen-year-old began to sing. As the song eased out of her mouth, some of it in English some of it in Spanish, she was transformed. The music took possession of her. She was an adult woman who knew all the suffering that the blues describe. Her man had done her wrong. She was too young to know such suffering, but the music knew the suffering and she put it on like a form-fitting dress. Her voice was deep and rich and sultry—and somehow, like all good blues singers, carried a little touch of hope.

She wasn't Billie Holiday. Rather she was Bessie Smith at the very beginning of Chicago jazz.

She smiled and nodded at each of the instruments as they improvised around her and she wrapped them into her soul. She gave a special smile at the good April as the piano joined in.

We were all in heaven.

Chuck rolled his eyes.

"Now," said the good April, "poor Mrs. O'Malley was always good at this song. Maybe, Maria Elena, she can back you up vocally."

"Gee, that would be wonderful," the girl, fourteen years old again, said awkwardly. "If you can."

"I wouldn't miss it for the world, dear."

So Kevin's mother and his current crush blended their voices, one soprano, the other alto around and about and in and out and up and down. She grinned impishly at me, briefly a fourteen-year-old again, and then urged my voice up to the top and let me plummet down to the bottom, where she gently caught me. We bonded in that song and I hoped that my son would never let her get away. The good April ended with a Count Bassie three-note, Maria Elena echoed it, and then I added a final fading echo.

Much applause at the end.

"Maria Elena," my husband said, turning on his full charm, "I always let my wife express our family position first, but before she does, I think you have an enormous talent and should take very good care of it."

Sometimes the poor man says exactly the right thing.

"Thank you very much, Mr. O'Malley," she said, blushing deeply.

"Sometimes, dear," I added, "Mr. O'Malley says exactly the right thing, not very often, but this was one of those times."

"It's the pain pills talking."

Might I call her mother and propose she join us at Long Beach for the Labor Day Weekend? Oh, yes, I might. So I called Mrs. Lopez, a very gracious woman. I told her what a wonderful talent her daughter had. I said if she would give her permission, I would protect her like she was my very own at the Lake. If it wasn't too much trouble, her mother said. She is still very young. No trouble at all.

When we stopped by Maria Elena's spotlessly neat home in the Back o' the Yards neighborhood (west of the yards), the child and I did our little improv together, to the delight of the large and handsome Lopez family. Her mother hugged me.

"We have played mariachi in our families for generations. We are very proud of Maria Elena."

I hope, Kevin, you know how much I'm investing in your future.

That evening, while the band (including the good April) performed on the porch of our house against a harvest moon smiling benignly over the Lake, I whispered to my husband, "It's only a kid's crush, Chucky."

"I remember we both had kids' crushes when we were about their age."

I replied with the immemorial exclamation of parents, "Times were different then!"

"The hell they were, Rosemarie my darling . . . You really co-opted that poor kid."

"Just like the good April co-opted me."

"That's not the way I remember it . . ." He closed his eyes again and reentered the world of sleep.

Earlier when she had jumped into the warm waters of the Lake, she was wearing a very modest one-piece swimsuit. Someone, doubtless either Carlotta or April Rosemary, provided her a bikini for the rest of the weekend, much to poor Kevin's delight.

It was a wonderful weekend, lovely weather and the sweet and low-down melancholy of summer coming to an end. It would be a long time before we had another like it.

Chuck and I were mending slowly, the hot days and the warm nights erased temporarily the horrors of 1968. Only April Rosemary seemed quiet and not quite present.

"Something wrong, kid?"

"It's all so happy"—she burst into tears—"and I'll miss it so much!"

"Boston is only two hours away from Chicago, dear."

"I know . . . Now it seems like two million miles away."

I hugged her and we cried together.

There was one last disaster—Richard Nixon won the election by less than 1 percent of the vote. The media folks insisted that the election had been lost in Chicago in August. In a way they were right. Humphrey's campaign lagged badly through September and early October because the big money people in the Democratic party believed the media story. Then in the middle of October as Hubert soared in the polls, they had second thoughts and began to contribute—just a little too late. The real experts agreed that if the election had been in the middle of November instead of the beginning, Hubert might have pulled off the biggest upset since Harry Truman. I hope Walker Cronkite et al were happy.

There was, however, a more basic reason why Humphrey lost—the war. Nixon announced that he had a "plan" for ending the war. Americans were so desperate to end the mess that many of them believed him. In fact, he was lying as he did on so many other occasions before it all caught up with him.

Hubert's people told him in early September that his only hope was to firmly disown the war. They drafted a speech which, while respectful of the good intentions of the administration, made it clear that he would end it as soon as he was elected. He liked the speech. He said he had to show it to Johnson first. Lyndon tore the hide off him. Nothing was ever heard again about the speech. Humphrey would go to his grave knowing that if he had delivered the speech he would have been elected. Lyndon had won the final round with the rest of us. His war went on and became Nixon's war. More than twenty-five thousand more Americans would die, to say nothing of the hundreds of thousands of Vietnamese.

Why did Hubert lose?

The Mayor was not talking Malaprop when he said that Mr. Humphrey lost because he didn't get enough votes. He should have . . .

Several months after the election, Chuck showed me a clipping that he had carefully underlined.

⚜

DOVES SUPPORT DALEY, MICHIGAN STUDY SAYS

According to a report by the University of Michigan's National Election Study, the majority of American voters who wanted immediate withdrawal from Vietnam approved of the way Chicago's Mayor responded to the convention riots in Chicago last August. Forty percent of the Doves, those who wanted immediate withdrawal, approved of the amount of force the Chicago police used, twenty perent more of them said that the Chicago police had not used enough force.

So the media had deceived itself. The public, even the antiwar public, did not accept their interpretation. Funny thing—Walter Cronkite never mentioned that finding on his program.

We encountered the Mayor later in the winter at a political party. He shook hands with us vigorously and asked how our health was. I assured him that it was fine, given the fact that he had not passed an ordinance against winter weather.

"Heh, heh," he said. "That's a good idea . . . I want to thank you for standing by us in that time of trouble."

After our magical Labor Day weekend was over, we settled down to the demands of the school year and autumn. We drove April Rosemary to her Radcliffe dorms in Cambridge. The place looked like an Ivy League school is supposed to look. The preppies had been replaced, however, by hippies. Our daughter was a very unhappy-looking young woman when we prepared to leave.

"It's up to you, kid," I said, when we were saying good-bye. "We can turn around and all three of us drive back to Chicago."

She shook her head. "No, Mom. I'm not a quitter . . . Daddy, happy fortieth birthday. I'm sorry I won't be there for the party."

After we had picked our way through the traffic mess of Boston and eased onto the Interstate, I said to Chuck, "I'm not sure that this is a good idea."

"I'm not either, Rosemarie . . . What can we do? I'm sure we couldn't talk her out of it. We could refuse to pay the bills. She'd rebel against that."

"I don't want to do that," I admitted. "Did you notice that before the cops broke up our little party in Gene McCarthy's offices, she told her friends how proud she was that we had marched with Martin at Selma?"

"You bet I did."

"She's so young, Chuck, so young."

Chuck's birthday on September 17 was an uproariously funny event as always, songs and stories and jokes and even impromptu dances by Moire, who had started to "take" Irish step dancing. Chuck reacted bravely to the critical turning point in his life. However, he seemed quite satisfied with his life so far.

"All I ever wanted to be," he told us, "was an accountant, a quiet man with a good, steady, conservative job. The monstrous regiment of women, as John Knox called them, in my life, that is my mother, my sister, and my wife, ordained otherwise. So here I am, a harmless little fellow with a camera permanently attached to my hand. I want to take a picture now of that monstrous regiment giving me my orders!"

It was a great party, as all the O'Malley family parties are. We all missed our eldest, who had never been missing before. We now knew how important she was to the family.

At Christmas, the week of our nineteenth wedding anniversary, as improbable as that seemed, she was with us, but not really with us. She seemed distant, preoccupied, unhappy. Her preliminary grades were terrible. She solemnly promised that she would have passing grades in all her subjects by the end of the year.

"We don't care about the grades, April Rosemary," I said to her. "We care only about your being happy."

"I care about them," she said grimly.

"You do any photography?" Chuck asked her.

"Right now that seems silly," she said.

When she kissed us good-bye at O'Hare, there was a certain air of grim finality about.

I worried. So did my poor husband who, poor man, has fewer ways to express his worry.

We had, it would turn out, a lot to worry about.

In early February of 1969, Chuck was invited to the White House to do a formal picture of the new President. Neither of us wanted to do it. We did not like the man one bit. On the other hand Chuck had done portraits of three presidents in a row and hated to break the string. After all, he was our President, like it or not.

Nixon had been courting many of the old Kennedy

friends, perhaps thinking he could win them over. His proposed domestic policies were radical for a Republican. He'd brought Pat Moynihan into the White House to be his principal domestic adviser.

So we flew to Washington and were picked up by a Secret Service limo. Pat Moynihan was there to greet us and create out of whole cloth, so to speak, the social niceties. I had the impression that both the President and his wife looked to Pat as to a tutor as to how a president should act.

Nixon seemed a genial and gracious man and welcomed us warmly, as did his wife. Both were quite nervous in our presence. As if the little redhead punk from the West Side of Chicago was armed and dangerous.

"The only trouble with him," I later told Chuck, "is that his smiles don't match what he says and his gestures are either one sentence ahead or two behind."

"He's not a disturbed man like LBJ was. He's disturbed in his own unique and special way. How do we ever get these losers as presidents?"

We could not have anticipated then what a loser he was.

The shoot was difficult because the President had a hard time sitting still and being quiet. He wanted to talk about Whittier College in California. Southwest Texas State Teachers College and Whittier College! We knew how to pick them, didn't we?

Chucky's philosophy of portraits is that they are supposed to be honest but not insulting. You don't try to make the subject someone he's not, but you also want to present him as the best of him is. With Tricky Dicky that was tricky. We ended up with a portrait of a man who was very smart and very determined. Others would come to see Tricky Dicky in the portrait. However, they were reading that into the picture. Both the President and the First Lady loved it.

"What's going to happen?" we asked Pat later in his tiny cubicle in the basement of the West Wing as we drank tea.

"I think you'll be surprised on how liberal he will be on domestic issues. He really would like to bring Americans together. I wish he and the men around him were not so defensive and suspicious."

"Paranoid?" I asked.

"Ah, Rosemarie, you speak with the Irishwoman's instinct for the honest word!"

"And the war?" I asked.

"That's Henry's domain . . . Henry Kissinger. Just now our policy on the war is very intricate, very complex, and very *Mittel* European. They both want the war to end. Neither wants to compromise American prestige, as though it were not already compromised beyond repair."

"He seems a bit odd," Chuck observed.

"It is worth remembering that Henry does not lie because it is in his interest to lie but because it is in his nature to lie."

With that happy thought we drove back to National Airport in a Secret Service car and took the shuttle up to Boston. We drove over to Cambridge in a Hertz car to visit our daughter. She did not seem particularly happy to see us.

"How could you take that awful man's picture?" she began.

"He's our President," Chuck told her, "the President of all of us."

"He's not my President," she insisted.

"Spoken like a true Democrat," I said.

She didn't laugh at that. Indeed she didn't laugh much at all.

She was thin, pale, and tired. She wore a sweatshirt and jeans and no makeup, not that she ever used or needed much. Her studies were very hard, she admitted, much harder than at Trinity, though she had to admit that the education she had received at her high school was better than that which most of the other Harvard students had received.

"They're very smart," she said, "and they talk big, but most of them are phonies. It's taken me a while to figure that out."

"So you're as smart as they are?" I asked cautiously.

"Smarter actually"—she laughed mirthlessly—"not that it makes any difference. It's all a silly competitive game around here."

She mellowed a little as the day wore on, mostly because of Chuck's funny stories about the band and about Moire, who wanted to be a member and was permitted to clang the tympani triangle.

"Kevin still have the hots for Maria What's Her Name?"

"I think," Chuck said smoothly, "that he still has a certain romantic attraction toward her, a very discreet one."

"She's sweet." My daughter frowned. "Probably too good for bro."

Then she laughed, the first and only laugh of the visit. By the time we left for an evening flight back to O'Hare, she actually hugged and kissed us affectionately.

"She doesn't like it there," Chuck said to me on the plane. "She's going to prove to herself that she can do it, then she'll come home."

"It's a lot more complicated than that," I said.

"How do you know?"

"Womanly instincts."

"I know better than to disagree with those."

"There's trouble brewing, Chucky, terrible trouble."

I didn't know the half of it.

❧ 24 ❧

Dear Mom and Dad,

I am writing to tell you that I passed all my courses as I promised I would. It doesn't make any difference to me whether I pass or fail because studies are irrelevant. But I know it matters to you that your investment wasn't wasted. So I hope that makes you happy.

I am not returning to Harvard. It too is totally irrelevant. I can't imagine a place more irrelevant. I hate it. I will never return here.

I am also leaving your family. I know this will hurt you and I'm sorry for that. I must live my own life and find my true self. I cannot do that as part of your family. I would like to be able to say I'm grateful to you for all you've given me, but I'm really not grateful at all. You have made me a spoiled irrelevant young woman. You have cheated me of the opportunity to discover who I really am. You have made me a silly, adolescent child.

I know you did not intend to do that. You are part of the capitalist system that makes us all what we are, a system of greed and exploitation and injustice. I can't forgive you for raising me in the same system. I do not however blame you for it.

I hate your family environment. While you sing and dance and carouse and enjoy your two beautiful homes and your fine cars, young men and women my age are suffering all over the world, including this country. You must know this is true, yet you say nothing about them. Young Viet-namese boys are dying at this very moment because of your capitalist greed. Young black men and women are suffering from genocide while you have your silly parties. The whole world is dying from hunger and starvation while you sing your silly songs. How can you possibly be innocent of all these crimes?

How can you spend so much time in the voyeuristic en-tertainment of photography which violates the privacy of people and exploits their poverty and suffering. I have given away all my equipment. I never want to take an-other photograph again.

I have little hope that you will ever change. That is why I have to disown you. I must break away completely from the capitalist greed and oppression in which I was raised. I do not know what will happen to me. I'm not sure I can ever become authentic or ever find my true self. I must try, however.

I ask you to let everyone in the family read this letter. I am disowning them too. I never want to see any of them again. I never want to see you again.

I will disappear from your lives. Do not search for me. Treat me as though I were dead. You may try to hunt me down with capitalist police. Believe me if you do I will simply disappear again. To try to find me will be a waste of time.

I do not want to rot in your capitalist slime ever again. I will not.

The one you call April which is no longer my real name.

PS You may collect my things—despised remnants of a life I'm giving up—at my residence hall. They will tell you where they are. Do whatever you want with them. Burn them! I don't care.

I brought the letter down to the darkroom, where Chuck was working on his *1968* exhibit and gave it to him.

He read it carefully and then read it again. He slumped into a chair.

"I knew we shouldn't have sent her there," I wailed. "I tried to tell you that and you wouldn't listen."

He glanced at me, trying to read my mood.

"It won't help, Rosemarie, if we become angry at one another."

"Did you ever hear such nonsense in all your life! Who has filled her innocent little head with such shit! It's your fault!"

"Didn't we hear the same thing from some of our young teachers at THE University. We just laughed at them."

"Times were different then."

"She is different from us," he said slowly.

"That's no excuse."

I was losing it. I knew I was. I wanted to calm down. I tried. I couldn't quite make it. I would struggle with this conflict for many years. I tried to be reasonable on the subject of the disappearance of my first child. Often I could be reasonable. Other times I could not.

"This is a lot of bullshit"—he gestured at the

letter—"that she absorbed from some idiot of an instructor."

"What does that have to do with it? We've lost her."

"For a while, Rosemarie, only for a while. She'll be back."

"She'll never come home, never."

I realized even then that my anger was aimed at my daughter. Since she wasn't there, I turned it on my poor husband. I must stop this, I told myself, I must stop it or I'll lose him too.

"I think she will," he said. "She'll be back."

"What are we supposed to do? Just sit around and wait for her?"

"The first thing to do is to drive down to Boston, collect her belongings, and see if we can learn anything about what happened."

"I will NOT go to that place ever again!"

"All right, I will."

"I don't think we should show this to the other kids or the rest of our family."

I was trying to make him fight with me. He wouldn't do it. Not ever.

"How can we not show it to the kids or tell the rest of the family? They won't understand what's happening if we don't?"

"Well, I won't show it to them!"

Which was a lie. I could hardly wait to share the letter with Peg.

"Not till after Kevin's graduation anyway."

"Do whatever you want."

Chuck drove down to Harvard by himself, leaving me to do all the work for Kevin's graduation from Fenwick.

"Where is Sis?" Kevin asked one day. "Shouldn't she be coming home about now?"

"She's not coming home!"

"Huh?"

"She has disowned us because we're materialists. She never wants to see us again."

He shook his head sadly. "Sounds like Sis . . . Poor kid, she goes off on idealistic tangents because she hasn't developed enough common sense yet."

That was as perceptive an analysis as we would ever have—not that Kevin would display much common sense either.

"She never wants to see us again."

"She won't be able to make it stick. She'll be back just like she never left."

"That's what your father says."

"Yeah, well Dad is usually right."

I could not dispute the truth of that assertion. So I ignored it.

"She wants us to read her letter to all of you. We were planning on doing it after graduation."

"No way! She can't make us listen to her crap and we won't do it! To hell with her!"

"Kevin! She's your sister!"

"And I love her. No way I have to listen to her bitchy crap. Forget about reading it to us. I'll tell Seano and Jimmy."

That was a great relief. My cavalry son did not tolerate crap gladly.

There was still poor little Moire.

"April Rosemary isn't coming home this summer, honey. She thinks she needs some time off from our family."

My youngest accepted my announcement with little surprise.

"Well, Mommy, maybe we need some time off from her too."

"We'll miss her a lot."

"Maybe she'll stop being bossy when she comes back. You know, Mommy, she doesn't act like a real grown-up."

That settled that.

"The little bitch," Peg said when she had read the letter. "The stupid selfish little bitch. She'll regret this letter for a long time."

"Chuck thinks she'll come back eventually."

"Of course she will. She can't survive without her family . . . It may take a while."

"I don't care if she ever comes back."

"Yes you do . . . How's Chuck taking it?"

"You know what he's like. All calm and reasonable, figure out what happened before we try to find her."

"That's how he would be. He is a man after all. He's hurting too, Rosie. Don't blame him."

"He should never have let her go to Harvard. That was a terrible mistake."

My best friend through the years looked at me for a moment as she contemplated what to say next.

"Don't take out your grief on him, Rosie. Don't, whatever you do, let it ruin your marriage."

It was a solemn warning. She was right. I had been acting like an idiot.

"I can't believe she'd be so cruel," I said, and deteriorated into tears.

"Carlotta says that April Rosemary has kind of freaked out. She uses a lot of pot, some LSD. That is probably part of the problem."

"A drug addict! Dear God in heaven!"

"Not an addict exactly. Not yet. A lot of kids their age are into drugs but they never quite become addicts because they're too well stitched together."

"Her mother was an addict," I said, close to tears.

"A long time ago . . ."

"She was old enough to know. She had to be a little mother for the other kids."

"A completely different situation, Rosie. Don't blame yourself. That won't help anybody . . ."

Solid sensible advice with a lot of warm support. What good were advice and support when you have lost forever the first child you carried in your womb?

Dr. Panglossa, my lovely mother-in-law, as always viewed the incident benignly.

"Poor dear little April Rosemary." She sighed. "She just needs some time off from the family. She'll be all right I'm sure."

"How can you be so confident, April?"

"Well, dear, everyone loves her so much that she'll just have to come back."

"What if something happens to her?"

"We'll have to pray to God that nothing does."

The trouble with the good April's Panglossa was that she was so often right. That was no consolation to me in my pain and rage.

"You blame yourself for this letter?" Maggie Ward raised one of her damn eyebrows at me.

"Did I say that?"

"Not in so many words."

"I suppose I do," I admitted

"So you take out your anger on your poor husband?"

"If you say so . . ."

"I don't say so. I'm asking what you say."

"Sure, I blame him. He's there."

"Not a good idea for the marriage."

"No," I admitted. "Yet Harvard *was* his idea, not mine."

"Come now, I think we both know better than that. It is absurd to blame the school. She probably fell under the influence of some overpowering instructor who exploited her naïve idealism. That's no one's fault except his. She could have encountered the same kind of person at Notre Dame these days."

That was certainly true, even if I didn't want to admit it.

"Maybe," I replied.

"You are hurt because of what she has done as any parent would be when a child writes a foolish letter.

That's understandable. You must grieve . . ."

"As though she were dead?"

"As though she was accurate when she said you would never see her again. Do not postpone the grief."

"Everyone says she will come back eventually."

"That is a reasonable expectation. I would not be surprised if she did. Nonetheless, you must work through the grief of the present moment as if she will not return. Otherwise, it will poison your life and your marriage."

"I resist that."

"Resist it all you want. It's still true."

"Yes, I guess it is."

"Your real anger is at yourself because she may have inherited your addiction tendencies?"

"Yes," I said sorrowfully.

"You brought those tendencies under control long ago. The dominant example for your daughter was of a woman who beat addiction."

"Maybe it's in the genes."

"For which you are not personally responsible."

"I know . . ."

"Many young people who use drugs today don't come from addictive backgrounds."

"I know . . ."

"Moreover, all the explanations for drug usage are multivariate, a combination of many different variables. April Rosemary uses drugs because she freely decided to use them."

"Will she ever be able to freely decide to stop?"

Dr. Ward hesitated.

"Given her family background, her intelligence, and her character, I would think there's a good chance of that. But, Rosemarie, don't count on it."

"Tough words."

"I know that. You are suffering terrible pain. It will not go away immediately. You will have to live with it. Gradually it will diminish. There will always be a residue of pain in your life, the sort you are not unfamiliar with from your own family experiences ..."

"Can I handle this?"

"Certainly you can ... Should your daughter return to your family the same person that she was only wiser and more experienced, that must be a wonderful surprise."

I understand.

I did understand. I was one very tough, strong-willed woman. I had survived. I would continue to survive.

No easy way out, Clancy. There never has been for you and never will be.

So when Chuck returned from Cambridge, morose and beat, I apologized.

"Chuck, I was a terrible bitch. I'm sorry. You've put up with a lot from me through the years. You always forgive me. I hope you'll forgive me this time."

Pretty stiff and formal, huh? That was the best I could do. Besides, I knew how my husband would react.

With his wide grin, which took in all the world and the whole solar system.

"Have I ever complained, Rosemarie?"

"No ..."

He put his arm around my shoulders.

"This is a hellish experience. We'll survive it and be better for having survived. We may fight sometimes about what to do. But we won't blame each other ever again. Okay?"

"Okay," I agreed.

I meant that when I said it. I tried my best to keep my promise. Usually I did. However, guilt and anger are as persistent as they are pernicious. They did slip back into my soul through the back door and cause me and Chuck many serious problems.

That day, however, I told myself firmly that he was suffering as much as I was.

"What should we do with her trunk?" he asked.

My answer, inspired by Kevin's attitude, was, I think, brilliant.

"Nothing! Nothing at all! We'll just leave it in the storeroom downstairs. If she ever comes home, she can open it herself. I don't want to give her the satisfaction of hurting us more."

Chuck nodded. "Good idea."

"What did you learn in Cambridge?"

"The dean at Radcliffe was no help at all. She knew that April was under stress, but she had no idea that she was leaving school or cutting her relationship with her family. She gave me the impression that she couldn't care less."

"Ugh, secular nun!"

"Not all nuns would react that way . . . Anyway, I found some students who were more open. April was very popular, they said. Fun and funny. She took the school too seriously, however. Should have been able to beat Harvard without any trouble at all. Wouldn't admit it to herself. Worried about everything. Eventually stopped being funny and had no fun at all. Brightest kid we knew. Really had trouble with this Professor Agostino. Sociologist who's hung around here for years. Hasn't finished his dissertation. Pretends to be one of the kids, though he's at least thirty. Gets off on attacking rich kids or kids he thinks are rich. His family has plenty of money. Corrupt slime of American capitalism, that kind of stuff. No socialist country would tolerate him. Harvard dumped him this year. He got to Rosemarie. I don't know why. Last person in the world you'd expect to be guilty about being upper middle class. Some kids say her idealism was really deep. He exploited it. No romantic involvement, I believe. He's still hanging around acting like the asshole he is. 'I was astonished when

April told me that she wasn't coming back. She never said she intended to disappear. We'll really miss her.' "

"Dear God in heaven . . . Such a strange story."

"We raised her to be an idealist, Rosemarie. She happened to be in the wrong place at the wrong time. Lots of reason to be hurt, no reason to be angry at anyone, not even at the poor kid herself."

"I hate to admit it, Charles Cronin O'Malley, but you're probably right."

I told him that all the kids knew. Family too. He smiled slightly, as if he were not surprised. I told him also that at Kevin's suggestion we would not read the letter to the others.

"Kevin has grown up with common sense." He smiled.

We would have reason to doubt that too in the years ahead.

The two of us went over to St. Ursula, to our court of last resort, John Raven, the young assistant at the parish when we were growing up and now the white-haired but always youthful pastor.

He read April Rosemary's letter with an expression of increasing pain on his red face.

"The poor kid!" he exclaimed.

No sympathy for us, but lots of it for the little brat.

"Oh?" I said with a note of disapproval in my voice.

"It must have broken her heart to have to write this letter."

"Huh?" Chuck said. "What do you mean?"

"Look, guys, you're the gifted firstborn of a West Side Irish Catholic liberal family which has inculcated more by example than by word, a powerful idealism. Your idealism, naïve and inexperienced, turns against the way your family lives. You can only be true to your ideals if you break with them and find out who you are. What else could she have done?"

"Talked to us?" I asked. "Come home and have it out about the way we live?"

"Wouldn't work. Because she loves you so much and you have so much influence on her life, she knows she'd lose the argument. She has to find out for herself."

"Will she find out who she is?" Chuck demanded.

"If she does"—John Raven glanced at the letter again—"she will discover that she is the very gifted daughter of a West Side Irish Catholic slightly zany liberal family."

"What are the chances of that, John?"

"I don't know, Rosemarie. She's a smart kid. Clearly she saw through Harvard. I wouldn't write off the possibility she will. Then she will return as if she'd never gone away."

"I can't see that happening," I said. "She cut her ties too completely."

"Had to if she was going to find out who her true self is."

"Maggie Ward says that we must assume that we will never see her again and work through our grief."

"Heaven forbid that I should seem to be in disagreement with that good witch of the west. She's right of course. However, another part of you should always be ready for surprise. That's how God wants us to live."

"All right," Chuck interrupted, "I see your point. She's out in the world by herself trying to find an identity. What if she becomes a druggy in the process?"

"I have enough confidence in her intelligence and strength to bet that, while she may experiment with drugs, she'll never completely succumb to that culture."

"She's an innocent," I protested.

"A tough innocent."

"She hurt us terribly, John."

"I know that, Rosemarie. She doesn't realize how much. When she does sorrow and guilt will over-whelm her . . . Are you two ready to forgive her?"

"Damn you, John Raven," I snapped, "for demand-ing that we be Christians when we don't want to . . . We've forgiven her already, haven't we, Chucky?"

"That's what Christians do, isn't it?"

"Do you think we ought to try to hunt for her?" I asked. "Hire a private eye to find out where she is . . ."

"I don't know about that, Rosemarie. If you do find out, leave her alone. The more you push, the less likely the story is to have a happy ending."

"Why, John, why?"

"The times, Rosie, the times! Three years ago she would have gone to Africa with the Peace Corps, three years from now she would be in South America with the Jesuit volunteers. These are terrible times to grow up."

We talked about it as we walked back to our house.

"What do you think, Chuck?"

"I agree with John Raven. We should leave her alone."

"Couldn't we at least know where she is and what she's doing without interfering in her life?"

"Do you think if we find out where she is we can then leave her alone?"

"We'll have to, won't we?"

"I hope so. John is right. If we push her too hard, we might destroy whatever little hope we might have."

"She's not John's daughter."

"Do I get veto power about what we do if we find her?"

"We're in this together, Chuck. I don't want to push her. I just want to be in the background if she needs us."

"And wants us?"

"And wants us."

So it was agreed. We hired a top-flight agency to see what they could learn. Initially they found no trace of her. It was as if my firstborn child had disappeared from the face of the earth.

Nonetheless we made Kevin's graduation from Fenwick a glorious event. The band played with the good April on the piano, Maria Elena as the lead singer, and myself as the backup. We bought out all the ice cream at Petersen's. Chuck and I did our expanding repertory of musicals. Peg, now concertmaster of the West Suburban Symphony played a Vivaldi sonatina. We all sang the night away. Kevin would stay home with us and commute downtown to DePaul, where he would study composition and the trumpet, a surprising admission that someone could teach him anything about that instrument. Maria Elena had already started voice lessons there.

With the boys working in Chicago, we drove back and forth from the Lake often because we thought that Moire was entitled to her summers at the Lake too.

Toward the end of the summer there was a rock festival in Woodstock, New York, to which a hundred thousand kids, it was claimed, flocked. For that generation it was a landmark event. For those of us who were in earlier or later generations it was a disgusting orgy. Despite all the peace symbols that were displayed, politics hardly mattered. Rock and roll really didn't mean peace; it meant sex and drugs. Despite TV commentaries marveling at the vigor of this "historic" new youth movement, clips showed half-dressed young men and women cavorting around with pot in their mouths and booze in their hands. Their bodies were painted wild colors, their hair was long, they bragged that since they were being "natural" they did not have to worry about the shortage of toilet facilities. The men looked like hairy satyrs frolicking around a Renaissance painting, the women were, it seemed to me, less happy in their role of endlessly violated virgins. One news program allowed a dissent from its wild-eyed enthusiasm. A boy, as satyrlike as the rest, told the camera, "This is a freak show here. Everyone is zonked out on LSD. I came here to listen to music not to fry my brains."

Our April Rosemary couldn't be there, I told myself.

The next night our man landed on the moon. All of us cheered at our house at the Lake as mankind took that one step, though I could not for the life of me understand what was the point in going to the moon. Because it was there, maybe. I did cheer with the rest of them.

"How can we land on the moon and not be able to end a war?" Jimmy asked.

"Landing on the moon is easy, Jim," my husband replied. "It requires good logistics and lift power. Ending a war requires wisdom."

The week after at our routine lunch, Peg said, with some hesitation, "I think there's been a sighting, Rosie."

"Woodstock?"

"I'm afraid so . . . Do you want the details?"

"No, don't tell me . . . Yes, I want to know."

"Some of Carlotta's friends from Rosary College went down there. They report that it was like totally gross. However, they claim to have seen April Rosemary."

"In what condition?"

Peg drew a deep breath.

"Totally naked, her body painted red, zonked out on LSD, cavorting around with a crowd of naked boys."

"I suppose we might have expected that," I said, too angry to weep. "It's a wonderful way of finding out who you are."

I told Chuck when I came home from lunch. He put his face in his hands and wept.

1970–71

❧ ❧

❧ 25 ❧

Nineteen sixty-nine turned into 1970. The war went on. Nixon and Kissinger talked and negotiated and lied to us. The Vietnamese knew they had won and were not prepared to deal with us. Boys kept dying.

One of the boys who died was Maria Elena's brother Batiste—twenty years old. We went to the funeral at St. Francis of Assisi down on Twelfth Street. We expected an emotional funeral—public grief, weeping and wailing and hysteria. Instead the Lopezes were grim and restrained, even more controlled in their sorrow than we Irish are. Thus for our stereotypes.

Nixon went to China and made some sort of peace with Chairman Mao, not enough for the Chinese to lean on their allies to end the war. Why should they? What was the payoff in it for them? Still it was a major diplomatic victory because we had detached the Chinese from the Russians. Big deal, I thought, when boys like Batiste have to die in a foolish war.

Chucky and I began to drift apart. At first neither one of us noticed. It was a slow, gradual, and pernicious drift. He was wrapped up in his *1968—Year of Violence* exhibit, which he now planned to be his biggest and best. When you're forty, you want to do something really big. Worry about my children pre-

occupied me. I was still writing my secret stories—
with the door closed to my "study" so no one would
know what I was doing.

There were fewer conversations between us and
fewer fights too. We didn't laugh together much anymore. We made love less frequently, which ought to
have been a signal. We didn't want to see it. I stopped
seeing Maggie Ward and joined one of the first
"consciousness-raising" groups in our neighborhood.
Most of the women were the wives of doctors who
resented their inferior status as "doctor's wife." They
wanted to be their own person, just like April Rosemary, to have an identity of their own. They hated
their husbands, who did indeed sound like arrogant
insensitive fools. Bitter words at the group's meetings
were a substitute for telling them off. The women
agreed that "doctor" would not hear what they were
saying.

I figured that my relationship with my husband was
different. Chuck was not an insensitive jerk. Yet my
identity was clearly "Ambassador O'Malley's wife."
No one ignored me, not twice anyway. But I was not
doing anything that would give me a special identity
distinct from my husband. I was writing and polishing, rewriting and polishing my stories. However, no
one knew about that. Why I wondered at first did
these women need to have careers of their own? Had
they not willingly submerged themselves in their husbands' careers? Was it not unfair to blame "doctor"
for their own decisions?

Still, Betty Friedan had written her book *The Fem-
inine Mystique* and the feminist movement was taking
shape all around us. I agreed with most of their goals.
Chuck probably did too if he noticed the emerging
movement. We didn't discuss it. However, I didn't
hate men. Or so I told myself.

There were more sightings of our daughter. Someone thought they had seen her on the beach at La Jolla

with the surfing crowd. Better that than Woodstock.
Jimmy, who went to one of the many antiwar marches
in Washington, was positive he had seen her from a
distance.

"What did she look like, Jimmy?" I asked him, my
stomach turning with fear.

"She looked like Sis, except she was wearing old
clothes. When she saw me, she ran away in the crowd.
So I was certain it was her."

"Was she on drugs?"

"Didn't seem like it. I think she's okay."

The Harvard girl we had talked to called us to say
that some of her friends had seen her in a drug commune in Vermont.

Our private eyes checked out these stories. They
were unable to find her, though it did appear that she
had been in the drug commune for a while.

The "Red Army" faction of the "Weathermen" faction of the SDS came to Chicago for their "Days of
Rage" demonstration, which was supposed to be a
repeat of the battle in front of the Conrad Hilton.
However, few Chicago kids joined them and the police were paragons of restraint.

Hundreds of them in motorcycle helmets and with
clubs in their hands swarmed up Michigan Avenue
and into the Gold Coast. They smashed store windows, attacked doormen in elegant apartment buildings, stopped autos, pulled out passengers and beat
them, and shouted, "Ho, Ho, Ho Chi Minh!"

The Governor sent in two thousand National
Guardsmen. After a couple of days the Weathermen
had either been arrested or left town.

It's hard to know what they were up to. Did they really think they could launch a revolution in Chicago?
Or were they symbolically attacking their parents in
the Gold Coast. It was an era of demonstrations for
their own sake, "liturgical protest" Father Dan Berrigan called them.

I absolutely forbade my husband from rushing downtown and photographing this nonsense.

"Those kids are killers, Chuck. You're the ideal target, an old white male."

He didn't give me much of an argument. He'd done enough scenes of violence.

We were both worried that April Rosemary might be among them—which is really why Chuck wanted to photograph the melee. Peg asked Vince, who was still working for the Mayor, to find out anything he could about her.

"None of them have ever heard of her, Rosie," he said, with a shrug of his shoulders.

Sometimes I thought I saw her in TV clips among the protesters in one march or another. Chuck would get the tapes, which we would watch carefully. It was evident that she was not in the crowd, though I refused to admit it to him.

Then in the spring of 1970 Nixon and Kissinger decided it was time to invade Cambodia and set loose the furies which would lead to the genocide in which several million people were slaughtered by the Communists. The campuses of America blew up in protest. At Kent State University in Ohio, nervous National Guard kids opened fire on protesters and killed seven of them. Then the campuses really went crazy.

"It used to be panty raids in spring," my husband mused. "Then there was streaking naked across campus. Now it's protests. Anything but study for exams."

"People don't get killed in panty raids," I snapped.

"Yeah," he said glumly.

Students and faculty went on strike at many schools. They demanded a "moratorium" on classes in October so that they could campaign for a "peace Congress" in the November elections.

"Strange kind of strike," Chuck commented. "Teachers get paid and students get final grades. Can't beat it."

I ignored him as I usually did in those days.

Vince confided to us that the Mayor was hoping the colleges in the Chicago area would approve the moratorium.

"Look," Chuck protested, "the current Senator from Illinois is Ralph Tyler Smith who was appointed to fill the place of the late Senator Everett McKinley Dirksen when he went to his reward. Senator Smith is a Republican and wears electric green suits. Against him we are running no less a person than Adlai E. Stevenson III, who is as lazy as Gene McCarthy but who has a great name and is against the war. He is, as they say, an odds-on favorite to win. You turn posses of hippie kids loose on the electorate and they'll vote for Ralph Tyler Smith."

"Oh, the kids won't campaign."

"What will they do?"

"Play basketball and drink booze. What else do kids do when they don't have to go school?"

"Then why let them loose on the grounds that they will campaign against the war."

"Otherwise," Vince said, "they might burn down the schools."

Vince's cynical prediction was accurate. Once again I understood that it doesn't take many people to create a riot or a protest march or even a Woodstock. Most of the other kids hated the war and experimented a little with drugs. Otherwise, they weren't much different from previous generations, my own included.

While Peg and I had always been best friends, we rarely discussed my marriage as best friends usually do. My husband was her beloved brother. I could hardly talk about him with her. She could tell when things were good and when they were bad and would occasionally make a very general comment.

Like "Tough times with Chuck these days."

To which I would reply, "You know how he can be, Peg."

She would nod solemnly, though I don't think she knew at all. So she would worry about me. It was nice to have someone worry about you.

I attacked him now at the consciousness-raising meetings. He was an arrogant jerk who thought he was funny. He did not care about my career. I was merely a useful adjunct to his work. I kept the books, paid the bills, helped in his lab, and received no credit for any of those things.

Deep down I knew this was unfair. Looking back at those times, I understand that rage at poor Chuck had become a kind of substitute for drinking. Oddly enough, or perhaps not so oddly, I was never tempted to turn to booze in those awful times. I could kill myself with that stuff, just as my poor mother had.

Then Kevin came home from school one day, gathered the two of us together in the kitchen, and told us that he was giving up his draft deferment.

"I don't believe in the war," he said, "yet I know that it's not fair that guys from poor families have to fight it and I don't. It's part of the experience of my generation. I have to do it."

My heart stopped beating. Why did all my kids have to be idealists?

"Batiste's death?" Chuck whispered.

"I've been thinking about it all winter. I made up my mind at his funeral. As you can imagine, Maria Elena does not want me to go."

So formal, so carefully rehearsed.

"No woman ever does," I said softly.

"Is there any way we can talk you out of it?" Chuck asked.

I wanted to strangle him for being so calm and rational about it.

"No, Dad, there isn't. I've made up my mind. I

know that you and Mom will be unhappy about it, especially with Sis on her hiatus. I can't do anything else. Besides, Sis will be home soon, I'm sure of that."

Two children lost to the damn war.

"Mom?" He turned to me.

What was I supposed to say?

"I don't want you to go, Kevin," I said slowly, feeling my way, "but I respect your integrity and maturity. If you feel that's your duty, I'm not going to throw myself on the floor at the doorway and make you walk over me."

We all laughed, somewhat hollowly.

Dear God in heaven, you made me say that. You made me sound heroic. I don't feel that way at all.

We had our usual family party for him at the Lake before he left for Fort Benning. Like all our parties it was a jolly, madcap affair. The Crazy O'Malleys were still crazy, even if their hearts were breaking. Maria Elena, now a senior at Providence High School, watched Kevin's every move with sad, adoring eyes.

Without Kevin to pull it together the jazz band fell apart that summer. After basic training they sent him to Officers' Candidate School, waiving the requirement that he should be a college graduate because he was so intelligent. Lt. Kevin Clancy O'Malley, combat infantryman.

"Ranks me," Chuck said stupidly.

"Second Lieutenants in the infantry have the highest casualty rate," I said reprovingly.

"I know that, Rosemarie. I know that."

"Then why didn't you stop him?"

"Do you think I could have stopped him?"

"No."

My heart was a lump of lead, beating only under protest. I tried to write a story about losing a son to the war. I couldn't put words on paper after the first couple of paragraphs.

We had another family party at the end of the summer (I invited Maria Elena and she accepted, as if she already considered herself a member of the family). This one to send Jimmy off to St. John's University in Collegeville, Minnesota, on a basketball scholarship.

"I thought they played only hockey up there in the polar regions," Chuck said.

"It's a great Benedictine cultural center," the new collegian said proudly.

"We may have told you that on occasion," Chuck replied.

We had always said that St. John's was one of the bastions of our kind of Catholicism.

"No way," Jimmy argued. "I'd remember."

It was good that he didn't remember. If he had, he might have rejected the school out of hand.

"Don't anyone worry about me," he added. "I'm going to stay in school till the war is over."

Somehow I felt secure about Jimmy, safe in a monastery.

Our house was almost empty, only two kids left, Seano would leave the following year, perhaps for St. John's too, and ten-year-old Moire—or Moire Peg as she now wanted to be called—who was turning into a young beauty.

Her baptismal name was Mary Margaret, after her aunt who was Margaret Mary. Moire is Irish for Mary and is properly pronounced (not by us) as Mary. Soon she decided that she wanted alliteration (she didn't call it that) so she became Moire Meg.

"Poor little Moire," the good April observed, "is developing into quite the darling little character, isn't she?"

"Little character anyway," I agreed, fearful that the last of our children had to be a character to gain any attention at all in our family. Had I failed her too?

"Kids all gone," Missus said sadly. "No need Missus anymore?"

"We'll always need you, Missus," I said firmly, guilty that I had perhaps neglected this wonderful woman.

"Not enough work. No mess."

"You come three days a week now and we'll pay you for five anyway."

"Not fair."

"Is fair."

"Hokay. Is fair."

A Weathermen bomb factory blew up in New York. Those who live by the bomb will die by the bomb. I was convinced that April Rosemary was one of the unidentified female bodies found in the ruins of the brownstone house. I insisted that Chuck send her dental records to the New York police.

"I don't think she was there, Rosemarie."

"I don't give a damn what you think! Send the dental records!"

"Making bombs isn't her style."

"Renouncing her family isn't her style either . . . Send the goddamn records."

So he did. The New York police thanked us when they returned the records. Our daughter was not one of the victims of the blast.

The next sighting was in Boston. Back in Harvard country again? A couple of guys from Harvard who had known and apparently admired her reported that they'd seen her in an Irish housing project in South Boston.

"I didn't know there were Irish projects," I said to my husband.

"Neither did I . . . What were the Harvard kids doing there?"

"Working in some kind of settlement house. They were sure they saw her coming out of a bar. They tried to find her later but couldn't track her down.

They say they're still looking. One of the kids told me they admired her gumption and honesty in class."

"Sounds like our daughter," I admitted.

Another one of our goddamn idealists.

The kids promised they would keep looking. Our detectives said they could not "verify" the report.

It was suddenly 1971. I was forty years old. Life had happened so quickly. You marry, you have kids, you struggle through their early years, you worry about them as teens, you watch their first tentative steps toward love, you celebrate their graduations and then, just as they seem to become semiadults with whom you can talk as a fellow semiadult, they disappear. You grow old so quickly.

I absolutely forbade a party. I didn't want to celebrate getting old and I didn't want to celebrate when two of my children could not come to the party.

That was mean and selfish of me. Worse, I knew it when I was doing it. I am, after all, an O'Malley not only by marriage but by early childhood association. I would say that I ought to have known better except I did know better.

There were some gray strands in my hair. I could still fit into my clothes because of my exercise routine, which was necessary anyway for letting off steam. However, I felt old.

There were also touches of white in Chuck's hair about which I did not kid him since we didn't kid anymore.

His exhibit *1968—Year of Violence* opened at the Art Institute and then was going to travel to New York and Washington and Boston. There was the usual gala opening with black tie dinners. I wore a strapless gown—blue and white (blessed mother colors in honor of the Beatles song "Mother Mary")—just to show people I could do it. I was convinced that everyone was dismissing me as "oh, that's his wife. I hear she's very difficult to live with."

The reviews were ecstatic. "Major Contribution to the New Photography." (Whatever the hell that was.) "O'Malley's work of genius." "After twenty years of brilliant contributions to American photography, O'Malley has established himself in the very top ranks." "There can be no doubt after his dazzling and powerful re-creation of that troubled year that Charles Cronin O'Malley is a master of photographic history. His oeuvre is a profound memorial of our times." And that last from the *New York Times*—which made it officially true!

The *Boston Globe* observed, "Clearly a number of people wanted to inflict severe physical harm on Mr. O'Malley during 1968. A sensible person would have run. A courageous photographer would hold his ground and fire away with his camera. Mr. O'Malley chose the latter course, which will surprise no one. Yet one feels the need to say, 'Chuck, already all right enough. Keep out of those tight spots in the years ahead. We need you.' "

Amen to that!

I was not such a bitch that I resented his success. After all, I had driven him into his art, had I not? Even if I wasn't getting credit for any of it, I was proud of him. Yet I felt sorry for myself. I had sacrificed my career for his.

What career? Singing? I still did funerals and weddings and an occasional recital, though no recitals in recent years. Sometimes, before Kevin left, I had sung with the band. I didn't have the voice of a great concert singer or even of a jazz singer like Maria Elena.

Obviously my writing career. I was too busy being the wife of a great man to pursue that career.

Was this bullshit? Sure it was. I half knew that it was, but that half wasn't operating.

Finally, my self-pity reached its limit. I blew up at him, poor man.

I stormed into his workshop next to the darkroom and dumped on the table all the bills for the opening of the Exhibition.

"I'm sick and tired of being your servant," I screamed. "Pay your own goddamn bills!"

He was startled. He should not have been. He must have known that an explosion was coming.

"If that's what you want, Rosemarie," he said guardedly, his eyes trying to figure out quickly what was going on so he could respond.

We had been through this a long time ago when I had retired for the first time as his factotum. Maybe he thought the same thing was happening now. Well, if he did, he was wrong.

"I'm fucking tired of being the woman at whom people point and say, oh yes that's his wife. I want to be my own woman from now on."

A direct quote from my daughter. Wisely he refrained from pointing that out.

"I've never heard anyone say that," he said cautiously. "The adjectives beautiful and gifted are usually added."

"I am sick of that goddamn horseshit. I've sacrificed everything for your goddamn career and I have nothing to show for my work. I want to be someone else besides just your wife."

He might have asked if I still wanted to be his wife. He didn't however.

"Have I ever interfered with your singing? If I did, I'm sorry . . . I didn't realize it!"

"Fuck the singing."

I note in my own defense that I almost never talk that way, not when I'm sober and I was sober then.

"I see . . . What do you want to be?"

"A writer, that's what I want to be!"

His face lit up in a smile.

"How wonderful! I think you'll be a great writer! What can I do to help?"

Clever comeback, Chucky, but that's not nearly enough.

"How can I be a writer when I have to spend all my time on this shit!"

I gestured at the bills and realized that I was raging beyond all sense. I had been writing secretly for years.

"Spend all the time you want on your writing. I'll do whatever I can to help!"

So generous, so reasonable, so besides the point.

"Goddamn you! You're not listening to what I'm saying!"

I stormed out of the workroom in full fury.

Back in my study I broke down and wept. Somehow everything was going wrong. What was I supposed to do next?

I could go on with the battle and ruin what was left of our marriage and family life.

Or . . .

Or what?

Pick up the phone and call Maggie Ward, the smart little bitch.

❦ 26 ❧

"There's one area of possible exploitation by your husband that you apparently did not mention with your consciousness-raising group," she said softly. "That puzzles me."

She seemed unperturbed by my long absence. She did not raise an eyebrow at the mention of consciousness-raising. She expressed no surprise at my account of the deterioration of our marriage.

"What's that?"

"You didn't seem to think that his use of you as a model, often clothed just within the limits of modesty, was exploitive."

"I don't think it was!"

"Many feminists would have thought it was. I'm sure the women in your group would have said so."

"I didn't think the pictures were dirty!"

"So I understand, but it would seem to me that if you were determined to awaken your husband to his lack of concern about your independent identity, you would have used that as prime proof. He subjected your body to his artistic vision."

Good point.

"It just didn't occur to me."

"Did he resist your announced intention to pursue a literary career?"

"No."

"Did he warn you that it might very well be an unsuccessful pursuit?"

"Uh, no, he didn't."

"How then did he react?"

"As though any success I had as a writer would redound to his fame."

"Did he say that?"

"Not exactly."

"Ah, what did he say?"

"That he'd support me in any way he could," I admitted reluctantly.

"That made you even more angry?"

"Yes."

"Why?"

"Because he wasn't listening to what I really meant."

"And what did you really mean?"

"Uh, well . . ."

"That you felt worthless?"

That was unfair. How dare she say that.

"Yes."

"That your life had always been worthless?"

"All right."

"Tell me, Rosemarie, let us suppose you had published four or five novels and a successful book of short stories, would you not still feel worthless?"

Tears formed in my eyes. I fought them back.

"I suppose so."

"Only then your husband would not have been such a convenient target?"

"I would have blamed him anyway," I admitted honestly.

"I see . . . Could you have found the time to write during the last twenty years of your marriage?"

"Yes, if I worked hard at it."

"But you didn't?"

"Oh, no," I said, realizing that the game was up. "I've actually written some."

"How many?" she demanded implacably.

"I donno . . ."

"Five?"

"A little more than that."

"Rosemarie, I will not tolerate this game playing!"

"Shrinks shouldn't say things like that."

"I just said it."

"Well . . . maybe between twenty or thirty . . . maybe closer to thirty."

For the first time in our relationship, Maggie Ward permitted herself to look astonished.

"And who has read them?"

"No one."

She was backing me into the corner. I was scared of the corner but willing, indeed eager, to be backed into it.

"And who knows about them?"

"No one . . . Well, you do now . . ."

"And you blamed your husband for inhibiting your career as a writer, although you have secretly written thirty stories?"

"Uh-huh."

"Wasn't that terribly unfair?"

"Uh-huh."

"Why did you not show him any of your stories?"

"Maybe he would have made fun of them."

"Has he ever made fun of anything serious you've done?"

"He wouldn't dare!"

"You nonetheless think he would have ridiculed your stories?"

"He might have."

"Rosemarie!"

"If they were weak, he would have said so very gently and if they were any good at all, I'd be like a female James Joyce."

"Aha!"

"I thought they were probably worthless."

"Like you yourself are?"

"Kind of . . ."

"You didn't want to expose one more aspect of your worthlessness?"

"I suppose . . ."

"And you've been willing to risk your marriage to hide that worthlessness?"

"Kind of . . ."

I hadn't looked at it that way. Pretty dumb, huh?

"Kind of?"

"I was trying to blame Chucky for my fears."

"Rosemarie, you are paying a heavy price for clinging to this low self-esteem, despite the fact that you know it's wrong."

"I don't know it's wrong!"

"Come on! At the opening of Chuck's exhibit you wore a daring dress that only a woman who knows she's beautiful would wear!"

"How do you know what I wore?"

"In addition to seeing the picture in the papers and on television, I was there. Remember?"

"Spying on me."

"Do you think your stories are any good?"

"How would I know? A lot of them are humorous. I think they're pretty funny . . . Oh, all right, I'll say what you want me to say . . ."

"I only want you to tell me what you think is the truth."

"Uh . . . Well, I think they're great, but I'm the author . . ."

"Rosemarie, this nonsense has to stop. I understand its origin in your childhood experience. However, at this stage in your life, you clearly know who and what you are. What is the cost of abandoning your old self-concept?"

"Then I'd be free!"

"And that is terrifying!"

"Yeah."

"It's almost time, Rosemarie. I insist you show your husband all the stories."

"NO!"

"That is an order! You will go home and do it, understand?"

"Shrinks don't give orders!"

"This one does and has, especially when she knows the client came here today to get that order!"

Bitch, bitch, bitch.

I went home, took all my stories out of the locked cabinet in my study and went down to Chuck's workshop, where he was reading a German economic journal, and dropped the whole untidy mess on his desk.

"Read these," I said.

He looked up, confused. "What are they, Rosemarie?"

"My stories."

"The one's you haven't been able to write?"

"Yeah . . . Maggie Ward said I should show them to you."

"Did she now?" A faint grin appeared on his leprechaun face.

"She did. Read them today. Now. I want your honest opinion. No bullshit, understand?"

He leafed through a few pages.

"I promise that I will be dispassionate and objective."

"You'd better be. If you think they're not much good I want to know it. I'm no James Joyce."

"No reason you should be."

He turned aside from his journal and began to read the stories. I escaped as quickly as I could and fled back to my ornate study with its red silk walls and thick drapes and oak furniture. I tried to begin another story, one about a husband telling his wife that her work was worthless. I couldn't get beyond the first paragraphs of pain.

"Goddamn it, Chuck," I cried. "They're not worthless!"

I made myself a pot of tea and drank it all. I thought I might take a shower. However, he might come to my study looking for me and not find me there.

We had a dinner date at the Conways' that night. Why doesn't he hurry up?'

Finally, there was knock on the door of the study, a shy tentative knock. I knew him well enough not to trust Chucky Ducky when he was shy and tentative.

"Come in, damn it!"

He peeked in, like he was making sure I wouldn't throw something at him. He looked very satisfied with himself.

"Well," he began as he put the pile on my desk, "I've read them all."

The pile had been transformed. Compulsive neatnik that he is, Chuck had placed each story in a separate folder with the title neatly printed on the cover and then arranged all the folders in a loose-leaf notebook.

"I note with interest that many of the stories are about a marriage."

Damn him, why was he grinning that way? He knows I find him irresistible when he grins that way.

"Yes," I said carefully.

"I personally find the husband a rather charming person. He's a dull oaf, I admit, stupid, unperceptive, and obsessed with sex. Yet I quite agree with the wife that he's not without his appealing aspects."

"It's not you!" I shouted.

"Rosemarie, the hell it isn't!"

"Well, he wins most of the time."

"Only because his wife makes him win."

He was grinning broadly, delighted to have found

me out. Maggie, drat her, would insist that all along I wanted him to find me out.

"That's what happens in most marriages . . . I'm just using the particular to rise to the general . . ."

"And while no unseemly details are provided, it is broadly hinted that he is not without skills in bed."

"He does improve over time," I conceded.

"He seems quite harmless as a lover, doesn't he?"

"He's obsessed with it."

"In her own, uh, modest way, she is too. Arguably more so."

"It's supposed to be comedy."

"Oddly, Rosemarie, I did comprehend that."

"You haven't told me what you think of them."

"Oh, I thought I had . . . Well"—he opened to the first story and hesitated—"you know, Rosemarie my darling, why do I have the sense that another story is already taking shape in your agile imagination?"

Oh, damn. He'd be watching me for the rest of our marriage, looking for hints that I'd be taking mental notes.

"Get on with it, Chuck! Are they publishable?"

"Oh, is that the question?" he feigned surprise. "I thought the answer to that was obvious."

He fingered the pages of the top story again, as if weighing the proper answer.

"Well, the first three are in their present highly polished condition sure *New Yorker* material. That doesn't mean they'll publish them because they are a persnickity lot . . . You would need an experienced and influential agent . . . The rest of the stories are also brilliant light but telling comedy. In short, Rosemarie my darling, you've got it."

"I don't know any agents," I grumbled, thinking to myself I would surely be ravaged before the day was over, which wouldn't be all bad.

"If you wouldn't accuse me of interfering in my

wife's career because I wanted to claim credit for it, I might be able to find one such . . ."

"Damn it, Chuck, don't be an asshole all the time."

"Well, then I'll make a few phone calls."

"Thank you," I said. It was time I changed modes. I should stop pretending to be angry, like the idiot girl in the stories often did to cover up her fear.

"Sometimes that woman is an awful idiot," I observed, trying to change the mood. "I don't know why he puts up with her."

"Possibly"—Chucky sighed—"because he's hopelessly in love with her. Implacably in love. He could never not love her . . . Something like God loves us."

"Possibly," I said, averting my eyes so I wouldn't lose all control and break down completely.

"You are not fair, Rosemarie," he said, suddenly very serious.

"I know I'm not, Chuck. I know I'm not. I'm so sorry."

The waterworks behind my eyes opened. I began to sob, this time great, heaving sobs of pain and guilt, real guilt not neurotic guilt.

"And?" he said, kneeling besides me, his arm around my shoulders.

"And?" I gasped.

"What comes after contrition?"

"A firm purpose of amendment?"

"Uh-huh."

"Chucky, my love, I promise I'll never do it again . . . Well not more than once a week."

Then we both laughed and wept together.

Then I added the magic words that I had wanted to say for twenty-one years.

"Chucky Ducky, my magical darling, I surrender."

This would, I reflected, make a great story for the series.

Then he slipped his hand inside my blouse and tickled me.

"Chucky," I cried, "you know what that does to me!"

Quickly his fingers ignited my body chemistry. The chemicals had been dormant for a long time.

He kept right on with his deadly work.

"We're going to the Conways' for dinner." I sighed.

"And I'll take every opportunity this evening to tickle you some more," he warned.

"I'm not a sex object for male fantasy," I protested with a patent lack of sincerity.

"You're not a sex object. You're Rosemarie my pride with whom I'm about to have a second honeymoon right here at home. You said you'd surrendered."

"Third," I said, like the woman in the stories always correcting. "The second was after I gave up drinking."

As we walked through the soft spring air to the Conways', Chuck said, "So the gypsy woman was right."

"What gypsy woman?"

"The one in Dad's painting. The one who told your mother that she would have a daughter who would be a very great woman. Those stories are the frosting on the cake."

"I'd forgotten about that prophecy."

"No one else has."

This was my fourth second chance. I'd better not let it slip through my fingers. God would certainly not give me a fifth. Well, maybe he would.

I'm afraid I was incoherent at the dinner party. My poor body, denied what it wanted for so long, was punishing me by rampaging out of control.

However, I did manage to accomplish one important goal of my life.

"If any of you guys want to have a surprise fortieth birthday party for me," I said to Peg, who was also at the dinner, "I wouldn't mind, just so long as you tell me the date."

My best friend, whom I rarely surprised, was astonished. "Rosie, you said you didn't want a party."

"I changed my mind," I said imperiously.

They all laughed.

Our love that night was like that when Chuck came home from 'Nam—gentle, healing, and like rich dark chocolate. We ritually enacted my total surrender to implacable love which would never, never let me go.

In the early phases—I still had my panties on—I looked into the eyes of my lover and saw there for the first time what I had always refused to see before. He loved me as a beautiful woman. He had always loved me that way. I was in truth beautiful—I twisted in an agony of pleasure at that idea. If I took care of myself, I would always in some way be beautiful.

Maggie Ward, I thought just before I stopped thinking about anything, had been right all along.

1972–1974

❦ 27 ❧

Kevin's letters from 'Nam were always funny. He wrote about the inconveniences of military life, the different men in his platoon, the sickness of life in Saigon, the fun he had in teaching Vietnamese kids how to play basketball, the irony that the American involvement in the war would end in 1973 (as everyone was predicting) just when it was time for him to come home.

There was never any hint of either fear or danger.

Maria Elena and I compared notes on our letters. She would graduate from high school in the spring of 1972 and go on to DePaul. I sensed that she had become more confident and more mature in the last three years and that her heart ached as much as mine, no, more than mine, for Kevin. He was the love of her life. Dear God, I prayed, protect them both. They're so young.

Seano also was rewarded with a basketball scholarship to St. John's. He hesitated about taking it.

"I know Jimmy likes the place," he said. "He's half a monk anyway. I don't know whether I belong in a monastery."

"It's up to you, Sean," I said. "Thanks be to God, we can afford to send you anywhere you want."

"Well, that's probably not fair either . . . I'll give it

a try. Kev says we can win their championship and start a jazz band too."

"Can one do jazz in that cold a climate?" Chuck asked.

"Dad," said my third son, "you can do jazz in any climate, so long as you have soul."

"I'll have the house all to myself," crowed twelve-year-old Moire Meg. "No more messy boys around."

"Except Daddy," I corrected her.

"Mo-THER, you know that Daddy isn't messy at all."

Politics that year were enough to make my husband and I want to vomit. The various "movements" had captured control of the Democratic party. Politicians were being replaced by "the people."

"So long as," my husband said, "they are people with a Ph.D."

A committee headed by George McGovern had introduced "reforms" into the Democratic party which would put it in a wilderness for a long time. The idea of the "reforms" was "balance." Blacks, minorities, young people, women, and gays were to be represented at the convention in their exact proportion in the population. Delegations which did not honor this rule could be challenged before the credentials committee.

The media kept telling the world that this was the most "balanced" convention ever, another "historic first." Professional politicians, party hacks, and their backroom deals were forever banished. The party no longer needed the kind of delegates who had nominated Franklin Roosevelt, Harry Truman, Adlai Stevenson, John Kennedy, and Hubert Humphrey. Rather they needed the kind of balanced delegates with Ph.Ds from Harvard who would nominate a sure loser like George McGovern.

As for smoke-filled rooms, that hateful and mean Frank Mankiewicz engineered a deal by which the credentials committee rejected a duly elected Illinois delegation headed by Mayor Daley for a self-selected delegation elected at caucuses by so-called "activists and reformers" who displayed the required "balance." Mayor Daley, the commentators said gleefully, was being punished for the police riots in Chicago.

Somehow, there was no room for George Meany either. The labor bosses were a burden to the party as well as the urban machine bosses. The Democrats no longer needed them because they had the minorities, and the women, and the gays, and the young.

Chuck turned off the television in disgust.

"Just an accident that they're both Irish Catholics," he snorted.

"Honey," I said, "who needs Irish Catholics when you have the gays and the young?"

McGovern himself knew better. He chose a Catholic senator from Missouri as his vice president, said he was a "thousand percent" behind him when it was reported that the poor man had undergone some psychotherapy, and then dumped him for Sarge Shriver, a Kennedy in-law.

It didn't do any good. The President's campaign was a carefully orchestrated triumphal procession. No one realized at the time that dirty tricksters from CREP (the Committee to Reelect the President) were breaking into Democratic headquarters in the Watergate complex.

My renewed love affair with my husband continued unabated. We had a huge party to celebrate the publication of my first story. Kevin would be home soon. Who cared about politics anyway? Camelot was dead and buried long ago.

April Rosemary? Although, she was still a dull ache in my soul, I was resigned to the likelihood that I would never see her again.

It was evident that McGovern might carry Massachusetts and nothing else. The columnists who had celebrated the "balance" at the convention, hoped without much confidence that, as one *New York Times* guy put it, the "legions of the young" would turn out for Mc-Govern and spoil the predictions of all the polls.

We went to the polling place and with heavy hearts voted the straight Democratic ticket, like we always did.

The "legions" of the young did not turn out and those that did, like everyone else, voted for Richard Nixon. The "young" in the balance crowd at the convention turned out to represent no one but themselves.

Chuck had put away his cameras. The 1968 show was enough for a while, he said. There was nothing left to photograph. An occasional portrait maybe and a lecture somewhere, though not at Catholic colleges who were afraid of their bishops.

Well, he took some pictures of me, which I felt were really soft-core porn—forty-year old woman as Playboy Bunny.

That's completely untrue. They were in fact wonderful pictures of a woman whose beauty turned out to be durable. I had to say something didn't I?

The week after Nixon's triumph two officers in Army dress blue uniforms rang the front doorbell. As soon as I opened the door I knew why they were there. Kevin was dead.

I resolved that I would not, repeat not, break down. The task of these two men, one of them a chaplain (Southern Baptist) and the other a captain was a difficult one. I would not make it any more difficult for them.

"Come in, gentlemen," I said. "I think I know why you're here."

I served them tea. They informed me that our son Kevin Clancy O'Malley had been killed in action in Vietnam. The captain told me that Kevin had died fighting for America and freedom. The chaplain told me that Jesus would make him lie down in green pastures. I readily agreed with both comments, though

I didn't believe the first and thought that the green pastures damn well better have a lake and a beach.

The body would be returned to America for burial, if we wished, at Arlington National Cemetery. We didn't wish. He would be buried in the family plot at Queen of Heaven Cemetery in Hillside. Would we like a military burial—taps, a fourteen-gun salute. I thought not. If we did, I could call them at the number on a card they had given me. They presented me with a flag for the burial ceremony.

Chuck found me later sitting on the couch, the cold teapot next to me, the flag in my lap. I could not move, could not think, could not feel. He glanced at the flag the two men had brought for Kevin's burial, sat down next to me, and put his arms around my shoulders. Then we both wept bitter tears.

We were also notified by the Defense Department that he had been recommended posthumously for the Distinguished Service Cross.

Big deal.

Those were terrible days. I felt that my heart had been cut out. I wished that I was the one who had died. I lost faith in God, but I couldn't sustain that for long. I tried to hate Lyndon Johnson, but that wouldn't do any good either.

I was, for public purposes, a brave and resilient mother. I had to hold the family together, protect my husband from despair, assuage the grief of my surviving children, console poor devastated Maria Elena.

That's what brave Irishwomen did, wasn't it?

I wondered if April Rosemary knew.

How could she?

While we were waiting for the return of Kevin's body, Monsignor Raven presided over a memorial Mass at St. Ursula's. The new funeral ceremonies were like an Easter Festival. O death where is thy victory, O death where is thy sting! John preached a beautiful homily about idealism and heroism.

Chuck's cameras never came out of their cases.

No body, however, appeared.

Chuck called the Department of the Army. An indifferent bureaucrat assured us that the "process was under way" and would be carried out.

After two weeks, he called the President. He was put right through to the President, who remembered him very clearly. Naturally I was listening on another phone.

"Best picture anyone has ever taken of me. How's your beautiful wife?"

"Not very well at the moment, Mr. President. Our son was killed in Vietnam. The Army seems to have misplaced his body."

"Dear God, how terrible. My sympathies to you. I'm so sorry. I really am. I wish I could . . . Anyway I will call the Secretary of the Army personally and ask him to be in touch with you."

"Thank you very much, Mr. President. Congratulations on your victory."

"Thank you very much, Chuck. I'm looking forward to four more years of service to the country."

"He was very nice," I said.

"Yes, he was." I felt guilty for all the terrible things I've said about him.

However, the Secretary of the Army did not call that day. The next day, while Chuck was out, a Colonel called from the Department of the Army.

"Mrs. O'Malley, I'm calling you with reference to your son, First Lieutenant Kevin Clancy O'Malley."

"Yes, sir."

"We have no record of the death of Lieutenant O'Malley. Obviously, then, there is no body to be delivered to you."

"I have right here in my own hand a copy of the notification that he was killed in action."

"No, ma'am, we have no record of sending such a notification."

"But I have it!"

"You can't possibly have it, ma'am. We never sent it."

"And another notification that he was awarded posthumously the Distinguished Service Cross."

"We show no communication with reference to First Lieutenant Kevin Clancy O'Malley. I'm very sorry."

"I'm his mother," I screamed. "I brought his body into the world and I want it back."

"We cannot provide any information about his body."

I hung up.

I was hysterical when Chuck came home.

He said some very bad words and then grabbed the phone.

"Pat, Chuck O'Malley here. I need a favor."

I was listening on the other line.

"You got it, Chuck," Moynihan replied in the best Chicago political fashion.

Chuck spilled out the story.

"Oh, damn, damn, damn! Those idiots. As the war runs down, they have lost their ability to cope with casualties. I'm sure the President did his best. I'll be back to you."

He called us at midnight.

I answered being the lighter sleeper.

"O'Malley residence."

"That you, Rosemarie?"

He sounded very tired.

"Yes . . . let me wake Chuck up."

I jabbed him and he grabbed the phone.

"I've some very good news for you . . ."

"You found his body!"

"Much better than that. I found him. He's alive. Wounded in action. I'm afraid he lost a foot to a land mine. He's very much alive and is being flown back to this country for further medical treatment at Great

Lakes. And they did award him the Distinguished Service Cross. The Secretary of the Army apologizes both for the mistake and the behavior of the idiot who called you."

"Alive!" I said in disbelief.

"Are you sure?" Chuck gasped.

"Quite sure. I didn't call you till I had checked all along the line. He's alive and, please God, he'll lead a long and happy life."

"Is this a dream, Pat?" I said between sobs.

"It's the wide-awake world, Rosemarie. I think the O'Malley clan had better prepare itself for one of its legendary parties."

"They reported me missing in action when I was over there," Chuck said.

"The wish in your case, Ambassador O'Malley being, as my wife would say, the father of the thought. Come visit us in India and teach me how to be a diplomat."

He said we would. That's another story.

Before anyone else I phoned Maria Elena.

Several anxious and excited days later the three of us waited in the drab lounge of the Great Lakes Hospital, where families met with maimed young men. Maria Elena was already weeping. Indeed she had been weeping tears in which sadness and joy mingled in equal parts since I had called her that night. I was my usual, calm, self-possessed self that I always am under pressure. Chuck was grim-faced and angry, still seething at the mess the Army had made of Kevin's story.

"They did the same to you," I had told him.

"That was the Navy and I wasn't really missing."

I was so happy that my son was still alive, I couldn't be angry at anyone.

"Will he still love me?" Maria Elena wondered. "After what he's been through?"

"Wanna bet?" I replied.

She giggled.

Then, after a long purgatory of waiting in which the medical profession seems to specialize, a nurse appeared helping a young man on crutches.

"Kev," I gasped.

He looked awful—thin, worn, tired, as he hobbled toward us, in a medical gown and a dark blue robe. However, his cavalryman grin, appropriate now because he had been in the First Cavalry Division (which hadn't seen horses in forty years), lit up the whole lounge.

"Hi, Mom, Dad, who's the mysterious woman you brought along?"

The nurse arranged him on a chair.

I motioned to Maria Elena that she had first claim on a kiss. She leaned over her lover and kissed him with sweet and gentle love to which he responded in kind. Now I was crying. There were even tears in the great photographer's eyes.

"Thank God you're home," I whispered as I kissed him.

"You bet!" he said genially. "God really had to work on this one."

Chuck hugged him.

"Well done, Lieutenant," he said.

"Carry on, Sergeant." Kevin laughed.

Our wounded son was in a better mood than we were.

"What's a foot?" he said. "I have another, don't I? When they fix me up, I'll be just fine. No basketball, but I can still shoot around and water-ski and maybe snow ski. I don't think this gorgeous woman will mind my hobbling around a bit. I'm lucky to be alive."

"I don't mind at all," she said, kneeling on the floor next to him and pressing his hand to her lips.

"Can you tell us what happened?" I asked.

"Sure, I was dumb. Remember, Mom, how often you told me to look where I was going?"

I didn't remember saying that at all.

"Well, this time I didn't look but bumped up against a mine. Fortunately for me it was mostly a dud, so I'm still alive and all right."

"They reported that you were dead," Chuck said, "and that they were sending your body home. We even had a memorial mass!"

"A story to be told for the rest of my life! I hope the guys did a little New Orleans funeral music."

"They did indeed; it was all very sad."

"Did Sis show up for it?"

"No, dear, but then she had no way of knowing . . ."

"Well, she'll be back eventually."

"And the DSC?" Chuck asked, still the military man, albeit a quirky and critical one.

Kevin sobered up.

"Well, there's two versions of that. The first is that Captain O'Malley . . . yeah, Dad, they gave me a second bar, but Gramps still ranks me . . . took command of his augmented platoon when its commanding officer had been killed, repulsed a concentrated enemy attack, and then led his men through the jungle for two days to return to their base with no further casualties. Often he exposed himself to enemy fire to facilitate the orderly redeployment of his command."

"Sounds impressive," Chuck nodded. "And the other version?"

"I'm not sure how much of that the Army knows or wants to know. They gave me the medal, I think, in hopes I wouldn't tell the whole story. There's no point in doing that now anyway."

"Army foul-up?"

"Incredible! Our platoons are understrength in country because we're withdrawing now pretty quickly. Some of them are down to fifteen, twenty men. They combine them so they have enough guys to send out on combat patrols."

"Why dear?" I asked. "Aren't we about to leave?"

"Because some of the commanders still want to make a name for themselves. All they know is combat patrols. Anyway, this group of ours is a mixed bag of misfits and malcontents and guys hoping and praying that they get home alive. No one wants to fight. No one wants to find Charlie. No one wants to be a hero—except the Captain who is in command of the enhanced platoon. He's jerk, a psychopath who believes we have to fight the enemy till the bitter end. That's taking a chance out there these days because it can get a guy fragged—blown up by a hand grenade throw by one of his own men.

"Anyway, we're picking our way through the jungle on this hot, steamy day, hoping that Charlie has enough sense not to be looking for any action. Well, we're wrong. Suddenly there's small-arms fire in front of us and on our right. Charlie isn't shooting very well, so he doesn't hit any of us. Then he stops, leaving the next move to us, since he can see us and we can't see him. Our Captain gets the bright idea that we should attack. Charge them, drive them out into the open, and kill them.

"He gives the order to charge. There are two really bad guys in the unit. Spent time in the stockade outside of Saigon. They've been looking for trouble ever since they joined our outfit.

" 'Let's get the hell out of here,' one of them yells.

" 'Kill the officers and run,' the other shouts as he throws a grenade at the Captain. He dissolves in the blast, poor guy.

"The first guy aims his weapon at me. I shoot him with my M-1 before he can fire. Pure instinct and luck because I'm not much of a shot. The other guy fires a round over my head. A big, black Master Sergeant, from my own outfit, kills him before he gets a chance to fire a second round.

" 'Thank you, Sarge,' I say.

" 'Don't mention it, sir,' he says. 'Now get us the hell out of here.'

"You see with my guys I have this reputation for being the best redeployment officer in the Army. That Kevin, they say, he's a real wily snake when it comes to retreating. Runs away quicker and slicker than anyone else."

Chuck interrupts, "Not an unimportant skill, Captain."

"Probably inherited," Kevin says with a big laugh. "So we redeployed, slipped out even though we were apparently surrounded. Charlie is shooting at each other after a while."

Phil Sheridan didn't retreat in the Shenandoah, but that's all right. Different war.

"Apparently we foiled a major ambush on a whole regiment from our division, which was retreating behind us. Maybe Charlie didn't know the war was over. The rest of the story is true. I stepped on the mine outside our base, one of our own probably."

He told the story with professional ease. I wondered if the images would haunt him for the rest of his life.

"Bad place," Chuck said.

"Terrible. Worse than I expected. Worse than most people know. Damn stupid war, Dad, just like you said. A lot of good men killed over nothing."

"No regrets?" I asked.

"You mean about going? No, I figured it was the thing to do. I made it home alive, which is more than a lot of them did. I'm glad it's over."

No foolish claim that the war had made a man out of him.

Suddenly I laughed. "Runs away quicker and slicker than anyone else!"

We all laughed.

"I figure," Kev said, serious for a moment, "that maybe I saved a couple of hundred guys' lives be-

cause I was so good at getting the hell out of messes.
Maybe that's why God wanted me over there."

Damned idealist.

"What's next, Captain?" Chuck asked.

"School, Sarge, doctorate in musicology, I think.
Teach, compose, perform. I'll get money from the
government for the rest of my life. I guess Mom has
taken pretty good care of me too. Do a little jazz too,
maybe duo if I can find a woman who will do Latin
blues with me on the trumpet. You know, Billy and
Pops sort of thing?"

"I don't know where you can find someone like
that," Maria Elena said with a laugh.

"Dear God," he sighed with relief. "Am I glad to
be home."

He was home with us for the Christmas of 1972,
the best we had in a long time. The band played
again, complete with Grams on the piano and Mom
backing up the Latin blues with wordless improvs.
God forgive me for it, but I hardly thought about
April Rosemary.

"Wedding before 1973 is over," Chuck said that
night as we were getting ready for bed.

"I sure hope so," I agreed.

Maria Elena confided in me that Kev was talking
to a psychiatrist because of his terrible dreams.

"He'll be all right, Rosie, won't he?"

"Sure he will . . . I'm glad to hear he is talking to
someone."

The major political event of the year was the beginning of the Watergate revelations. At first it
seemed unlikely that the President knew about the
Watergate break-in, a minor and foolish dirty trick.
Then as the story grew, it began to look like he had
bungled the minor event into a major crime.

In a way I felt sorry for him. He was not quite the
kind you'd expect to find in a Greek tragedy. He had
given the enemies he so feared the tools they needed

to destroy him. Yet he had opened the door to China, signed the Environmental Protection Act, founded the National Endowment for the Humanities, forced integration on primary schools, and in many other ways followed the liberal agenda. Like LBJ he let his tragic flaw destroy him.

Chuck and I continued our rituals of mutual surrender. Our love prospered through the year. He was much more relaxed with me, so much so that I finally noticed how careful and cautious he had been through twenty-three years of marriage. What a nebbish I had been.

I felt guilty at that until Maggie said, "So, Rosemarie, now you have another guilt?"

I was improving at shooting down the guilt raiders as they flew by.

"Big change between you and Chuck?" Peg said at our usual lunch.

"Oh?"

"Everyone notices it."

"Oh?"

"There's some debate as to who has changed."

"You should be able to answer that one."

"It wasn't Chuck."

I sighed.

"Poor dear man, he has the patience of a saint."

Then I broke all the rules and told her about dark chocolate love.

She actually blushed, something that Peg rarely does, and rolled her eyes.

"We'll have to try it."

Several weeks later, she ended a phone conversation with the comment, "I like dark chocolate too."

A veteran of the *Vinceremos* Brigade, a band of young American radicals who went off to Cuba to help Castro harvest his sugar crop reported in an article in *The Nation* that one of her co-workers was

April O'Malley, the estranged daughter of famous photographer Charles X O'Malley (sic).

No more details.

We tried to check the story, but could find no confirmation.

Then she had been seen back in Boston working in a photography lab at Boston University. However, the university had never heard of her.

The last American combat troops were withdrawn from Vietnam that year and the prisoners of war came home, eight years after the war began and five years after Chuck and the other senior advisors told LBJ that the war could not be won. It dragged on two more years with the ARVN doing the fighting until the NVA overwhelmed them. The United States made an undignified exit from the roof of its Embassy, leaving thousands of its employees and allies behind. We had not preserved our credibility.

The return of the prisoners was not much help to Richard Nixon during the long death agony of his administration, which would drag on to the summer of 1974.

Chuck commuted back and forth to Washington to take pictures at the committee hearings of Nixon's people—Dean, Mitchell, Ehrlichman, Haldeman, Colson, Hunt, the whole scurvy crowd. It was frightening that such a group of incompetents could flood the West Wing, though our Ivy League friends were hardly more effective once they lost their President.

Chuck portrayed Nixon's cohorts compassionately— men frightened despite their bravado, vulnerable, hunted. He called the series *Cornered.*

"They're people like us," he said. "Way out of their depth, caught in a quagmire of their own making and struggling hopelessly to get out. They're entitled to some compassion."

"Like all crooks," I said, thinking of my father.

"It was hard with John Mitchell," he said of the Attorney General. "Not much to sympathize with there."

"Except the meal the media are making of his poor alcoholic wife."

We celebrated our twenty-third wedding anniversary at St. Francis of Assisi Church on Roosevelt Road at the first wedding of our family. With John Raven and Luis Ramirez presiding, Kevin Clancy O'Malley and Maria Elena Lopez were joined in Holy Matrimony. Kevin's two brothers and his suddenly gorgeous sister and Maria Elena's brother and two sisters joined in the wedding party. Moire Meg was content for the day to be beautiful and left her "Craziest of the O'Malleys" persona at home. Thank God. Kevin walked down the aisle without a trace of a limp.

A Mexican mariachi band played at the reception in an American Legion Hall. The jazz group, however, did a few numbers. Without the good April, for whom there was no piano, but with Kevin's mother.

"They are so young," Maria Gloria, the bride's mother, whispered in my ear.

"I was the same age when I married Chuck."

"My dear," she replied with an impish grin, "I thought you were much younger."

"Things were different then," I said lamely.

"I think I like these Mexican weddings better than our Irish weddings," my husband informed me.

"How so?"

"No drunks."

"I remember a guy who was drunk before he left the wedding dinner."

"No statute of limitations?"

"Course not!"

The rehearsal dinner the night before at the Country Club went off smoothly enough, despite the hostile glares from some of the locals. The Lopez family either did not notice the glares or were too classy to pay any attention. A jerk made a nasty comment to Chuck as we were leaving after dinner. My husband would have slugged him if I had not dragged him away.

Chuck's prediction of a wedding before the year was out had been right only by a few days.

The summer of 1974 was the best in a long time. Our children went back and forth from the city to the Lake, except for Moire Meg, who refused to go into the city no matter what pretext was offered.

"Rosie," she said to me, "this commuting stuff is totally gross."

She also denounced my propensity to arrive at the house and then promptly drive over to the mall to shop as "vulgar."

Somehow we survived the energy crisis created by the Arabs to punish us for the victory of Israel in the Yom Kippur War the year before and aggravated by American government policy.

Chuck and I devoured books and argued about them. He denounced David Halberstam's *The Best and the Brightest* about the Vietnam War because Halberstam never acknowledged that he and most of the journalistic establishment had at first supported it. I told him that the author's analysis was no different from his own. He thought that *Gravity's Rainbow* was unintelligible and refused to finish it. I argued that Thomas Pynchon was one of the great novelists of our time, which I really didn't believe.

We both hated *Last Tango in Paris* because it made sex dull and loved Bergman's *Smiles of a Summer Night*, because it brought back memories of our own youthful summers at the Lake.

Maria Elena told me that she was pregnant, which was hardly a surprise.

"If the child is a boy, we will call him Kevin, of course. If we have a girl, she will be Maria Rosa after her wonderful grandmother, who has been so good to me since the first day we met."

We hugged and cried together, of course.

I remember the awkward but very lovely fourteen-year-old who sang in our parlor only a few years ago. She looked the same but somehow had transformed herself into a poised and sophisticated wife and expectant mother. Not for nothing was I the daughter of a trader; I knew a good future when I saw it.

"If you can't beat 'em, join 'em," I sobbed to Maria Elena.

We both cried some more.

The family watched the endgame of the administration—the pained face of Peter Rodino as he called the roll for the impeachment vote in the House Committee and the pall of sadness with which the votes were cast. No one was happy that night, except for the fanatic Nixon haters around the country. We saw the anguished conversation between Alexander Haig and Mike Wallace the night before Nixon resigned. We marveled at the veneer of bluster with which the President protected his disgrace in his final talk.

The media were already screaming for an apology, as though it would make any difference.

His final departure on a helicopter from the White House was bizarre. He turned toward those who were bidding him farewell from the door of the helicopter and waved as he had so often before in his hands-over-the-head gesture of triumph, dissociated as it always was from his artificial smile.

As much as I disliked the man, I felt that it was an ignominious end to twenty-two years of life in the center court of American politics.

The talking heads on the screen debated whether the "system" had worked.

"We survived 'Nam and Watergate," I said. "Of course it worked."

"We would not have had to survive either," Chuck replied, "if it had not been for two assassins."

That was as good a summary of the last fourteen years of American life as any. Years, I reflected, that found me in my late twenties and left me in my early forties.

That was the summer that jeans became fashionable, especially for women. Chuck alleged that he disapproved. It deprived women, he contended, of their femininity.

I laughed at him.

One morning we had a completely empty nest—Moire Meg was at a basketball camp. We were eating breakfast in our robes. My husband was reading the self-righteous editorials which the *New York Times* editorial board can grind out in their sleep. He periodically snorted derisively, like a judge hearing a government lawyer trying to pull a fast one.

"Do you ever get tired of me, Chucky?"

"Hmm?" he said, as if he hadn't heard me, which of course he had. He always hears me.

"I mean a little bit bored?"

He folded the paper and placed it on the table, promptly soaking it in the maple syrup left over from his waffle.

"Bored?"

"I mean, like making love with the same woman all these years. No variety."

"Well, Rosemarie, you do tire me out often, on the tennis courts and in other places . . . But bored? The last adjective I would use to describe you is boring . . . in bed or anywhere else."

He picked up the paper and, oblivious of the maple syrup, continued to ridicule the pomposity of John Oakes and his buddies.

"You wouldn't call me exciting, would you?"

He cocked his head thoughtfully.

"That word might not be strong enough."

"What word might be strong enough?"

He pondered for a moment. "How about enchanting?"

"Nice word."

One wife now reassured.

Chucky Ducky, once on a roll, couldn't keep his mouth shut.

"You cast a spell on me at Lake Geneva when you were ten years old the day you kissed me . . ."

"You kissed me!"

"Regardless," he said, stealing my word and my dismissive gesture. "The spell has only grown more powerful with time. It will never fade."

Very good lines, Chuck Ducky.

His fingers found my ribs underneath the robe. This time he was only touching, not arousing. We leaned on each other's shoulders for the longest time. Then I sobbed and collapsed into his arms.

Late in the summer, Trudi and her husband and their seventeen-year-old daughter Rosemarie visited us for a long weekend at the Lake. The blond kid was a dead ringer for the picture of Trudi in Chuck's first book, without the pain and the terror in her mother's eyes in those days. Jimmy and Seano were delighted to squire her around the beach.

Their son, Karl, was now a pilot for Lufthansa.

I did not invite Ed and Delia Conway from down the beach. There was no reason to line up Chucky Ducky's previous loves—though he had never slept with Delia.

We had a grand time, singing songs in German and in English, especially "You Are the Sunshine of My Life," and telling stories and eating massive meals that Trudi cooked for us. She rolled her eyes at me when Chuck used the camera she had given him to record the event.

Since my husband does few things without a reason, I was sure that he displayed the camera to assure her that he still treasured it and her.

"What memories, Chucky?" I asked him in bed that night.

"Bittersweet mostly. And more sweet than bitter."

"You saved her life and she saved yours."

He knew I meant that she had saved his life by disappearing and thus not permitting him to bring her home to America for a marriage which she knew would have never worked.

"Still love her?"

"Sure," he said. "Not the way I love you . . . It's all in a golden haze of youthful days that perhaps never existed."

"They weren't very golden then."

"They were drab and dangerous and boring and bitter cold . . . Even in August."

"Still she taught you how to love . . ."

"And maybe I taught her that men could be tender."

"I'm sure you did."

"Do you mind that I still love her?"

"Certainly not! You would be a monster if you didn't."

We were invited to photograph the new President Gerald Ford in November. He served the same Michigan wine at his White House dinners as we served at our meals at the Lake. I warned Chuck that I might hit him over the head with a bottle if I heard him say once more, "It is a simple wine of the countryside, but I think you will find its pretensions amusing."

April Rosemary was still a painful ache in my soul, one of which I was often not conscious. There were so many other matters which required a mother's attention and worry.

Then it was Labor Day and the summer was over. We deserted the Lake. The leaves had begun to fall. Only the dazzling, daffy Moire Meg remained in our house.

One more September song as our days declined to a precious few.

❧ 28 ❧

On the first Saturday after Labor Day, Moire Meg and I went shopping in the fading Oak Park Mall. I had delayed this expedition too long, because she absolutely refused to come in from the Lake to prepare for her freshman year at Trinity High School or shop with me at the Marquette Mall in Michigan City.

"You just want to feel melancholy, Rosie," she informed me, "because I'm the last teen you'll have to prepare for high school."

"It's thirty years since I started at Trinity," I said with a sad sigh.

"Well, there's always a way to find yourself another freshman, like fourteen or fifteen years from now."

"You, young woman, are a little brat!"

She chuckled complacently.

Somehow we had become best buddies and with that relationship she assumed the right to ask me confidential questions and give me advice.

For example, "Do you and Chucky still make love, Rosie?"

"That's a very personal question, dear."

"You sound just like Grams . . . Well, do you?"

"Certainly we do. We love each other very much."

I remembered with a pang that April Rosemary had once asked me that question.

"Uh-huh . . . How often?"

"Quite often . . ."

"And you enjoy it?"

"More than ever."

She grinned happily.

"That figures."

We did not bicker during our shopping expedition, an unusual phenomenon.

"Don't think I'm getting soft, Rosie. This is your big day and I don't want to ruin it."

She was saved from being an obnoxious little brat by her humor and her instinct about how far to go.

"Why do you call your mother 'Rosie'?" her father asked the first time he heard that name. "Isn't 'Mom' good enough?"

"I never call her *Mom*, Daddy. When other people are around I call her *Ma*. When she says something silly, I call her *Mo-THER*. And when I'm being affectionate and intimate, she's *Rosie*. Is that all right, *Chucky*?"

That broke my husband up.

"Her real name is Rosemarie."

"That's your pet name for her and I don't want to desecrate it!"

"What will you be like when you're eighteen?"

"Probably a lot more cautious than I am now!"

It was a lovely late-summer, early-autumn afternoon when we returned from the mall, leaves under our feet, a haze in the air, a tinge of color on the trees, a mildly erotic breeze on the face.

Too early autumn, I thought. We don't need death yet.

Chuck was waiting at the door of the house. I unloaded my packages into his arms. That's what husbands are for, aren't they?

"We're having a couple of overnight guests," he said cautiously.

"Who?"

"Our daughter and a boy named Jamie . . . In separate bedrooms . . . They're not sleeping together she tells me."

"Holy shit!" exclaimed Moire Meg, grabbing me before I collapsed.

I didn't have the strength to warn her about her language.

"The little brat! She thinks she can return without any warning!"

"Cool it, Mo-THER," Moire Meg instructed me as she helped me to a chair in the parlor. "If she wants to come home, we have to welcome her with outstretched arms."

"What did she sound like?" I asked Chuck.

"Like April Rosemary. Very nervous. Frightened."

"And what did you say?"

"That we would look forward to their visit with great joy!"

"Chucky swallowed the Blarney Stone," my younger daughter observed, quoting one of my favorite aphorisms.

"What are we going to do?" I asked, aware that my head was whirling and my brain racing.

"We're going to have a very polite reception for her and the young man . . ."

"I think Jamie is a cool name," Moire Meg informed us.

"I informed the senior matriarch and told her to spread the word that everyone should stay away from the house until we said it was all right to come over and then we might, just might, have a big O'Malley party."

"She doesn't deserve a big party!"

"ROSIE, why don't you go read the gospel about

the man who had a feast for his son who came home?"

Ouch.

I took a deep breath.

"How come you know so much, Moire Meg?"

"Because I'm a *Catholic*!"

"I can hardly wait to see her," I admitted, with a catch in my voice.

"Now, as for you, young woman, as soon as we see their cab pull up, I want you to go upstairs and wait till we see which way the wind is blowing. When I tell you, call Grams and tell her to unleash the party. Got it?"

"Yes, Pa," she said with fake docility.

"Was the good April surprised?"

"She said that she always knew that poor little April Rosemary would come back."

"Did she know?"

"She might have . . ."

"If you wanted to find out," I said, twisting a tissue which had appeared in my hand, "whether the coast was clear for a return, whom would you call?"

Chuck nodded his head.

"Seems reasonable."

"There's a cab out front," Moire Meg announced, peeking out the window. "Hey, this Jamie guy is really cool!"

"Upstairs, young woman!"

"Yes, Pa."

I dashed into the powder room to make sure my face was on right and that I looked calm and collected. The doorbell rang.

I stood behind Chuck while he opened it.

There was no question that the young woman in the brown autumn suit at the door was April Rosemary, relatively unchanged, a slightly more developed figure perhaps, but the same dancing eyes, the same infectious smile, the same jet-black hair.

"Daddy." She threw herself into Chuck's arms. Doubtless she knew from the phone call that she would receive a warm reception from him.

"Mom!" She opened her arms, a bit hesitantly for me.

Fresh little brat.

I enveloped her in my own arms. Our two trembling bodies came together and our hearts beat in unison. We clung to one another as though nothing and no one could ever tear us apart. She rested her head on my shoulder. We were both crying, of course.

"April Rosemary," I said, "you look absolutely fabulous!"

"So do you, Mom. More beautiful than ever. I knew you would."

And so that was that.

"Mom and Dad, this is Jamie. Excuse me, James Nettleton, M.D., my fiancé."

She was wearing a very large diamond ring. Not bad, kid.

The young man was a giant, taller even than my cavalry raiders and more solid, yet another Black Irishman. He wore rimless glasses, a navy blue suit, and a sweet smile.

"I trust," Chuck said, "that Captain Polly and Colonel John are both well!"

His superior officers from Bamberg! God was a humorist!

"Very well, indeed, Staff Sergeant O'Malley. They send their compliments. They have fond memories of you and are eager to meet you again."

"And great stories too, Daddy. You were a real character over there . . . and terribly brave."

"I deny all charges."

Then this witty giant kissed me on the cheek.

"Mrs. O'Malley, April told me how beautiful you are. I see now that you are even more beautiful than her descriptions."

"Rosemarie, Jamie," I said.

The young man talked funny as everyone from Boston does. He had also swallowed the same stone that his future father-in-law had swallowed.

"You're both most welcome," Chuck said. "Come in and sit down. Let's talk."

April Rosemary, tense and worried, plunged into a preliminary explanation. I wanted to tell her that it could wait, but she had to speak her prepared piece.

"Jamie is about to begin his residency at Northwestern," she said, "and I have to finish up my college requirements this year before I enroll at the Art Institute for my master's. We hope to be married a year from December and plan to live in Chicago . . ."

"So," I said, "you'd like to live here while you attend Rosary and be married from this house at St. Ursula's?"

She gulped.

"If no one minds."

"You're certainly welcome, as far as I'm concerned. You'll have to learn to put up with your no longer little sister who is like totally bossy . . . Chuck?"

"I'll be outnumbered by three bossy women. It gives me an idea for a new sequence. I'll call it *Bossy Women.*"

April Rosemary's shoulders slumped in obvious relief.

"Thank you," she said, desperately resisting the impulse to bubble over. "I can hardly wait to see Moire."

"Moire Meg as she calls herself now."

"Speaking of pictures"—April Rosemary straightened her shoulders—"Dad, that exhibit of yours was overwhelming. Your best work ever. Only I hope you read what that man in the *Globe* said about not taking any more chances . . ."

"Whether *I* read it is not the issue, kid," he said.

"Your mother read it and it's now official family policy."

"And Mom," she raced on, "I can't believe how wonderful your stories are. Dad is just perfect in them, every detail right."

"They're not about him!" I protested.

The three of them laughed at me.

"And he always wins!" I added.

"Only," Chuck said, "because the wife makes him win!"

"WELL," our daughter was fitting back into the family banter, "that's the way it should be, isn't it!"

"Could I make some tea for all of us?" she then asked.

I should have made it myself. However, she needed time to breathe.

"Everything's where it always was, dear, even the cookies for your father."

She rushed out to the kitchen.

Jamie Nettleton, M.D., beamed at us approvingly.

"You guys done real good," he said.

"Did you save her, Jamie?" I asked.

"April saved herself, Rosemarie," he said. "I might have helped a little the last couple of years. She's a very resourceful and tough young woman. However, I don't have to tell you that. She's fine, terribly nervous today, but you don't have to worry about her anymore . . . You have to understand that she wanted to be sure that she had everything together before she came home."

"We don't believe in budgeting the Holy Spirit's time," Chuck added.

"You noted," he glanced at both of us, his pale blue eyes dancing, "when we've scheduled our wedding?"

"Next Christmas," I said . . . "On our silver anniversary!"

"On or about." He grinned.

Great torrents of tears welled up behind my eyes.

I restrained them, but only with enormous difficulty.

Then Moire Meg peeked around the corner of the door, a tray of cups and saucers in hand. She was wearing the grim frown with which on occasion she greets the world.

"*She*"—she nodded toward the kitchen—"said I should bring these out."

She had donned the beige miniskirt and matching sweater which we had purchased at the mall, just so there would be no doubt about her budding figure.

"Ma, he's cute"—she pointed at Jamie—"I vote for him."

"The fabled Moire Meg." Jamie stood up and shook hands with her.

"She didn't know I'm now Moire Meg," she said suspiciously.

"I'm psychic," he replied.

My younger daughter then deigned to smile, which has the same effect as a battery of flashbulbs exploding.

"Thanks for bringing her home, Dr. Jamie," she said demurely. "It's good to have her back."

"Would you make that phone call I mentioned, Moire Meg?" Chuck said.

She looked blank for a moment, then nodded and rushed up the steps.

"What an adorable little brat!" Jamie marveled. "And so sweet!"

"She wears a thousand faces," I admitted. "The one you just saw is the deepest one . . . She beat me to it. Thanks for bringing her back!"

"You done real good too, Jamie," Chuck agreed.

April Rosemary returned with the teapot and a large plate of cookies.

"What happened to my helper?"

"She'll be right back," I said.

"She's really special," April Rosemary said. "Absolutely unique. She told me that she was glad I had come home because, in her very words, taking care of Rosie and Chucky is too much for one poor little teen."

"That's just the beginning," I warned.

"She's authentic," Moire Meg's big sister said. "She loves to play. Actress maybe?"

Moire Meg thundered down the steps and into the parlor.

"Boys, boys, boys," she said, "they drive me crazy!"

"What will you be doing your MFA in, April Rosemary?" I asked.

Her eyes darted around the room anxiously.

"Photography," she said, her voice quavering.

I was not even close to saying something nasty, like it's not parasitic anymore. Instead, I said, "Why am I not surprised?"

"April supported herself in Boston last year," Jamie said proudly, "by her photography. She specializes in pictures of children, and especially babies."

"You haven't become a Republican, April Rosemary?" Chuck asked suspiciously.

"Like great-grandfather O'Malley?" she asked, revealing a terrible family secret that we had tried to hide from the children.

"Different times," Chucky mumbled.

"Not a chance, Daddy," she said with a happy laugh. "Jamie would disown me if I did. Besides, being a Chicago Democrat is part of my identity! When I run for political office I'll run as a Democrat!"

Before anyone could comment on that, the Crazy O'Malleys began to arrive, carrying food, drink, and musical instruments. The good April and Vangie, Peg and Vince and their kids, Jane and Ted McCormack and their kids, Father Ed, Monsignor Raven, Jimmy and Seano, who had been sidetracked by Vince, and then Kev and Maria Elena.

April Rosemary and Kevin stared at each other for

a moment. They had been on opposite sides in the war. Or had they really? Who knew? Who cared?

He embraced her.

"Sis, welcome home!"

She broke down completely and sobbed in his arms. He held her tightly.

Well, that was over!

She hugged Maria Elena and congratulated her on the baby, who was just becoming visible. No problem there either.

I glanced at the good April, who had put on her cat-and-canary smile. Yes, she was the spy within the family.

My elder daughter, I reflected, may look like me. She has her father's charm, however, and can turn it on full force when she wants to. She worked the room like a polished precinct captain.

Her first encounter with Carlotta was initially tense. In her businesslike second-year-law-school suit, my niece tried to look distant and superior. Then April Rosemary turned on all her charm. Her cousin melted.

"Same old April Rosemary," Carlotta whispered to me. "Pure charisma."

The boys were into bebop these days, though they would never threaten the reputations of John Coltrane or the Bird. My two daughters kicked off their shoes and danced with the band, to the enthusiastic applause of the crowd.

As the music and singing continued, April Rosemary seemed to wilt. A wistful glaze spread over her face. She's thinking about all she missed.

I followed her into the kitchen as she carried out a stack of dirty plates. She leaned against the fridge, her whole body sagging.

"Kind of overwhelming, isn't it?" I said gently.

"I wouldn't have it any other way, Mom . . . Yes, the Crazy O'Malleys, no, we Crazy O'Malleys are overwhelming! . . . I thought it would be so difficult.

Now it seems like I was here only yesterday."

"And you've provided them with another excuse for a party!"

"There's so much to talk about, Mom. Right now I'm so dragged out . . ."

"There's all the time in the world, dear, for the talking."

"I'm so sorry, so very, very sorry."

I touched her shoulder.

"It's taken me a long time in life, April Rosemary, to realize that real love is implacably forgiving."

She nodded.

"I better get back in there. They all want to see how I've changed."

"Not at all, dear. A little older, a little more self-possessed."

"And a lot less obnoxious, I hope." She grinned, dumped her pile of plates in the sink, and rushed back to the party.

That night, after we said our prayers, as we cuddled in bed, both of us emotionally drained, Chuck whispered, "Well we won that one."

"By a landslide."

"How did we come to think it would end any differently?"

"Mostly my fears that I was a poor mother."

"And now?"

"She's damn lucky to have one like me."

I'd save that line for Maggie Ward.

✤ 29 ✤

Not that night, but some night shortly thereafter, we conceived our sixth child.

"Unplanned pregnancy?" Peg asked

"Definitely planned . . . If my daughter-in-law is pregnant and my daughter will probably be soon, I might just as well be, right?"

"Chuck . . . ?"

"It takes two to plan. We both want another kid around the house."

"You are the craziest of all the O'Malleys." She embraced me. "And the best of the lot too."

So in due course and with remarkably little fuss, there appeared in the world a certain Siobhan Marie O'Malley.

All that needs to be said about her can be summed up in the comments of her sibling, Moire Meg:

"Gosh, Rosie, she is like totally cool . . . Are we ready for a third redhead in the family?"

AUTHOR'S NOTE

The O'Malleys are a fictional family. This story is an exercise in historical fiction. Thus the conversations between the O'Malleys and people who exist in God's world are fictional, as are incidents involving such people. Pat Moynihan's comment about Henry Kissinger is in his *A Dangerous Place*. The rescue in the South China Sea is based on a true story. *The Limits of Intervention* by Townsend Hoopes tells the story of the decision by the Senior Advisers of the President to recommend the termination of the war in 1968.

What happened to all the young radicals of those years? Most of the young people of that era were not all that radical. They couldn't sell out because they had never really bought in. For some of those who did buy in, sex, drugs, and rock and roll were the outer limits of their radicalism—combined with an occasional protest march. Most of them returned to the upper-middle-class fold from which they came. Some would say they "sold out" and permit themselves to feel fashionably guilty about that while they enjoy the good life with some superficial and self-indulgent modifications of life style (which David Brooks has described brilliantly in his book *Bobos*). Others repudiated their radical experimentation and became at least as conservative as their parents. Others abandoned more or less the trappings of radicalism but continued their intense political commitment, as my colleague Doug McAdams has argued.

April Rosemary's return to her family is in many ways typical. Her radical roots were not all that deep. However, she gives a hint at the end of the story that she remains politically committed, perhaps in the style of her family's pragmatic liberalism. What will happen to this young woman whose charisma her mother is only beginning to appreciate? Will she seek political office of some sort, following in the footsteps of her great-grandfather O'Malley, save at the opposite end of the political spectrum?

We'll have to wait and see.

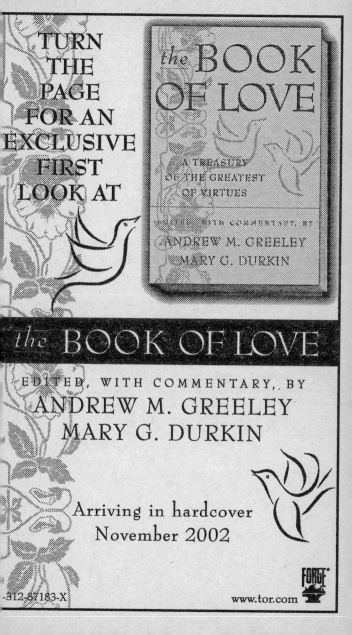

TURN THE PAGE FOR AN EXCLUSIVE FIRST LOOK AT

the BOOK OF LOVE

A TREASURY OF THE GREATEST OF VIRTUES

EDITED, WITH COMMENTARY, BY

ANDREW M. GREELEY
MARY G. DURKIN

the BOOK OF LOVE

EDITED, WITH COMMENTARY, BY

ANDREW M. GREELEY
MARY G. DURKIN

Arriving in hardcover
November 2002

0-312-87183-X

FORGE

www.tor.com

It is God that God has chosen the name of Love.

Maybe it's only a human name that we ascribe to God. Maybe we've imposed it on God without his permission. Or her permission. Christianity is more explicit about the name. St. John says flatly that God IS love. Other religions, as the selections in this Book of Love will illustrate, say pretty much the same thing, though perhaps more cautiously. Even the saints and the mystics who may have had more contact with God than the rest of us claim that they encounter overwhelming love.

If God didn't like the name, She could have easily rebuked those who use it, one way or another. If one is a Christian, one has to say that St. John's naming of God is inspired, that in some fashion God and St. John conspired to Call Her Love.

Odd.

All right, all our efforts at naming God are pale metaphors which reveal to us a little about God, a lot less than they don't reveal. God is like human love but also unlike it. Less passionate, less forceful, less determined, less enraptured? We can hardly say that because if we do the metaphor collapses. Love in its very nature is passionate, forceful, determined, enraptured. So if the metaphor has any validity at all it must mean that God is like human love only more so, more passionate, more forceful, more determined, more enraptured.

Scary.

Persistently passionate human lovers can be very scary. However, we can cool them off in various ways. A God who is infinitely more passionate? A God whom we can't cool off? A God from whom we can't escape? Very scary indeed.

And very odd.

Love is not just hearts and flowers and St. Valentine's day lace—though it is that too. Love is essentially a raging torrent rushing inexorably towards union. A river tumbling irresistibly towards the ocean, the ocean sweeping up into the river mouth in its high tide. Love is usually very messy, very troublesome, very dangerous, very consuming. It is, as Father Martin Darcy S.J. wrote in his classic *The Mind and Heart of Love*, finally not so much the desire to possess as the desire to be possessed. God is like that?

Most odd.

We are tempted to say that God doesn't really mean that. She conspired with St. John to say She was something sweet and nice, not something turbulent and demanding and fearsome. The word doesn't mean the same thing at all when it is used of human love as when it used as God. Certainly Love is not love, right?

Wrong! Unless you want to argue that God plays word games as well as dice.

Love emerged in humankind not as a result of our being human but as a precondition of our becoming human. In our hominid ancestors the bonding between male and female, already passionate enough, had to extend to the female's children for humanity as we know it to emerge. The bond of love produced a family and by so doing produced humankind. Moreover to really bond the family together humans had to develop in such a way that the male and female were capable of sex not merely episodically (once a month, once a year) but all the time. Now that is really messy!

Did God really want to compare Himself to the hunger of man and woman for one another, a hunger which in its pervasiveness is unique among the species about which we know? A hunger which causes all kinds of trouble in the human condition? A hunger which has developed out of the bonding propensities that we share with other less passionate species? A propensity to bond rooted in the earth and in bodies? Did God want us to think that He's really like that?

If He did, that is outrageously odd. However, one learns, like Job, not to argue with God. If God wants to be Love, then that's His business. One can understand, however, why many people try to pretend that God doesn't really mean it or to pretty the name over with sentimental veneer. The implications of the notion that there is something in the messy joy of human passion that is very like God are too disturbing to have to take seriously.

Not only then, do we pretend that the passion between man and woman is totally different from God's passion for us, we also try to pretend that all the other varieties of love that are part of human life are totally different from sexual passion. The word obviously means three totally different things—God, human sexual attraction, and all the other loves in our life. There is love[1] love[2] and love[3]. The first is God, the second is sexual attraction, the third is the way we feel about our friends and relatives. All are different. They merely happen to have the same name.

Stated that baldly, our attempt to eliminate the body from our friendships and from God may seem hilarious to some. Nonetheless, it is the implied conventional wisdom of those who want to escape from the scary implications of love as passion.

In fact, we know of no other species which has as many different kinds of love as we do. Clearly all our other loves are possible only because we are a species endowed with a very unique kind of sexuality, one oriented not merely and not even principally towards reproduction but towards bonding. Humans can have a wide variety of loves because they have such a powerful capacity to bond. The other loves are not the same as passion between man and woman, but the ability to engage in passionate sexual bonding makes possible all the other loves. They are not watered-down versions of sexual love but rather the result of our vast, amorphous, and desperate need to bond. Close friendship is not the same as sexual love, but it's not completely different either and is possible because we are creatures who can bond.

That leaves unanswered the question of why God wants to identify Herself with human bonding, why She wants to create the impression that it is in Her nature to bond with us. We often wish She would go away with that metaphor but clearly there is no escaping it though we pretend to try.

Perhaps that is the reason that in so many of the current spate of books about virtues (Books of Virtue, so-called) love is absent. In these books one encounters much about various stoic virtues as honesty, reliability, industry and suchlike—all doubtless admirable virtues. However, one reads nothing in these inestimable anthologies about love.

One wonders why. Did not St. Paul say the greatest virtue was love? Have the anthologists dismissed him because love has somehow come to be identified with nineteen sixties hedonism (as in "make love not war"), drugs and rock music? Might it be that love is perceived as a soft, mushy, self-indulgent, undisciplined quality that hardly deserves the name of a virtue? How could one who writes editorials for the *Wall Street Journal* and cries for more outrage from Americans possibly sing the praises of something like love, for which there is anyhow little room in a free market economy? Why, of all things, should parents want to put in the hands of their children a book about love? Given the very conservative orientation of the anthologists, that may well be the case. Too bad for St. Paul. And for St. John too.

If love is a torrential force towards a union which bonds, it will bring sustained happiness only when it is focused, disciplined, intent, experienced, mature, patient, kind and all those other nice things St. Paul says about it. The ability to love wisely and well is the most important trait parents can pass on to their children. It is not, however, sentimental mush.

Thus it seems to us that the omission of Love from those anthologies is passing strange. So we decided to prepare a book which might be a supplement or a corrective or even a challenge to these books of virtue, minimally a polite reminder from St. Paul that without love the stoic virtues are sounding brass and tinkling cymbals.

Therefore we commit this book to two fundamental propositions:

God is Love

The greatest of all virtues is love.